BOOK TWO OF THE SAND TRAVELER DUOLOGY

DUNES
OF
WATER

JESSICA FLORY

IMMORTAL WORKS
SALT LAKE CITY

Immortal Works LLC
1505 Glenrose Drive
Salt Lake City, Utah 84104
Tel: (385) 202-0116

Cover Art by Lenore Stutznegger
www.lenorestutz.com

ISBN 978-1-953491-85-5 (Paperback)
ASIN B0D9WV85J4 (Kindle)

For Dad, for showing me the stars.

1

———

NORAH

The ocean of sand is merciless.

It doesn't care who it hurts. The sand, wielded by enemy Shakers, tears through the To'Morat lines. The Shakers use their gift to control the sand, sharpening it into knives, tearing through flesh and bone.

A foreign ship, long and black and narrow, hovers before the plateau, lifted by streams of sand wielded by Shakers. Far below it the ocean of sand crashes and shifts, pulled by the moon's gravity into waves. I can hardly hear it over the screams.

I stand on the plateau, the fiery sun high above making sweat drip from my neck down my spine. Sand blows in gusts across the open expanse of desert. The city of To'Morat is behind us, and a small group of warriors are all that stand between it and the enemy.

Agriad Zul—the leader of these strange warriors—stands aboard his ship, watching with colorless eyes. He's holding a corpse.

A corpse that looks exactly like me.

Who is she? Why do we look alike? I swallow. And what happened to her?

Warriors of To'Morat, my former enemies and now allies, fight and rage around me on the flat expanse of sand. But as I watch them shout and throw spears of sand, I realize something. We're losing. The mighty To'Morat, warriors of legend, are losing.

The enemy fights from aboard their ship. They're dressed in black paneled armor and blow darts from long tubes, and the To'Morat soldiers who are hit drop immediately. The darts must be soaked with toxins because it doesn't matter where someone is hit. They instantly fall.

The edge of the To'Morat plateau is littered with bodies, and blood soaks the sand. Guilt and dread make my stomach heave. All this fighting, it's over me. This man, Agriad Zul, wants *me*.

Over half of the foreign Shakers dedicate their sand Shaking to holding the enemy ship aloft. The To'Morat warriors aren't giving them space to dock. But even with only half of their fighters attacking, we're being beaten.

My hands clench and unclench at my side, longing to hold a spear, to fight, to do anything.

The warriors battle hard to defend me. Quartz-tipped spears shoot through the air, powered by an Extractor taking energy from the sand and using it to achieve inhuman strength. Knives of sand, hardened to quartz by Forgers, fly toward the opposing side.

Love used to weaken the sand gifts. But thanks to me and Zadock, things were made right again. And now love strengthens the sand gifts, as it should. I can see the difference in their powers now that love is fueling them and not hindering them.

But still, they're falling, the poison darts hitting with terrifying accuracy. The mighty To'Morat, the strongest nation on the ocean of sand, are dropping like sand mites.

Zadock, my beloved, screams, shooting spears of sand toward the attacking force. "Norah, get behind me!" He pushes me behind him with one arm, shielding me with his body. His sandy hair blows in the wind, and his tanned arms are covered in grit and sweat.

Fear paralyzes me. Not for myself but for the people dying around me. For Zadock.

I wish I could do *anything* to help here. But my sand gift is different. Sustaining, it can't take life. It can only give. In the desert, it's a blessing straight from our enormous moon and goddess, Atoille. But it means that right now I'm helpless while people are dying to protect me.

Agriad Zul's long black hair blows away from his face, his expression determined and cold. He stands behind a line of his warriors. His pure white eyes are on me, watching with an eerie gaze. He is calm and still, even while his warriors battle around him.

The To'Morat warriors are dropping fast. Imwraeth Jeriyah, Favored One of To'Morat, yells from behind me, calling to his people for reinforcements. Off to the side, I see the glow of Absorbing. My friend, Lylahn, is using her sand gift to heal those that have fallen.

And I stand behind Zadock. Helpless.

This man—Agriad Zul—said that he wants me. That's why they're here, on the edge of the To'Morat plateau, slaughtering warriors. Because they want me to go with them. Because for some reason, that corpse looks just like me.

My heart pounds, yet I stand here and do nothing. The darts never come near me. Agriad Zul wants me alive.

My beautiful Zadock stands in front of me, Shaking the sand with everything he has, blocking darts as fast as he can and returning attacks of his own.

I take a step back. Everyone expects me, the Sustainer, to be their savior. These past two moon cycles, Zadock and I have sailed from plateau to plateau, Sustaining plants and trying to heal the world from an unnatural famine that lasted over three years. All of the desert nations were on the brink of starvation. I've done my best, but it's not enough. I'm only one person, and everyone expects so much—

Zadock reaches out with sand and yanks a man from the ship, hurling him into the ocean of sand. How easily Zadock does this now, after how much fighting he's seen. We used to talk about how he was nervous to fight a real person, not a practice dummy. We used to wonder if he could really take a life.

One of the foreign warrior's comrades lashes out with sand to grab at their companion, but Zadock wrenches the sand away so the man continues to fall. And falling into the ocean of sand is a death sentence. He'll be sucked away in an instant, left to suffocate under the crushing waves.

My shoulder-length brown hair blows into my eyes, and I brush it away. My gaze is riveted on the battle.

Zadock focuses his full power on the sand underneath the ship. He moves his arms in a pulling motion, straining, the muscles in his biceps taut. The sand that's supporting the foreign ship jerks. The ship tilts at an angle, and the people aboard cry out. The Shakers lifting the ship work their arms, furiously trying to right it.

Zadock is the most powerful Shaker To'Rahn, our home plateau, has seen in generations, and I think he might actually do it. He might actually overturn their ship.

For a moment, the To'Morat warriors gain the upper hand. I hold my breath, watching them throw their spears of sand and knives of quartz. Several of the enemy warriors go down.

Agriad Zul's cold eyes turn toward Zadock, and my heart stops. He points.

A warrior next to Agriad puts a blow dart to her lips, and, through the haze of dust and sand, the dart zips toward Zadock. I cry out in warning, terror jolting through me. The dart strikes him in the cheek. Zadock flinches, and his body crumples to the sand.

Something within me rips open. I'm screaming, but I can't hear myself. My eyes are only for Zadock, my beloved, my Anointed, fallen in the sand.

"LYLAHN!" I cry for my friend, the only Absorber I know who might be strong enough to heal this.

She rushes to kneel at his side, yanks the dart out of his cheek, and grabs handfuls of sand to place on his skin. The sand glows with a white light. I kneel beside Zadock, my breath coming fast. *Please, please, Atoille, let her be able to heal him.*

Screams, war cries, and the sounds of the dying echo around us.

Lylahn removes her hands from Zadock's cheek to grab more sand. Tears fill my eyes. I can't lose him. Not like this. Not ever. Not so soon after we finally have each other.

Zadock's skin is going gray. Where the dart bit into his cheek is a horrible, swollen red lump. Blood drips down his face and into the sand.

I grab a spear from off the ground and hurry to stand in front of Lylahn. She is a target, with her Absorbing.

A dart zips through the air toward us. I whack it out of its path with a growl.

Agriad Zul shouts indistinguishable words from aboard his ship, yelling at whoever blew the dart my way.

"It's poison," Lylahn says, still working. "Some kind of neurotoxin. I'm trying to push it out."

I fight to keep the panic at bay. She can heal him. I *have* to believe that. I stand before her, crouched in fighting stance, a human shield.

"He's still alive, but Atoille, this works fast." Lylahn grabs another handful of sand, places it onto his skin, and breathes.

After what seems like an eternity, she pulls her hands away.

I turn and look from Zadock, still unconscious on the ground, to Lylahn. Zadock's cheek looks better, not so swollen, but the red bite of the dart is still there.

"I did what I could," Lylahn says, pushing her curls out of her face with the back of one hand.

"And?" I don't want to hear the words from her lips. That he's dead. Not after all this. Not after we've been through so much.

Zadock's eyes blink open. "Nors...?"

I gasp in sharp relief, dropping the spear and rushing to kneel at his side. The tears spill down my cheeks. "You're alive!" I clasp Lylahn's hand. "Thank you." I sob. "Thank you."

"That poison is strong," she says. "If I hadn't started to work on him immediately, or if I had been a weaker Absorber, he would be gone." Lylahn gives my shoulder a comforting squeeze before hurrying away toward another fallen To'Morat warrior.

I take in the battle around me. The To'Morat numbers are dwindling fast. Imwraeth, easy to spot with his vivid red hair, alternates between shouting orders and glancing at Lylahn, worry plain on his face.

We're losing. The enemy ship is still filled with warriors. If one of theirs falls, another replaces them. They have the high ground and the advantage of superior weapons.

Zadock sits up and takes my hand. His face is a pale shade of green. "Norah, don't..."

I squeeze his hand. "Rest."

All this fighting, it's over me.

Agriad Zul still stands at the head of his ship, the body in his hands. He hasn't moved throughout the battle. His Shakers are vigilant in protecting him, Shaking away any sand that threatens him. He catches me watching and smiles.

My head spins, my stomach churning. There's so much I don't know here. So much that is at stake. So much to decide and no time to do it.

I stand, slowly, on shaking legs. I take a deep breath. "I'll go!"

The fighting is too loud. No one hears, no one stops to turn. Except Zadock. He holds out a hand. "No, Nors!"

I ignore him. I have to, or I'll lose my resolve. I wave my arms. "I'll go with you!" I yell. "Just STOP!"

Agriad Zul's eyes are blank and pupilless. They hold my gaze, sending chills up and down my spine. Finally, he holds up a hand, and the battle stops. Imwraeth signals for his warriors to hold. The quiet that overtakes the battlefield is sudden and stark, a sharp contrast to the chaos of only moments before. A few warriors moan on the ground, wounded and bleeding, and Lylahn attends to them.

"I'll go with you," I repeat.

Fingers grab at my hand. Zadock.

"It's all right," I whisper. "It's all right."

Imwraeth looks at me, his face torn. "Norah, you can't—"

"Come," Agriad says. His face is a passive mask. He nods, and one of his Shakers moves her arms, forming a platform of sand before me.

I stare at it.

What will it mean, if I go with these people? Where will they take me? Will I ever come home? Will I ever see Zadock again? My motah, my little sister? Fear makes my stomach turn.

"Nors, no. Don't do this." Zadock struggles to stand.

The sand platform inches closer. I step on.

"DON'T."

"Goodbye, Zadock." I turn to meet his gaze. His dark blue eyes are filled with anguish. "I'll find a way back to you," I whisper. "I promise."

"Bring that one as well." Agriad points straight at...Zadock.

"What?" I yell. "No. That wasn't part of the deal!"

The enemy Shaker controlling the sand platform lifts it into the air, and I wobble on my feet. Another Shaker wraps sand around Zadock and brings him up beside me, and we're carried to the black ship. Zadock doesn't fight it.

This can't be happening.

"No! Leave him be!" I cry.

"Norah!" The shout comes from behind me, and I don't dare turn to see who spoke, not while I'm being carried across the gap between the ship and the plateau. The voice sounded like Lylahn.

I look down, and my stomach drops. The ocean of sand churns and spits far below.

The sand platform passes right by Agriad Zul. His eyes study me with an intense stare, the only color in them the tiny red veins. I jolt back in disgust.

Zadock and I are dropped onto the middle of the deck near the central mast. I stumble and fall into him, and he catches me, wrapping protective arms around me. I send a silent prayer of thanks to Atoille that Zadock's skin is getting its color back and he's strong enough to stay on his feet.

"Cast off," Agriad says to his people.

His warriors obey, preparing the ship to sail. Shakers at the stern move their arms, lowering the ship back into the ocean of sand. The To'Morat stare after us or tend to their wounded. Imwraeth watches us go, worry etched into his expression. He knows exactly what this means—his people are losing their only Sustainer.

Without me, there's no one to grow food for them in the desert. The famine will return, and it will be worse than ever.

But I can't—I can't think about that right now. I'm just trying to save everyone... I'm just trying—

"It's ok, Nors." Zadock strokes my hair. "It's ok. I'm here with you."

No. No, no, no. It was supposed to be *me* I was sacrificing. Only me.

I have no idea the fate that awaits us.

The black ship sails downward, and we land in the ocean of sand with a jolt and a spray of dusty waves. Shakers work the sand, hurling us forward in an eastward direction.

Agriad Zul stands at the head of his ship, looking out over the sands. A warrior in black armor takes the corpse from him. Agriad closes his eyes and says a few words. Then he bends and tenderly smooths the corpse's brown hair from her face. The body looks fresh, so her death can't have happened that long ago.

Agriad lowers his forehead until it touches hers. Then he straightens and nods, and then the body that looks so much like me is thrown overboard to the sands.

I watch as her face—my face—is pulled under. The ocean of sand sucks her away in an instant. I swallow.

Zadock's arms squeeze me tighter. "I'm here."

The swelling in his cheek has already gone down, and there's only a tiny dot of red that hints at where the dart hit. I put my finger on Zadock's cheek and stroke the spot. "Zadock, I—"

I'm cut off when Agriad turns and looks at me.

I expect to see anger, hatred, disdain.

Instead, I see joy.

What? I lower my hand from Zadock's face.

Agriad strides over to us in the center of the ship. His warriors bustle around us, paying us no heed. Many have changed out of their black armor into soft white pants and shirts.

Fear swirls in my stomach. I have no idea what he wants, no idea what this man is capable of.

To my utmost surprise, Agriad embraces me.

Revulsion crawls within my stomach. I don't push away because I'm frozen in horror. He smells of iron and...salt?

Agriad pulls away, clasps his hands on my shoulders. His face is tender, and he smiles. "You have been returned to us. My daughter."

2

ZADOCK

Umm... What?

Agriad Zul, or whatever his name is, embraces Norah. I step back in shock, and the ship seems to sway beneath my feet. The desert sun beating down on us feels unbearably hot, the To'Morat plateau an impossible distance away.

What the speck is happening?

Norah's expression is flabbergasted. She doesn't embrace him back.

Agriad lets go and looks into her eyes. "My daughter." He turns to the members of his crew, who are busy working the ship. "My daughter has been returned to us! She has been born again!"

The sailors raise fists and cheer.

"To the sea!" someone shouts.

The sea? Does he mean—? No. He can't mean the ocean of water. Just thinking about that place makes my heart skip a beat.

Atoille, our enormous moon and goddess, is close enough to pull the sand into waves. I've seen firsthand what that gravity does to waves of water.

"We can't—we can't go there," I whisper.

Norah meets my eyes. She agreed to go with these people to save everyone. Why is it always her? She saved the desert nations from famine when she discovered her Sustaining gift. Sustaining used to be as common as Shaking, generations and generations ago, but it was lost. Until Norah. She thought she didn't even have a gift for most of her life, and I saw firsthand how hard it was for her, being the only one without a gift.

For so long we weren't allowed to love, for fear of weakening our much needed gifts, and now that she's mine... I would do anything for her.

Norah takes my hand. "It's going to be all right."

Agriad looks tenderly at Norah. "What is your name, child?"

"Um. Norah Saranyi. I'm not—"

Agriad smiles. "Norah."

The way he looks at her... I wrap my arm around her shoulders. *I'm here.* I want to say. *You're not alone.*

"Saranyi," Agriad says. "That is a common last name here?"

Norah frowns. "Yes."

Agriad turns to me, and his expression darkens. "And who is this?"

Norah takes my hand. "Zadock Penvaren, my Anointed."

I wonder if being Anointed means anything to him, if he knows it's a promise to wed. Are our cultures similar in this?

Agriad appraises me. "Ahhhh. I understand." His voice is low and raspy, almost like a desert snake's hiss. It gives me the creeps. Blue veins swirl beneath his paper-white skin. That complexion can't be healthy, not out here in the desert sun.

"You must have many questions," Agriad says.

Norah nods.

"Come with me to my cabin."

Norah tightens her grip on my fingers. "We want to go back to our people. I don't understand what you want with us. I'm not—"

"All will be explained." Agriad gestures behind him.

Norah and I glance at each other. Every instinct inside of me is fighting to protect her, to get her out of this situation. Our people *need* her. She is the only Sustainer. I don't know what these people want with her, but it can't be good. I don't know what else she could've done, what other options there were back on the plateau. We were losing the battle; that much was clear.

But without her, everyone will starve.

We follow Agriad across the black wooden deck. As he walks, his warriors salute him, grinning. A few clap him on the back. Agriad returns their smiles and nods to each of them.

We descend a narrow spiral staircase into the depths of the ship. We enter a hallway lined on one side with round glass windows that look out across the ocean of sand and let in light.

We follow Agriad's long stride down the hallway to a door at the end. The wood has been carved to look like a ship spraying through sand, or is that water? Before I can inspect further, Agriad opens it, and we follow him into a room bigger than my bedroom at home.

Everything is stuck to the floor with a rim of Forged quartz—the carved wooden desk, the cushioned armchair, the seats in front of the desk, and the chests of drawers at the sides of the room. There is another door to the left, leading to other chambers, I assume, and the right and rear walls of the room are windows. Enormous glass windows that look out over the desert.

The plateau of To'Morat is gone. It's nowhere in sight.

I clench my fists. *Oh, Norah... What are we going to do?* We're going to escape, that's what. We've been in worse situations than this. We're going to escape tonight, and I'll fly us back on a platform of sand. Yep. That's what we'll do.

Feeling a bit better, I sit in one of the chairs, and Norah sits beside me. The cushions are velvet soft, and the chairs are wood. Everything is made of black wood.

"Do you not have Forgers, where you're from?" I ask. It's a stupid question and the last one on my mind, but it's what comes out. Do they not have Forgers to turn sand into quartz and make their furniture? Why else would they waste precious wood like this?

Agriad smiles and sits behind the desk. "We do. Our Forgers are artists. Why make a chair out of quartz when wood is so much more comfortable and pleasing to look at? And so plentiful."

I jolt. Norah meets my eyes. Plentiful?

"Please," Norah says. "What do you want from us?"

I reach out and hold her hand.

"I want to take you where you belong, my daughter," Agriad says.

"But I am not your daughter!" Norah says.

I'm afraid that Agriad will get angry, and who knows what he is capable of? If he realizes that Norah is not his daughter, will he let us go? Or will he just have us killed?

But Agriad only gives her a fond smile. "You are; you simply do not realize it yet. But you will, in time. The miracle of rebirth is part of Sustaining. It is part of you, and it is part of me."

Norah's eyes widen. "You're a Sustainer?"

Agriad nods, his smile broadening.

I jolt in surprise. Another Sustainer? I frown. "And somehow that makes Norah your daughter?"

Agriad's face falls, and I worry I've offended him. The sudden change in expression is alarming. He stands and walks to the window where the waves of sand crash outside. The ship is speeding forward.

"I lost my daughter, Cale, two moon cycles ago." Agriad stares out at the sand waves. "I woke in the night to a jolt, and I knew something had happened. I knew it deep in my heart. I went to check on her, and she was dead."

"Eight weeks?" Norah says. "But the...Cale...she looked so fresh." She grimaces.

"I Sustained her body," Agriad says. "Kept her perfect until her burial."

I swallow. Two moon cycles ago. That was...

Norah's eyes go enormous. "Was it the night Atoille rose on the eastern horizon?" She asks the question quietly, tentatively.

Agriad turns back to look at us. "Here, yes. Yes, it was. I knew that

Sustaining had happened here, something strong enough to take my daughter's life. A Sustaining greater than anything that had occurred before." Agriad turns his white eyes on me, and my skin crawls. "A Sustaining strong enough to bring back the dead. A life...for a life."

Norah's head swivels to look at me. I meet her eyes.

Eight weeks ago, Norah saved my life. I was gone. I don't remember much of it, but it was the moment that Norah uncovered her Sustaining ability. Up until that point in her life, she'd thought that she didn't have a sand gift, and that she was the only one. She brought me back from the brink of death. Apparently, there was a cost.

Norah hasn't been able to repeat the feat, and Sustaining cannot heal, not like Absorbing can. But I was...well, I think I was dead. It's all black. But Norah did something to bring me back that she hasn't been able to replicate.

Agriad returns to his seat. Suddenly, I feel the urge to move, to run, to be anywhere but here, but I'm frozen. I am Norah's best chance of escaping this mess.

Agriad sighs. "I don't know what happened that night, but it's clear you have an idea of what I'm talking about. Sustaining is always a balance. You cannot grant life without taking it from somewhere else."

"So these weeks, all the plant life I've been Sustaining..." Norah leaves the question dangling.

"Has been taken from *my* home," Agriad says. "Upsetting the balance of the world. But, daughter, all will be made right. Do not fear."

"Why..." I swallow as Agriad's frozen stare turns toward me. The way he looks at me is a stark change from the loving glances he gives Norah. "Why does your daughter look like Norah?"

Norah looks to Agriad, waiting.

"Norah is my daughter," Agriad says again. This time, anger tints his voice. "That is why she and Cale look the same." He looks again at Norah, smiling. "Cale, you have returned to me. But I will call you Norah if that is what you wish."

This is getting weirder and weirder.

"What do you want from us?" Norah asks. "When can we go home?"

Agriad's smile widens, his eyes glittering. "We *are* going home."

3

LYLAHN

I jolt awake, sweating and gasping. My eyes scan the room, looking for threats, before I realize I'm in my own bed, safe. I had another nightmare.

I was back in that night. The night the To'Morat attacked, and my older sisters died. I lived on the plateau of To'Shahera with my three sisters. Our life was a simple one, tending herds of camehl and selling their milk and butter. Until the famine hit, and the bloodthirsty To'Morat decided that the only way to survive was by taking from others. They *obliterated* my home. Burned it to ash.

I grabbed my younger sister, Kaera, and ran, screaming, from the house. Hyria and Bellah told us to go, get out of there.

"Remember," Bellah said, one hand cupping my cheek. "Remember—"

What? Her last words to me are gone.

And then they ran to help put out the fires. My older sisters were Shakers, both, and even though they weren't very strong, they ran to help smother the flames with sand.

I fled, taking Kaera with me. But I looked back. I saw a warrior in black and red armor stab a spear into Hyria's gut.

I screamed and shoved Kaera aside so she wouldn't see. I ran back to Absorb, to heal her, to fix her.

Bellah Shook the sand at their attacker, throwing up a screen of dust to blind him.

The warrior sliced off her head.

The To'Morat found me trying to heal two corpses.

I shouted for Kaera, and of course, she came running to me. I couldn't leave her. So they took us, thinking that both of us were Absorbers, not just me. I didn't correct them, because I knew that they'd kill her. The To'Morat have never been known for their mercy.

My hands tremble. I curl them into fists, but it doesn't help.

We became their prisoners, tasked with healing their Favored One, who was burdened with a congenital heart failure that still prevents him from running. I failed in that healing, but I did fall in love with Imwraeth Jeriyah, Favored One of To'Morat.

And now this is my home.

My bedroom is enormous, and it doesn't feel like mine, not yet. The violet and cream bed is too big, the armoire has a dozen dresses I didn't choose, and the high ceilings make the room seem empty and looming, especially at night.

And when I walk through the halls during the day, every time I see a To'Morat warrior in black and red armor, I flinch.

I step out of bed and cross over to the window. Atoille is a low orb on the horizon, leaving a clear view of the stars. Kaera sleeps in her own room and goes to school with the other To'Morat children. She is happy here, has learned to eke out a good life. Seeing her smile steadies me.

But I can't let things go.

I sit on the window seat. It's still the middle of the night, and I should go back to bed, but I can't.

The window nook is cushioned and cozy. It's my favorite thing about the room, besides the many bookshelves lining the walls. I'll choose a new book to read by moonlight in a moment, but for now, I need to breathe.

The window overlooks the palace gardens and the winding path where Imwraeth and I took our walks with Kaera. Where I listened to him talk of his childhood, of his struggles of being a ruler.

I smile. It was on those walks when I fell in love with him.

I'd been planning escape since the beginning. I had to find where they were holding Kaera and go. I'd even gotten Imwraeth to believe that he could be healed if Kaera and I both worked on him all day, and then I searched for an opening.

But I couldn't do it. I couldn't leave him.

Imwraeth didn't order the attack on To'Shahera. He was a puppet in the hands of his councilors, Lienos and Therah, who are now both gone. Without them, Imwraeth has blossomed into an incredible leader. I have forgiven him.

The rest of the To'Morat people are a different story.

I bury my head in my hands. I can't live like this. I can't live here, day to day, seeing them always. The people who murdered mine.

I stand and choose a new book off the shelf. A lot of the books are on warfare theory, but many are also stories.

I snuggle into the cushions on the window seat and turn to page one.

☾

By the time the sun rises and engulfs Atoille's light, my eyes are drooping, and my head is pounding. Reading by the light of the moon is maybe not the best idea.

I force myself to get back in bed and under the covers, revulsion making my skin crawl. The bed is perfectly fine. The nicest I've ever slept in, actually. But this is where I relive the horror. Every. Single. Night. I brush sweaty bangs out of my face and attempt to make myself presentable.

A female servant, about fifteen years old, enters the room. She is small for her age, with spindly limbs. She is my maid, and she's here to help me get dressed, something that I don't think I will ever get used to.

"Breakfast in bed or at the table, Favored Lady?" The maid steps forward, carrying a breakfast tray full of berries and a creamy grain porridge.

"Oh, no. The Favored One and I aren't Anointed." I blush. "Favored Lady" is a title I don't have.

The maid bows her head. "My apologies, Lady Lylahn."

"At the table, please." I take a seat at a small crystal table, still wearing my nightgown, my hair a mess.

Imwraeth wants to be Anointed, promised to each other to eventually be wed. He still brings up the subject occasionally. But I'm just—not ready.

Even though my stomach is in knots, I force myself to eat. It is delicious. The berries are fresh and ripe, and the porridge smooth as cream, sweetened with cactus nectar. Food is plentiful, thanks to Norah.

Norah.

"Anything in particular you'd like to wear today, Lady Lylahn?" The maid pulls open the armoire door.

"No. You choose."

When I'm finished eating, I sit in front of the sand glass mirror. I'm given a tiny bowl of water to wash my face, a luxury. I'm stripped and scrubbed, cleaned and polished, and the maid does up the back of the dress she has chosen.

Today's an important day. Imwraeth must address the people and tell them what's happened with Norah before rumors fly out of control. And then we must council with his higher-ups to figure out a plan of what to do next.

I close my eyes. My shoulders sag with dread.

I sit while the maid teases my dark curly hair into something presentable. The gown she has chosen is lovely—a sky blue dress made of soft, flowing silk, so smooth compared to the camehl hair clothing I'm used to. It's cinched at the waist, and the skirts flow and swirl about my feet, almost like water. The neckline is a V plunging down a little lower than I would like, and I blush when I think of Imwraeth seeing me in this.

I glance up at the maid and startle when I see that she's crying. With a stab of guilt, I realize I've been so wrapped up in myself that I didn't even notice.

"Are you all right?" I wonder if she won't like me drawing attention to the fact that tears are sliding down her cheeks.

The girl scrubs at her tears with the back of one hand before continuing to work on my hair. "I apologize, Lady Lylahn."

I shake my head, and my curls slip from the maid's fingers. "No need. I understand. Is there...anything I can do?"

Her eyes well with tears again. "No, but thank you, Lady Lylahn. I lost—I lost my Anointed in the recent skirmish with those foreigners. We'd only just found out we'd be able to love, that our love would *strengthen* our sand gifts, and now—" Her voice breaks.

My heart sinks into my toes. I put one hand on top of hers. "I'm so, so sorry." I don't know what to say. There's nothing that can make this kind of pain better. "I've lost people, too. That kind of pain never really leaves." I wish this was something I could heal. Absorbing can do so much, but when it comes to pain within, I'm at a loss.

The girl takes a few deep breaths to compose herself. Deft fingers move through my hair, skillfully weaving it back out of my face without pulling or hurting me.

"What's your name?" I ask. I smile when I think of Imwraeth, a lifetime ago, asking me the same question.

"Amantha, Lady Lylahn."

"I'm happy you're here to help me, Amantha. Before I came here, I took care of a herd of camehls. I wasn't anyone special. This is all new to me."

She smiles. "Don't worry, Lady Lylahn. That's what I'm here for."

"Will you call me Lylahn?"

The expression on her face goes from shocked to horrified, and I shake my head. "Never mind. Lady Lylahn has a nice sound to it, doesn't it?"

Amantha nods and smiles, relieved.

She finishes with my hair and moves on to my face. She powders my cheeks and paints my lips and eyelids. I've never seen half of the tools she uses. I've never had the money or reason to buy powders to do up my face.

When Amantha steps aside and lets me look in the mirror, I'm shocked. I stand and get closer to the mirror, turning this way and that, examining my face.

My hair is lovely. She's somehow accentuated the curls and brought half of them up in a sweeping up-do. She's covered the permanent dark circles under my eyes and made my long eyelashes pop. My lips look rosy red. The dress highlights my natural curves, and the color looks magnificent next to my skin.

"Amantha, I don't know what to say." I take a step back from the mirror. "You've made me look…"

"Perfect." She smiles. "You look perfect, Lady Lylahn."

I smile back. It's probably inappropriate, but I turn and wrap my arms around her in a hug. She stiffens with surprise, but then softens. "I'm so sorry about your Anointed."

Amantha takes a deep breath. "Thank you, Lady Lylahn."

There's a knock on the door. Amantha steps away, and we both turn. My heart pounds. Will it be Imwraeth? Or will it be his guards, come to take me away? I'm certain they've realized that even though their Favored One wants me here, I don't belong. Imwraeth would never allow me to be imprisoned again, I remind myself.

Imwraeth enters the room, and I sigh in relief. His eyes light up when he sees me. His red hair looks almost gold in the morning light, and his dark eyes seem lighter, less burdened.

"What do you think?" I twirl the skirts, blushing.

"I love it." He looks me in the eyes. "I love you."

"I love you, Imwraeth." How good it feels to be able to say those words and not worry that I'm going to lose Absorbing. What an incredible gift Zadock and Norah have given us.

But even still. There's a tiny stab of bitterness in my heart, of anxiety, of fear. Worry for our future together. And what it means for me.

I haven't even known Imwraeth that long. On my home plateau of To'Shahera, potential partners may court for years before they decide to make a match and become Anointed. I've known Imwraeth for mere months. How do I know if this is love? Could I really spend the rest of my life with him? Here?

Am I in love with him because I have nowhere else to go?

I take his hand, nausea swirling in my stomach. I wave goodbye to Amantha, who's already making the bed and cleaning up, and we exit the room. We walk down the hallway. I try to glide, but it's nearly impossible in the heels Amantha is making me wear. They're short heels, thank Atoille. Imwraeth isn't that much taller than me.

Imwraeth holds out his elbow, and I weave my hand through it. It steadies me.

"You look gorgeous, Lylahn," Imwraeth says. "Your beauty blew me away when you were in prisoner's rags, and now...you're breathtaking."

"Thank you." I try to hold onto the compliment, to let it fill up some of the emptiness inside me. "Thank you for having all these dresses made for me."

Imwraeth waves his hand. We turn a bend in the marble corridors decorated with flourishing plants. "I would do anything for you."

Every step takes us closer to addressing his people. Our people?

The further we go, the more I have trouble standing up straight. My feet drag.

Imwraeth glances sideways at me. "Are you all right?"

I can only nod.

Four guards fall into place around us as we exit the palace, and my spine stiffens. Luckily, they're not wearing the red and black

To'Morat armor that haunts my dreams, just palace livery with spears at their hips. We begin the walk through the city. We could take a retahn-drawn carriage as we sometimes do, but today Imwraeth wants to be seen by his people.

The heat of the day is already scalding. I hope Amantha knows how to get sweat stains out of silk. We descend the palace's crystal steps, making our way into the streets of To'Morat. Imwraeth smiles, looking around at his people, at the full grow walls and gardens next to every home. It will be enough to last us a while longer, at least. Hopefully long enough for us to figure out what to do.

The guards make me uncomfortable, and I wish we could do without them. But of course, I don't say anything. It's not my place, and I don't understand the protocols here like Imwraeth does.

The people stare at us as we walk by. I hold Imwraeth's elbow a little tighter. He looks over at me with a reassuring smile and puts a hand on mine. "Don't worry. I'll do all the talking."

I breathe in and out. But the people's staring has me on edge. Many of them smile when they see us, but some look at me with hostility. Already, people expect to be fed again, and the miracle of what we helped Norah achieve has lost is shine. Or people don't know my part in it, that I was the one who rushed the red moonstone through the streets of To'Rahn and put it in its rightful place, and they only see a fragile prisoner turned royalty.

We reach the central plaza of To'Morat, and I follow Imwraeth up onto a raised dais. An enormous crowd is crammed into the dusty square, a large open space that is normally filled with people leading camehls and others bartering around market stalls. Even the alleys between shining quartz buildings are full of people. My breath catches at the sight. Most of the city has come to hear Imwraeth speak.

People are worried. Imwraeth is going to attempt to placate their fears and announce that we have a plan. I have no idea what he's going to say. We don't have a plan.

Imwraeth steps up onto the dais, practically dragging me behind him. I step on the corner of my dress and almost trip. Great. Very dignified. I hunch in on myself even more, wanting to disappear.

Imwraeth puts a hand in the satchel he wears at his side, and the sand within glows. Imwraeth needs to carry sand everywhere he goes and Extract from it to power his malformed heart, the heart I was unable to heal. People still give him funny looks, but not as many as he used to get. His people have accepted his malady just as he has.

A surge of pride fills my heart, and it reminds me why I'm here doing this. Being here, adjusting to this way of life, is so difficult, but it's not for me; it's for him.

I plaster a smile on my face and stand next to Imwraeth. The four guards stand at each corner of the dais.

The crowd stares at Imwraeth with solemn faces. It's good to see that those faces have filled out a little, that the hollow, blank gaze that plagued everyone during the famine is missing.

"People of To'Morat," Imwraeth begins. He Extracts sand from his satchel again, not to strengthen his heart but his vocal cords. His voice is amplified and spread throughout the plaza. People gather in the side streets and lean out of the windows of their homes. Every inch of space is filled.

"What you have heard is true," Imwraeth says. "The Sustainer, Norah Saranyi, has been taken from us."

"And who did this?" a man near the front of the crowd calls.

"A man called Agriad Zul and his warriors," Imwraeth says. "People who say they come from across the ocean of water."

It seems impossible, but Agriad Zul did say that. He could've been lying. His ship, though... It was unlike anything I've ever seen.

The people murmur. I'm not sure how well this is going. Imwraeth is meant to be easing their fears, not building them up. I resist the urge to push my bangs out of my face, forcing my hands to stay at my sides.

Imwraeth holds up a hand, and the people quiet. "We do not know much about these people other than they have taken our Sustainer from us."

Heated shouts and raised fists explode throughout the crowd. These are war-faring people, and they are disposed towards action. My heart speeds up, my eyes scanning the crowd, taking in the angry faces.

A flash of blood.

I blink and shake my head. No, no. There was no blood.

"But we will get her back!" Imwraeth cries.

"We will fight!" someone yells.

Imwraeth gives a sharp nod. "Plans are being made to retrieve Norah Saranyi in any way we can. We will—"

"What?" A woman near the front shouts. "You will do what? How do you plan to cross the ocean of water? It's outrageous!"

Imwraeth falls silent. "My people, we are strong. We will find a way. We will—"

Shocked whispers echo through the crowd.

"He doesn't know—"

"We're doomed."

"This is impossible—"

Imwraeth holds up his hands again, but the people don't silence this time. The voices get louder and more fearful, more insistent.

These are the warriors who attacked my people. The very same ones who hurled torches to burn my home to the ground.

"My people, please. Together we can come up with—" But Imwraeth's voice, even with his enhanced vocals, is being drowned out.

Someone near the front throws something.

A spear. Hurtling towards my sister.

I scream and duck my head, cover my ears with my hands. "Hyria, NO!"

Imwraeth looks down at me, his mouth open. "Lylahn, are you...?"

I open my eyes in horror and realize what I've said. The To'Morat people are quieter, and some stare at me in confusion. But others call out their anger and dismay. I see what was thrown—a plantain peel.

I have to get out of here.

My head feels full of fuzz as I stumble off the dais. I hear Imwraeth's voice calling for me as if from far away. Every step I take is a flash of fire, of sand, of blood.

I close my eyes and shake my head.

But when I open my eyes, I'm not here.

I'm there.

There's flame and chaos all around me, To'Shaherans screaming and running for their lives. Kaera's hand in mind, tears streaming down her ashen face. A burning home collapses in front of me, and I scramble to get away.

I fall off the dais.

The sky is blue above me, like my dress. The moon is a washed-out orb. I'm lying in the sand.

I stand on shaking legs and hurry away. Shame courses through me.

Imwraeth calls out my name, but I run back to the palace.

4

NORAH

I stare out over the ocean of sand at the rise and fall of the waves. Listen to the sound of the flowing and ebbing of the sand against the ship's hull. It's comforting. Familiar.

"Careful standing so close to the edge." A woman with black hair in braids warns us as she walks by carrying a coil of rope. "You don't want to fall through the sand."

I nod, but then I frown at her odd choice of words.

Zadock walks to stand next to me. Instead of looking at the sand waves, he stares at the people around us. They've taken off their armor now, and they wear loose white clothing with forearm and shin wraps. Shakers at the stern take turns steering and keeping the ship afloat. Agriad Zul walks among them all, clapping people on the shoulders, smiling and chatting with his crew. He wears a white tunic tied with a black sash about his waist.

Cheers follow Agriad wherever he goes. The people are happy for him, congratulating him on my rebirth or whatever. Do they genuinely believe that I am his daughter?

I close my eyes for a moment and inhale. The desert smells comforting, the sand earthy. I've always loved sailing. My potah used to take me all the time when I was young, before he fell into the ocean of sand and was sucked under, lost forever. That smell takes me back to simpler times. To times when my only worry was learning the constellations so I could navigate our small boat, trusting that even if I made a mistake, my potah would know where to go and what to do. I could breathe in that smell forever.

The wind shifts, and I get hints of Zadock's scent, warm and calming, and I change my mind. *This* is the smell I could breathe in forever.

When I open my eyes again, Zadock is looking at me. His brown-blonde hair is messier than I've ever seen it, and he attempts to flatten it with a hand, but it does no good. He places a hand on my back and leans toward me. "What are we going to do, Nors?"

"I don't know."

"We've got to escape somehow." Zadock lowers his voice even more and glances around. "We can't go with them. First of all, they're supposedly crossing the ocean of water, um what? Second, we can't leave our people. They need you. Things are just starting to get better."

I attempt a smile, though my stomach twists in knots. "So what do we do?"

Zadock opens his mouth but closes it again when Agriad strides toward us. He puts a hand on my shoulder, and my hackles rise, but I don't shrug him off. I'm afraid to offend him, afraid of what he'll do. "Welcome back, Cale. Norah. Just wait until we get you home." He smiles and stares over the side of the ship. "The ocean of sand is calming, is it not?"

I stand up straight, letting his hand fall. I'm not sure what to do here or how to play this game. What will he do if he realizes I'm not his daughter? Would he send us back or kill us?

"Yes, it is. Beautiful." I swallow. This is painful. "But, Potah..." Oh, how those words hurt. I can barely choke them out. I miss my true potah so much. Every moment since he died three years ago, I have missed him. Zadock squeezes my hand.

Agriad glances down at me. The smile on his pale face broadens, and the whites of his eyes seem to alight.

"I'm worried," I say. "I'm worried about the people we're leaving behind. I'm their only Sustainer. They need me."

Agriad shakes his head. "There is no need to worry, my daughter. You will soon understand. We are bringing you home. Then you will see."

I swallow and look away. Zadock's grip tightens on my hand. I hate this. If Zadock and I managed to escape, what would this man do? I don't believe that he'd just let us go. He would come back after us. It could mean a full-scale war.

I put my head in my hands. I don't know what to do.

One of the warriors approaches Agriad and bows low. "High Sustainer," he begins, "there is a colony of sand moles up ahead."

I perk up, remembering the one Zadock and I saw on the *Norah*, the small boat my potah named after me, so long ago. I always liked those creatures. I peek over the ship's edge and see three of them bobbing up above the sand waves, their antennae floating in the breeze, the hard backs of their shells rising and falling in the sand.

I point them out to Zadock. "Remember those?"

Zadock smiles. "Yeah. The antennae are poisonous, right?"

I manage a smile back, thinking of how I teased him on our small boat.

"High Sustainer, shall we go around them or go straight through?" The warrior asks. "They cannot survive the impact of the ship."

Agriad waves a dismissive hand. "Going around will lose us precious time. Go through."

My mouth falls open. "Wait, but—"

Agriad cuts me off with a frozen stare that sends chills up and down my spine. It reminds me that this is a dangerous man. "Norah. I will forgive this insolence this once because you do not remember the way of things. This one time, I will remind you of your place, girl.

You are my daughter, and you will obey me. You will not question my orders. Do you understand?"

I nod, my throat scratchy, like it's coated in sand. Zadock puts his arms on my shoulders, steadying me.

The warrior heads off to the Shakers, telling them to plow ahead through the colony of sand moles. Grinding shrieks fill the air, along with the cracking of shells. My stomach turns. All those creatures are dying because Agriad couldn't be bothered to turn the ship.

Agriad looks me in the eyes, locks his gaze onto mine. The whites of his eyes have bled to black again, and I jolt. Does this mean he's angry? His stare is terrifying. Agriad leans forward, and I back away further into Zadock.

Agriad's rough cheek grazes mine as he whispers in my ear. I swallow, trying to take in the feel of Zadock, Zadock behind me, strong arms protecting me. Not the sharp, metallic scent of this man's skin.

"Norah." His voice is a breath. "If you do not obey me, if you make one more step out of line, then this boy that you love will die. I promise you that."

Agriad straightens, and I gasp, the breath wrenched out of me.

"What?" Zadock says. "What did he say?"

I grip the sides of the ship. Agriad is called away.

That's why. That's why Agriad ordered Zadock to be brought with us.

Agriad is going to use him to control me, and I realize with dismay that it's going to work.

5

ZADOCK

The sun sets, and Atoille shines on the horizon. The ship plows onward.

I didn't hear what Agriad said to Norah, but something has shaken her. She clutches the side of the ship like it's a lifeline. Maybe it's just this weird boat, being here with these bizarre people, being kidnapped. I don't know. I'm just glad I'm with her.

Agriad brings us bowls of food. I don't recognize the small, round grain that's served, nor the white and green vegetables swimming in broth atop the grain.

I try to smile. "Thank you."

Agriad scowls.

Norah sits next to me on the deck, stirring her food and staring into it. The other warriors laugh and joke with Agriad and pass around a flask of something, cheering and toasting their victory. Every once in a while, one of them glances at Norah and raises the flask to her, but Norah doesn't seem to notice.

I nudge her with my elbow. "You need to eat." I lower my voice. "I don't know how long it will take us to get back to To'Morat floating by sand platform if we leave tonight."

Norah glances at me with enormous, dark eyes shining in the moonlight. My heart squeezes. She becomes more beautiful to me every day.

The desert is cooling, and no one has offered us coats, so I slide closer to her. How wonderful it feels to have her hip pressing against me, the bare skin of her arm touching mine.

"Zadock—"

Agriad Zul approaches us, and Norah cuts off. "Are you feeling well, my daughter? You haven't eaten much."

Norah looks at him and then back to her food. She takes a bite.

Agriad smiles. "When you are finished, I will show you both to your room."

I sputter around a spoonful of soup. "Um, room? Do I have a room?"

"Yes, of course. With Norah."

I swallow. I glance at Norah. I wonder how she feels about that. Yes, we slept on the same pallet for a week while we traveled across the ocean of sand on her small boat, but that was out of necessity. I guess this is, too. Speck, I loved that week.

But something feels different now that we're Anointed and promised to be wed. Every touch means more to me, and I think it also does to her. On To'Rahn, it's traditional to wait until after marriage to...do anything about your relationship. I swallow. Of course, in the past, love was discouraged since it weakened the sand gifts, so maybe traditions will change, but this still feels wrong.

Norah must have too much else on her mind because she doesn't react. She lifts the spoon to take another bite.

Agriad frowns. "You are Anointed, are you not? Is it so strange to share a room?"

I don't want to argue with this man. I don't want to explain our traditions. And Norah doesn't seem to want to, either. So I nod and try to smile. "Yes, we're Anointed. Thank you."

Agriad's smile toward me looks predatory, like he sees something he can devour. My stomach turns, not liking the foreign food. I find myself coughing out an awkward laugh, and then it turns into a real cough. I clear my throat, and Norah pats me on the back.

"I'm done. Are you, Zadock?" she asks.

I nod, still coughing.

"Then I will show you where you may sleep," Agriad says.

We follow Agriad, passing the rest of his crew, the warriors who, just earlier today, were blowing poisonous darts at me. They're drinking from multiple flasks now, and I don't want to know what's inside. I notice with a jolt that some of their eyes are tinted green. What the...?

We descend the same steps that lead to Agriad's cabin but take a right down the narrow hallway. Everything is made of the same black wood, and it's smooth when I run my hand along it. So strange. Where do they get the wood to make a ship of this size?

Agriad opens one of the doors to a cabin. There's one bed—wider than the pallet was, at least—and desk and chair, both Forged to the floor with a rim of quartz. The room is decorated with a painting of the ocean of water and a ship traveling on it. I'll examine it later. There's a blue-dyed rug on the floor and a small glass window on the far wall.

"This is your room, Cale." Agriad shakes his head. "Norah. It's going to take me a while to get used to that."

When he talks about his daughter, he sounds a little less like a snake.

Norah swallows and glances around the room.

Agriad nods to a large chest at the foot of the bed. "Your clothes are in there. They should still fit." He turns to me. "I'll have someone bring you something to wear." Agriad smiles once again at Norah. "Good night." He reaches out to touch her hair. Norah recoils but then freezes. Lets him stroke her brown hair. Ugh.

Agriad leaves—thank Atoille—and closes the door behind him. I wait and listen. I don't hear a lock click.

"Ok, so, what's the plan?" I pace the length of the room. "We're getting out of here, right?" I start planning in my head. All we have to do is wait until most of the crew are asleep. There will be someone keeping watch and Shakers moving the ship, but if we can avoid them, all we have to do is get to the deck, I'll form a platform out of sand, and then we'll be gone. Agriad doesn't know the extent of my power. He thinks he's safe from us escaping, out here in the middle of the ocean of sand. Well, he's wrong. I've done this before. Though I don't relish the prospect of traveling a long distance by sand platform again, I'll do it for her.

I'd do anything for her.

"The longer we wait, the farther away we'll be from To'Morat, so we should—" I cut off when I glance at Norah.

She's staring straight ahead, her focus lost.

"Nors." I put my hands on her shoulders, alarmed. This is so unlike her. She's the strong one. *She's* the leader, pulling me along. "It's going to be ok. We'll get out of here."

She looks into my eyes. Speck, she's gorgeous.

"It's going to be ok," I say again. I squeeze her shoulders.

Norah gives me one small, tight nod. "Zadock, why did that dead girl look like me? Not just similar." Norah shakes her head. "She looked exactly like me."

"I don't know, Nors. It's strange."

"Do I have a hidden twin sister I never knew about? Someone Motah somehow shuttled across the ocean of water to a foreign land at birth?"

I look at her with a raised eyebrow.

She sighs. "But then...was my potah not really my potah?"

"What? Of course he was!"

"But then what? How is this possible?"

"I..." I pause. "I don't know."

Norah closes her eyes. "Zadock, we have to stay."

I jolt back in surprise, dropping my hands from her shoulders. "What? No—"

"We can't leave. Think about it." Norah's eyes blink open.

"Ok. I'm thinking."

"He won't let us go. If we escape, they'll chase us back to To'Morat or wherever we go. They'll hunt us down. There will be war."

I walk over to the tiny round window and look out at the crashing waves of sand. I don't see a plateau anywhere in sight. Just desert and stars. No ocean of water, not yet. "The To'Morat can handle it. They'll fight for you. They need you. All the desert nations need you."

Norah walks over to the bed and sits down on a patchwork quilt of different shades of blue. She puts her head in her hands. "I don't want a war. Not again."

I turn to her and square my shoulders. "The people will die without you, Norah. They would all say the same thing I am—that you're worth fighting for."

She looks at me, her eyes wide and liquid, full of tears. "Agriad said—" She pauses. "Agriad said he would kill you if I don't do what he says."

I freeze. That's what's been eating her up, making her do whatever he wants.

No...

"Nors, I..." I don't know what to say, so I sit on the bed next to her and put an arm around her shoulders. I swallow. "I still think we should run. The To'Morat will protect us both. We'll—"

"No." Norah stiffens under my arm. "I won't risk that. I can't."

I grit my teeth. We've been given an awful choice. Escape, and know that there will be a war and lives will be lost, that Agriad will target me? Or stay and know that without Norah to Sustain, the famine will strike again, and people will starve?

Norah grips the quilt. "Zadock. You are *everything* to me. I can't lose you." Her voice trembles. "I can't."

I hold her tight, and she melts into my chest. "I feel the same way, Norah. My wild girl."

We stay like that for a moment, arms wrapped around each other.

"I want to know why that dead girl looked like me," Norah says.

"Maybe we can figure out a way to leave without a war, without more people dying. Maybe I can convince him that I'm not really his daughter."

I raise an eyebrow. "You think that's possible? Nors, he's not going to change his mind. The longer we stay, we'll only get deeper in. Now is the time to escape. Tonight. We'll get back to To'Morat and make plans to defend you."

Norah shakes her head. "We don't know what kinds of resources these people have. What defenses, what weapons, what numbers. They can kill with a single blow. How do we fight against that? This could end in everyone we love dead." She sits up, and her eyes meet mine. They say what she's really thinking. *Including you.*

"Maybe they're not strong," I say. "Maybe they're a wimpy little village in the middle of nowhere."

"With the ability to cross the ocean of water? With poison that can kill almost instantly? We don't know what we're up against."

I open my mouth to argue, but Norah continues. "Zadock, I'm— I'm afraid that if we fly off this ship on a platform of sand, one of them will see us." She pauses. Swallows. "They'll shoot you with a blow dart, leave you to fall into the ocean of sand, and a Shaker will carry me back to this ship." Her eyes fill with tears. "I'll be alone, surrounded by enemies, and you'll be—you'll be—"

I freeze. She's right. *Speck.* She's right.

Norah takes my hand.

I sigh, resigned. I give her hand a squeeze. "All right. We'll—we'll find a better way." *I will get you out of here, my love.* "How did he even know about you?"

Norah shakes her head. "I don't know." She glances up at me with a shy smile. "Is it weird we're in the same room? Again?"

I lift a hand and stroke her cheek. "Not at all."

Yeah. It's totally weird. Everything is different now that she's mine. I swallow, feeling longing rising within me. I'm done with being Anointed. I'm ready for more. I know what I want, and it's her.

"Are you ok with sleeping in the same bed?" I ask.

"You're not sleeping on the rug," Norah says. She lays back down on the bed, yawning. The night has gotten darker, and the pale light of Atoille shines through the window. I lay down next to her and stare at her lovely face.

Norah turns to face me, our noses inches apart. I reach out and tenderly brush the hair from her forehead, tingling going up and down my spine just from that simple touch. Norah closes her eyes. I cup my hand around her cheek and stroke back and forth with my thumb.

I lean forward and press my lips to her forehead. Her skin is soft, her scent comforting, and a rush goes through me.

"It's going to be ok, Nors," I whisper. "I'm here with you. This time, I am going to take care of you."

Norah tilts her head to look up at me, her brown eyes shining. My breathing quickens.

Norah closes the distance between us, coming in for hungry kisses. Her lips are smooth and tantalizing. I kiss her back, wrapping my fingers in her hair. She adjusts to lie atop me, her body fully against mine, only the thin fabric of our clothing keeping our skin apart. I wrap my arms around her and hold her close. The feeling of her... It's everything.

"Holy speck," I breathe in between kisses.

Norah smiles. Her eyes are warm and wet, her lips full and rosy. She kisses me again like she's desperate, like she needs me more than anything, and it fills me with joy. How did I get her? What did I do to deserve her?

I hold her in my arms like she's precious and delicate. Our clothing is getting mussed, and the bare skin of her stomach touches mine. Something like fire shoots through me. And speck, her lips—

Norah kisses me once, twice, full and long and slow. Then she pulls away and presses her forehead against mine.

"I love you, Zadock," she breathes.

"You are everything to me, my Norah."

She rolls away and gets under the blankets, and I follow, a little disappointed but also, I get it. Tradition and all that.

We sleep in our clothes because I don't have anything else, and Norah doesn't look through the trunk of a dead girl's clothing. I tuck in tight next to her, and she curves her body into mine. I wrap my arms around her and lay awake for a long time.

If Norah won't escape, then I will protect her at all costs.

6

ZADOCK

The next morning, we emerge from below deck and are greeted with cheers and raised fists. The sailors wear heavy wool coats to stave off the freezing cold of the night, but some are already shucking them off.

Only one, I notice, does not seem happy about us being here. A girl about our age crosses her arms across her chest and frowns. The whites of her eyes darken to gray. She has light blonde hair swept up into a tail.

Agriad Zul strides toward us, and I turn my attention to him. He walks forward with open arms, a huge smile on his face. "Daughter." His eyes narrow in on me. "Zadock."

I swallow. Somehow, I manage to give him a nod.

Agriad produces two cloaks, one for Norah and one for me. Both are finely made, soft and thick, lined with some kind of animal fur. Norah's is dyed blue, and mine is black.

"This is yours, Norah." Agriad does the clasp of the cloak for her. "Blue is still your favorite color, is it not?"

Norah gulps and nods.

Her favorite color is not blue! I want to shout. *It's orange, like the sand.*

Agriad beams. "Well then." His eyes fill with tears. "It's so good to have you back." He frowns. "But you're not wearing your own clothes, my daughter. You must change." Agriad barks orders for some new clothes to be brought to me as well. "But first, breakfast."

Agriad leads us across the deck to the other side. My hackles raise. Sailors turn to watch us, their eyes merry, but I see cunning in them. The blank, white eyes give me the chills.

We descend the other set of stairs and come into a dining room. Black wooden tables and chairs are stuck to the floor with quartz, and there's a countertop and a cook serving up food. It smells good, and my stomach growls.

"We shall eat together, of course," Agriad says, taking a seat. Norah slides into a chair, and I sit next to her. "I'm sure you have many questions. Rebirth is never easy."

I glance at him. I do have many questions, but I don't know how much I can trust his answers.

"Rebirth," Norah says. "Has this ever happened to...me before?"

Steaming bowls of soup are placed in front of us. Soup for breakfast? It's strange. But I'm so hungry I don't care. I pick up my spoon and take a bite. It's sweet and savory at the same time, with some kind of white chunks of vegetables floating around in the aromatic broth. It's different but good.

"Not to you, no," Agriad says. "But to other Sustainers, yes."

"And you said that you are a Sustainer?" Norah asks. She hasn't touched her soup. I pick up her spoon and put it in her hand. Without looking away from Agriad, Norah takes a bite.

Agriad sips at the broth. "Yes. I am. Just like you, just like your motah was."

Norah bristles, but Agriad doesn't seem to notice.

"Was?" She asks.

Agriad stirs his soup. "Yes. She passed on a long time ago."

I finish my first bowl, and a boy, only a little older than Norah's sister, Shrey, comes to refill it. A platter of some kind of squishy steamed bread is brought to the table, and I take one for Norah and then for me.

"Have you been reborn?" Norah asks.

"No." Agriad shakes his head. "In fact, the process hasn't happened in many generations until now. The people on this side of the ocean of water have not had Sustainers for very long, yes?"

Norah nods. "Yes. So why—"

Agriad cuts her off with a sharp shake of his head, and Norah closes her mouth. "That's enough questions for now. Let us enjoy breakfast. Our Shakers are making good time, and we'll reach the ocean of water soon."

Soon. I take a bite of bread, but I find that my appetite has vanished. I drink some water from a wooden mug. Wood. Not quartz.

There's a commotion up above deck. We can hear it even from down here, cheering and shouting. What's going on?

"Ahhh." Agriad smiles. "I believe we are here." He stands. "Come, daughter, if you have finished. Let us see the ocean of water."

7

———

LYLAHN

"My councilors." Imwraeth leans forward, his hands clasped before him on the table. "What do we do about this?"

I sit next to Imwraeth in the council room, trying to force myself to pay attention and shake off the nightmare from the previous night. Imwraeth had someone remove the small table that was here before and replace it with a larger one. With Therah gone and Lienos in prison, Imwraeth has appointed more councilors, including me. I've been to a few of these meetings now, and I'm not very valuable in them, but I try. For him.

He wants me to feel like I have a place here. He hasn't said that outright, but I know that's the reason he's appointed me as a councilor. Me, who has no experience with this and who doesn't know these people or their needs.

Amantha has dressed me in a lilac gown today, along with a tiny chain necklace that has a crystal sphere at the end. It's pretty, but it feels like a collar. A collar put on a stubborn camehl to lead it in the right direction.

I try to sit up straight and pay attention. Imwraeth is explaining our circumstances to his councilors. There are three besides me.

General Riah, the woman who stayed loyal to Imwraeth despite his previous general trying to take control, sits at Imwraeth's left, looking serious as she listens. Her short black hair is getting longer, down to her neck now, and it curls slightly. The spear she always carries leans against her chair.

The other two are new to me, and I'm not sure how Imwraeth knows them or why he chose them. There's Councilor Sahlas, a woman in her mid-thirties with dark red hair and straight-across bangs. She sits with her hands folded in her lap, watching Imwraeth. Her eyes look like a desert hawk's.

Next to her is Councilor Danosrin. He's tall, and even sitting, he towers over the rest of the council. His cropped hair is dark brown, and he appears to be about the same age as Councilor Sahlas. His eyes are gray and soft, kind. Absorbing is a rare sand gift, but I've been told that he is an Absorber like me. His face always makes me feel a twinge of recognition, like I should know him from somewhere.

He notices me staring and smiles. I look away.

The room is decorated with portraits of To'Morat leaders. Imwraeth's painting was only recently added. He looks handsome as ever in the picture, and I can't help but smile when I look at it. He looks stern and commanding, yet there's a hint of a smile on his face and a twinkle in his eye. I sat and watched while his portrait was painted, and the smile was for me.

Potted plants line the walls. Plants that used to be thriving under Norah's care but are already starting to wilt.

"That, my friends, is our plight." Imwraeth finishes and clasps his hands in front of him on the table. He looks at his councilors with an expectant face, a confident one. It makes my heart happy to see him like this, sure of his place and his role. Only two moon cycles ago, he was quivering as the puppet leader of the To'Morat, certain that he could not be a good leader to his people while his heart was sickly. He still carries the satchel of sand that he must Extract from to power his heart, yet he appears confident and strong. He's a new person.

Danosrin clears his throat. "So. Norah Saranyi has been taken from us. How long can we survive on what we have now?"

Imwraeth sighs. "With what Norah's given us? We have about two months until we're completely out of food. If we ration and Extractors take turns using energy from sand to go without eating, a little longer."

Riah gasps, and I meet her eyes across the table. Only two months. Norah worked hard, but she's only one person. We're doomed without her, and the other plateaus of the desert are in the same plight.

"We don't have much time, then, to come up with a solution," Sahlas says. Her voice is crisp and sharp.

"What can we do, Favored One?" Riah asks.

I glance from her to Imwraeth. He looks at me, tenderness in his eyes. Eyes so dark they're almost black, at odds with his striking red hair. I could lose myself in those eyes.

"What do you think, Councilor Lylahn?" Imwraeth asks.

"I—uh—" I swallow and sit up straighter. I think for a moment. What can we do? "You're right about rationing. We need to be careful about the food we have left. We don't know how long it will take to rescue Norah." I pause. "Are we going to rescue her?" I look from Imwraeth to the faces around the table.

"We don't have much choice," Sahlas says. "We cannot go on without her."

"Councilor Lylahn is right." Imwraeth smiles at me, even though all I did was repeat the need Imwraeth pointed out. "Councilor Sahlas, oversee the rationing of food. Take stock of what we have and dole it out wisely. Work with food merchants to make sure prices don't get out of hand. I want everyone to make it through this, not just the wealthy."

Sahlas purses her lips and nods. She takes every assignment Imwraeth gives her the same way, with a grunt of affirmation and a frown. But she does what he says and follows through.

"We've got to make that food last as long as we can," Danosrin says.

Imwraeth nods. "Include the palace on those rations, Sahlas."

"I will."

Imwraeth suddenly looks weary, older than his eighteen years. "And how do we get Norah back?"

The table goes quiet. Sahlas drums her fingers on the table, and Danosrin stares into his lap. Riah frowns.

"We have to build a ship," I say.

The entire table looks my way, and I feel myself shrink. *Not good enough. Don't belong here. Can't do this.*

I swallow.

"Go on, Councilor Lylahn," Imwraeth says.

"Those people said they came from across the ocean of water, right?" I say.

Danosrin nods. "Yes. One of the many hurdles facing us."

"We don't have a ship capable of crossing it," I say. "So, we build one. Copy their design as best we can."

"Impossible," Sahlas scoffs. "The ocean of water cannot be crossed."

"And yet," Imwraeth says, "it was. If we believe them."

"Why would they lie?" Riah adds.

"They might have lied," Sahlas says, "so we'd pursue them to our deaths!"

Imwraeth holds out a placating hand. "Calm, Councilor Sahlas. You're right. They might have lied. But think. We've never seen a ship like that, narrow instead of wide, with black wood. Those people looked different from any around here. They are not like us."

They are not like us. How many times did Imwraeth and his councilors use that rationale when they attacked and decimated other plateaus? I look down at my hands on the table and find that they're shaking. I put them in my lap.

"I believe that they were telling the truth." Imwraeth looks to me. "And I believe that Councilor Lylahn is correct. We have to cross the ocean of water if we're going to get Norah back. We need a ship that's capable of doing it." He turns to Danosrin. "Councilor Danosrin, will you gather our best engineers and have them research how this can be done?"

Danosrin nods. "Yes, Favored One."

Imwraeth gives him a small smile. "Thank you, Councilors. Together, we can figure this out."

The grave faces around the table nod back at Imwraeth. My shoulders tighten with dread. How are we going to accomplish this?

Imwraeth turns to Riah. "Councilor Riah, I want you to send out a scouting boat. It's possible the foreigners haven't made it to the ocean of water yet. Find them. Instruct our warriors to watch them, but don't engage unless there's a clear opportunity to get Norah back. These people are powerful. We need to research how best to defeat them."

"It will be done right away."

Imwraeth takes a deep breath. "I also need you to prepare our warriors for war."

The words send ice up my spine.

"When the ship is built, we'll need our strongest contingent of warriors to accompany me to fight these people and rescue Norah. Get them ready."

Riah nods.

We break at last, and I'm heading for the door when someone puts a hand on my arm.

I jump, and my heart leaps into my throat. A scream rises within me.

But I turn, and it's only Danosrin.

I swallow, taking a deep breath. His expression is concerned, and he removes his hand from my arm.

"I'm sorry." I shake my head. "Yes?"

"You did well, Lylahn." Danosrin smiles. "That was an excellent suggestion."

"Thank you." I flush from the compliment. Out of the corner of my eye, I see Imwraeth glance back at me while he finishes his discussion with Riah and Sahlas.

"Are you all right?" Danosrin asks. "I can't imagine doing what you're doing."

"Doing?"

"Living here." He gestures. "Amidst us. The bloodthirsty To'Morat."

I force a laugh, but it's pained.

Danosrin's expression softens. "Not all of us are like that, Lady Lylahn. Some of us wanted peace all along."

Tears spring up in my eyes, and I hurry to blink them away. "Thank you. That was kind of you to say."

Danosrin squeezes my shoulder as he walks by.

I watch him go with a sigh. It was kind, but his words put into stark relief the truth—I don't belong here.

8

NORAH

The ocean of water is stunning.

I'm struck dumb as we ascend the stairs and stare at the enormous waves. Taller than any plateau, the waves slam down onto the sand and suck it under. I've seen it before, but the sight is so incredible that it takes my breath away again. Each collision of water against sand is a roar. We're close enough that droplets of water splatter against my face and clothes.

It's the answer to a question I've had since I was small—if the moon is so close and so large that she pulls the sand into waves, what does her gravity do to the ocean of water?

The answer is terrifying, and my stomach churns with dread. We're going to sail that?

"How?" Zadock stammers. "How is it done?"

Agriad turns to me as if I asked the question. "You will see."

Zadock takes my hand in his and squeezes it almost too hard. He's told me about his experiences in the ocean of water, where he fought for his life and the red moonstone. Zadock retrieving the red moonstone and reuniting it with the blue is what fixed everything and made it so that love powers the sand gifts instead of hindering them, but still. I wish he hadn't had to go through that. I wish we weren't here right now, bringing up his terror.

We don't have a choice here. We have to trust these people.

The crew starts readying the ship, and I watch with interest. They fold in the sails, which makes sense. Cloaks are handed out that look like sand cloaks, but they're stiffer, slicked down with oil. I wrap mine around myself. Much of the crew goes below deck, and those who remain above tie sturdy ropes around their waists, with the other end attached to the mast.

"Do you want to go down?" Zadock asks. "Or stay above?"

"We—we need to stay above," I whisper. "We need to see how this is done."

Zadock nods. He raises a hand, and a sailor about our age with white-blonde hair brings us each a rope. She stares at us before moving away to attend to her duties.

Zadock ties the rope around my waist and then triple-checks that it's secure. I'm shaking. This whole journey has me unhinged.

I'm afraid for myself. I don't know what is ahead or what Agriad will do when I am not the daughter he wants or when I don't live up to whatever he has planned. I'm afraid for Zadock. Afraid of losing him.

That is the one thing I can never allow to happen.

"High Sustainer!" one of the crew calls. "A ship!"

I whirl around. Quickly approaching on the horizon is a ship with black and red sails.

"The To'Morat," Zadock breathes. "They've come for you."

I catch my breath.

Zadock's voice goes quiet. I can barely hear him over the spray of the water waves. "Nors. I could get you to that ship. We could escape."

I hesitate, but then I shake my head. "They'll shoot you down out of the sky and take me back. We couldn't make it in time."

Zadock looks stricken. "You're right." He chokes out the words.

Agriad Zul turns to look at the ship in the distance. I get a better look. It's a smaller boat, so not a warship. Probably scouts sent to gauge the situation.

"Zadock," I whisper. "I don't think they're going to engage. I don't think they're here to—"

"Attack!" Agriad Zul cries.

His warriors rush to their stations. The ocean of water roars and sprays before us, but their attention turns to the stern.

"Shakers, now!" Agriad calls.

Shakers adjust the ship so that the starboard side faces the incoming To'Morat. Dread swirls within me, and I want to do something, but I'm helpless.

"Nors, we have to warn them. Something—"

"Shakers, attack!" Agriad yells.

The Shakers gather along the starboard in a line, their blank white eyes lighting up. They're each still tied to the central mast, but it doesn't seem to hinder their movements. As one, the row of warriors moves their arms, Shaking the sand. The boat is a good distance away, so far that it must require a tremendous amount of strength and skill, but they Shake the sand underneath the boat. It tips and rocks. The cries of the To'Morat are carried to us on the wind.

"Stop this!" I cry.

Agriad doesn't acknowledge me. "Again!"

The Shakers move the sand as one. They're working together. This is a maneuver they've practiced.

"Stop!" Zadock cries. "Leave them alone!"

"Again!" Agriad is relentless.

The Shakers move again, the sand undulating underneath the To'Morat ship. It tips back and forth, their Shakers frantically trying to right it, but they are so few. It's only a scouting boat.

Zadock subtly outstretches his arms, and I know he's Shaking, trying to help the To'Morat. My fists clench and unclench. I hate this. I *hate* this.

The To'Morat ship tips over.

"NO!" I shout.

The crew screams, and most of them are sucked under the sand immediately. One Shaker rises on a platform of sand, but it's immediately yanked out from under him by one of Agriad's crew. He falls, screaming, until he's pulled into the ocean of sand.

My hands fly to my mouth. *No...*

Zadock releases his hold on the sand and puts one arm around my shoulders, pulling me close.

Agriad gives one satisfied nod and his crew cheers. "Well done, everyone."

"How could you do this?" I turn to Agriad, anger and fire within me.

He raises one eyebrow, then looks from me to Zadock with a calculating, cold gaze. I fall silent.

"Onward!" Agriad calls.

The Shakers resume their posts, pushing the ship closer and closer to the ocean of water. The boat speeds up. The air tastes salty, and water mists on my face. I touch my cheek, and my finger comes away damp.

Zadock and I are quiet. I'm shaking with fury.

"The To'Morat shouldn't have done that," Zadock says. "Sent a scouting boat."

I can only nod.

Zadock scrubs a hand through his hair. "Why not send the whole fleet, To'Morat? Come on," he mutters.

I glance sideways at him. He's getting harder to hear over the roar of the water. It's like a beast, looming closer and closer, the waves smashing into the sand.

"If they had sent more, more would've died," I say.

Zadock stares at me. "But...it's the To'Morat. If they can't fight these people, who can?"

"I don't know." I stare at a hulking wave tearing toward the shore.

"Norah." Zadock's voice is low. "We can't go in there. Look

around you." He glances from side to side. The howl of the ocean of water grows louder. "They're distracted. Let's go. Now."

"Zadock." I take his hands in mine. Press a kiss to his fingers. "I know you're scared, but—"

"Scared?" Zadock laughs, on the verge of hysteria. "I'm specking terrified."

This is what unhinges me the most. I've never seen him like this.

"We have to—"

"These people are insane." He shakes his head. "This crossing can't be done. Their ship is different than ours. So what? This isn't—" His voice is cut off by the rushing roar of a wave. It's taller than To'Rahn. The ship falls into its shadow.

Zadock looks up, pure panic on his face.

Agriad stands at the helm, his black hair whipping in the wind. He outstretches his hands, and I see something in his right, something glowing green.

"What is—"

The wave peaks and then moves down toward us. I look up. I can't help it. The crew shouts, and Zadock throws his arms around me. I look up as the wave crashes down. We are underneath it, completely in its shadow. The wake of the wave is white and foamy, the tangy smell of salt overwhelming. Outlines of creatures, some big and some small, swim within the wave. My heart jumps, terror and adrenaline blotting out all thoughts.

I scream. Zadock grips me tight.

The wave crashes.

I shut my eyes and put my hands over my head, bracing myself. But then...nothing. When I open my eyes, we're dry. The wave isn't above us anymore.

What just happened?

Agriad still stands at the helm, but he's lowered his hands. The green glow is gone. We're sailing on the water, and the ship dips and rises with the waves. Shakers still move their arms at the head and rear of the boat.

"Are they using sand to steer the ship?" I have to yell over the spray. We tumble down the crest of an enormous wave, and my feet leave the deck for a moment before crashing back down.

"I think so!" Zadock calls. Even though he's looking at me with pure terror, he says, "Are you ok, Nors?"

I hang onto him. We crouch low together on the deck. It's slippery, and we slide toward the bow of the ship.

"I'm—I'm—"

Another enormous wave of water looms above us. It's a beast, going to swallow us. Zadock was right. We should've left. And now there's no sand to get us away.

I see Agriad out of the corner of my eye. He raises his hands once more. There's the green glow again.

This time, I force my eyes to stay open.

We go through the wave.

The water parts around us, starting at the narrow tip of the ship. The curtain of water gets bigger, like a waterfall cascading down around the ship. I look up and see the point, the tip of water that goes above the masts, just skimming the top. A fish the length of my arm with spiny fins flops onto the deck. It's bigger than any of the tiny fish that swim in the canals or oases back home. A nearby warrior spears it with a grin.

I swallow. My stomach can't handle this much longer.

"Did you see that?" I ask.

Zadock nods. "What is happening? How is Agriad doing that?"

I shake my head. We emerge through the wave and plummet down the other side. This one is slightly less steep, but my stomach still churns. Droplets of water collect on my slick cloak and slide down. We slip across the deck, and we're closer to Agriad now.

He's lowered his hands, and he stands, his footing somehow solid, as we cascade down the wave, leaving a white wake in our path.

"These are the dunes, daughter!" Agriad shouts. "We're riding the dunes of water."

We reach the bottom of the crest and settle into the water. I realize the narrow design of the ship is made for cutting through waves, how quickly she rights herself at the bottom. Still, this way of traveling, it's pure recklessness.

And even worse is the nagging voice in the back of my head. *We'll never go back. We'll never get back through this on our own.*

Our chance to escape has passed. I blew it because I was afraid.

Zadock's got his eyes squeezed shut, and he's turning green, but he's alive. *He's alive.*

Agriad raises his arms again, and the water parts above our heads. We drop down the other side of the wave, and it's smaller than the previous waves, but still a steep decline.

I swallow bile and hold my stomach. I'm glad I only picked at my breakfast. Zadock is not as lucky. He stumbles to the railing and vomits over the side of the ship.

Agriad laughs, and part of me wants to punch him in the face. Instead, I stand by Zadock's side and rub his back with one hand, the other gripping the railing. It's unnerving, being this close to the edge. Schools of fish swim through the rocking water, glinting silver in the sunlight. A larger creature with spikes trailing along a sinuous body snakes through a wave to our right. A shiver of fear courses through me.

"Agriad, are we—"

"Potah," he snarls. "You must call me potah."

I swallow. The water is calming down but still rocky, and Zadock looks green. "Potah." I choke out the word. It strangles my heart on the way out. "Are we safe from these creatures in the water?"

Agriad smiles. "You are perfectly safe."

I gulp.

"Watch, Norah," Agriad points with one hand. "There it is. A dune that will take us home."

I glance to the right, and I gasp. One of the waves is still, the water frozen in a crest. The foam churns and bubbles at the top, but the wave doesn't move. The strangest thing is that the wave glows green. The same green that emanates from Agriad's hand.

Zadock lifts his head and inhales sharply.

"Feel a little better?" I ask.

He nods and wipes his mouth. Then he shakes his head. "No."

The Shakers steer the ship toward that green wave.

"Po...Potah," I call. "What is that?"

"A dune of water," Agriad yells over the roar of the waves. "This dune is special. Atoille herself has touched it."

The ship pierces the green wave. Agriad raises his arms, and there's the green glow again. I catch a glimpse of something in his hand.

It's a moonstone. A faceted, shining green moonstone.

What...?

I expect the water to part above us, but instead, we crash into it.

The green glow explodes.

9

———

LYLAHN

My pale pink dress swirls around my feet when I walk. I don't understand why Amantha insists on doing my makeup and hair and dressing me up every day, even when there's not an event to attend. It's tiresome, but it's always worth it to see Imwraeth's face.

I stroll through the hallways without direction, mostly trying to avoid another meeting with Imwraeth and the other councilors. I study the tapestries in the hallway, glance at the wilting plants, and listen to the swish, swish of my skirts. I pass servants but luckily no guards. No one dressed in To'Morat armor. It's easier to pretend that way, that these could be my people.

My people.

Sometimes, it strikes me out of nowhere. All the To'Shaherans are gone. Kaera and I are the last of our plateau.

I stop and put my hand on a wall to steady myself.

I hear voices, and I see that the doorway I've stopped next to is cracked open a tad. I peek inside and see a group of familiar faces, people I know to be Imwraeth's best engineers. There's a design hung on the wall that they're arguing over.

A ship.

This is the meeting where they're trying to decide how to build a ship to go after Zadock and Norah. I glance at the design. It looks a lot like the pointed black ship that took Norah and Zadock away, but something sits uneasily with me.

How did *that* ship cross the ocean of water?

We're missing something.

I hear a clatter of footsteps behind me, the clink of someone walking in armor. I gulp and rush down the hallway, leaving the meeting of engineers behind. I'm sure they know what they're doing much better than me.

I hurry along, trying to look like I have a purpose. The footsteps get softer, farther behind me, and I breathe a sigh of relief. I blow my bangs out of my eyes.

My stomach growls, and I shake my head. How quickly I've gotten used to full meals; the reduced rations already have my stomach complaining. I'm not the only one. I pass a pair of servants arguing about food and how to divide it up.

I find myself passing through the doors that lead to the palace grounds, nodding at the servants holding open the doors for me. I'm not sure where I'm going, but I'm happy to breathe the fresh air. Happy to be able to come and go as I please.

The desert air is warm and dry, and I'm already sweating in my dress as I descend the grand crystal steps of the palace, but I don't care. I cared for the camehl herd on To'Shahera, so I'm used to being outside a lot.

The pang of loss surges forward, but I shove it back.

I pass a few people coming and going from the palace, lords and ladies dressed similarly to me, petitioning Imwraeth with their worries. Servants carrying burdens. No guards. No warriors.

I don't know if I'm ready to walk through To'Morat city by myself quite yet. And Imwraeth has asked me not to go anywhere without a guard, so I take a right to stay within the palace walls.

I walk along a sandy path, letting the movement loosen the knots in my chest and throat.

A long whinny startles me out of my thoughts, and I look up to see that I've found the retahn stables. Before me is a large quartz structure divided into stalls, a retahn in each. In front of me is a dusty, fenced-in arena. A girl about my age with short, yellow hair poking out from a sweaty cap runs a retahn in circles.

The retahn is skittish and young, and she doesn't want to do what the girl wants. The gorgeous creature skirts away from the girl, its black horns glinting in the sunlight. Her black coat is glossy in the sunshine.

The retahn tosses her head, whinnying, and the rope flies out of the girl's fingers. Her expression is so startled that I can't help but giggle.

The girl whips her head toward me, and she scowls. "If you think you can do better, then go ahead!" She stalks out of the arena. The retahn prances off to the side to graze on some brown grass poking out of the sand.

"I'm sorry."

The girl puts her hands on the railing and stares at the retahn, frowning.

"I didn't mean to laugh. I thought you were doing great."

She glares. "And you're an expert somehow?"

"No. But if retahn are anything like camehls..." I pause, not knowing if it's my place to say something. "You should never let her graze without your permission. Food is what she cares about. If you let her eat while you haven't given her leave, you're letting her take control."

The girl glances at me with a softer gaze, surprise in her eyes. She lets out a sigh. "This isn't supposed to be my job, you know. The retahn master was killed in the battle with To'Rahn."

"I'm so sorry."

"Don't be. He wasn't a kind master." The girl eyes me sideways.

"I want to do this. But some help would be nice." She looks me over, taking in the silks and finery. "You have some influence with the Favored One, yes? Can you ask him to appoint more stable hands? People who know what they're doing?"

"I—"

Without waiting for a reply, the girl goes back into the arena and picks up the rope, jerking on it and clicking. The retahn protests but obeys, going back into her circling loops around the arena.

I find something like longing inside me when I watch the girl and her retahn. I enjoyed caring for the camehls on To'Shahera. It was something I was good at, and it was a simpler life.

A presence stands next to me, and the hairs on my arms raise. I turn and relax when I see Imwraeth.

"I wondered where you were," he says.

"I had to get away. Just for a little while."

Imwraeth sighs. "It's all right, Lylahn. I know you're going through a lot." He takes my hand in his and strokes my thumb.

Guilt swirls in my stomach. "I know you are, too." I want to be there for him. I just don't know how.

"It's fun to watch the trainers and the retahn, isn't it?"

I smile. "It is."

"Maybe you could come down here and learn to ride," he says. "You know, whenever we have time."

My smile widens. "I'd like that."

Imwraeth turns to me, and my heart beats a little faster. That spark of love started back when he was a weak, powerless leader. I fell for *him*, the goodness inside of him. And now he's come into himself even more.

I've watched him come alive, but I am withering.

And truly, how well do I know him? Not well enough to seal my life to his, not with everything that comes with that choice.

Imwraeth leans to press his lips to mine under the awning of the retahn shelter. The smell of the retahn, clean and fresh, is overtaken by the smell of him, the feel of him in my arms and his mouth against mine. My heart flutters, my body flooded with warmth.

Imwraeth pulls away too soon. He takes my head in both of his hands, running his thumbs over my cheeks. I close my eyes.

"Tell me about your sisters." Imwraeth lowers his hands.

I blink my eyes open in surprise.

"If...if you want to," Imwraeth adds, heat creeping into his cheeks. "I realize that might be difficult."

I swallow and lean against the railing, watching the retahn go around the arena.

I let the memories overcome me. Hyria, laughing in the kitchen while she chopped vegetables, always dancing and singing. Bellah was solemn and serious, but Hyria could get her to laugh.

I take a deep breath. "Hyria was the oldest. She is—was—four years older than me. Bellah was two years older than me. They were both very protective, especially after we lost our parents to the blood plague." I take a moment to steady myself.

Imwraeth puts a hand on my back. "What were they like?"

It's so, *so* hard, but I keep going. "Hyria loved growing things. Taking care of our small garden was her greatest joy, besides tickling and chasing Kaera. Bellah loved to read, like me." I let a small smile creep onto my face. "We both spent hours at the tiny stall in the market that sold books, haggling over prices and then arguing over who got to read which book first." The smile fades. "She would've loved it here."

Imwraeth's hand on my back wraps around my shoulders and pulls me to him. "Thank you. Thank you for telling me about them." He pauses. "I love you, Lylahn," Imwraeth whispers. "I know I'm asking a lot. I'm asking you to lead the people who—" He swallows. "Who killed yours. I know I don't have the right to ask this of you—"

"Imwraeth," I say.

He stops. Looks at me.

"I want—"

"Favored One!"

Imwraeth jolts. Councilor Danosrin approaches, taking Imwraeth away to discuss something with him, and I turn back to watching the retahn.

Maybe it's best that we didn't get to finish that conversation, because I have no idea what I want.

10

ZADOCK

This can't be real.

I'm holding tight to Norah to keep her safe just as much as to comfort myself. Once more, I check the knots that are holding us tight to the central mast.

Agriad glows green, his hands outstretched above his head. The crew yells over the roaring of the waves, Shakers working at the rear of the boat. They must be doing something with sand to help Agriad, but what? Droplets of water hit my face and slide down the slick oil cloak.

I can't help the thoughts that rage through my mind. We should've escaped when we could. We should've left, and now it's too late.

The wave emits a sickly green light, the same shade as whatever's glowing in Agriad's hand. The peak is a frothy lime color, churning down, ready to swallow the ship.

We go straight into it.

I clutch Norah, my arms around her back, and hold her to me. I brace myself.

Agriad takes us into the wave. The sharp point of the ship pierces the water. It doesn't part around us this time like the other waves did.

No. We can't go in that water.

"Agriad!" I call. "Turn the ship around. We can't do this!" He must be mad. That's the only explanation.

Agriad ignores me, and the ship goes farther into the wave. Where the water meets the ship, the green glow is strongest. It's blinding.

Norah wraps her arms around me tighter.

I squeeze her into me like I can protect her from sheer force. My arms are shaking, whether from strain or fear, I can't tell.

Agriad passes inside the green wave. It's almost to us.

Every muscle in my body goes taut. Norah and I are one, melded together.

The dune of water hits.

It doesn't feel wet and cold like I expected. The water falls upon us, but it's soft and warm, and it bubbles away. My clothes stay dry.

And then, in a moment, we're through.

The green glow is behind us now. The ocean of water rages around us, but the waves look...different. They're tinted purple, not deep blue. And there are more of them, but smaller.

Well, that's a relief. I guess. But this is strange. What is going on?

"Norah," I say. "Open your eyes."

Norah lifts her head and looks around. Her eyes widen.

The rest of the ship pushes through the green glow, and Agriad lowers his hands. The light around Agriad fades, though the dune of water, as he called it, stays lit.

Agriad puts something into a pouch at his side.

The purple waves peak and trough, and they're huge, but they don't loom over us quite like before. We still go through them via whatever Agriad is doing to part the water, but we probably could sail over them if we wanted to.

Yep. The water is definitely purple.

I look up in the sky for Atoille, and to my utter shock, the moon's not there.

"Norah, look up," I say.

She does so, and her mouth falls open. "Atoille, she's...gone."

I soften the tight hold I have but keep my arms around her, stroking her back. A pit of fear starts to grow in my belly. I am so out of my depth here, so unsure of what to do and how to keep Norah safe.

"Where are we?" Norah yells to Agriad over the waves. "What just happened?"

"You will see, daughter," Agriad says. Another purple wave parts around us, the water falling around the ship in a foamy curtain. "All will be explained."

Norah turns to me and buries her face in my shoulder. "Did you see, Zadock? Did you see what he held?"

I shake my head. "What was he holding?"

"It was a moonstone, Zadock. A green one."

What?

But then all thoughts of that flee from my mind. The shore is in sight. The ocean of sand is in sight!

"Land ahead!" one of the sailors calls.

Agriad grins.

We push forward, the Shakers working as much as Agriad to bring the ship out of the water.

Waves foam and bubble against the sand, and finally, the boat lands in the desert with a splash of water and dust. We're on land again.

Somehow, we made it.

Sailors untie ropes from about their waists and unfurl the sails. Someone comes to collect our ropes and cloaks, but I barely notice. We shoot forward through the sand. The heat is scorching, as if the wind is on fire.

"Norah, the sand," I say with dismay.

She puts a hand over her mouth in shock.

The sand. It's white.

Pure, sparkling white, like crystal glittering in the sunlight. This can't be happening. The ocean of sand is orange. Norah and I have sailed it probably more than anyone, and it's orange. Always.

I don't know what happened or where we are, but it's not home.

11

NORAH

The days drag. There's not much for me and Zadock to do besides stare out at the ocean of sand. It's pure white and blinding in the sun, so different than the deep orange that we're used to.

I don't know what I was expecting, but this is not it.

Zadock takes to helping the Shakers and learning things from the sailors. He's friendly and talkative with them despite the fact that these are the people who attacked us and kidnapped us only days ago. They like him. They joke with him.

But I'm used to being different. Apart.

Bitterness twists within me. I grew up believing that I didn't have a sand gift, that I was the only one. I was an outcast my entire life, scorned by my village and looked down on by almost everyone I interacted with. But as soon as it was discovered that I could Sustain, their attitudes flipped, and all of a sudden, I'm everyone's hero. Treated like I'm something special.

I'm expected to save everyone.

And I can't.

Not now, of course, because I'm not there. But even before

Agriad took us away, it was just *so* much. I loved traveling the sands with Zadock. But going from plateau to plateau, seeing the starving faces, knowing that they expected me to save them... It was a lot. I am only one person.

No matter how much food I was able to Sustain, it wasn't enough, and we'd have to move on to help the next village. Their disappointed eyes followed me, haunting.

I would be lying if I didn't admit to myself that a part of me, a very small sliver, is relieved to be away from that.

But then guilt overwhelms any other thought. I should be back there, helping them. I would if I could.

I stare out over the vast ocean of sand. Atoille isn't in the sky, so it's calmer without her direct pull, the waves only tiny peaks and valleys.

What does this mean, that Atoille isn't in the sky? She was low on the horizon when we left, a few days away from sinking below and making the journey to the other side of our world. And now she's not in the sky. Could it be...could we really have traveled to the other side of the planet?

No. That's ridiculous.

I avoid thinking about that for now. There are so many more creatures in this desert than back home, and they're fascinating to watch. Sand moles by the dozens poke their heads out with their feathery antennae, their colorful shells bright and sparkling in the sunlight. They give me a pang of longing for my potah. He would've loved this.

I wonder if the dangers of the ocean of sand are more rampant here as well, the bloodworms and deathstalker scorpions.

Creatures that we don't have are out there, too. Fish with silver and golden scales that leap up above the sand and soar across it, flying with wide sail-like fins. They make me smile. If I wasn't so terrified for the future and for my people, I would love this.

The grain of the wood is rough beneath my bare forearms, the sun beating down on my skin. I've changed into Cale's clothes, a white tunic and belt matching Agriad, and they fit well. It feels wrong.

Agriad comes to stand beside me at the railing of the ship. He's been busy leading his crew, so I haven't been able to talk to him for the past few days of travel. Now might be a good time to get some answers.

"It's beautiful, isn't it?" Agriad says.

"Yes, it is," I say. "But so different than the ocean of sand that I'm used to." I watch Agriad out of the corner of my eye.

"Yes. The orange ocean of sand is very different from ours. Your Shaker will find that working the sand feels different here, as well."

"Where are we?" I ask.

"We've crossed the ocean of water."

I bite back a frustrated sigh. "I get that. I don't understand how, but I get that we've crossed somehow. But where did it take us?"

Agriad breathes in and out. "It's hard to explain, Ca—Norah."

"Try." I watch a fish soar across the sand. Is that how they get their air? Search for food? The explorer in me longs to know.

I've studied the skies at night. The stars are wrong for this time of year, but they're stars I know, so at least something is familiar, even if it doesn't quite make sense.

"We're on the other side of the world."

I stare at Agriad. Slowly shake my head. There's no other explanation for what I'm seeing, but...

He nods. "Our home is on the opposite side of the planet. Traveling through a dune of water is a shortcut, if you will. A unique pathway to get from one place to another."

"That's why the stars are wrong," I say. "That's why Atoille is gone."

Agriad smiles. "It's good to have you back, Cale."

I frown. "How is it done, traveling through a dune?"

"Someday, I will pass that information on to you, but not yet."

"You don't trust me?" I ask, even though I already know the answer.

"I trust my daughter."

"I saw the stone." I'm taking a chance, treading dangerous water here. Putting out antennae and seeing what they feel.

The sailors shout behind us, and Agriad turns to watch them work before turning back to me.

Agriad's eyes, those white, strange eyes, turn cold and hard. "Yes. The moonstone. That is a small part of it, Norah. Only a small part. There is much yet that you don't understand, but you will."

I look out over the sand. I don't know how much information I can get from him, but if Zadock and I are ever going to get home, I've got to try.

But not now. I've pushed hard enough.

Agriad puts a hand on my shoulder and squeezes. Goosebumps rise on my arm, and it takes all the willpower I have not to shrug him off, but then he's gone, issuing more orders to the crew.

I stare out into the desert, thinking over everything that Agriad said. We're going to have to get the moonstone from him if we're ever going to get home, and I'll need to know how to use it.

When I look up, I see something new on the horizon.

"Zadock!" I call.

He's at my side in an instant, a hand on my back. "Nors?"

"Look," I point.

Zadock looks out over the ocean of sand at the hulking shape in the distance. "It's a...plateau?"

The biggest plateau I've ever seen juts out of the ocean of sand. It takes up the entire skyline. It fills the horizon.

"It's more like a land mass," I say.

Agriad joins us, standing beside me and grinning. "There it is!" he calls. "Our home."

My breath catches. That's our destination. We're almost there.

"Welcome, daughter," Agriad says. "Welcome to To'Sharazad."

1 2

LYLAHN

We're in a war meeting. Again.

I forget when they stopped being called councils and started being called war meetings. But it's accurate.

No more killing. Imwraeth's promise to me feels like forever ago. It was an unrealistic vow.

I sit at Imwraeth's right hand. Danosrin and Sahlas sit across from us at the quartz table that's covered in a red cloth. Crystal goblets of chilled wine are served, but it looks too much like blood, and I only take one sip before setting my cup down. A platter of peeled and sliced bristlebrush fruits sits in the center of the table, but no one's touched it.

Riah sits at Imwraeth's left, drumming her fingers on the table. I'm grateful she has chosen to wear formal robes rather than her armor today. Next to Riah sits Imwraeth's head engineer, Fenrick. He's a tall man with deeply tanned skin and one ear torn halfway in two. It's hard not to stare at it.

Before the meeting this morning, I sent word via sand gull to Norah's motah, Katiyah Saranyi. Since she's on the To'Rahn council, she'll be able to pass on what's happened. Maybe they'll be able to offer some aid, and we can work together to solve the problems before us.

And she deserves to know what's happened to her daughter.

"Welcome, everyone," Imwraeth says. "I'm grateful for your hard work and attendance at this meeting today."

Sahlas gives a report on how the food rationing is going. My stomach growls even now. The blushing red bristlebrush fruits on the table look good, but I'm too nervous to take one.

Danosrin gives an update on the engineer's progress. "Fenrick, can you tell us more about how construction of the ship is going?"

The ripped shreds of Fenrick's ear wobble as he nods. "Yes, I can. Thank you for inviting me to this meeting today." His face is grave. I wonder if he ever smiles. "The ship is progressing well. The outer hull is halfway complete, and I have a team working on designing masts that can withstand the great pressure of water. I'm afraid we'll have to roll the sails when we're out on the water. The risk is too great to—"

I tune him out, thinking about the foreigner's ship. Yes, it was narrow. It had thick masts. Everything Fenrick is saying makes sense. But I can't help but feel that we're missing something.

Imwraeth focuses solely on Fenrick, gives him his full attention. Fenrick continues to gesture and describe the ship. He lays the plans on the table, and everyone leans forward to see them. I can't make sense of them at all.

My mind wanders again. I blink my eyes several times, trying to banish the exhaustion.

"Lylahn, what are your thoughts?" Imwraeth asks.

I startle and glance at the plans, but I still can't make sense of the diagrams and drawings.

Sahlas rolls her eyes while Danosrin looks at me with a placating smile. I feel sick, knowing what Imwraeth's real councilors think of me.

An idea strikes. My initial reaction is to dismiss it, but if I can help, I have to. "What if...what if we built a barge?"

"A barge?" Sahlas snaps. "Have you been listening to anything Fenrick is saying?"

Danosrin frowns, but Fenrick tilts his head, thinking. The drumming of Riah's fingers stops.

"What do you mean, Councilor Lylahn?" Imwraeth asks.

I take a deep breath. Now that my mind has hold of this idea, I can't let it go. "A round barge would be able to withstand the punishments of the ocean of water better than a pointed ship. We could all go below deck and—I don't know, secure ourselves into seats with straps or something. It's still dangerous, but—"

"It's absurd." Sahlas throws up her hands. "Favored One, surely—"

Imwraeth holds up a hand, and Sahlas stops. "Let her finish. All ideas are welcome at this table."

Sahlas' dark red bangs frame her angry eyes, but she silences.

I force myself to square my shoulders and sit tall. "I realize the foreigners had a pointed ship, one like this design. But I think we're still missing something. Maybe building a ship like theirs is the wrong choice."

Fenrick nods. "Some of our engineers have been voicing the same thoughts. We don't know how the black ship survived the trip across the ocean of water. It doesn't seem possible. And yet, that is how it was done."

I swallow. "You're right. But..." I am a part of this council, whatever Sahlas thinks. "I think the barge design may be superior."

Fenrick looks thoughtful. "We can only choose one. A quartz-reinforced ship will be too heavy to float on water. With wood being as scarce as it is, we can only build one ship."

I swallow. One ship. Even if we make it across the ocean of water by some miracle, how many warriors will we be able to bring?

Imwraeth nods. "Your idea is a good one, Councilor Lylahn. I think you're right." He frowns over the papers of the pointed ship a little longer. "Fenrick?"

Fenrick sits back in his chair. "I will talk to my engineers. We will discuss the idea of a barge."

Something warm sparks within me. When Imwraeth smiles at me, it gets even brighter.

"How many warriors will we be able to fit on this barge?" Riah asks. She's been oddly quiet.

"That is another question we will look into, General Riah," Fenrick nods to her.

She sighs. "I'm worried, Favored One. Even if by some miracle we make it across the ocean of water—"

Riah is cut off by the door slamming open. I jump. Four warriors enter the room, dressed in full To'Morat armor.

Words come out of their mouths, addressing Riah, but I don't hear. My vision goes red and black, and I'm back there in that night. The heat of the fires is scorching. The screams burn my ears. Kaera's pulling on my arm, begging me to come back into the house, but our house is going down in flame.

A flash of red. Bellah's blood. It's on me. It's on my shirt.

I stand, throwing back my chair, wiping my palms on my dress, frantically trying to get the blood off.

And then I freeze. I'm back. I'm in the war room.

Just a flashback. But it felt real.

"I have to g-go." I manage to get out. I push through the opposite door and down the hallway, leaving the room. Leaving behind the warriors of To'Morat.

Was it one of them? Was one of them my sisters' killer?

Terror powers my feet, and I hardly hear Imwraeth calling after me. I'm blinded by panic so overwhelming it blocks everything else out, and I dash down the hallway. I hear footsteps behind me, and I pick up the pace.

I knew it. They're coming for me. They're coming—

"Lylahn!" Imwraeth grabs my hand, and I gasp and yank my grip out of his. I take deep, shuddering breaths. I'm shaking all over.

"Lylahn. It's all right. I'm here." Imwraeth wraps me up in his strong arms, and I sink into him, breathing in his scent, burying my face in his shoulder. I can't help the sobs that wrack my body.

"You've been through so much," he whispers. "And I keep asking more of you. I'm sorry."

I calm my breathing and stifle my cries. Imwraeth needs me to be strong right now. "I'm ok," I say. "I'm ok. I was startled, is all."

Imwraeth raises his eyebrows. "So startled you ran panicking from the room?"

"Yes."

Imwraeth pulls me aside to a smaller hallway where we're less visible to the servants walking past. "Lylahn. You are everything to me." He tucks a curl behind my ear, and I close my eyes, savoring the touch. He wraps me in his arms and holds me close. "I'm here for you."

I nod into his chest. "I know."

"If you..." He hesitates. "If you ever wanted to talk about that night, I would listen."

I catch my breath. I'm not ready to talk about it. I can't burden him with—

Imwraeth grips me harder. "I would do anything for you. So if you want to talk, I'm here, if you think it would help."

I shake my head. "No. I don't want to relive it. I just want the past to be gone."

He doesn't say anything for a while, and slowly my trembling subsides. "I understand."

People in the hallway call for the Favored One. Imwraeth pulls away and gives me one brief, full kiss. "Get some extra rest, all right?" He brushes a finger down my cheek and then leaves.

I watch him go, and my heart sinks. The panic starts to return.

I will never be rid of this horror. I will never escape that night.

Despair washes over me, black and crushing. I breathe faster, feeling like I can't get enough air.

I fall to my knees.

Will it always be like this? Will I always be tormented by the past? Will I ever—

A thought strikes me.

If I can make it right, then maybe their voices will stop haunting me. My breathing evens out. The trembling stills.

That's it. I'm having these flashbacks and visions because my sisters' blood goes unavenged. If I could find their killer and...take care of him, the fear would be over. I could be at peace. Maybe I would even be happy here.

I look down at my hands. Who am I to avenge them? Could I ever find the warrior who killed them among all the warriors of To'Morat?

But then, I realize, I could. His face, in his black and red To'Morat helmet, is etched into my brain. I would recognize him if I saw him. I know I would.

But even then...could I take a human life? Me, a healer?

I try to shake the thought. Seeking out someone with the intent to kill? That's not me. That's not who I am.

But the thought won't leave me alone. I stand, new strength filling my limbs.

My sisters. They need vengeance.

13

ZADOCK

The sand is the wrong color. Atoille is gone when she should be in the sky. And that plateau before us is specking huge.

I put an arm around Norah's shoulders as the ship is lifted up the side of the plateau, To'Sharazad or whatever Agriad called it.

Norah puts a hand on mine.

I kiss the top of her head. Somehow, we'll get through this. Together.

The Shakers call out to each other, and Agriad shouts orders. Norah looks over the side of the ship, down at the white ocean of sand far below. I think about how she used to jump off the plateau for fun, knowing I would catch her, and I grip her hand tighter. I don't think she'll do it, but just in case.

We reach the top, and my mouth drops open.

The Shakers ease the ship into an enormous boat port. Rows and rows of ships stretch down the sandy expanse of the plateau, but behind it is what's truly incredible.

Trees. Trees and plant life crowd against each other. Vines and flowers dangle from long, hanging branches. The black trunks are as thick around as I am, with green leaves sprouting from their tops.

There wouldn't be room to walk through them except for the quartz-paved path that leads up to an enormous city, a jewel shining in the sun.

"Whoa," I breathe.

Norah's eyes are enormous. "They live in a jungle."

A word I've only read about in books. Not something I thought existed.

A gangway is extended, and we exit the boat. I step onto white sand. It's soft and fine, sparkling in the sunlight. I grasp Norah's hand. Agriad directs his soldiers to begin unloading supplies that camehl-pulled carts are waiting for.

The sailors begin their work, and Agriad turns to us. "Come, daughter. I will take you home."

Norah looks at me. I tighten my arm around her shoulders. What have we gotten ourselves into?

We follow Agriad to a carriage-type vehicle that looks like it's made of pure crystal. The sides are open, the seats cushioned in blue velvet. On top is a sparkling quartz overhang, like a flower petal attached to a stem, to provide shade. There's no camehl to pull it, and there are no wheels. There are quartz propellers attached to the back and the...bottom?

"What the...?" I ask.

Agriad laughs. "I forgot. You don't have these where you're from." He grins at Norah. "You're in for a treat now that you're home."

We follow Agriad up the steps into the carriage. I look out, marveling again at the jungle all around. Brown furry creatures leap from tree to tree, eating some bright yellow fruits.

A man dressed in a blue and white servant's livery climbs the steps and takes a seat outside the carriage near the propeller. He puts his hands on it, and it starts to glow.

The propellers on the side and bottom whir to life, and I gasp as the coach lifts into the air.

"We're flying!" Norah calls.

Agriad smiles.

The vehicle zooms forward along the quartz road, straight for the city. I look out the window and watch the jungle trees zip by, marveling, eyes wide.

The engineer in me is fascinated. It's my concept, similar to what I built to power that boat across the ocean of sand to get to Norah, but a thousand times more evolved. The man must be an Extractor, using energy from the sand to power the propellers.

I watch the jungle go by in a blur. The black trees are nearly impossible to see through, but I catch splotches of colorful flowers and fruits. Every so often, I glimpse the movement of creatures.

We reach the city in almost no time at all. There's a high quartz wall all the way around, and two guards stand at the ready at a solid crystal gate. It takes two Extractors to push the gate open. They bow to Agriad and wave us through.

"Their eyes," Norah whispers. "Did you see their eyes?"

I shake my head.

Norah sees Agriad watching and shuts her mouth.

"You're safe now, daughter," Agriad says with a smile. "Out in the jungle, there are many dangers. You must stay in the city." He looks at her with intensity. "You must not leave the city walls unless I give you permission."

Norah swallows, glances at me, and then back to Agriad, and nods.

He turns away, satisfied.

I take in the city. This is incredible! I mean, we might die at Agriad's whims, and who knows how we're going to get back home, but wow!

The street is made of paving stones of quartz. People walk down the road wearing brightly colored clothing and carrying baskets of food or other goods. We pass some coaches like ours, powered by an Extractor. The streets are crowded, with towering homes and businesses on either side. There's so much to see, I almost don't know where to look. The quartz is sparkling and bright but somehow not blinding. The Forgers have figured out a way to change its color, and the quartz buildings are in every color of the rainbow.

And the people! Quartz jewelry dangles from their necks and wrists, even on the men. I notice their eyes now. They're normal. Agriad and his warriors are the only ones with the pure white eyes.

Interesting.

We pass through a wide plaza and a market with shops and vendors selling everything from food to jewelry and clothing to children's toys and books. The smells make my stomach growl—savory spices and smoky cookfires.

The streets are so crowded that the carriage has to slow to a crawl. There are so many people and so much plenty. The city is thriving.

Agriad leans out of the carriage and smiles and waves at the people. They cheer and point where they see him. He's holding a fistful of sand, I notice, and it begins to glow. All around us in the plaza, plant life springs up and stretches towards the sky. Trees sprout red and orange fruit, and bushels grow plantains, yellow and ripe for picking. The people clap and cheer.

I meet Norah's eyes. "Whoa."

Something like jealousy darkens Norah's face. "He's very powerful."

A group of children scream with delight and rush up to the carriage. They stretch out their hands. Agriad laughs and reaches into his pockets, pulling out handfuls of date-sugar candies. He hands them out with a grin, the children approaching him without fear to grab for the sweets. Agriad pats each one on the head.

I'm so shocked I don't know what to say. This evil, horrible man who's stolen Norah and dragged me along... His people love him.

Agriad leans back in the coach and smiles. "Welcome home. There will be feasting and celebrating at the palace tonight."

"Palace?" I ask.

"Of course. Sustainers are royalty here."

"There are more of us?" Norah asks in a quiet voice.

"Oh, yes, Norah. There are a lot more."

"Look at that!" I cry. A boy a little younger than me flies by on some kind of quartz glider.

Agriad glances to where I'm looking. "There are many wonders in To'Sharazad."

We pass crystal fountains with water gushing in intricate patterns. The people's dress gets finer as we get deeper into the city. The ladies wear dresses and carry lacy umbrellas to keep off the sun, and the men wear large-brimmed hats. There are more coaches now than there are people walking.

The homes grow in size and are less crowded together, with large green grounds. So much green. I have never seen so much green. Where's all the sand?

I turn to Norah. "What do you think?"

She stares at me with wide eyes. "It's a bit much to take in."

"It will all become normal soon," Agriad says. "Soon."

Finally, the coach comes to a halt. More guards wave us through a shorter quartz wall. These guards' eyes, I notice, are pure white. Why? How? The coach pulls into a circular driveway area and comes to a halt.

I gasp. We've stopped in front of an enormous palace. The walls are made of blue crystal, with turrets and balconies towering high above. A wide staircase leads up to doors of black wood carved in intricate designs. Green grass is all around, split by a path of blue quartz gravel. Orange and yellow flowers bloom along the walkway, and a burbling fountain sparkles in the sunlight.

Another servant dressed in the blue and white livery comes hurrying down the stairs. He opens the door to the coach before I can get a handle on it. A blue carpet is rolled out.

"Ummm. What's that for?" I ask. The servant jolts, staring at me.

I descend the steps and turn to help Norah down. She squeezes my hand hard, like I'm a rope keeping her from falling into the ocean of sand. Agriad descends behind us, and the Extractor drives away.

"Here we are." Agriad inhales. "Home."

14

NORAH

I gape at the palace. It's so tall I have to crane my neck to look at the top spires. The heat here feels different, muggy and wet. Zadock stands next to me, mouth open in awe.

If Agriad is a Sustainer, he somehow used Sustaining with that moonstone to get here. If I can get him to trust me and teach me—and get that moonstone from him—then maybe we can get home.

I swallow. It seems like an enormous task.

Zadock takes my hand, and once again I'm struck with how glad I am that he is here with me. I feel guilty for that because he'd be safer back at home, but *would* he? Without me, our side of the world will die. I don't know how long they have until that happens.

Agriad might know. I will try to get that information out of him.

We follow Agriad up the carpet. It's lined with servants wearing white and navy livery. The guards wear the same black leather armor that the sailors wore when they attacked us, and they all have the distinct colorless eyes.

"P-potah." My heart aches as I spit the word out. I imagine my real potah, dead for three years now, even though it feels like it's been longer.

Agriad turns back to me with a smile. "Yes, daughter?"

"What will happen to the other side of our world without me?"

Agriad stops on the walkway, servants on all sides, the sun beating down on us. Sweat gathers on my temples.

"It will die, of course, as it is meant to." Agriad moves on, eager to get to the palace.

"Wait, as it's meant to?" Zadock asks, anger darkening his voice.

"Yes, of course." Agriad gestures around him. "Haven't you noticed? The beauty of this land, the pure white of the sand, a sacred color. Like Atoille herself. The plenty and fertility all around. This land is meant to be Atoille's paradise."

My mouth opens in surprise.

Agriad continues. "And the other side of our world is meant to be Atoille's Hell." He puts a hand on my shoulder. "Now that you're here, everything can be made right again. Now, come."

I turn to Zadock and share a glance. "How long?" I say to Agriad. "How long until this happens?"

Agriad sighs. "I can't be sure, but do not worry, daughter, the change won't take long. Without a Sustainer on that side of the world, the land will die. A few weeks? A month at most."

A month. A month is how long I have to learn from Agriad, get the moonstone from him, and get back home. And somehow figure out how we're going to do all that without starting a war. Without putting Zadock in danger.

Dread sinks my stomach into the ground. I don't know. I don't know how to do this. And everyone, *everyone* is counting on me.

I'm supposed to be their savior.

The palace doors open wide, and we enter.

"Here we are, Norah," Agriad says with a smile. "Your home."

Glass windows stretch to the ceiling, and crystal chandeliers hang up above, catching and spreading rainbows of light. A long blue carpet extends down the grand entryway, and two staircases lead upstairs. The walls are lined with porcelain vases and flourishing plants.

Agriad turns to a brown-haired servant standing with a rigid posture near a stairway. "Show Norah and Zadock to their room. Send servants in to help them prepare for the feast tonight."

"Yes, High Sustainer." He bows and turns to us. "Follow me, if you please, Great Ones."

We follow the servant up the left staircase and down carpeted hallways, leaving Agriad behind. It's a relief to be out of his presence.

Paintings hang on the walls, images of Agriad. A portrait of me stops me dead. I stare at it. I'm sitting in a chair, posture tall, wearing a gown of midnight blue. My honey-brown hair is long, much longer than I like to keep it. A small smile plays on my lips.

Zadock stops beside me. "It's—"

"Follow me, please," the servant urges, and we continue in silence.

At last, the servant stops in front of an ornate crystal door. "Here we are. Your room." He opens the door, and we enter.

"I will leave you to rest from your journey." The servant closes the door, and his footsteps retreat down the hall.

There's an enormous bed. The blankets are blue, of course. And the floor and walls are the same navy crystal. Two tall wooden armoires are set against each wall, made of the same black wood as the ship. There's a small black table with cushioned chairs around it and a crystal wash basin in the corner.

A painting of—me?—is on the wall. Next to my portrait there's one of a boy about my age. Handsome, despite the pale skin. Short, straight blonde hair with streaks of brown, and broad shoulders. A strong jaw.

"Who's that?" Zadock asks.

I flop down on the bed. It's soft, the sheets exquisitely smooth. "I have no clue." I put my hands over my face. "One month. He said one month. One month until everyone we love starves to death."

"Hey, hey." Zadock sits on the bed and puts a hand on top of mine. "It's going to be ok. We'll figure this out."

I swallow and stare at him. My love, my Anointed. I sit up, take a deep breath. "I can almost believe anything when you say it."

Zadock smiles and leans forward. My heart beats faster. I move closer.

There's a knock at the door. "May I enter?"

We break apart and stand. "Yes," I say.

Another servant enters. He's a short, plump man, the livery buttons on his coat almost bursting apart. His outfit looks a little different than the others. More lace at the collar.

He bows to me, and then to Zadock he gives a quick nod. "Welcome home, Ca—Norah." He smiles. "And welcome, Zadock Penvaren of To'Rahn. We are so pleased you're here with us." His gritted teeth suggest otherwise. "My name is Bernan, and I am head of the staff here." His smile becomes genuine as he turns to me. "You don't remember, Great Sustainer, but I have served you since you were a child, and I have served your family my entire life." He bows once again, and I exchange a flabbergasted look with Zadock. This is all so overwhelming and strange.

I nod my head in what I hope is a dignified manner. "Thank you, Bernan." I don't know what else to do or say.

He tsks when he sees our worn travel clothes. "This will not do for the feast tonight. Do you wish to bathe separately or together?"

My face goes crimson, and I can't look at Zadock. "Separately."

Bernan nods. "I will send in attendants to draw you each a bath and prepare you for tonight." Bernan beams once more at me. I might be seeing things, but his eyes seem teary. "Welcome home, Great Sustainer."

Bernan bows once more and exits the room.

"This just gets weirder and weirder," Zadock says.

We hardly have time to breathe before two more servants enter, a man and a woman. The woman has ebony hair, and she's tall with a stern face. She wastes no time in giving a curt bow, approaching me, and attempting to pull my shirt over my head.

Zadock blushes and turns away.

"Hey, wait!" I try to yank my shirt down, but she's ruthless.

"I must bath and dress you, Great Sustainer. The feasting will begin soon."

More servants trail in, crossing the room and opening the door to what I assume is the washroom. I hear water and catch swirls of steam.

I sigh and allow her to remove my clothing. My face burns.

I see out of the corner of my eye that the male servant is treating Zadock in the same way, but then I quickly look away.

"I am Jeru," she says. "I'll be taking care of you while you're here."

The way she says it makes me wonder if she doesn't think it will be very long. Maybe not everyone is convinced that I'm Cale.

I'm stripped down and herded to a quartz-paved room. The bathtub is an enormous crystal thing filled with steaming hot water. My eyes go wide at the sight.

"That much water is for bathing?" I have always only ever in my life taken sponge baths.

Jeru gives me a tight nod and gestures for me to get in. I hurry to comply, sinking into the warm water with a sigh of pleasure. That's when I notice a second bathtub on the other side of the room.

"Umm..."

Jeru wastes no time scrubbing and polishing away the dirt on me like it's done her a personal offense. I barely have time to register the pleasant heat of the water or the bubbles kissing my skin. Or the fact that Zadock walks in, followed by a male servant. I gasp and turn away before I see more than his perfect bare chest.

Jeru scrubs oils and ointments through my hair. I studiously ignore Zadock in the tub next to me, receiving the same treatment.

"All right," Jeru says. "You're clean. Let's get you dressed." She holds a towel for me, thank Atoille. I stand and hurry to wrap it around myself. I follow Jeru from the room without looking back.

She strides to the wardrobe, and I stand there, practically naked. Jeru throws open the wardrobe doors. There's a gorgeous array of dresses hanging there in all colors. Jeru chooses one, dark blue, of course, and returns to me.

Jeru throws some kind of silk shift over my head, and then on goes the dress. My breath catches as the silk slides over my skin. It is beautiful, the most beautiful thing I've ever worn. It gathers at the waist and fans out. The sleeves are two thick straps over my shoulders in a square neck. Crystals are sewn into the bodice and skirt, so when I move, I glitter.

I feel dazzling. I feel like an utter fool.

"Thank you, Jeru." I must've said something wrong because she looks at me with surprise.

I glimpse Zadock when he exits the washroom, towel around his waist.

Jeru walks me over to a dresser and mirror and plonks me down on a velvet cushioned stool. She brushes my hair, being only slightly gentler than she was when she washed it.

Jeru shakes her head as she examines my hair. I assume it's at the length, which is just an inch or so beyond my shoulders. She grabs a handful of sand, and a soft glow emanates from her fingers. So she's an Extractor. Jeru moves her hands expertly around my hair, and the heat from her Extracting dries it quickly. Steam rises from my head.

Once it's dry, Jeru settles on pinning half of my hair up with a gorgeous crystal flower pin. She clasps a matching necklace around my throat.

This is all so beautiful, but it isn't me.

At last, I turn, and there's Zadock. He wears a fine shirt of navy blue with a matching crystal flower pinned to his chest pocket. Silk white cloth, bedecked with glittering pieces of blue quartz, is wrapped around his middle and tied at the side. Black pants complete the outfit. His messy hair has been somewhat tamed. He gives me a grin.

"Norah, you look incredible."

My blush deepens. "You look nice, too, Zadock."

He extends his elbow, and I thread my arm through it. I feel better already with him close.

Jeru and Bernan bow. "You will follow us to the feast, if you please," Jeru says.

I look at Zadock, nerves squirming in my stomach.

Zadock nods to me. Smiles.

I tighten my grip on his arm and turn to Jeru. "Lead the way."

15

LYLAHN

I walk alongside Kaera on the garden path, the same one where we walked as prisoners. It's her favorite place. Under Norah's care, the plants were flourishing and beautiful, but they're already dying.

Kaera, as always, runs ahead and then turns back, stopping to look at a creature or plant, and then runs ahead again. I walk along the path, pausing to ooh and ahh over whatever treasures she finds.

I've been mulling over the problem before me all day. It's simple in theory. Execution is the complex part.

Find the warrior who killed my sisters. Avenge their deaths.

If I see his face, I know I'll recognize him. He haunts my nightmares. He's a tall, lean man in bulky armor. Eyes gray and bloodthirsty.

I will know his face if I see him.

The problem is that Imwraeth's warriors are stationed all over To'Morat. How do I find him?

My weary brain can't come up with anything, but I renew my determination. This is how I banish the nightmares and flashbacks. Once I overcome them, I will finally, *finally* be of use to Imwraeth and not just a burden.

We reach the garden wall, and Kaera looks back at me with a grin. "I'm so happy here, Lahnnie."

I smile. "I'm glad."

She takes my hand and walks beside me for a moment. "But you don't seem happy."

"I am, Kaera. I'm happy here." I sigh. "I miss home sometimes, that's all. I miss…" I trail off. I don't want to bring up fresh pain for Kaera. Not when she seems to be moving on and handling things ok.

She looks up at me with those wide blue eyes. "I miss them, too. But I'm glad we have Imwraeth."

"Me too."

"Let's go through here!" She points to a gate in the wall. It's unguarded, which is a relief. The first thing I have to overcome is my aversion to looking at Imwraeth's warriors.

"Umm. All right." We open the gate and step through, right into the retahn's dusty training arena.

The girl is at it again with the gorgeous black retahn. She's riding her around the circle, and she's carrying a stick tied with several pieces of quartz, clinking and jangling.

Kaera and I stand to the side and watch, and the girl waves her stick in the air at us. Kaera laughs with delight.

"Lahnnie, the retahn! She's so beautiful."

I smile. The retahn is midnight black and glossy. It's a shame that these animals are bred for violence only.

The girl completes her turn in the circle before stopping her mount next to us. "Hi." She grins. "I'm glad you came back."

Kaera looks up at me with a pout. "You've been here before and you didn't show me?"

I ruffle her hair. "Sorry, sis." I look up. "What's your name? And why the stick?"

"I'm Sharise. And you?"

"Lylahn."

"Kaera."

Sharise shakes the stick. The quartz pieces jangle together. "I'm getting Darkest Night used to anything. On the battlefield, there are lots of unusual sounds. I'm sound-proofing her."

I nod. "Darkest Night. A beautiful name."

Sharise looks at me with hope in her eyes. "I could use some help. If you're willing, she needs to get used to carrying someone other than me."

Kaera grins at me. "Lahnnie, do it!"

I grit my teeth together and attempt a smile. "I can't Kaera, I have to..." I let out a breath. "Oh, all right."

Sharise beams, swinging her leg over the saddle to dismount.

"I am not holding that stick," I say.

Kaera giggles.

I take careful steps to stand next to the retahn. She's a big animal with wicked curved horns and sharp hooves. The retahn were there the night all of To'Shahera was slaughtered.

They're animals, I remind myself. They were doing what they were trained to do. It's not their fault.

I take a deep breath and hide my fear. I've always been a good liar. Imwraeth can always tell when someone is lying, but I even fooled him.

"All right," Sharise says. "You mount up by putting your foot here," she points, "and grabbing here. Let me know if you need help."

I put my foot where she suggested and grab the handle. I'm clumsy in my fine silk dress, but I manage to swing my leg up and around the retahn and find the loop to put my foot in—is it called a stirrup?—on the other side. My silk dress rides up to my knees, but I try not to care.

"Now what?" I ask.

"Click your tongue like this." Sharise demonstrates. "And she'll go. Use the reins to guide her. Right now, I'm teaching her what's called neck reining, so if you want her to go right, rest the reins on the left side of her neck."

I nod and clutch the reins.

"Later, she'll learn to be guided by your feet only," Sharise says.

"In a battle, you've got to hold your spear and shield. But she's not ready for that yet."

"Neither am I."

Sharise laughs.

I take a deep breath, click my tongue, and Darkest Night takes off.

I hear Sharise calling to slow down as if from far away. I'm bouncing in the retahn's saddle, gasping, the air blown from my lungs. But she won't slow down. She races around the arena, and I barely have any thought for the reins save to hold on for dear life. Darkest Night knows where to go, and she follows the outer edge of the dusty circle.

Soon, I lean forward. I can feel the rhythm of her hooves pounding into the sand, kicking up dust that licks at my feet. I ease into a pattern. She moves beneath me like the waves of sand.

My heart pounds and a grin lights up my face. This is amazing!

After a few more times around the circle, I call, laughing, "How do I stop?"

Sharise puts her hands around her mouth. "Pull gently on the reins. Say, 'whoa'."

"Whoa!" I shriek and yank on the reins a little too hard, but Darkest Night gets it, and she lurches to a halt in front of Sharise and Kaera. I'm breathing hard and sweating, and I don't want to look at the state of my dress, but I'm smiling as I awkwardly dismount.

"That was incredible! You're a natural." Sharise glares at Darkest Night. "How come you won't do that for me?"

I pat her on the neck. She's sweating, too.

"You know," Sharise says, "the retahn are more intelligent than people give them credit for. They can tell when you have true courage, and they connect with that."

True courage. I hold back my scoff.

"She likes you, Lahnnie!" Kaera turns to Sharise. "Can I have a turn?"

Sharise laughs. "Of course. But let's get you a calmer mount." She winks at me. "This one is for the Favored Lady."

I blush. "Oh, I'm not—The Favored One and I aren't—"

But Sharise is already leading Darkest Night back into the stable.

"That was incredible!"

I whirl around and see Imwraeth, leaning against the arena railing, grinning like an idiot.

I flush. "You saw?"

"Almost the whole thing." He's still smiling.

My blush deepens when I think about how high my skirt was on my legs.

I walk over to the railing and lean beside him as Kaera and Sharise step back into the arena. The retahn she leads for Kaera is a reddish-brown mare, fat and lazy looking, with burnt orange horns. Sharise lifts Kaera and then walks the retahn around the arena. Kaera waves.

I smile.

"It's good to see you happy," Imwraeth says.

I lay my head on his shoulder. "It's good to feel happy."

He takes my hand in his, and I savor the feeling of his skin, the smell of him that is uniquely him.

"Lylahn." He hesitates. "If this means so much to you, I want you to come out here and help Sharise train the retahn. I've been trying to find help for her like you asked, but I haven't had much luck."

I jolt and look up at him. "Really? That's all right with you?"

Imwraeth smiles. "Yes. I'd do anything for you. Just remember that I still need you, too. Please don't walk out of any more war meetings." He laughs, but there's a strained sound to it.

I swallow. "Thank you, Imwraeth."

He puts an arm across my shoulders and pulls me close to him. Kaera laughs with delight as the retahn goes around the circle. I feel some measure of peace, watching my sister, Imwraeth's arm around me.

But. I can't let myself get distracted from my true goal.

"I was thinking…" I swallow. "I was thinking I could inspect the warrior barracks for you." I cringe at the tone of my voice, how it shakes.

Imwraeth looks at me, eyebrows raised. "You want to inspect the warrior barracks?"

I swallow. Will he see right through me? "Yes. And the warriors. If it would be helpful to you."

Imwraeth blinks. "Yes. It would be very helpful. I'll arrange for it to be done…tomorrow?"

I force myself to nod. The thought of being surrounded by them makes my skin crawl. Bile rises in my throat, but I remind myself that this is the only way.

16

ZADOCK

We make our way through lavish blue crystal hallways, plush rugs on the floor and intricate tapestries on the walls. Flourishing potted plants decorate each corner. Blue crystal lamps are affixed to the walls, and I stop to examine one. It glows with its own internal light. Extracted and stored energy? I shake my head. Amazing.

The décor can't take away from the eerie feeling of perpetual night, of being encased in blue.

The hairs on my arms rise as we follow the servants through a twisting maze of turns and staircases. Norah and I do our best to keep up, walking hand in hand. I get this feeling that someone is watching me, that we're surrounded by enemies. These people put us in a palace, yes, but we're still glorified prisoners.

We turn a corner and stand before an imposing black doorway carved with a design of the moon and clouds in a night sky, encrusted with shining quartz "stars."

"Here we are," Jeru says. "The feasting hall of To'Sharazad."

The servants open the doors, and we follow them through. My

mouth drops open. I have never seen anything this grand. My entire home on To'Rahn could fit in here.

It's an enormous crystal room that sparkles in gold-blue light. Lanterns float around the perimeter of the room. Extractor work? Eight long tables fill the room, each packed with people, and servants bustle around with trays of food. The loud conversation taking place quiets when we enter.

Norah shifts her weight from side to side, adjusting her skirts. I grip her hand, even though she's crushing my fingers.

All heads turn to look at us.

Jeru announces our presence. "Great Sustainer Norah Saranyi of To'Sharazad and Zadock Penvaren of To'Rahn."

People murmur at our announced titles. My brain gets stuck right after Jeru says, "Great Sustainer Norah."

Norah and I exchange glances.

"I can't do this, Zadock," she whispers. "I'm going to mess up, Agriad's going to—"

"Nors," I say. "It's going to be all right. Let's just make it through tonight."

The conversation slowly resumes throughout the room. Agriad stands at the head of a center table. He glides across the room toward us, and where he goes, people's gazes follow. They watch him with admiration on their faces.

Agriad is dressed in an outfit similar to mine, but the sparkling quartz bits attached to the fabric around his middle are larger and cut in a way that makes them catch and reflect the light. His silk shirt is navy blue, and he wears a gold chain with chunks of blue quartz around his neck. In the center of the chain are three gems—one green, one orange, and one yellow. They're not quartz; they don't have that milky look. The gems are clear and so bright in color I almost have to turn away. They look like—

"Moonstones?" Norah breathes.

My mouth parts. She's right. He's wearing three moonstones.

Agriad takes Norah's hands and kisses her fingers. She barely hides her look of disgust. His white eyes fixate on her and then shift to me.

"Welcome, daughter!" Agriad says. "Welcome, Zadock." Agriad turns back to the feasters. "My daughter has been returned to us!"

The people cheer and raise glasses in toast. They're all dressed as elaborately as we are, in sparkling dresses and smooth silk shirts in bright colors, crystal jewelry at their throats and wrists.

Norah exchanges another nervous glance with me.

"Tonight, we celebrate her rebirth!" Agriad says. The people cheer again. "Please, everyone, enjoy yourselves. A wonderful gift has been delivered to us." Agriad smiles at Norah, and there's something in his smile, something wicked and barely restrained. It makes me want to punch him in the face.

Agriad guides us to the central table where he feasts. The room fills with the chatter of the partygoers, knives and skewers clanking against plates, servants bustling about the room, loaded with trays. "Here is your seat, Zadock." Agriad gestures to an empty seat at the end of the table, surrounded by other nobles dressed in finery. I clasp Norah's hand tighter. I think we're going to break each other's fingers.

"There's no seat for Norah," I say.

Agriad's snake-like smile widens. "She will be seated by me. The arrangements are done according to rank. We don't know what your rank is, so here you are."

I turn to Agriad. "Listen, we—"

Norah quickly shakes her head. "Let's just do what he wants." Her eyes go wide. "Please. Just do what he wants."

My stomach turns.

I sit by strangers and watch Agriad guide the love of my life away to the head of the table.

I keep my eyes lowered in an effort to not look at those around me. I'm aware of all the eyes turned my way. I'm a curiosity. A foreigner. I feel like a specking fool.

A servant places food in front of me, a bowl of some kind of soup with a greenish tinge. I pick up a wooden spoon with a deep well and dip it in. I'm about to bring it to my lips when a girl across from me says, "No, no. You don't eat that yet. It's to cleanse your pallet between courses."

I glance up, startled, and she smiles. She's got hair so blond it's almost white, and it falls halfway down her back. She wears a green dress, glittering with small beads of quartz. "Tap the spoon against the bowl. It means you're ready for the next course."

What's with all the rules? I tap my spoon like she indicates, and sure enough, a servant comes with a plate of food in hand. My soup is moved to the upper left corner of my table setting and replaced by a plate full of steaming plantains sliced lengthwise and filled with some kind of green, pulpy mixture.

I swallow and attempt a bite. At least the plantains are familiar. The pulp tastes like coconut, so that's not too bad.

The girl takes a sip of purple wine out of a crystal glass. Winks at me.

Ugh. I don't want to deal with this. I start shoveling down food just to avoid conversation.

"You don't recognize me?" the girl asks.

I look at her more closely now, surprised. "You were one of the Shakers on the ship."

She grins, and her smile reminds me of Agriad's. Predatory. Her eyes are the same as his—white, blank, and unreadable. "Yes."

"Oh."

"So, Zadock, is it?" The muscular man to my right smiles. His eyes, though not blank, are beady and sharp. "Let me introduce myself. I am Lord Brassock of the east Strathon estates. My family—"

And on and on he goes. When Lord Brassock stops to take a breath, the woman next to me, who is all skin and bones, introduces herself as well. These people seem to be clamoring to talk to me, to get to know me. *It's because I'm close to Norah.* They want to get closer to her through me and to Agriad through her.

When I've finished my plate of plantains, I glance up at the girl. She catches my eye and smiles. Then she picks up her spoon, takes a sip of the green liquid, and taps it twice against the side of the bowl. I copy her actions. Servants appear immediately. My empty plate is taken away, and another course is set before me, a plate full of rice with some cubed yellow fruit and round, grayish beans. What the—?

"Where's the meat?" It bursts out of me.

The man and woman next to me look horrified, but the white-haired girl across from me erupts into laughter. "Meat? We don't eat meat."

Oh no. Not only have we been kidnapped, but we've been kidnapped by vegetarians. I chew rice, frowning. The gray bean things aren't bad.

The girl catches my eyes and shakes her head subtly. I freeze mid-chew. "What?"

She sighs. "You are never supposed to eat the next course before someone ranked higher than you, and for you—" She pauses. "That's everyone at the table."

I sigh and set down my spoon. I wait until she and my other two neighbors have all taken a bite, and then I pick up my spoon with a raised eyebrow.

The girl nods, and I continue to eat.

"My name is Kemelah," she says. "I'm pleased to officially meet you, Zadock."

She was one of Agriad's chosen Shakers on the boat, so she must be very strong. And she's looking at me like I'm the next course, vegetarian or not. Her eyes are white, with only the tiny red veins showing any color.

I swallow and remember my manners. "Nice to meet you, Kemelah." My brain scurries for a topic. "Have you been a Shaker on Agriad's ships for long?"

"Oh, you must call him High Sustainer or Agriad the Great, never just Agriad," she says with a coy smile. "People around here get offended easily."

"Um. Of course. Have you been a Shaker on the High Sustainer's ships for long?"

"Nearly all my life," Kemelah says. She chews on a bite of rice. "He saw the potential in me when I was quite young. Cale and I were good friends." Kemelah's eyes glitter. "I'm sure Norah and I will rekindle that friendship."

Suddenly, I understand why Agriad placed me here, away from Norah. Everything he does has a purpose. If Kemelah's as strong as she says she is, and she's going to be close to Norah, this could be dangerous.

The food is taken away and another course brought. I'm already stuffed, but everyone around me digs in, so I try to take a few bites.

I can't help but wonder if Agriad is using Kemelah to threaten me, then what is he doing to Norah?

I risk a glance down the table, trying to get a glimpse of her. She's seated next to Agriad, and she looks frozen in fear, her eyes enormous. I long to go to her, comfort her.

I will keep her safe. Whatever it takes.

17

NORAH

I try to meet Zadock's eyes from down the table, see how he's doing, but he's surrounded by people trying to talk to him.

Some green soup is set before me. It looks odd, but I see Agriad watching me, and I pick up my spoon.

"I've had all your favorites prepared for the feast tonight." Agriad smiles.

I swallow and take a sip of soup. It's not bad, cool and refreshing and tastes of mint and something else. "It's...good."

But that seems to be the wrong thing to do because he frowns.

I am seated to his left. I don't know what that means here, but in To'Morat, seating arrangements are important. The chair to Agriad's right is empty, even though every other chair is occupied.

Agriad picks up his spoon and taps the side of his bowl. A course of plantains is brought to him. I feel silly, but I copy him.

A plate is set before me, plantains with some green mush stuffed down the center. Everything is so different, but I'm afraid of offending Agriad, so I dig in. The plantains are sweet and the green mush kind of earthy. Agriad frowns as he cuts into his plantain, and again, I think I'm doing something wrong.

"I hope you and your friend are enjoying yourselves." Agriad takes a bite.

What am I supposed to say to that? "Um…yes?" Agriad has taken us captive. Now that I think of it, why invite Zadock to the feast at all? Zadock's only here to get me to do what Agriad wants, so why treat him well? Why not put him in a cell?

The thought makes a tendril of worry squirm inside me.

"Why treat us so well?" I ask. "Aren't we your prisoners?"

Agriad looks at me with those blank eyes. "You are my daughter, and he is your guest. You clearly care for him, and I care for you." His face softens. "I am glad you're home."

Hmm.

Someone a few seats down the table asks Agriad a question, and he turns to them. I chew my food.

The boy seated to my left is about my age. I do my best to keep my elbows in and avoid poking him as I cut into my plantain. I rack my brain for something to say to Agriad, some way I can go about asking all the questions swirling in my brain.

"Are you enjoying the feast tonight?" the boy asks.

I turn toward him, lips parted to say something, and then my mouth falls open. I nearly drop my skewer and knife. "W-what?"

He smiles, showing perfect, white teeth. His eyes are brown and warm, not the pure white of Agriad and some of his elite. "I asked if you're enjoying tonight's feast?"

I blink, dumbfounded. This is the boy. The boy in the painting in our room.

"Um. Yes. Thank you." I turn back to my plate and stab my food. "I like this stuff?" I mutter under my breath.

The boy next to me laughs. Oh, no. He heard. I hope Agriad didn't. I glance at him, and he seems engrossed in chatting to someone a short way down the table, across the empty seat.

The boy holds out his hand. "I'm Elandor." His hair is golden with streaks of brown, his skin the pale white of Agriad's people but not quite as transparent. He has a tattoo on his left cheek, three diamonds with a teardrop shape in the middle.

"I—I'm Norah." I hold out my hand to his. Instead of a handshake as I was expecting, he intertwines his fingers with mine in the sacred symbol of Atoille's promise. I jerk my hand back.

"Sorry." He looks abashed. "Cale is my...was my...Anointed."

My eyes widen. I blink. I should have seen this. I should have guessed.

I turn back to my food, my breathing speeding up. There's a reason Agriad placed Zadock so far down the table. There's a reason he has me seated right next to this boy.

Agriad glances at me and sees that Elandor is looking in my direction. "I'm glad you two have become reacquainted." Agriad turns back to his discussion with his nearest neighbor and laughs at something that was said.

Thoughts race through my brain. Zadock is useful to Agriad as long as he thinks that killing Zadock will lose my obedience. He won't get rid of Zadock. Not yet.

Elandor looks nervous, but he places a hand on top of mine, trembling on the table, food forgotten. "Ca—Norah. It's all right. I understand that you don't remember anything."

"I'm not her."

"I know you think that, but Agriad says—"

"Agriad says a lot of things." I remove my hand. I'm being rude, but I don't care. I should play along with Agriad's game to save Zadock's life. But right now, I can't think. It's too much.

I have a sudden longing for Motah. She would know what to do.

"I'm willing to wait," Elandor says. "I know we don't have to get re-Anointed right away. Or ever, if you don't want to."

I look at him sideways. "So, me and you, we're not Anointed?"

"No. It was broken when you—when you—" He clears his throat and turns to his plate.

"I'm so confused," I murmur, stirring food around my plate.

Elandor nods. "Agriad said you may never get your memories back."

I grind my teeth in frustration. I'm not Agriad's daughter reborn, whatever he believes, and my memories are my own.

"You should get the next course." Elandor picks up his spoon and taps on the bowl of soup. "This is your favorite dish. I promise the gray things are really good."

I eye him sideways. But I copy him, and within moments, my plantains are taken away and a new plate is brought to me. I take a bite. He's right. The gray things are berries of some kind, and they pop with sweetness in my mouth. "You're right. They're good. Thanks." I'm a great conversationalist, that's for sure.

"It's going to get better, Norah," Elandor says. "You'll see. I don't want to pressure you or rush you into anything, all right?"

I look at him. Earnest, and ok, yes, handsome. Not like Zadock, who is attractive in a rugged, scruffy kind of way. Elandor is neat and perfectly put together in a camehl-butter-yellow silk shirt. It's all I can do to nod.

Out of the corner of my eye, I see something that stops all thought. I drop my spoon. I turn and look at the man walking into the room. He strides next to Agriad and takes the chair to his right.

He's a tall man with light brown hair like mine, but it's curly like Shrey's, my little sister. He sits at Agriad's right and taps his spoon against his bowl. Agriad claps him on the shoulder, and they begin talking.

I stand, jolting out of my chair so fast that it tips over behind me. Agriad stares in shock before frowning in disapproval. The conversation around us quiets, but I can't hear anything anyway over the ringing in my ears, the pounding in my heart.

My voice comes out in a whisper. "Potah?"

18

———

LYLAHN

My body wrenches from sleep after another terror-filled night. I dreamed again of flame and blood, of the To'Morat warrior. I see his face every night.

I'm exhausted. I feel it in my bones. My body is wearing down from no sleep night after night.

I reach beneath my pillow and check for the dagger I swiped from dinner. I don't know how to use it, but I feel better knowing it's there. If I find him, now I have something. It's a start, anyway.

I make my way to the mirror and splash a small amount of precious water on my face. Bloodshot eyes stare back at me. Amantha enters with a curtsy and a murmur of "Lady Lylahn." She dresses me in a scarlet dress today with cascades of lace at the waist and sleeves. I swallow at the color but don't say anything. She works on my hair and then turns to my face, frowning at the dark circles under my eyes.

"Is there something wrong with the bed, Lady Lylahn?" Amantha asks. "Would you like another pillow or blanket?"

I shake my head. "No, it's fine, Amantha, thank you."

She continues to apply the face powder.

I hurry to eat breakfast—the portions are getting smaller and smaller under Sahlas' rationing eye—and then there's a knock on the door.

Amantha lets in Imwraeth. I smile when I see him, but it's a grim, tight smile.

"Lylahn, you look...fierce," Imwraeth says.

"Thank you."

"I thought I might go with you to inspect the barracks," Imwraeth says with a questioning glance.

"I would like that." I'm relieved, actually. I'm not going to kill the warrior today. Just find him.

Guilt squirms within me, but I shove it aside. I push my bangs back and straighten my shoulders.

Imwraeth extends his elbow, and I loop my arm through his. We walk down the hallway and leave Amantha to straighten the room.

I walk with my head high and try to still the trembling of my fingers.

We exit the palace and walk down the steps. I try to practice gliding and walking regally like a lady should, though it's difficult in these long skirts.

The sun is bright in the morning, the air fresh and still holding on to the evening chill. I take a deep breath and feel my chest loosen just a little. I try to focus on the moment, on walking with Imwraeth, on this brief time we have together.

We cross the palace grounds and hurry past the execution arena. I shiver and look away. We're almost to the barracks now.

"I'm sorry we haven't had much time for each other lately," Imwraeth says.

I give his arm a squeeze. "I understand. It's a difficult time."

"Yes, but, I want you to know—" Imwraeth turns to me, and we stop walking. "You are my priority," he says. "Even if I haven't been very good at showing it."

I smile, and my heart warms. "I know."

Imwraeth pulls me close to him, wrapping his arms around me and holding me tight. It takes my breath away, this simple contact. I bury my face in his shoulder, and, for just a moment, I think about pouring my heart out to him, sharing my burdens. But no... I can't do that to him.

"You're everything I've ever wanted," Imwraeth says. "I want to be officially Anointed to you. I want you to be my Favored Lady." He pulls back to looks at me with those large, black eyes. Waiting.

"Imwraeth..." Fear chokes me. I'm here, I'm trying, but I fail him, I—

His face falls briefly before his expression softens. "Whenever you're ready, all right?"

I can only nod. We continue walking down the path, a breeze blowing sand around our feet.

"I know something is wrong," he says. "I know it's hard for you here. I know you lost your people not that long ago." He looks at me. "I wish you would open up to me. Let me help you." Imwraeth stops again and touches my cheek before letting his hand fall. "Please," he says. "Don't shut me out."

There is one thing I need to do, I want to say. *I can't be yours until this pain is gone.*

Instead, I say, "I just need a little time."

The barracks loom ahead, an enormous square building that almost rivals the palace in size. We walk past groups of warriors walking in formation across a large expanse of open sand, some practicing with spears or sand sparring. Blood Ranked leaders shout out orders.

My breathing quickens. Warriors in black and red armor. Everywhere I turn. I grip Imwraeth's elbow tighter, grateful that he came with me.

I freeze on the path, forcing myself to watch the soldiers spar.

Imwraeth stops with me. "Lylahn, I know you want to help, but—"

I make myself walk forward. One step. Another. "I can do this." My voice trembles. Blood and fire flash through my mind. I focus on Imwraeth's touch, grounding me in the present.

We walk forward, and I search the faces.

Warriors stop their activities and salute. Imwraeth hails his Blood Ranked captains by name. Two of them fill him in on their drills, pointing out the things they're doing to prepare the warriors. The military lingo goes over my head.

And that's when I realize deep down that Imwraeth is humoring me.

I'm not of use to him.

It hits me like a punch, but I swallow and try to force it away. I need to keep my goal in my mind. That's how I'm going to heal.

I scan the sea of faces. Shaking, I force myself to let go of Imwraeth's arm. I walk up and down the rows of warriors. They salute when I walk by, with murmurs of, "Lady Lylahn."

None of them match my memories.

I hurry back to Imwraeth and release a breath. My chest still feels tight. But I did it. I'm doing it.

"Well done. Keep up the good work, Blood Rank Three Siahn." Imwraeth says. His warriors salute and continue their drills.

We walk up the steps into the barracks, and my body responds as if I'm walking into a den of deathstalker scorpions.

The hallway is neat and ordered, with warriors stationed at every doorway. We walk through their eating hall, their bed chambers, their weapons rooms. I clutch Imwraeth's arm and stay silent, feeling my skin crawl. He stops to talk with his warriors, boosting them up and congratulating them on their order and discipline.

Panic grips my throat. I scan the faces.

Finally, I think we've seen it all, and we exit the building into the fresh air. The clamp around my chest loosens just a tad. I step away from Imwraeth and fall to my knees. I can't help it. My arms are shaking. The red dress is probably getting torn and scuffed, but I can't bring myself to care.

My breathing comes in rapid gasps. Imwraeth is at my side in an instant. "Lylahn!"

I swallow. I try to stand, but I'm shaking too badly. "I—I—"

He wraps his arms around me and pulls me to him. "I appreciate your help. I really do. You can help in other ways, all right?"

I didn't find him.

"Ok." We looked in every warrior's face. I'm sure of it.

Was he killed? Is this a hopeless cause? No. I can't believe that. There are other warriors out on patrol or serving in the palace.

He's still out there. I know it.

19

NORAH

"Potah?" I say again. He's here. He's alive. How?

My aching heart longs to be filled with joy, but something holds me back. Why won't he look at me? Has he been here this entire time, these entire three years I thought he was dead? Why didn't he come back to me?

Agriad looks up, annoyed. "Yes, daughter?"

I shake my head. "No." I point. "Potah?" I plead again. I step around the table. People are quieting their conversation, turning to watch. My fingers tremble as I walk to my potah.

I bend down close to his face. Still, he refuses to look at me. "Potah? It's me, Norah." Tears fill my eyes. It's him. He's here!

A chair scrapes back, and Zadock is at my side in an instant. "Raen Saranyi? Is it really you?" Zadock looks closer at my potah's face, and then he looks back at me, his face lit up with a smile. "Norah. He's alive."

The tears spill over my cheeks.

Potah looks at me, and I step back in shock.

His eyes. They are pure white.

"Potah?" I whisper.

Agriad stands. "Norah, come with me."

I hold my ground. "Potah...? Please, say something."

The man who looks like my potah stands to his full height. It's him, it's him. Everything about him is so familiar and warm, it makes me want to rush into his arms. Except his eyes. They're wrong.

"I am not your potah."

It's his voice! A cry wrenches from my lips. It's the voice that guided me through my first steps, my first sail.

"I'm sorry, but I am not who you think I am."

The joy in my heart twists into despair. What's happened?

Agriad frowns, his expression dark. "Norah, you will come with me. Now."

I follow Agriad on wooden feet, Zadock at my side. Before we leave the room, Agriad turns back to his guests. "Please, enjoy yourselves. We will return momentarily."

I look back once. Potah is focusing on his meal.

We leave the banquet room and enter an empty hallway with dusty portraits lining the walls.

"What's happening?" I demand. "Why do you have my potah?"

Agriad sighs. His eyes look weary, but I could be misreading them because of the white. Zadock puts an arm around my shoulders.

"Norah." Agriad's voice is tight, angry. "I realize that you may not get your memories back as Cale, but there are certain protocols that must be met. You are my daughter and my heir, and you have embarrassed me tonight."

I open my mouth, angry, but Agriad plows ahead. "It will be remedied. I will find you a teacher, someone to remind you of courtly ways. How things are done here. But I warn you." The white eyes bleed to black.

I swallow. I forgot where we are, the danger that is in every moment.

"I warn you," Agriad says, "this cannot happen again."

I nod. I need to play his game if I'm going to get answers. "Yes. But...please..." I try to look contrite. Zadock's grip around my shoulders tightens. "Please tell me why that man looks like my potah?" I choose my words carefully. "My potah from my...previous life." The words come out strangled, but Agriad's eyes fade back to white.

Agriad sighs. "Raen Saranyi is the general of my armies. He came to us oh...three years ago?"

I look at Zadock. Three years.

"So, he's not..." How do I say this? "Reborn? Like me?"

"No." Agriad shakes his head. "That is something that happens with only the most powerful of Sustainers."

Interesting. I tuck the information away. For now, I cling to every word coming out of Agriad's mouth.

"Raen Saranyi came from your world, yes," Agriad says. "But he came through the sands. Not the safer way, through the ocean of water."

"He came...through the sands," I repeat. The horrors of my potah's death snag in my mind. Me, reaching out for him. His hand slipping through mine, the force of the ocean of sand pulling him under.

A servant carrying trays of food bustles down the hallway and into the feasting room. We step aside to make way. Sounds of conversation float through the doorway and then go quiet.

Agriad nods. "Yes. It can be done. There are points in the ocean of sand that function like a dune of water, areas where travel between our sides of the planet is possible. Most who fall through these don't survive the trip, and the very few that do emerge with a madness that cannot be cured." Agriad leans in. "You understand, right, Norah? He doesn't remember anything about his past. Only his life here."

Despair crushes my heart. He doesn't remember me.

But he's alive. It's him. My potah didn't die. He came through the sands somehow. It doesn't seem possible, but Potah always said there was something magical about the deep ocean of sand.

"What's wrong with his eyes?" Zadock asks.

Agriad frowns. "Nothing. Nothing is wrong."

I bite back a sigh of frustration and try another question. "How did he come to be your general?"

Agriad waves a hand and glances toward the door to the party.

"Please," I whisper. "Please. I need some answers. For your daughter." I gag on the words.

Agriad smiles, but it doesn't touch his white, glittering eyes. "He came to us, babbling from the trip through the sands. He's a Shaker, so he was able to travel a short distance by sand platform before we found him. He was rambling about getting home, getting home."

I put a hand atop Zadock's on my shoulders. This is too much, the hope and despair warring within my heart.

"We rescued him. Brought him here. And then he saw my daughter, Cale, and something inside him snapped. The madness clicked in." Agriad shrugs. "He became somber, serious and quiet. We nursed him back to health, and he found a life among us. I came to realize that his skills at navigation and strategy were invaluable. He's a good man, General Saranyi, and smart. He's recovered from his ordeal, but it's likely he'll never get his memories back."

No... It's not true.

"Now," Agriad says. "Are we ready to return to the feast?"

I want to shout that no, I'm not, and at the same time, I want to see my potah again. Even if he doesn't remember me.

He's alive. It's him. Not a copy, not a body that looks like him. It's *him.* "Yes. I'm ready to return."

We turn back and walk down the hallway. Agriad grips my arm in cold fingers and whirls me towards him.

"I'm warning you, Norah. Do not embarrass me again."

And then he walks ahead of us and opens the door to the banquet hall, greeting his guests with a loud call.

Zadock looks at me. "Are you ok, Nors?"

I choke back the tears threatening to spill. "I'm ok. We better get in there."

I follow Zadock back into the banquet hall. People raise glasses when we enter, and I try to smile, though I'm sure the look is pained.

And there's my potah. Sitting beside Agriad, engaging him in conversation.

I take my seat and keep my eyes on him, studying his face. It's really him. I know every curve, every sharp line, every inch of stubble. It's the face I looked into as a child, as a young girl sailing a ship on the sands. The face of the first person who loved me.

I clench my grip around my fork and hear Elandor talking in my ear, but I don't register anything that comes out of his mouth.

Potah.

I'm not leaving here without him.

20

ZADOCK

I close the door to our room and breathe a sigh of relief. I lean back against the wood and slide down until I'm sitting on the floor. Norah sits beside me. We stare together at the blue crystal walls, the painting of her and that other guy. At the enormous bed and the dressers full of clothes that aren't ours.

"Hey. Do you think I'm wearing that boy's clothes?" I ask.

Norah looks at me, surprised. "Who?"

"That guy. In the painting. I saw him sitting next to you. Do you think these are his clothes?"

It's so ridiculous after everything that's happened that Norah bursts out laughing. She laughs and laughs until her shoulders shake with sobs.

"Nors. Shhh." I wrap her up in my arms, and she cries into my chest. I stroke her smooth hair, whispering in her ear. "It's ok. You just saw your potah. All these years, you thought he was dead."

"He's alive," Norah whispers. "He's really alive."

I tighten my grip on her.

"And he doesn't know me." Norah chokes back a sob. She hurries to wipe her eyes.

"Norah." I tilt her chin so she's looking up at me. "You don't have to fight it. You don't have to be strong for me. You can let it out."

Norah's eyes fill with tears, but she still hurries to brush them away again. Atoille, she's so beautiful. Even with swollen eyes and puffy red cheeks, she's as beautiful as the moon goddess herself.

"I've got to make him remember, Zadock." Norah's voice steels with resolve. "When we escape, we've got to take him with us."

"Nors..."

"I'm not leaving without him."

I sigh and stand. I walk across the plush carpet to a dresser and start untying the sash thing from around my waist. "Norah, he's on Agriad's side now."

"Yes, but—"

"He won't come with us. He'll turn us in if he knows we're trying to leave. And then—"

"Agriad will know we're trying to escape. I know."

I give up on the sash and walk back to her. I extend my hands to help her up. She stands, and I wrap my arms around her and pull her in close. I breathe in her scent.

"I can't leave him, Zadock."

I stare at the wall above her head. "I get it. I get it." I sigh. "We'll try to make him remember. Like you said. We'll make him remember."

She holds me tighter. "Thank you."

"For a month," I say, even though it's painful.

Norah backs away from me, her face confused. "What?"

"We'll try for a month. If we can't make him remember by then..."

"No. We've got to—"

"Nors." I cut her off gently, but her face reddens. "People back home need you. You heard what Agriad said, they've got a month, maybe less, before the food supply runs out."

Norah spins me around and yanks at the knots on my sash. "He's my potah, Zadock. I thought he was dead."

"Yes. But our people will die without you."

The sash falls to the floor with a tinkling of crystals. I turn back around and take in Norah's face, her stubborn expression.

"They were getting along fine without me before."

I frown. "What?"

"Before we found out that I'm a Sustainer. No one needed me then. No one wanted me then."

My stomach twists. "Norah, I—"

"I'm tired." Norah crosses the room and opens the enormous armoire. She's still wearing the gorgeous blue silk with glittering crystals. She digs through the clothes.

I cross the room and touch her bare shoulders. She freezes. I long to wrap my arms around her, but I'm afraid she would push me away. We've never fought. "*I* always needed you. *I* always wanted you."

It must be the right thing to say because she relaxes within my arms and turns back to me. "I'm sorry, Zadock. This place... It's been a lot."

"Yeah."

Norah laughs softly. "One room. One bed. Things sure are different here." Even with only soft starlight coming through the windows, I see her rosy blush.

"They are." I turn around to give her some privacy.

"Zadock... I—I need help," Norah says. "I can't undo this dress by myself."

"Oh. Um. All right."

I turn back around. Norah shows the back of the dress to me. It does look complicated, the ribbon laces crossing over each other up the back and tied at the top. I work at the bows and ribbons for several minutes. The dress falls away a little at a time, revealing smooth, tan skin beneath. My breath catches in my throat at the sight of her bare back. My fingers graze her skin as I undo the last of the ribbons.

With every ounce of willpower I have, I turn back around so she can finish getting changed in privacy.

"Thank you," Norah whispers.

"You're welcome." My voice comes out ragged. I walk to my own dresser and grab something to wear to bed before hurrying to take off the ridiculous silk shirt and pants.

Norah's lying in the bed, her back to me, by the time I climb in beside her. The bed is soft and big enough that we can sleep without touching, and I'm disappointed. I'd take the pallet in our small boat over this any day.

"Good night, Zadock," Norah says.

"Good night, beloved," I whisper.

I lie there awake, mulling over the events of the day. Whew. It was a whirlwind. And we're sleeping in this strange place, surrounded by enemies.

Starlight shines through gauzy curtains over the window. I can't sleep. Neither can Norah, if her tossing and turning is any indication.

"Nors. You awake?"

Norah lets out a sigh. "I can't sleep."

"Me, either." I hesitate. "Do you...want me to rub your back?"

In the dim light, Norah's eyes turn toward me. "What?"

I clear my throat. "Umm. Rub out the muscles in your back." I hurry to explain. "Sometimes, when I was little, I couldn't sleep. Ki'Rhen Dalayn would rub my back. It helped."

Norah smiles. "She's always been so kind."

"She has."

Norah rolls over onto her stomach. "All right. If you think it will help."

It might not help me *sleep,* I think as I sit up next to her. The bed is soft and sinks beneath my knees.

I catch my breath at the sight of Norah, lying face down on the bed, her head turned to one side. Her soft brown hair is splayed out behind her, and her skin shines in the starlight. The thin, sleeveless nightgown she's wearing is almost sheer.

I swallow.

I reach out with both hands and massage Norah's shoulders. The feel of her skin sends sparks up my fingertips. I start out soft and hesitant, then increase the pressure when I feel knots.

Norah moans.

I startle. "Are you ok?"

"Don't stop."

I smile and resume working out the knots.

"I've never had anyone do this to me before," she whispers into the quiet.

"Anytime." I shift my fingers lower, going over her shoulder blades and mid-back. Her skin... *Speck.*

And yeah, maybe it's a little selfish when I say, "I could get a better angle if I..." I can't bring myself to finish the sentence. I love this girl so much.

Norah only nods. Her eyes are closed, relaxed. Good. This is what I wanted. If I can help her in this small way, it will be worth it.

But speck, it's torture.

I lift one leg over Norah to straddle her, taking care not to touch anywhere indecent. Even so, my pulse races.

This is not good for my sleep.

Her legs are barely touching mine through the thin gown, and the heat that courses through me is enough to push back the cold of the night.

I focus on the knots in her back, trying to ignore the feel of her warm skin beneath mine. I only want to help her relax.

"Thank you, Zadock," Norah breathes. "That was heavenly. I think I can sleep now."

"You're welcome." I pull the blankets up around her shoulders and lay back beside her.

"Can I do the same for you?" She asks.

My heart races at the thought. "Another night. You go to sleep."

She murmurs something and shifts onto her side. Her breathing deepens, even and slow. Good.

I will my body to *cool it,* for the love of all that is holy, and lay there, thinking of anything except the feel of her.

I think of her potah and her determination to make him remember her and bring him with us. I let out a deep breath, wondering how we can possibly do this.

Her potah is Agriad's general. That high ranking didn't happen by chance.

21

NORAH

When I wake up, my first thought is for potah. He's here. He's alive! Tears prick my eyes, and I blink them away.

I roll over and smile when I see Zadock. His eyes are closed, and he's breathing deeply. His face is as strong and kind and adorable as ever, his biceps highlighted by the way his arm is positioned behind his head. The other arm stretches across the space between us, reaching for me.

That back rub last night...that was something else.

I have to keep him safe. I'll do what Agriad wants, and I'll find my potah and make him remember me. I must walk a fine balance. Zadock's life is on the line.

I look at his sleeping face, at the sandy hair falling into his eyes, and I harden my resolve.

Zadock blinks his eyes open and yawns. He smiles. "Good morning."

"Good morning." I lean forward for a kiss.

The door slams open, and Jeru and Bernan barge in. I hurry to lean back and cover my chest with the blankets.

Jeru gives me the briefest of curtsies, not a hint of a smile on her face. "Great Sustainer, it is time to arise and prepare for the day."

Bernan smiles at us warmly, the lace at his throat tickling his chin. "Good morning to you both."

I grumble, but I get out of the bed when Bernan's focus is on helping Zadock. Jeru bustles me into a dress slightly less ornate than the one I wore last night, though it's still the same shade of dark blue. The silk is fine, and there are crystals glistening about the neck and waist. The skirt is more...twirly...than the last one. I can move a little easier, but still not what I'm used to.

Jeru sits me in front of a mirror and is running a comb through my hair when she asks, "Will you be breakfasting in your room this morning or in the dining room?"

"Umm...in here."

Jeru frowns like I've said the wrong thing, but she rings a bell for our breakfast to be brought.

Zadock and I sit at a small table on the far side of the room next to a window. While we wait for the food, I look out at the vast palace grounds. Quite a distance away, a low quartz wall encircles the palace. Flowers burst and bloom along the winding paths, and the black trees with their tangling vines grow in intervals. Beyond it, there's the city, and then, far into the distance, I can see the outer city wall and the thick jungle of black trees beyond. The ocean of sand is too far to make out.

Suddenly, I feel stifled. The dress feels too tight. I glance at Zadock.

He reads my expression instantly. "It's so different here, isn't it?"

I nod, my throat tight. "I don't see sand anywhere. I miss it."

"Me, too."

More servants bustle in with trays bursting with food, and my eyes go wide. Is every meal going to be a feast like last night?

There's camehl cream and floral tea, yellow and orange fruits that look like stars, coconut milk and cardamom-scented rice porridge, and balls of dough fried and rolled in cinnamon and coconut sugar. I choose the porridge, and Zadock, grumbling, takes dough balls and fruit. Even more choices are laid out on another table off to the side for us.

The rice porridge is warm and delicious. I savor a sip of creamy tea. "Mmmm."

Zadock stirs his food around and mumbles, "No meat."

The servants bow and leave us in peace. Jeru and Bernan stand ready at the door.

I take another bite, but it feels awkward with them watching. "Umm. You may leave us?"

The two look at each other and exit, closing the door behind them.

I can finally take a breath.

Zadock and I exchange glances, and I laugh at his expression. The tightening in my chest loosens. I'm starting to feel hope.

"You know, as far as being kidnapped goes, this isn't so bad," I say.

Zadock frowns. "Speak for yourself."

I laugh, but then my expression turns serious. I stir my porridge and take another sip of tea. I try one of the star fruits. "Zadock, how are we going to get my potah to remember me? And how are we going to get out of here after that?" I take care to talk quietly. I'm sure Jeru isn't far away.

Zadock sighs. "We have to hope that the more you spend time with him, something will click, don't you think?"

"Yes, but how am I going to spend time with him?"

Jeru opens the door, and I jump. "I present Agriad Zul, the High Sustainer of To'Sharazad." She bows and backs away off to the side, and Agriad enters. My chest constricts.

Agriad frowns when he sees our breakfast spread. "I will forgive your ignorance, just this once," he says. "But from here on out, you will take your meals in the dining room. You will get to know your fellow Sustainers."

Annoyance swirls within me. Why were we given the choice if it was the wrong thing to do all along? "Yes, Agriad."

Anger flashes across his face.

"I mean, yes, Potah."

The cold smile is back. He takes a chair and joins us at the table, though both of us have stopped eating. "In ten days, the palace will hold a gala celebrating your return. Some of the most powerful people in To'Sharazad will be there to celebrate you." Agriad looks me over, and shivers go up and down my spine. "We must get you ready. This version of Cale is quite ignorant, but that is to be expected."

I stiffen.

Agriad leans forward. "Do not disappoint me, Norah."

Zadock grips the table and looks like he's going to say something, but I tap his foot with mine, and he closes his mouth.

"What am I supposed to learn?" I try not to sound rude, but it comes out like that anyway.

Agriad ignores my tone. "You will learn court etiquette and manners, first of all. To behave like a royal Sustainer. I already have a teacher prepared for you."

Zadock and I exchange a glance.

"And you will learn Sustaining. From me," Agriad says. "The nobility will expect a display of your power, and it must be strong. All High Sustainers are."

"I have been practicing. I can—"

Agriad shakes his head. "What you can do at this time is not enough. Not nearly enough. But. There is time yet. I will teach you many things."

I should be excited by the prospect of learning more about my sand gift, but all I feel is dread.

"I will join her," Zadock says. "I can be there to help."

Agriad looks at Zadock like he's a speck of sand, disdain on his face. "No, boy. And you will do well to remember your place."

I give Zadock a meaningful look, but he misses it. He's only looking at Agriad, his eyebrows turned down in anger. Zadock opens his mouth, but Agriad presses on.

"You will be at the gala as well, of course." Agriad doesn't sound thrilled about it. "We must introduce Norah's new Anointed to the court." He smiles, but it doesn't touch his icy white eyes. "Don't worry, Zadock Penvaren. I have a teacher for you as well. We'll start today. As soon as you're ready."

I swallow down the lump in my throat. "I want to...I want to learn more about your—I mean our—armies. How they work, how to lead them." I cringe under Agriad's intense scrutiny, but I press on. "If I'm going to be High Sustainer, I have to know these things, right?"

Agriad blinks. But then he smiles. "Of course. You have many things to learn about our people, but there is plenty of time to do it."

I grip the chair underneath me. I can't sound too desperate. "I want Raen Saranyi to teach me." I swallow. "He's the best, right?"

I brace myself, but Agriad only shrugs. "Very well. But the military lessons are secondary. You must learn court etiquette and Sustaining; that comes first. Do you understand?"

I stifle the thrill in my heart and attempt a gracious nod. "Yes. Thank you, Potah." It's rolling off my tongue now because I picture my potah—my real potah—in my mind.

Agriad stands. "Well, if you are finished, I will show you to your first lessons."

Zadock nods. "We're ready."

I can't help the smile that blooms on my face as we follow Agriad. My potah is here, and I'm going to get to spend time with him. There's one small tendril of worry that whispers that it was too easy. Agriad agreed so readily.

We follow Agriad to the door, where he pauses and turns back to me. "And Norah." He lowers his breath to a whisper. "Don't disappoint me."

22

LYLAHN

"Lylahn."

I jerk awake with a scream. The nightmare was worse last night, so much worse. Panic has me in a vice. There's someone in my room.

I grab for the dagger under my pillow.

It's him! I realize with a jolt, my vision clearing. It's him. The same tall, lean figure. The gray eyes.

It's the warrior who killed my sisters. He's in my bedroom. He's come for me!

"Lylahn, wait—"

I don't think. I just act. Fire pounds through my veins, rage at what was taken from me, and a deep, primal fear that forces my hand. With a cry, I plunge the dagger into his chest.

A guttural groan slinks from his lips. He falls to the floor.

I stand on trembling legs. I did it.

The nightmare fades, and my vision clears. The red and black in the forefront of my mind soften into the background.

It's Danosrin.

I scream.

"Danosrin!" I kneel at his side, watching the blood gush from his wound. In my fevered state, I missed his chest. The dagger is buried in his stomach. Blood spurts from his mouth.

How could this happen? How could I do something like this? *No no no no no.*

I scramble for a vase of sand kept on my nightstand, tipping it over and dumping it all over the quartz tiles. I grab handfuls and place them on the wound. It's gritty, and I'm sure it hurts, but once I Absorb, the sand will disappear, taken within me and within him, turning into the pure energy required to heal.

"I'm going to heal you." The sand glows underneath my touch, and I focus on the healing. It's complex, requiring a deep knowledge of the body and tissue structure. I have to guide his body in how to heal, what to do. I close my eyes to focus.

When the sand dissipates, I open my eyes. Danosrin lies on the ground, breathing hard, a trail of blood making a line down his mouth. But his eyes are open, and the wound in his abdomen is sealed.

I gasp with relief and fall back onto the ground. "Danosrin—I'm so, so sorry. I—"

"It's all right." He sits up, wincing. "Still a little sore."

I cover my hand with my mouth and rock back and forth, ashamed and mortified at what happened. What I did. "I'm so sorry," I whimper.

Danosrin watches me for a moment and then puts one hand on top of mine. "Lylahn, don't worry. I startled you. I shouldn't have done that."

"Please don't tell Imwraeth!" The words rip from me.

Danosrin's eyes widen, but he nods. "The Favored One doesn't need any more worries right now."

I nod, still rocking back and forth. I can't stop trembling.

"It's all right, Lylahn. Everything's ok."

He's comforting me. The man with dried blood on his face and stomach. The man I almost killed.

"I can't tell you how sorry—"

"Shhh." Danosrin smiles. "Truly, it's all right. I understand. My people killed yours. You must be wary of us." He glances toward the knife I was keeping under my pillow. He shakily stands and then holds out a hand for me. He's so kind, so forgiving. I take the hand he extends and stand on quivering legs.

"The Favored One asked me to come get you. I'm sorry to wake you, but he said it was urgent."

I realize suddenly that I'm only wearing a thin night dress.

Danosrin seems to notice it at the same time, for he quickly turns around. "I'll call your maid to help you dress."

I nod at his back as he rushes from the room.

There's a puddle of blood on the floor. The sight makes me nauseous. I'm not sure what I'm going to do about that. I can't think right now, I'm so in shock.

I almost killed—I almost killed—

Amantha enters the room, and she stops, frozen, when she sees the puddle of blood. The quartz tile is freezing under my bare feet, but I barely feel it.

"Oh, Lady Lylahn! Are you all right?" Amantha rushes over to me, and her kindness brings tears to my eyes.

She skirts around the blood and takes my hand. "Is it your womanly time?"

I jolt, surprised, but I find myself nodding. What a child she must think I am. What everyone must think of me here.

"Don't worry, I'll take care of everything."

Amantha helps me to the washroom and gets me cloths to take care of myself, and then she goes to clean up the puddle of Danosrin's blood.

I turn to the washbasin and vomit.

☾

Imwraeth enters in a rush. "Lylahn." He looks at me with enormous eyes.

I'm sitting at my small breakfast table, forcing down the tiny portion of boiled plantains and shriveled dates. Amantha miraculously cleaned the floor of blood, and it's one more note on the list of things I have to thank her for. I'm shaking less now and trying to get my breathing under control.

I was startled, is all. Danosrin startled me. I've been so on edge, forcing myself to stare into the faces of Imwraeth's warriors. It's no wonder I jumped to conclusions.

I wiped the dagger clean and put it back under my pillow.

Imwraeth's face is stricken. Does he know what happened? Did Danosrin tell him? "Imwraeth, what's wrong?"

He extends his hand in a daze. "Come with me."

I take his hand, and we rush through the palace corridors. The palace is a flurry of activity, with servants darting every which way. There are extra guards placed, and I try to look at their faces to see if recognition sparks, but we're going too fast.

"What is it?" I ask again, out of breath.

Imwraeth stays silent as we exit the palace. We turn right toward the gardens and the stables. Imwraeth nods to the guard, and he opens the gate. I make myself look in the guard's face. Not him.

Dread makes my footsteps drag. Why the garden? What could be wrong?

Imwraeth steps aside, and I get a view of the garden. My mouth drops open. I fall to my knees.

"No..." It can't be. "No."

The garden. It's dead.

The plants look even worse than they did during the famine, before Norah Sustained them. Where there used to be flourishing life, vegetables and berries and beautiful flowering plants, there are black, shriveled stems. They're ashen, dark. Wrong, somehow. Like something that's been left to rot for a long, long time.

I walk along the garden path, stunned, and I kneel next to what used to be a bristlebrush plant. A fruit is there, waiting to be picked. It would be fully ripe, except it looks like it's been burned in a fire. I reach out to touch it, careful of the spines, and it crumbles to dust. I gasp and yank my hand back.

"What happened?" I breathe, standing and meeting eyes with Imwraeth.

He plops down on a nearby bench. I notice the dark circles under his eyes, and something tugs on my heart. My Imwraeth. He's shouldering so much.

I sit next to him and take his hand.

"I don't know." Imwraeth hangs his head and runs his free hand through his red hair. "I assume it's something to do with Norah's absence, but I don't know."

I stare around us at the ashen plants in shock. "Is everything like this?"

Imwraeth sighs. "Not everything. The plants around the palace and edge of the plateau got hit the worst, for whatever reason. Some of the grow walls within the city survived. The food that was already picked and stored is fine. But this cuts our survival timeline in half... at least. And that's if I work with Sahlas to ration the food even further." Imwraeth lets go of my hand and puts his head in his hands. "Lylahn, I...I don't know how we're going to get through this."

I grit my teeth and wrap my arms around him. I lay my head on his back. Dread and worry are making me sick.

Imwraeth trembles underneath my grasp.

"You are the leader the people need right now," I say. "You can do this." But even I don't believe it.

"No. No, I can't. How am I supposed to help them get through this? How?" His voice rises in volume.

I grip him more tightly. "I don't know." I hook my finger under his chin and tilt his head to look at me. "But I know you can." I place a gentle kiss on his lips. His mouth barely responds.

"I don't know what to do. I don't know how to fix this."

I place my forehead against his and breathe in his smell. I close my eyes. "I'm here," I say. "I'm here with you. We'll get Norah back. It's all we can do. We'll hold out until then."

Imwraeth nods against my forehead.

"Is the barge ready?" I ask.

Imwraeth stands, removing himself from my embrace. The stark blackness of the plants strikes me again. I swallow.

He holds out a hand to me. "Let's go see."

23

———

ZADOCK

Norah walks ahead of me down the blue crystalline hallways, her back straight, her hands in fists at her sides. She's trying to be brave for her potah, but I have this sinking feeling that won't go away. We keep getting in deeper and deeper. Meanwhile, people back home need their Sustainer. Agriad says we have a month, but who knows if he's telling the truth?

I don't like this. Not one bit.

We follow Agriad through the hallways. I take Norah's hand and give it a squeeze. She smiles at me, and my heart beats a little faster. For her. I'm doing this all for her.

I've got to make plans to get us out of here. I have to be ready for us to go if anything goes wrong. I hope we can get her potah to go with us, but my priority is keeping Norah safe.

We descend flights of stairs and go past the ornate doorway that leads to the feasting hall. We pass guards and servants who bow to Agriad and murmur, "High Sustainer."

At last, Agriad stops and opens a door. "Zadock, this is where we leave you."

I grip Norah's hand. "We're going to stay together. Norah's coming with me, right?"

Agriad frowns. "I have arranged for you to have separate teachers since you have different skill sets to work on."

I open my mouth to protest, but Norah squeezes my hand hard. "That will be fine."

I breathe out. She won't let me protect her. How am I supposed to do my job?

I grit my teeth and nod, and Agriad grins. Those eyes are downright freaky.

Agriad holds the door. "After you."

I move to walk by him and pause. On his shoulder, there's a dusting of sand. It's orange.

"You have something...there." I point. Orange sand. Not white.

Agriad glances at his shoulder and hurries to brush the sand away. He doesn't acknowledge the question in my eyes, just gestures through the doorway with a secretive smile.

I walk through the doorway, mind whirling. I saw Agriad last night. He didn't have time to cross the ocean of water and sail to our home. So where did that sand come from?

We walk through the doorway into a sitting room. There's a table and chairs and a large flowery rug on the floor. Kemelah is seated across the table. Her ice-blonde hair is pulled back into a long tail, and she wears the same white belted tunic that she did aboard the ship.

"Welcome, Zadock," she says.

I swallow.

"Kemelah will be your teacher," Agriad says.

Norah looks at me. "It's going to be ok," she whispers. "Do what she says."

"I'll see you soon," I say.

She smiles. "Soon."

Norah and Agriad leave through the door we came in. My

stomach sinks as she walks away. I have this irrational fear that something bad is going to happen to her if I'm not there.

"Well, Zadock Penvaren." Kemelah gestures to the seat across from her. "Shall we begin?"

I sit at the table. The silk shirt I'm wearing is tight and uncomfortable. I miss my regular clothes.

"Go ahead," I say, a tad irritated.

"First of all, you must know how to address the people around you properly," Kemelah says with a haughty air. She's enjoying this way too much. "When you sit down to any kind of meal, there are protocols to be followed, or you risk offense."

I put my elbow on the table and my head in my hand. "Yep. Ok."

Kemelah frowns. "No elbows on the table."

I move back.

"When you address someone higher than you—"

"Why do your eyes look like that?" For some reason, it's very fun annoying her.

Kemelah's blank eyes narrow. "Listen. I have been instructed to teach you and to report on your...cooperation. Please don't make me give a bad report."

I grit my teeth. *For Norah. I'm doing this for Norah.* I nod.

"My eyes are a gift, if you must know," she says. "From Agriad."

"How does—"

"Enough," she snaps. "Back to what I'm supposed to be teaching you."

The lesson becomes a blur of which fork to use and where to place your napkin and even when to use it, phrases to say to certain people and what not to say, and the order in which to say them. And on and on and on.

"I—I need a break," I say after what feels like hours. "My head can't take much more of this."

"Very well." Kemelah sighs. I'm a hopeless cause, and she knows it. I can't remember all this stuff.

I stand and walk around the room to stretch my legs.

Kemelah Shakes sand out of a vase in the corner, swirling sand around and through her fingertips. I watch her out of the corner of my eye. She uses the sand to lift a skewer and knife, pretending to cut with it.

"You're good at that," I say.

The cutlery drops. "Thank you."

An idea pops into my head. An idea that might make these lessons not such a waste of time. "What can you teach me about Shaking?" I ask. "I'm a Shaker, like you, but things are so different here. I'd like to learn more."

I'm hoping beyond hope that there's something I can learn about Shaking the sand while sailing the ocean of water. Something those Shakers did helped Agriad to cross. If I can learn from her, maybe I can be of help to Norah.

"I wasn't instructed to teach you that," Kemelah says, eyes narrowed.

"But—"

"Etiquette first," she says. "We'll see how you do. Shaking can be your reward." She gives me a coy smile.

This girl gives me the creeps.

I take a seat at the table. "All right. Let's get back to it."

24

NORAH

I watch Zadock go and send up a prayer in my heart to Atoille. *Please, be with him.* I'm doing what Agriad wants, but I still don't trust him. I don't trust any of these people.

I follow Agriad down more hallways, up the stairs, and then he stops. "Here we are." Agriad opens the door with a smile. "Your teacher should be familiar to you."

I walk through the doorway eagerly. *Potah?*

Elandor stands in the center of the room, hands in his pockets, a sheepish smile on his face. "Hey, Norah."

My face falls. I can't help it. "Oh. Hi."

"Elandor will be your etiquette teacher. When you finish lessons with him, I will teach you Sustaining."

I enter the room, and I hear the door click shut behind me. I'm alone with Elandor. Cale's Anointed.

The room is enormous, with a high glass ceiling overhead that shows the bright sun and cloudless sky. The room appears to be some kind of ballroom. Velvet-cushioned chairs line the walls. I'm at the top of a grand staircase, Forged to shine like gold. The walls are painted with stars, planets, and Atoille in full detail. I stare at it for a long time, mouth open.

"Those are accurate," I say.

Elandor notices where I'm looking. "The stars? You know star patterns?"

Taking care not to trip on my dress, I descend the staircase. "Yes. I do. Did...did she?"

Elandor glances down. I can't imagine how hard this is for him. I bite my lip and resolve to try to be civil.

"Yes. She loved it almost as much as I do."

"Oh? You like astronomy?"

Elandor grins at me. "I could study the stars all night. There's something magical about them, isn't there? That moment when you see a galaxy or when you find out that a planet has thirty moons." He blushes. "Sorry. I'm carrying on."

I smile. "Don't be sorry. I love it, too. I never get to talk about it with anyone." The last time Zadock and I star-gazed was months ago. We never get a chance anymore.

Elandor smiles back, hesitant. "Sometime, I would love to take you to see the palace telescope if you're interested. It's a beauty."

My heart starts to pound. I am interested, and I would like that. But...no. "Umm. Maybe."

"All right." He gestures to the table behind him, set with dishes and a placemat. "You want to get started?"

I nod and take a seat at the table. I can see why Cale would've liked him. He's handsome, with a kind face. His pale blue eyes study mine as we sit, and he begins discussing the fine points of dining. I try to pay attention and remember everything, but I'm failing miserably. I did not know there were so many things to learn about eating at a table with fancy people.

I sigh and put my head in my hands. "This is a lot harder than I thought."

Elandor sits back. "Let's take a little break."

I nod and stand. I walk around the room, studying the walls. "So does Agriad Zul have a thing for astronomy?"

"No." Elandor joins me. "Just his daughter."

My stomach twists.

"And he likes being surrounded by powerful things." Elandor waves a hand. "This is the room where the gala will be held. Agriad Zul likes to remind people what Sustaining can do."

I look at him with a cocked eyebrow. "Can Sustaining do something with the stars?"

Elandor shrugs. "I don't know enough about it. You'll have to ask him."

"And what's your sand gift?"

Elandor takes a handful of sand out of a small pouch at his side. He cups it in his hands and focuses. After a few moments, Elandor opens his hands, and there's a...flower? It's quartz, but it's shaped like petals, smooth and intricately layered. The flower is dusky orange, the color of the sunset. The color of the sand at home.

Did he know to choose this color? I shake my head. I am reading way too much into everything.

"It's beautiful," I say.

Elandor hands the flower to me. "It's called a desert rose. Under the right conditions, quartz crystals will form naturally this way."

I take the rose and examine it more closely. "That's amazing." I move to hand it back.

"Keep it. It's for you."

"I—" I don't know what to say. "I'm Anointed to someone else."

"Yes, I know. But you...you look so much like her." Elandor turns back to studying the wall. "And I miss her."

I swallow and close my hand over the flower. "This must be really hard for you."

"It is." Elandor looks at me sideways. "Agriad says you are her, reborn, but I don't know what to think. You look like her, but you don't act like her."

I shake my head. "I'm not her, Elandor. I don't know what's going on here, but I'm not her." I pause. "The tattoo. On your cheek. Does it mean something?"

Elandor touches his cheek, running his fingers over the three triangles and the teardrop. "It means I've lost my Anointed."

I look away. "I'm so sorry."

"Well. Let's get back to it, then."

Suddenly, the room darkens.

I glance upward, senses firing, and my mouth drops open. "A sandstorm!"

Elandor follows my gaze. We watch the sand pummeling the glass ceiling, driven by the ferocious winds. It hit out of nowhere. It didn't build, gathering force. It struck.

Oh no.

"That's odd," Elandor says. "I don't think there was a sandstorm predicted today."

My stomach turns sour. Before Zadock and I reunited the red and blue moonstones, events like this were hitting more and more frequently. Random sandstorms. Increased plateau erosion. Rain that didn't nourish the plants.

The sand drives in wild patterns against the glass ceiling, and I can almost hear the roar of the winds. Anyone caught outside in that will be cut to shreds.

Elandor catches my worried expression. "Norah, it's all right. I'm sure the High Sustainer will take care of it before it can do real damage. He's a powerful weather influencer."

I walk back to the table, my legs trembling. What does this mean? Why is it happening here? I step on the hem of my gown while sitting and fall into my chair with a *thunk.* My face burns, and I let out a deep sigh. "I am never going to get this."

"You will," he says. "You're smart, Norah. You can memorize star patterns. You can learn this. We have ten days until the gala."

Ten days. "Let's keep going."

❨

When Agriad fetches me hours later, I rush from Elandor's presence without saying goodbye.

Agriad hurries through the palace, and I follow as fast as I can without breaking into a run. The dress moves smoothly, but it's still difficult to walk. We go upstairs and through more crystalline hallways, then past the banquet hall and back to the main doors of the palace. "Potah? Where are we going?"

"You'll see."

We approach the doors that lead out of the palace, and I freeze. "The sandstorm?"

Agriad turns back to me with a reassuring smile. "Over already. I took care of it before many were hurt."

A cold, hard knot forms in my throat. Agriad "took care of it"—a sandstorm. I don't have much to compare him to, but his Sustaining must be ridiculously powerful.

We exit the doors of the palace, and the desert sun hits me in full. It's bright and hot, but the heat feels different than the dry heat of my world. It feels wetter, somehow, like every breath I take is laced with water. Sweat breaks out on my temples, and I'm pretty sure this goes against everything in etiquette I just learned.

Agriad descends the palace stairs, and I follow. He nods to guards who line the walkway. They salute him and bow low. The palace grounds unfold before me, and I get a better look this time. So many plants. So much green. How much Sustaining does it take just to keep the lawn growing?

Shakers line the walkway, Shaking the dusty sand brought in by the sandstorm and lifting it up and over the palace walls. I try to get a glimpse of the city beyond, but Agriad turns to the left, following the garden path.

The path is made of bits of Forged quartz, and it crunches under our feet. Again, how long did it take to make this? Who spent all this time Forging quartz just for it to become a walkway?

We come to an enormous, opaque dome. Agriad opens the door, and we step through.

I'm hit with a rush of warm, moist air. I catch my breath at the sight of so many plants. The quartz path continues to wind, but I can't see it past the first bend. Every inch of ground is covered in plants, growing and blooming, protected from the sandstorm by the glass dome. There are beautiful, foreign flowers and so much food. Every plant seems to be growing something edible, though I don't recognize much of it.

The smell is intoxicating. Bright and floral and rich with life. I breathe in deep.

To'Sharazad isn't just existing. They are *thriving* while the people of my home are scraping by.

I bend to smell a flower and take a minute to compose myself. My people need me. I have to get back to them.

And yet...I can't deny that it's nice being away from the pressure. The pressure of having to save everyone.

Agriad stops in the pathway and turns to face me. "Welcome to the palace gardens of To'Sharazad." He smiles. "This is where most of the food that the city eats is grown. Of course, there are other greenhouses like this one placed throughout the city, cared for by other Sustainers like you and me. That is why Sustainers are nobility. Naturally, we are above everyone else with their mediocre sand gifts."

The way he talks grates on my nerves. But I swallow and don't say anything. *Just learn what he has to teach you and get out of here.*

We walk down the winding path, me following a short way behind Agriad. Crystal fountains of water dot the way, with some of the plants growing straight out of the water.

"Rice paddies," Agriad says, gesturing to the green shoots.

There is so much life here I almost can't process it all. I've never been surrounded by green and vibrancy.

I stop to examine a bush with sharp red fruit growing out of it in bundles of three. They almost look like bristlebrush fruits but a brighter red and more cone-like.

"Achiote," Agriad says, noting my glance. "The fruits can cure fevers."

I look at him. "They can?"

"Plants are medicine as well. As a Sustainer, you'll need to spend time studying the properties of each medicinal plant. To have them in your arsenal, to grow when needed. Absorbing can heal much, but Absorbers are rare, and the more we can assist them, the better."

We keep walking, Agriad pointing out even more plants, their names and properties. I don't know how I'm going to remember it all.

I pause at a garden bed where green vines with camehl-butter-yellow flowers bloom. I bend to inhale their scent, but Agriad stops me with a hand.

"Take care, daughter. Some plants of the jungle are dangerous. This is the yellow oleander, and though it is beautiful, the nectar of the flowers is highly toxic. It's what we use to make the poison darts that our warriors are so well-known for using."

I stumble back.

"You will help grow and Sustain them, eventually, of course."

We continue down the path, me taking more care to not let vines and tendrils brush my bare arms.

We stop at a bend in the path surrounded by berry bushes. Agriad turns to me. "Show me what you can do."

"All right." I choose a bush with bright green berries. The plants, I realize, are growing out of sand. I know that sand is not fertile soil from all my time spent working at the grow walls, but I also know that the regular rules go out the window as far as Sustaining is concerned. I grab a handful of sand and clutch it tight. With my other hand, I reach out and touch a leaf.

It's been a while since I Sustained. I didn't realize the hole that was inside of me, wanting to be filled, until this very moment.

Love. I need to feel love. I think about Zadock. I think about Motah. I miss her. I hope she's doing ok. She was on To'Rahn, but I'm sure someone has gotten the news to her by now. She's probably so worried about me. I think about my sister Shrey, about her smile and her bouncing curls.

I squeeze the sand tighter.

The sand glows, and I channel the energy into the plant. It grows, the berries expanding, the leaves getting larger, the stalk shooting towards the sky about a foot higher.

The sand dissipates, and I step back, pleased.

Agriad stares at my work. "I'm disappointed, Norah."

My mouth falls open. "W-what?"

"Your skill is quite dismal."

"Well, I did only learn to do this less than three moon cycles ago."

Agriad glares at me. His eyes bleed to black. Oh no. Wrong thing to say.

"Yes. When Cale died." He swallows and composes himself. His eyes shift back to white.

I open my mouth, but nothing comes out. Three months ago. That was when I healed Zadock, brought him back from the brink of death, the first time I truly used Sustaining.

"Well. It's to be expected that you've forgotten much," Agriad says. "Though Cale was highly skilled in Sustaining. She was ready to take my place."

I look away, grinding my teeth. "So, what can I do differently?"

"Well," Agriad says. "To start, you can hold this." He unclasps a cord from around his neck and removes the green moonstone. I catch a glimpse of two others beside it, orange and purple gems glowing in the sunlight.

Three moonstones.

"Are those...?"

"Yes," Agriad says. "They are moonstones. A gift from Atoille. Your side of this world has its own. These are ours, what powers our sand gifts. Rather than place them in a statue for all to admire and ogle, we treat our moonstones with great care. I guard them. One day, this duty will fall to you, my daughter."

He tucks away the orange and purple moonstones and hands the green to me. I take it reverently. It gives off a green glow, and it's faceted and palm-sized, just like our moonstones back home. It's a perfect match.

"You seem to know a lot about our moonstones," I say. "Have you been to To'Rahn?"

Agriad ignores the question. "How does the moonstone feel? Pay attention to it."

I drop the subject. I'm still nervous about pushing him too hard. I need him to trust me.

This moonstone. This could be a crucial step to getting home.

I close my eyes and pay attention to how the gem feels. I never held the blue or the red, so I don't know what to expect, but it feels strange. Almost like it's calling to me. Almost like I can feel green tendrils trying to dig into my skin, go up my veins, and ooze into my heart. I don't like it. It feels wrong.

"Can I hold a different moonstone? Do they all do the same thing?" *Can any one of them get you through a dune of water or only the green* is what I want to ask.

"They are each slightly different, with their own properties and connections to the natural world. The green is what will help you Sustain the most."

Not a helpful answer. I turn the gem over in my hands, trying to get rid of the oily feeling. "It feels...it feels like..." I can't put my finger on it.

"Ambition," Agriad says. "The longing for power. The need for it."

"Ambition?" I open my eyes and hold the gem away from me. I try to swallow the lump in my throat, to get over it and just hold it. I need to know the secrets of this gem.

"Yes, daughter. The drive to become more. That is what you must feel when you Sustain." Agriad holds out a hand. "Here, let me show you."

I give the moonstone back to him, skin crawling. And all of a sudden, I realize why. I have felt what the moonstone is asking me to feel. Ambition. Power. The hunger for it. When I had nothing, no sand gift to call my own, I yearned for one. I would've given so much to have one.

I have a gift now. A powerful one. One that everyone needs. And I'm not sure if I—

Agriad takes the gem in both hands. "Once you understand, once you see more clearly, you won't need to hold the gem." He holds it close to his heart. "The moonstone can be a guide for you, a funnel for your power until you are used to how it feels." Agriad looks me up and down. My skin crawls under his gaze. "And you will become very powerful, indeed. The raw gift is there inside you. Cale's gift."

Cale's gift.

"Power. The need for it," Agriad says. The gem begins to glow brighter, and I realize that Agriad's not holding any sand. He's using the gem itself.

It shines with a green light until it's so bright it's almost unbearable. The trees, bushes, and flowers around us begin to grow. Higher and higher they climb until the path is almost obscured. The sun darkens underneath the shade of the plants, and still, they grow larger. The dome of the ceiling is high above, and the trees around me grow up until they are practically touching it.

This isn't natural. Plants aren't meant to loom this high.

The green berries grow so big that they pop, splattering juice all over my arms and face. But they still they grow, higher and higher. More berries sprout and pop just as quickly. The trees loom overhead, black vines dangling down until the sun is blacked out, and we're in a dark forest.

The plants are so getting so big now that they've encroached on the pathway and are now pressing into me. "Agriad," I say. "Stop." I'm going to drown in plants. "Potah!"

Agriad stops. The glow dissipates, and we are left in darkness. Then, to my utter shock, as fast as the plants grew, they shrink back down. The plants wither and retreat from me. I take a deep breath of air.

But the plants aren't just shrinking. They're dying. Black branches and vines turn brittle and crumble like ash. In moments I'm surrounded by a forest of dead things. I swallow.

Sustaining...it can't do that. No. *No.*

"You see, Norah," Agriad says, lowering the moonstone with a smile. "You can be so much more."

25

LYLAHN

Guards accompany Imwraeth and me in a retahn-drawn carriage through To'Morat. I looked into the guards' faces as we entered the carriage. Nothing.

Imwraeth sits next to me, silent, staring out over the side. I watch Imwraeth's people. There are relatively few in the streets, and they're despondent, dejected. People walk through their gardens and grow walls, touching plants that turn to ash, trying to coax them back to life with precious water.

"You should address the people." I turn to Imwraeth. "They need to hear from you."

Imwraeth closes his eyes and sighs. "I don't know what to say. I don't have a way to fix this."

I take his hand.

"But you're right," he says. "You're right."

The retahn's hooves make soft swishing sounds through the sandy streets, and the servant that sits up front holds the reins, tapping and clicking with his tongue. I find myself watching him, memorizing his movements.

The carriage halts, and I glance to the side and see the shipyard close to the western edge of the plateau. It's a large quartz building bustling with activity. I spot Danosrin pointing and directing someone carrying precious wooden planks. To'Morat is using all its wood resources to build this thing, for the quartz-reinforced cactus fibers they normally favor will be too heavy to sail on water.

Imwraeth helps me out of the carriage and gives a solemn greeting to Danosrin, whose long face looks even more forlorn than usual. We enter through the doors, and it's chaos and sound. I flinch but then take a deep breath to steady myself.

Engineers and workers barely pause in their activity to nod to Imwraeth. The building is one enormous dome, and the barge is being constructed in the center. One side of the building is open, facing the plateau's edge. I glance off into the distance at the ocean of sand, Atoille's face on the horizon. I can almost hear the roar of the sand spray, but then the din of the engineers fills my ears.

It smells strange in here. Not bad, but different. I smell fresh air and the hot desert sand, but there's an earthy scent underneath it all. Wood.

I let my eyes rest on the barge. I was almost afraid of what I'd see.

"It's ready, Lylahn!" Imwraeth grips my hand. "It's ready."

The barge is an enormous half-oval with a flat top, the wood smooth and light brown, the planks knit together. Ladders line the sides where engineers finish their final checks, and more workers load supplies up a ramp that extends down one side.

"It's ready," I whisper. I'm happy, but I also feel a worm of worry within me. We can go after Norah now. We can sail the sands and then the ocean of water.

Of course, Imwraeth will go. And I will go with him.

But I'm afraid.

This was my idea. And if it fails...if he dies because of me...

I step closer to Imwraeth and link my arm through his.

"How soon can we be ready to depart?" Imwraeth asks a passing engineer.

The woman bows her head. "Favored One. The barge is being

loaded with supplies as we speak. All our people are working to get ready to go as soon as possible. It will be ready to go tomorrow if you wish."

Imwraeth nods, and she continues on her way. He turns to me. "Tomorrow, Lylahn."

He takes my hands and kisses my fingers. "Finally, we have some hope."

I smile, but the unease within me deepens.

NORAH

Sweat pours down my face, and I'm breathing hard, but still, the plant I'm working on budges only inches.

"Again," Agriad says.

Tall black wood trees tower overhead, almost reaching the top of the garden dome. The heat within the glass walls is sticky and close. I feel disgusting, exhausted, and frustrated. I can tell by the furrow in Agriad's brow that he is not happy. He expected this to be easier for me.

Sustaining feels more difficult than it ever has. Even while holding the green moonstone, I'm not getting it.

Agriad sighs and glances towards the sun overhead. "It's time for your lesson with General Saranyi."

My heart leaps.

We walk back along the garden path to the palace steps, and Agriad nods for a guard to escort me the rest of the way.

"Norah." Agriad stops me as I'm about to leave. "I know what you're trying to do."

I freeze.

Agriad doesn't seem angry. Instead, his face takes on a pitying look. "Child, his mind is gone. Whatever association you had with him in your past life, it's over. He won't remember."

My hands squeeze into fists. I force myself to curtsy as Elandor taught me. "Thank you for the lesson, Potah."

Agriad nods.

I follow the guard through the palace doors and down the entryway. He's wrong. He's wrong.

I glance in the rooms we pass, but I don't see Zadock.

The guard stops at last at a door, and I enter eagerly. I'm in an office, with a black wooden desk and bookshelves lining the walls. The shelves are sparse, with only a few thick titles collecting dust. Miniature quartz sculptures in twisting shapes are artfully placed in between books. A window looks out to the palace grounds. On one wall, there's a painting of Agriad and my potah, both with serious faces. And seated in the chair at the desk, he's there.

My heart leaps into my throat. It's all I can do to stay where I am, not to run to him and throw my arms around him.

"Potah..." I breathe.

He looks up. There they are, the familiar features. A kind, gentle face. Dark hair that curls to his shoulders. And then, the only piece of him that is not him. The blank, white eyes unnerve me.

There are more worry lines etched into the corners of his eyes than there were before, and his eyes look vacant, distant. Is that the madness that Agriad refers to? If my potah is Agriad's general, it can't be that debilitating, right?

He stands and bows deeply. I stiffen. "You don't—you don't have to do that."

Potah straightens from his bow and resumes his seat. "You are a Great Sustainer, my lady."

I sit in the chair across from him.

"Norah, right?"

My breath catches in my throat, and I have to fight tears. "Yes. Norah."

The guard closes the door behind us, but I know he'll be there, listening.

"I'm Raen Saranyi." He holds up a hand in greeting, and I take it, clasping fingers together. The touch of his skin is dizzying. *My potah, my potah.* He's here. I hold his hand longer than necessary.

I'm flooded with memories. Potah swinging me over his head, laughing. Walking to the edge of the plateau, learning from him to discern the stars and to love them. Going to the market with him and Shrey, haggling over the ingredients for dinner, and then coming home and making it together.

He was the only one who could make Motah smile. Something in her died when he did.

If I could bring him back to her...

"Do I—" I swallow. "Do I look familiar to you?"

"Of course. You look just like Cale."

"Yes, but—"

"Well," he says. "We better get on with your lessons. Don't want to disappoint the High Sustainer, do we?"

My heart sinks. "Yes." I look around the room. "Why are we here? I thought we'd be in a sparring arena or..." I trail off and shrug.

Potah's blank eyes twinkle. "Eventually, I will teach you to defend yourself, but for now, we're going to discuss strategy. If you are to take the High Sustainer's place one day, you'll have to know basic military policy. Even if I or someone else will be here to help you."

I listen to his lesson, informing me of the basics of how the To'Sharazan military works. It's probably valuable information that I should be paying attention to, but it's hard to focus on what he's saying. I take in his face, his voice.

He pauses to take a sip of water from a crystal glass.

I lean forward. "General Saranyi, don't you think it's odd that you and I have the same last name?"

He shrugs. "Saranyi is not that uncommon of a name."

"Yes, but is it common here?"

"No, it's not." He sets down his glass. "So, you know."

My heart leaps into my throat. I hang on to his words like they're the edge of the plateau, and I'm dangling off it. "Yes?"

"I'm not from here." He spreads his hands wide. "I'm from across the ocean of sand. I came through it. Agriad has informed me of my past. I lost my memories and part of my mind on the trip through, and I'm not eager to repeat it."

"Yes." My eyes plead with him to go on.

"We really should get back to your lesson."

"Why haven't you gone back?" I ask. "To your home? There are ways—"

"Yes." He holds up a hand. "I know. Agriad has explained to me how he can safely travel through the dunes of water. And he's got that...purple moonstone that lets him come and go through the sand."

My mind latches onto that. Is he saying what I think he is?

"But my life is here now. I don't remember any of my life before the sands. And sometimes..." He stares into the distance, eyes blank. "Sometimes, I forget large portions of my life here. That is how the madness is affecting me." He shakes his head. "I can't go back. My world is here."

I squeeze my eyes shut. *Yes, it is. I'm here, Potah.*

I open my eyes. I've got to keep trying. "I know you," I start. "I know who you were on To'Rahn."

Potah looks away, grabs a sand gull quill, and starts making notes on a paper. "Oh?"

I reach out and touch his hand, and he stops writing. "You were my—"

Abruptly, Potah stands. "I don't want to know, Norah. Please."

My heart sinks into the ground.

"My life is here now. I'm not going back." His eyes are soft, his voice is gentle, but his words are crushing my soul.

"But..."

He sits again. "Let's continue with your lesson. Agriad will be disappointed if you don't show much progress."

I swallow the lump in my throat and nod.

LYLAHN

I stand on the edge of the plateau, overlooking the ocean of sand. The barge is perched near the drop-off, supported by cross beams and ropes until we're ready to depart. Ramps lead up to it, with warriors and servants carrying boxes of supplies and coaxing up retahn. Crates of weapons are also being loaded, along with boxes of black and red armor.

I rub my arms. It's evening, and the cold is setting in. A deep chill has penetrated my bones, and it will never leave.

I didn't find him.

I should be happy that we're leaving. We're getting off the plateau, we're going to save Norah and Zadock. We're going to save everyone.

The plateau's edge is a graveyard of charcoal plants. I touch one, and it crumbles to black dust. This is unnatural, this death that has struck the plant life.

I think about crossing the ocean of water, and my stomach turns.

"Lylahn?" Imwraeth wraps his arm around my shoulders, and I lean into him, appreciating his warmth. We watch the warriors loading the heavy crates and boxes. At least I can look at them with their armor on and not feel the urge to run now, even though my shoulders still tighten. I look into each of their faces as they pass. Not him. Not him.

"Lylahn, I—" Imwraeth swallows. I glance up at his face. "I want you to stay here."

I look back out over the ocean of sand, the crashing of the waves. "No."

"Lylahn—"

"I'm going with you." I grip his forearm around me. "If you're going, I'm going."

Imwraeth lays his head on top of mine. "I'm afraid, Lylahn. We don't know if the barge is going to work, and even if it does, there's going to be a battle. We're going to have to fight to get Norah and Zadock back. I don't want you in the middle of it."

I turn to face him. "I don't want *you* in the middle of it, either."

"I have to go. I need to do this for my people. And if there's any way we can get her back by negotiation, I have to try."

"I know." A breeze whirls sand around my feet. Atoille is setting, a low half-moon on the horizon, and everything feels heavier. "If there is a battle, you're going to need Absorbers who are ready to heal. I'll be there."

Imwraeth sighs. "I don't like it."

The flurry of activity continues before us, last-minute loading before the barge is ready to take off. We'll travel day and night, rotating the Shakers, never stopping until we find Norah and Zadock.

Suddenly, there's a cry, and I whip my head to the side. A heavy crate has fallen and pinned one of the warrior's arms to the ramp, and he's shouting in pain. Imwraeth and I rush over to help as a second warrior lifts the crate off his arm.

The warrior's face is twisted in a grimace, and I kneel beside him. I forget that he's a warrior of To'Morat. To me, he's a man in need of healing.

"It's all right," I say. "I'm an Absorber." I grab a handful of sand

and hold it against his wrist. The familiar light flows within me as I Absorb, and there's a connection between me and him.

Imwraeth puts a hand on my shoulder.

The edges of the crate were sharp, and the bruising is deep, but I am strong. The connection between us, made by the sand, allows me to regenerate skin, repair the tiny fracture to bone. Within moments, it's over.

The man stands, rubbing his healed wrist. He bows low. "Thank you, Lady Lylahn."

I smile. It felt good to do something useful for once. "You're welcome."

"Well," Imwraeth says. "If you insist on coming, I got you a little surprise." He turns with a smile, gesturing with his hand.

Sharise walks across the plateau, leading Darkest Night behind her.

My eyes go wide. I glance at Imwraeth. "Is she—?"

Imwraeth nods. "She's yours."

I beam and dash to the retahn. She whinnies and bucks against Sharise's hold.

Sharise hands the reins over to me.

I stroke the retahn's nose, and she nudges me with it, almost knocking me over with her strength. I laugh. I look to Imwraeth and then Sharise. "Thank you. Both of you. So much."

Imwraeth stands with his hands in his pockets, a weary smile on his face. "I'm glad you like her. She's coming with us." He nods to Sharise, and she takes the reins from me and leads Darkest Night away. "She'll be your battle mount if you think she's up to it."

"She is. She's perfect." I watch Sharise lead her up the ramp and onto the barge.

Imwraeth walks beside me and offers his elbow. "Shall we?"

I nod.

"Wait!" A tiny voice cries out.

I turn around. Kaera.

She throws her arms around my waist, and I hold her. "I'm

coming, too." Her voice comes out muffled against the folds of my skirt.

I can't help but smile. "No, Kaera. You're staying here."

She looks up at me with tears in her eyes, her long brown hair blowing in the breeze. "I'm going to miss you, Lahnnie." She turns her gaze. "And you, Imwraeth."

"I'll miss you, too, Kaera."

Kaera looks back at me. "Lahnnie, don't forget..."

I bend to her level. "What, Kaera?"

Her eyes shine with tears. "Don't forget what Bellah always told us. Do you remember? She said—"

I swallow and shut my eyes. The ringing in my ears grows so loud that I can't hear the rest of what Kaera says. Flame dances before my closed eyelids, their screams drowning everything else.

My sisters...

Vengeance. I haven't given up. No matter what it takes, I'll keep searching until I find him.

I hold Kaera for a moment longer. Warriors give the call that it's time to push off. The loading is done, and a crowd has gathered behind Kaera, including Sharise, waiting to see the barge set sail. Their salvation.

I stand, and Kaera walks over to Sharise, who puts an arm on her shoulder. "I'll take care of her," Sharise says. "She can help me with the retahn."

Kaera looks up at her, eyes shining. "I can?"

Sharise smiles. "You can. But no messing around. I need serious helpers."

Kaera nods. "I won't."

"Thank you," I say to Sharise.

I turn back to Imwraeth. "I'm ready if you are."

He reaches into his satchel of sand, Extracts, and turns to address his people.

"My people." Imwraeth's voice is loud and confident, and it carries on the wind.

A burst of pride explodes in my heart.

"We embark on a rescue mission to save Norah Saranyi and Zadock Penvaren." Imwraeth projects his voice through the crowd, enhanced by his Extracting. "We will sail across the ocean of water and find those who took them. We will show them that the To'Morat are a force to be reckoned with."

His words are met with cheers and raised fists from the crowd in front and the warriors on the barge behind.

"We will show them who we are! We are strong. We are resilient. We are hope!" Imwraeth cries and pumps his fist in the air, and the people follow suit.

My heart fills. If he can overcome his demons, maybe I can, too.

"I am leaving Councilor Sahlas to govern in my stead." Imwraeth catches her eyes, and she nods. "Councilors Danosrin, Lylahn, and Blood Rank One Riah will accompany me, including our finest of warriors"—more cheers —"on this rescue mission. We will be victorious, for we are To'Morat!"

We turn and make our way up the ramp, followed by the echoing shouts of the people.

Imwraeth steps onto the barge and then turns and extends his hand. I take it, appreciating the touch of his smooth, warm skin, an anchor in this darkness. I step onto the barge.

The deck is enormous and wide. The opposite of the ship the foreigners used. My shoulders slump forward. This could be an enormous mistake, and so much is riding on this.

Imwraeth gives some last-minute instructions to Councilor Sahlas, and then she steps off the ramp with a bow. "Good luck, Favored One."

"To you as well, Councilor Sahlas."

Sahlas fixes me with her solemn stare and gives me a nod. That's the most I can expect, I guess.

The warriors unfurl the sails, and a team of Shakers takes their place at the periphery of the barge, ready to lift her off, waiting for Imwraeth's signal.

"Push off!" Imwraeth calls.

The barge lurches and sand lifts us into the air. I grasp the railing, watching as we fall through the sky, fall into the oblivion of the stars, the ocean of sand getting closer and closer.

We hit with a *thunk* and a spray of sand, and then we're off, churning through the desert, heading southeast toward the ocean of water.

2 8

─────

NORAH

I sigh, tapping my foot on the ballroom floor. Elandor drones on and on about when to take a sip of water versus alcohol, and I don't know if I can take this anymore.

Zadock is in another lesson with what's-her-name, learning the same thing, and it's annoying being separated day after day. I'm not making much progress on my etiquette or Sustaining.

I'm still taking military lessons from Potah, too, and it's torture. He doesn't remember me. Not even a little. Despair is growing within me, a vise closing around my throat.

Maybe Zadock is right. Maybe we should focus more on escape instead of my potah.

"Norah?" Elandor says.

I snap my attention back to him. "Umm. Yes?"

"I asked you a question."

"I'm sorry. I'm a little distracted today."

"I noticed." He says it with a smile that crinkles that tattoo on his cheek. He stands. "You know what, let's work on something else. The gala is coming up." Elandor extends a hand to me and, for some reason, blushes. "The High Sustainer has asked me to teach you the steps to a traditional To'Sharazan dance that you and Zadock will be required to perform."

My eyes go wide. "A dance?"

He clears his throat, and the blush deepens. "I know it's awkward, but—"

"It's fine. You're just doing what you're told." I'm frozen in my chair.

"Right."

I force myself to stand and walk over to join him. "So, how do we do this?"

Elandor steps closer to me, his body almost pressing against mine. I hold my breath.

"Umm. So, I take your hand like this." He holds my left hand with the barest touch. "Er, I mean, Zadock will. And then your other hand goes here." He takes my right hand and puts it on his shoulder. I can't help it that I feel the hard lines of his muscular shoulders underneath his shirt.

"My other hand goes around your waist. If that's all right."

I nod.

He puts his hand on my waist. I meet his blue eyes, and I have to look away. He is attractive, yes, and I know he's fighting feelings for me—Cale. "This must be torture for you."

We don't have music, but Elandor moves his feet in a specific pattern, and I try to mirror him.

He sighs. "Yes. It is hard. I miss...you."

"I'm not her, Elandor."

"Agriad says—"

I let out a breath and accidentally step on Elandor's toes. "Sorry. It's just—I had a life before he took me away from my friends and family. I have a motah, a potah, and it's not Agriad."

Elandor frowns. "I understand. Agriad says that you and Cale became one when she died. That you're connected."

I refrain from rolling my eyes. "I'm not Cale. I'm me." I take a step back. "And I'm sorry I can't be what you want."

Elandor freezes.

"Why can't I learn this dance with Zadock if I'm going to be dancing with him, my Anointed, at the gala?" Elandor's face falls with every word. I'm disappointing him, but I have to stop this. Now.

"Like you said, I'm just doing what I'm told. Agriad wants me to teach you this dance."

I restrain the deep growl of frustration that rises within me. I remind myself that this isn't Elandor's fault. It's Agriad's.

"All right. Can we try again?" I step closer and open my hands wide.

Elandor stares at me and then looks away. "I thought you were dead, and now you're back, and...you don't remember that you love me."

Those words hit too close to home. I turn away before he sees the anguish on my face. "Let's take a break."

The door flies open, and Agriad enters. He doesn't seem to notice the tension in the room. "Practicing the traditional dance? Excellent. You'll have to keep at it tomorrow. We're going to spend extra time working on Sustaining today, Norah."

Atoille, I hate every bit of this. I follow Agriad out of the room. I can't look at Elandor.

We walk down the hallway, me trying to keep up with Agriad's quick pace. "The gala is in two days, and you will be formally presented to the court as my daughter and heir. Are you ready?"

I swallow. I don't know how to answer that. "Yes."

Agriad only nods, continuing his long strides down the corridors. I have to hurry to keep up. "Tomorrow, Norah, I need you to make an appearance with me at an event that is special to To'Sharazad. People are anxious to see that Cale—you—have returned to us."

"Umm. Ok. What's the event?"

Agriad turns and smiles. "It's called the Judgment."

29

ZADOCK

"You're weaker here because our moonstone is different than yours," Kemelah says.

We lead a party of To'Sharazan warriors through the city. The air is warm and humid, the city loud and busy. Kemelah and I cruise on gliders at the head of the group of about twenty or so Extractors and Shakers, people of Agriad's household. Kemelah waves to the guards at the city walls, and they let her through with a nod.

Just like that, we're out of the city. We ride on gliders, me wobbling and looking like an idiot next to Kemelah and the other warriors who have been doing this their entire lives. Kemelah took a few moments to show me how they work, which was invaluable information.

The glider is a small platform of sorts with a handlebar attached. I can turn the glider by twisting the handlebars. The brighter the glow underneath the glider, the more energy it has that's been stored there by an Extractor. So when it's starting to dim, it needs to be taken back to the storage shed to be recharged. The gliders move faster and smoother than someone going by sand platform. When Norah and I escape, these things are the way to go.

Kemelah is supposed to lead this hunting party gathering food for the gala tomorrow. We've still got etiquette lessons to accomplish, so she told me to come, and she grills me as we skim out of the city.

The warriors trail behind us in a group, giving Kemelah and me some distance. A glance behind tells me they carry spears at their sides and blow darts in their belts. We glide down the wide quartz road, jungle trees pressing in on either side.

"Aren't we going to gather plants?" I ask.

Kemelah throws back her head and laughs. "Not today, Zadock."

Kemelah halts her glider and hops off, then motions for the others to do the same. I follow her lead. We stash the gliders on the side of the road, and Kemelah moves to enter the wild tangle of trees. The jungle.

"Uhhh. Kemelah?" I ask.

She glances back over her shoulder. A few of the warriors behind me sigh.

"Are we really leaving the path?" I swallow. "Aren't there dangerous creatures out there?"

I hear a chuckle, and my cheeks heat.

Kemelah claps a hand on my shoulder. "Of course there are. That's why you've got to stick with me and don't. Touch. Anything."

I nod.

"I'm serious. You can't even trust the plants out there." The teasing glint leaves her eyes, and they turn somber.

"I'll be careful."

Kemelah nods. "Good." She turns to the other warriors. "Split off in pairs. We're hunting picuro today."

"Only the finest for the High Sustainer!" one of them says. They pair up and melt into the darkness of the trees.

Kemelah looks back at me. "You ready? We'll work on your Shaking as we go."

"Ready." Holy speck. "Though I don't see how I can avoid touching the plants." I follow Kemelah into the dense jungle, taking care not to let a single leaf or vine brush my skin.

Kemelah laughs like I've made a joke.

We're quickly surrounded by darkness, the light cut off by the dense canopy of trees. My eyes adjust, and I see Kemelah before me, the reaching vines and sharp leaves all around. The sounds of the jungle—birds cawing, creatures chirping, the crackling of leaves—become more intense.

Is this some elaborate ruse to get rid of me?

"What's picuro?" I ask, keeping my voice down. I follow Kemelah along a narrow path that doesn't look purposeful. It looks like it's been made by animals treading this way over and over, or maybe previous hunting parties.

A sharp, pointed leaf brushes my arm, and I yelp.

"Hush," Kemelah says. "You're fine."

"But you said—"

"Picuro is a large jungle rodent." Kemelah walks carefully, choosing her footing, cocking her head like she's listening for something. "Delicious."

"Ugh."

"You eat lizard, don't you? Gross."

I pause. "Wait. Meat. You eat meat?"

She turns back to me, a small smile on her face. "Only on special occasions." Kemelah holds out a hand, and I stop. "Get back. Get back!"

I stumble backward, and she follows. I hold my breath. A brilliant yellow and green snake slithers across the path. It's almost as thick as my neck.

I choke back a cry. We freeze.

The snake moves on.

Kemelah continues down the path like nothing happened, glancing at the sand every now and then, looking for something.

"Let's work on your Shaking while we walk," Kemelah says.

Finally.

"I don't know what you're used to, but here, you need ambition."

Kemelah holds out her spear, still walking with care. "What do you want most out of life? Think about that."

Norah. I want to keep Norah safe.

Kemelah stops and turns. "Let's see what you can do."

I Shake sand from the ground, trying to form a sand platform, but it's fighting me. My thoughts flit from fear to fear. *It's all up to me.* The sand reflects my mood, jolting and wavering.

"Think about what you want."

Norah. Safe. Home.

"Now imagine that you have the power to take it."

The sand steadies. I swirl it from between the trees, vines quivering with the blowing sand, grabbing more and more. All right. This is feeling more like myself.

Kemelah smiles. "Good." She takes a step closer and leans over to breathe the words in my ear. "You know, you're pretty cute when you do that."

"Gah!" I take a step back. "I'm Anointed, Kemelah. I love Norah."

She laughs. "I'm messing with you. If you can't handle me whispering in your ear, then you can't handle getting Norah home." She turns and walks down the path.

I drop the sand in shock. "What did you—?"

She shrugs, tossing her hair over her shoulder. "Of course I know. All those questions about Shaking the sand in water. What was I supposed to assume?"

"Are you...are you going to tell Agriad?"

She laughs again, enjoying this way too much. "No. I won't." Her smile falters. "Because you'll never get out of here." Kemelah swirls together her own sand, forming a platform and hopping on.

I follow her lead, shaping a sand platform and climbing on, moving myself forward, getting used to the feel of it here. "Why not?"

We sail over a patch of bright yellow flowers with curling green vines.

"Don't touch the flowers," Kemelah says. "You'll never get out of here because the plateau is way too guarded." She turns in the air, and I feel her pull, trying to take the sand from under my feet, testing me. I resist.

"Obviously the High Sustainer has thought that you'll try to escape. He's got guards on every perimeter and around the boathouse. You'll never get away from here without someone seeing. Then, there's the ocean of water itself. You can't cross it."

I jerk on the sand under her feet, furious at her words and my own powerlessness, but her platform holds. I'm impressed by her strength. "Why not?"

Honestly, this is good. I'm finally getting some information out of her. I know more of what I'm up against.

I try not to think about how deep we are getting into the jungle. A neon blue frog leaps onto a leaf at my right, and I jump.

"Don't—"

"I know," I say. "Don't touch it."

"Crossing the dunes of water is not just about how you Shake sand underwater. You need a moonstone, and you'll never get one from Agriad. He never takes them off. Guards them with his life." Kemelah shrugs. "So I'm not worried. Agriad's not worried. Try all you want to get back to your home, but you're stuck here. At least until Agriad's accomplished his purpose."

I freeze. "His purpose?"

Kemelah stops her sand platform, and I almost bump into her. "Please don't repeat that. Just..." She pauses. "Be careful. Watch yourself. And don't let Agriad Sustain Norah."

"Sustain Norah? Why would he—"

Kemelah's grin returns right as she jerks the sand out from under me.

I fall with a cry, but Kemelah catches me with a spray of sand before I hit the ground. She lands me on a patch of sand beyond the yellow flowers.

Growling, I leap to my feet. Kemelah shakes with laughter as she lands beside me. She holds up a hand. "Don't be mad. You're strong. You need more practice here is all."

I soften my scowl and keep Shaking, moving the sand in patterns as we walk, getting used to the feel of it. Suddenly, she holds up a hand. She bends to the ground, looking for tracks or something, and nods at what she sees. She puts a finger to her lips.

Kemelah creeps forward, lifting her spear. I assume she's not using the dart guns these people seem to favor because she doesn't want poison to get in the meat.

She stops, plants her feet, and in one swift motion hurls the spear forward. A mangled cry sounds from within the undergrowth.

Kemelah swirls sand. She lifts something over to us, a giant dead rat—picuro, I guess. Kemelah removes the spear and covers the wound with sand.

"This will stop the bleeding," she says. "And cover up the scent so we don't attract predators."

I gulp.

Kemelah carries the picuro behind her, floating on sand, and we head back the way we came, following the path precisely.

I can't even worry too much about where we are or the dangers of the jungle. Kemelah's words tumble through my head.

Until Agriad has accomplished his purpose.

30

NORAH

I walk down the palace hallways, so familiar and comforting. I grew up here. The maze of corridors gave up its secrets to me long ago.

Elandor's laughing beside me. We run through the palace, hand in hand.

I look at him, and I smile. I'm so lucky that he's my Anointed. Even though he's not a Sustainer, Potah is allowing me to be Anointed to him. Because I love him.

We round another bend in the corridors. We're on our way up to the Astronomy tower, my favorite part of the palace.

But then I hear my potah's voice. I stop. I peek around the corner, and I see him. He's in his bedroom, and his enormous bed is strewn with open bags of clothing and food. As I watch, he packs a white shirt into a bag and ties it shut. Is he going on a trip?

"Potah?" I say. Elandor stops beside me.

Potah turns and brushes his long black hair out of his face. "Cale. There you are." He smiles.

Even though we lost Motah, and that still hurts, Potah loves me. He is always there for me.

"Are you going somewhere?" I hadn't heard about a trip.

"Yes, my darling. But I'll only be gone a little while."

I frown at the satchels of water and food. "It looks like it will be a long while." Elandor rests a hand on my shoulder, and I put my hand on top of his.

Potah smiles. "It may be a long while. But we can hope not."

"Are you going through the ocean of sand?" I hate it when he does that. I know that he has the purple moonstone that technically makes it safe, but it doesn't seem safe.

Potah strides across the room and opens the door all the way. He wraps me in his arms. "Yes, my daughter."

"Why?" I ask. "Why are you going this time?"

Potah opens his mouth.

"The truth," I say. "You can tell me the truth."

Potah closes his mouth again. He smiles at Elandor. "She's a smart one, isn't she?"

Elandor's hand on my shoulder squeezes. "Yes, High Sustainer. She is."

Potah turns back to me. "Very well, my darling Cale. The truth." He pauses. "I'm going to cross the ocean of sand. There's someone I have to kill."

☾

THE DREAM RAGES through my mind even as I push food around my bowl at breakfast. It was no ordinary dream. That was...a memory? Was that me in Cale's head? Or a bad dream?

Zadock has already left to go hunting with Kemelah, and I stand, pushing back my chair at the breakfast table. Elandor follows.

"More lessons today?" Atoille, this is getting tiring. I don't want to dance with him. I don't want to go through the motions today.

Elandor seems to sense this. He smiles with one side of his mouth. "Why don't we break the rules, just today?"

I stare at him.

"Come with me," he says. "Please? I want to show you something."

Anything is better than another long morning being grilled on etiquette. "All right. Where are we going?"

Elandor smiles. "I think you'll like it."

We leave the table together, and I glance back once. Servants are already coming to clear away our dishes. Agriad smiles at me. I force a smile to my face. But then I quickly turn back around.

Elandor leads me down hallways and up stairwells. The palace is starting to become more familiar to me, but soon we enter sections that I've never been in before.

"Where are we?"

Elandor hushes me with a finger on his lips. "We're almost there."

We enter a room, a small library lined with bookshelves and plush chairs. In the back corner, there's a narrow stairway. He takes my hand to help me up, and I don't object.

The staircase winds around and around, and we continue to go up. I glance out a window and see the palace grounds stretch out to the low wall and the city beyond.

"We're so high!" I gasp.

Elandor smiles. "We're almost there."

Finally, he opens a door, and we enter. "Welcome to the Astronomy Tower."

My eyes widen, and I gasp. "What?" I can barely catch my breath, and not just from the exertion of climbing. The tower is a glass dome, and through it, I can see out into the sky. It's clear blue, an enormous Atoille hazy on the horizon. Telescopes line the walls.

"Elandor...this is amazing." I move forward to check out a telescope.

"I'll take you back here when the stars are out if you like," he says. "It's incredible."

I turn back to him. "I would like that." He's staring at me, and I look through the telescope. The blue sky holds nothing interesting for now, so I point it at Atoille. Every facet, every crater, comes starkly into view. I catch my breath. "This telescope is so well-made!"

"Everything in here is the finest quality glass from the most skilled Forgers in To'Sharazad. Agriad spared no expense setting up this place. Because it made his daughter happy."

I look at Elandor. He steps closer and closer until we're nearly touching. I back away.

"Elandor," I breathe. "What happened to Cale?"

"I was holding her," he says. "I was holding her when she died."

I catch my breath. I nod for him to go on.

"We were in the garden. She was showing me something new she learned about Sustaining, some way to amplify her power, that she was excited about." A small smile plays on his lips for a moment at the memory, but then it vanishes. "Then her eyes went wide, her body rigid." Elandor squeezes his eyes shut. The three-triangle tattoo on his cheek wrinkles.

I find myself putting a hand on his arm, holding my breath. "Go on."

Elandor opens his eyes and looks at where our skin touches. "You—she fell, collapsed into my arms. She shook uncontrollably, and I didn't know what to do. The Sustaining she was doing didn't vanish all at once. It was like watching water drain from a well. It went slowly, fading from her. And then the light was gone from her eyes."

Elandor turns away, breaking contact with me. "Nothing I did could bring her back. Agriad tried." Elandor's voice breaks. "Agriad tried everything a Sustainer can do, over and over. Then he called Absorber after Absorber to heal her. But she was gone." Elandor turns back to me. "I was heartbroken. But Agriad was *furious*. He kept saying that he should've listened. He should've listened to Cale. She could feel that this was coming, that you—" He cuts off with a shake of his head.

I suck in tiny sips of air. I close my eyes but nod for Elandor to continue.

"When Agriad said he was going to find you, to find his daughter, I didn't know what to think. But you're here, and—" His voice breaks.

I open my eyes and take his hand. He's a good person. "Elandor, I'm so sorry. I'm so, so sorry." I'm not sure what else to say, what else to do. "When—" I swallow. "When did this happen?"

He takes a deep breath, composing his face. "It was...almost three moon cycles ago now," he says. "Just as Atoille was sinking on our horizon. That's when Cale died."

I stumble backward, my breath stuck in my throat. I suspected this was the case, but Elandor confirmed it. It was *that* night. The night when I first Sustained, when I held the power of the world in my hands.

I'm the reason. I'm the reason Cale is dead. "Elandor." I hesitate. "I've been having dreams. I think they're Cale's memories."

Elandor looks at me, eyes wide.

I stare at him. I can't bring myself to ask the question. *Am I becoming her?*

At that moment, the door opens, and Agriad strides into the room. He beams. "I thought I'd find you two here together. You always loved this room, Norah."

I follow his movements, hardly daring to breathe, hardly knowing what to think, as he strides to the telescope nearest me and takes a look.

"P-potah," I say. "Please. Tell me. Why do I look like Cale?"

I expect the same answer he always gives, but instead, Agriad pulls away from the telescope and looks at me. "Norah. You are a Sustainer. A powerful one, even if much of it is untapped potential right now." He sighs. "Let me explain something to you."

Elandor bows, but then he turns to leave. "I'll meet you at the Judgment, Norah."

I watch him go. "Oh. All right." I turn back to Agriad. He puts a hand on my shoulder, and I have to force myself not to brush it off.

"Norah, while we talk, would it be all right if I Sustained your hair?"

I jolt and take a step back. "What?"

Agriad smiles. "Just to make it longer. The Judgment is today, and a lot of important people will be there. It would be nice if you looked more like you used to."

"Umm..." I'm not sure what to say. I *do not* want him Sustaining me.

Agriad cocks an eyebrow.

"Ok." The word slips out of my mouth.

Agriad grabs a chair and pulls it toward us. I sit woodenly, mechanically. And I brace myself.

He's going to Sustain me. What will that feel like?

Agriad grabs a handful of sand from a pouch at his side and puts a hand on my head. I see the glow out of the corner of my eye and feel a thrum of energy go through me, but it's not unpleasant.

While Agriad works, he speaks. "There must always be balance in our world. When Atoille creates a powerful Sustainer, she makes another to complement them. This must be, in order to keep the balance of the world right. The two complementary Sustainers look the same, and they are one, in a way. A foil to each other. For most of Cale's life, she was incredibly powerful. She had almost endless Sustaining ability. And you had none."

I open my eyes, trying to ignore the buzzing inside my head and the fact that my brown hair is inching slowly down my chest. "Does this happen with every Sustainer?"

"No," Agriad says. "It is very, very rare."

I want to ask if there are more he knows of, but Agriad plows ahead. "Very few Sustainers are powerful enough to need that kind of balance. You are one of them."

It's a shock after being without a gift for so much of my life, to discover that I have unbelievable power if I can figure out how to get to it.

My hair is down past my chest now. I want to ask Agriad to stop, but my thoughts are reeling. "So when one of the pair dies...what happens then?"

Agriad removes his hands from my head. I glance down at my hair, now longer than I've ever had it in my life. Agriad moves around to the front of me to examine his work. He smiles. "Beautiful. You are beautiful, my daughter."

The words send a chill through me. "What happens, Potah?"

"When you achieved your power, you stole it from Cale. You took her life force." His eyes become black for the briefest instant, but then they fade to white.

I look up at him, feeling like I'm lost in a sandstorm, alone in an ocean of sand. "I didn't mean to," I say quietly. "I only wanted to save...someone I love. I didn't know. I didn't know I would kill Cale."

Agriad crouches to my level. "Norah. You *are* Cale."

LYLAHN

I stare out over the ocean of sand, trying not to vomit.

I haven't sailed much in my life, and I'm not used to the constant swaying. The Shakers have a hard time controlling the barge. It's different than To'Morat's usual ships, and the journey has been rough.

Imwraeth stands next to me. "You ok?" He puts a hand on my back.

"I'm a little sick."

His hand goes up and down. "I think we're almost there."

To the ocean of water. The thought doesn't improve my nausea.

"What did Kaera say to you?" Imwraeth asks. "When we left. Something your sister always said. I couldn't quite catch it."

I swallow and look away. "It was nothing."

There's yelling behind me, and I turn to look too fast. My stomach lurches.

Imwraeth shouts and crosses the deck, trying to quell the fight before it comes to blows. Tensions are high for everyone. The threat of death hangs over us all, and hunger is constant. I've been eating even less, for fear that I won't keep it down.

Imwraeth returns to my side and sighs. "I don't know how much longer I can do this."

I take his hand. "You're doing great, Imwraeth." I lay my head on his shoulder.

I've been going to see the retahn every day and checking on Darkest Night. She has enough hay, and the retahn seem to be handling the journey well, thank Atoille.

"The ocean!" someone cries. "The ocean of water!"

I squint into the distance, and I see it—a shining thing on the horizon. The barge gets closer, and I see the waves, taller than plateaus, crash to the shore with the force of a hundred To'Morat warships. Fear grabs me by the throat. We are so tiny compared to those waves.

"Imwraeth..." I breathe. "I don't...I don't know if this is a good idea anymore." My chest feels constricted. The waves. They're enormous, frothing and raving, glittering like dark quartz in the sunlight. We have chosen to enter the ocean of water by day, hoping that the waves will be less intense than at night, when the moon's pull is at full strength. I don't understand it all, and I have to trust that the crew knows what they're doing.

Imwraeth puts an arm around me. "We don't have a choice."

My shoulders tighten.

We're almost to the shoreline. "Stop the ship!" Imwraeth calls over the spray.

The Shakers halt the barge, and we rock in the sand.

Warriors, sailors, and Shakers turn to look at Imwraeth, their Favored One, making this journey with them.

"Why are we doing this?" he asks.

No one says anything.

"Why are we doing this?" Imwraeth repeats. His voice is loud enough to be heard over the waves, but it's not forceful. He's calm.

"For our families," someone finally says, a woman near the front.

"For our families!" someone echoes the cry.

"For our families!" Soon, the whole ship is chanting the cry, and

Imwraeth joins in. I feel myself shouting along with him, tears in my eyes.

Imwraeth holds up his hands and the ship quiets. "Everyone, get below deck like we discussed. Shakers will steer the barge by feel from there."

Imwraeth ushers everyone down, one by one, descending the steps. He and I are the last to go. The ocean roars.

"I wish you would've stayed on To'Morat," Imwraeth says.

I shake my head. I pull him in close and kiss him roughly on the lips.

Imwraeth responds, kissing me back. He buries his hands in my hair and pulls me closer. I press my body into him and wrap my arms around his shoulders. Droplets of water hit my back.

"I wouldn't be anywhere else," I breathe.

Imwraeth presses his forehead to mine. "I love you, Lylahn."

Tears fill my eyes. "Don't say that like it's a goodbye."

Imwraeth smiles slightly, then nods. He descends the steps.

"I love you, too, Imwraeth," I whisper. I don't know if he hears me over the spray of the water. It's getting stronger now. We're drifting closer, being pulled into the jaws of the beast.

I follow Imwraeth into the dark and then shut the hatch behind me.

It's pitch black beneath deck. Everything's been closed tight as was planned. We have to trust the Shakers to feel the sand and know what they're doing.

People whisper in feverish voices, the panic and tension rising.

Imwraeth Extracts, and sand lights up in his hand, a soft glow pushing back the blackness. Other Extractors do the same. Imwraeth's voice rings out. "My people, my warriors. We will survive. Trust To'Morat's strongest Shakers to guide us."

The whispering stills, and soon, it's so quiet I can hear the sand crashing against the boat. The roar of the ocean grows in volume.

This has to work.

We enter a large chamber in the center of the barge, theoretically the safest area. People strap themselves in along the walls and in seats fixed to the ground with nails of quartz. It's crowded, stifling, the air already getting hot from so many bodies shuffling and getting settled.

The retahn have been secured. The caretakers knew what to do. Any supplies have also been tied down. The purpose of the barge is to be tossed around, after all. I pray to Atoille that we survive it.

"Strap in!" Imwraeth says.

We take our places in the room. Quartz buckles click as they are fastened and tightened. I find one next to Imwraeth and strap myself in, then put my hands in my lap to still their shaking.

Danosrin stands off to the side, solemn face watching to make sure everyone is secured. Then he takes a seat next to me and buckles in.

"We're here." His large eyes are vacant, his lips a tight frown.

I reach over on impulse and grab his hand, giving it a squeeze before letting go. "This is going to work."

Danosrin gives me a weak smile.

The Shakers move us forward.

I feel it the instant we hit the water. The barge shivers. The spray of the waves roars in my ears. Murmurs, whispers of prayers ascend to Atoille around me. Extractor lights blink off and on as sand runs out and then is gathered again.

The air is hot and close, and my breathing speeds up. I reach out and find Imwraeth's hand.

A force slams into the barge, and the jolt makes the straps dig into my shoulders and waist. But they hold. We tip, plunging almost straight down. I lift out of my seat and press into the straps. I scream.

The Shakers must catch us with sand because we land again with a jerk.

I chant a prayer in my mind over and over. *Please Atoille, protect us. Don't let us crash. Don't let the barge leak.*

The barge leans upward now, and I tilt the other way, my body straining against the leather holding me down.

Then a *snap*.

One of the straps on the other side of the room breaks, and a man goes flying. He screams and collides with the opposite side of the barge, and then he's quiet.

No...

I hardly have time to register what happened, for we tilt, plunging downward and forward. My stomach heaves. I vomit, and, judging by the smell and the sounds around me, I'm not the only one.

"Trust our Shakers!" Imwraeth calls out. "Trust our Shakers!"

The roaring in my ears grows, and I know we're hearing the ocean of water muffled through the walls of the barge. They're too thin to withstand so much force. What was I thinking?

Despair blackens my mind as we tilt backward again and go up, up a wave the size of a plateau, a wave that could crush the entirety of To'Morat in one blow.

The Shakers are strapped in at the rear of the barge, moving their arms, softening and guiding the ship, but I don't know how much of a difference they're making.

"Trust our Shakers!" Imwraeth calls. The call is taken up amidst gagging and screaming.

"Trust our Shakers!"

I cry out along with them.

"TRUST OUR SHAKERS!" Danosrin's cry is the loudest.

Suddenly, everything stills.

It seems to go quiet around me, even though I feel vibrations of Imwraeth yelling and the screaming, the sand reaching up through the waters to catch the barge.

A green light tinges my vision.

What is happening?

I feel the strong urge to Absorb. Sand clings to my clothes, like always, and I put my hands on it. I give in to the urge. I couldn't fight it if I wanted to. I Absorb.

The green light deepens.

I lean into the Absorbing, not quite sure what I'm doing, feeling my power going toward...something.

Atoille, is this the right thing to do?

I can only follow compulsion—Absorb with everything I have.

Something feels off. Something is different.

The ship stops rocking, and we have a moment of peace.

And then the green light vanishes. My Absorbing is yanked away, cut off. It feels different than running out of sand. It feels—

Then we're plunging down the steepest incline, and my stomach jerks. The chanting reaches a frantic level. We tilt up.

The barge has held so far. Just a little longer...I can feel it. We're almost there.

"The sand!" A Shaker cries. "The sand is dry!"

The barge steadies. It levels.

Cheers rise around me.

"We did it!"

"We're here!"

Someone near the front unbuckles and opens the hatch to look out. Water pours down the steps, and I cry out, thinking we opened the hatch prematurely, but it's leftovers from our trial by water.

People gasp. Some clutch the straps like they don't want to exit, and others throw off the straps and head for the stairs like they can't get into open air fast enough.

"Lylahn, it worked!" Danosrin's face lights up in a rare smile, his gray eyes shining. "You did it." He unbuckles, hurrying to stand and go above deck.

I stay seated, clutching Imwraeth's hand. Something feels wrong.

Imwraeth shouts instructions to his people, and we follow them up the steps. Imwraeth does a head count, and miraculously, we only had the one casualty. It's gruesome, and Imwraeth sees about organizing cleaning and a desert funeral.

I prepare my eyes to squint in the sunlight, but darkness meets me. Starlight. And moonlight. Atoille is hanging low on the horizon.

Did the travel really take that long?

The barge charges forward through the sand. The ocean of water is behind us.

We did it.

Cheers and shouting erupt on the deck, and people embrace. I can't help but grin.

I look out over the deck, and the sand—it's white. My mouth drops open, staring at the pure white ocean of sand shining in the moonlight.

The Shakers take us away, farther from the ocean of water and deeper into this white ocean of sand, teeming with sand moles and life.

Imwraeth wraps his arms around me. His satchel bounces against his body.

"We did it, Lylahn!" Imwraeth grins into my ear. "Your idea worked. We did it." He laughs with relief.

I smile, but the dread welling up inside me makes it difficult. "It's dark. It's...night."

Imwraeth stares at the sky as if this is the first time he's noticed.

I glance around the deck for sand to scoop up, but it's been washed clean. "Can I use some of your sand?"

He frowns but reaches into his satchel to grab a handful for me. "Of course. Are you hurt?"

"No, I—I don't think so." I take the sand. Absorb.

Absorb.

Nothing.

My eyes widen. My heart pounds.

I breathe in sharply. Absorb. Absorb. *Absorb.*

Nothing.

Nothing.

"Imwraeth." I choke back a sob.

Tender concern fills his face. "Lylahn? What's wrong?"

"My Absorbing." My voice trembles. "It's gone."

32

NORAH

Today's the day Agriad wants to present me to his court.

An enormous, dusty arena is before me, with stadium seating all around. We're at the top in a kind of spectator box. Ladies and lords dressed in all their finery wander through the box, eating delicacies off trays offered by servants and craning their necks to get a peek at me.

The stadium is packed full of people wearing colorful clothing, and their chatter fills my ears with a low background rumble. Agriad laughs with a group of nobles off to my right. Elandor is wandering the perimeter, eating the provided snacks with a glum expression.

I breathe a sigh of relief when Zadock ascends the steps to the spectator box. He's wearing a deep green silk shirt that makes his blue eyes look almost emerald. His sandy hair is messy despite Bernan's best efforts, and it makes me smile.

Zadock's grin at seeing me falls. "Nors. Your hair..."

I finger the ends of my long hair.

Zadock crosses the room and takes a seat next to me. He touches the ends of my hair. "How did this happen?"

"It's—it's nothing," I say. "Agriad asked if he could Sustain my hair—"

Zadock's eyes shoot upward to meet mine. "Agriad Sustained you?" His mouth drops open in horror. "Nors. Your eyes."

"What about them?"

At that moment, Agriad steps forward to take his seat beside me. "Zadock. You're here. I've seated you in the back, of course."

I open my mouth to protest, but Zadock beats me to it.

"What did you do to her? Why do her eyes look like that?"

"Calm yourself," Agriad says. "It will pass."

We're drawing the stares of nobles around us, but I don't care. Elandor pauses in the act of taking starfruit from a tray to glance our way.

"What's wrong with my eyes?" I demand.

"Nors, they're—" Zadock swallows. "They're washed out, faded. Almost like—"

"Like mine, yes," Agriad says. "It's a side effect of being Sustained. I needed to make her hair longer before she is presented to the general court, but it *will* pass. The eyes you love so much will return to their regular color soon." Agriad winks at Zadock. "Now, take your seat, please."

Zadock puts a hand on my arm. "Are you sure you're all right? You don't feel any different?"

I wish I could see my eyes. My stomach swirls with dread. Do I believe Agriad? Will they return to normal? "I'm fine, I promise."

Zadock presses his lips to my forehead before moving to the back to take his seat. Agriad frowns, watching him go.

I stare at the arena. I don't know what's going to happen there, but I hate to imagine.

Agriad is dressed in black silk with a blue, quartz-encrusted sash. He extends a hand to me, and I take it, skin crawling. "Come. There are people I'd like you to meet." Agriad leads me to two women chatting off to the side. One has enormous eyes and a tiny mouth, and the other is tall, with long black hair and blank eyes, like Agriad.

"Lady Robehla," Agriad gestures at the giant-eyed woman, "allow me to introduce you to my daughter, Norah."

Lady Robehla's eyes go even wider. I nod to her as I've been taught and spread my skirts, cobalt embroidered with gold today. I hope Agriad is pleased. Some of the etiquette lessons are sticking, at least. "A pleasure to meet you, Lady Robehla."

Lady Robehla gives me a deep curtsy. "The pleasure is mine."

The ebony-haired woman steps a little closer, and Lady Robehla mumbles something about finding her seat before making a quick exit. The woman's eyes fill with tears when she sees me.

"Norah, allow me to introduce you to Lady Zahrina, your aunt." Agriad smiles.

I jolt. "Umm. Hello." I remember my manners and incline my head to her. "Lady Zahrina."

The tears in her eyes spill over, and Zahrina hurries to brush them away. "Agriad, how is this possible? Cale is alive?"

Agriad puts a hand on his sister's arm. "She doesn't remember anything, Zahrina. She is Norah now."

Zahrina glances from me to Agriad. Her face goes colder. "So she's not Cale?" She glances at me. "She looks just like—"

"She is Cale," Agriad says. Agriad glances at me with a frown. "Though Norah has yet to show her talent. And with the gala tomorrow, where she will be formally announced as my heir and expected to show her gift, she has little time to improve."

I swallow. I have an idea I haven't tested yet, something that may help me show more strength, but I'm still far from the level Agriad expects. "I'm trying, Potah."

From the back, Zadock sits in his chair, elbows on his knees, eyes only for me.

"Well." Zahrina smiles, but it's cold, devoid of emotion. "I'm glad you've returned to us."

Agriad gestures to the seats. "Shall we?"

Zahrina nods, and he leads her to the front of the box.

I sigh when I see that Elandor is already seated near the front. "So I'm sitting by him?"

Agriad smiles.

I take a seat, and Agriad follows. From where we're sitting, we have a good view of the sandy arena. Nothing is happening down there yet.

"Hello, Elandor." I incline my head toward him in a polite nod.

"Very good. You're learning fast."

"I'm trying."

Out of the corner of my eye, I see my potah take a seat next to Agriad. Lightning goes through me. How will I get him to remember? He leans forward, past Agriad, and smiles at me. I smile back. Warmth fills my chest.

Agriad stands. A guard steps forward with a handful of sand and presses it to Agriad's throat. The sand glows. Agriad's raised voice echoes throughout the arena walls, amplified by the Extracted strength. "Welcome, people of To'Sharazad!"

Cheers sound throughout the stadium.

"Before we begin, I would like to introduce to you someone very special."

I stiffen in my seat.

"Someone has been returned to us who was lost, someone more precious to me than the riches of the world." Agriad motions for me to join him. I stand, feeling hollow. I walk past my potah.

"My daughter, Cale, has been reborn!" Agriad takes one of my hands and raises it into the air.

The people don't cheer. There are quiet murmurs throughout the stadium, people turning to each other and whispering. A few groups stand and bow, and then the rest of the stadium, bits at a time, follows.

"Your Great Sustainer. She has returned!"

I'm not her! I want to scream. *I'm me!*

Now, the crowd straightens from their bows, and cheers erupt. I hurry back to my seat.

Agriad grins. "Are you ready to see your traitors put to justice?"

More shouting, some booing. The stands are packed with people, and the noise is deafening. My stomach sinks with every word.

"Elandor," I whisper. "What is happening?"

He sighs. "It's called the Judgment. I hate it."

Agriad's voice booms. "These people were found speaking out against Sustainers, saying that we shouldn't rule."

More loud jeers.

"They were saying that the Sustainers, the very people that keep our city prosperous and growing, don't have a right to rule in justice over this city."

Shouts and boos. I feel sick.

"Well. Let us see how the Judgment treats them." Agriad waves a hand. "Bring them out."

Guards down below in the dusty arena open a side gate, and maybe a dozen men and women are herded into the ring. Their hands are bound, but the guards cut the ropes to free them, then hurry to leave the arena, closing the door.

We have a good seat, and I can see their faces. Dirty. Worn. Terrified of what's coming.

"Traitors," Agriad calls. "Choose your weapons!"

In a rack of weapons on the side of the arena there are spears, axes, bows, and others I don't recognize.

I'm afraid. Afraid for them.

I glance behind me at Zadock. His face is pale.

"Agriad," I whisper. "Potah. This...this is wrong."

"Daughter." Agriad lowers his voice but doesn't take his eyes off the crowd. "You will not question me."

I shut my mouth. There's nothing I can do here. But I'm gratified when Potah, my real potah, glances over at me and gives me an empathetic smile.

Remember. How do I get him to remember?

The traitors in the ring have all chosen a variety of weapons and Agriad grins. "Send in the bloodworm."

The audience goes wild, cheering and calling. The noble section applauds.

And then, from a wide gated area to the left, comes the biggest bloodworm I have ever seen.

Potah and I saw these creatures occasionally when we were out in the deep ocean of sand. They are vile things that will suck the blood dry out of any creature they come across. But they were small, no longer than the length of my arm, and easily pushed back into the sand with Shaking.

This thing...this thing is not like that.

My mouth drops open as the worm slides into the arena. It's massive. It takes up half the length of the arena alone with its swollen, puffy body. Four pairs of legs, each ending in vicious claws, help it scrabble through the sand. It doesn't have eyes, but sensory hairs stand up around its entire body, and I know from experience that even though it looks soft and squishy, its skin can harden to armor in an instant. Where a mouth should be, there's a tube-like circle.

I shiver. If a small bloodworm gets its tube attached to your arm, it's almost impossible to get off.

"Elandor," I whisper. "This is..."

"I know," he says. "It's cruel. But this is how things are done." He glances sideways at me. "Make sure that's never you down there, ok?"

I attempt to smile at the joke, but it's really not funny.

The worm charges forward. Some of the people scatter and scream, some stand and fight. One Shakes sand into the bloodworm's sucker, but the worm spits it back out.

Purple, metallic venom laces the sand that flies onto the fighters, and some of them who are hit fall, stunned. The worm snakes over to its victim and latches onto the body. The tube is large enough to nearly engulf the person. Horrible gurgling sounds ensue from the arena, and in a moment, the person is sucked dry, their body left a bloodless husk.

The spectators cheer.

Bile rises in my throat.

The bloodworm slides forward, crushing one of the fighters beneath its hulking body. Another falls victim to the bloodsucker. I try to look anywhere but there, while still appearing to watch. One fighter manages to get in a hit, a spear striking the skin. The bloodworm's skin shimmers, turning metallic where it was struck, and the spear bounces off.

"What?" I breathe.

"It's in its cells," Elandor says.

"The cells?" My voice shakes. I stare at the sky, the crowd, anywhere but the arena.

Elandor clears his throat. I turn to him, grateful to have an excuse to look away. I see Zadock out of the corner of my eye, watching me. Watching us.

"It's in the cells," Elandor repeats. "When the bloodworm is attacked, proteins in each of its individual cells crisscross and change structure, forming a network that supports the skin on a cellular level. The change happens almost instantaneously in response to stimulus." Elandor clears his throat again. "Uhhh. Pretty wild, right?"

I can't help but smile. "That's interesting."

Elandor smiles back. "I thought you'd like that."

The people erupt in cheers around us, and I can only assume that the last victim is gone. Agriad stands and says some more words, but they are hollow in my ears.

Agriad wanted me to be here to see this. He wanted to introduce me to more nobles and show me off to his court, but I can't help but think that there was more to it.

He wanted me to see. He wanted me to see how traitors are treated.

33

———

ZADOCK

The day of the gala is here.

I hold Norah's hand, and we wait in a side corridor off the ballroom. The sounds of guests talking and glasses clinking are muffled through the wall. We wait to enter. It's silly, but Agriad wants to formally introduce us as an Anointed couple or something.

"Are you nervous?" I squeeze Norah's hand.

"A little. I don't want to do anything wrong. There's so much to remember."

I turn toward her. "You're going to do great. *We're* going to do great."

Norah smiles, but then her face falls. "Yesterday was..." She shudders.

"The arena?"

Norah nods.

"It was specking awful. But we're still here, and Agriad wants you. Don't worry, ok?" I don't say who it is that Agriad doesn't want.

Jeru enters the corridor and smiles when she sees Norah, one of the first smiles I've seen from the woman. "You look lovely, Great Sustainer."

"Thank you."

Jeru stands by the doors, listening for the signal that it's time for us to enter.

"You're beautiful," I whisper in Norah's ear. "Captivating. There aren't words to describe the way you look, my wild girl."

Norah smiles at me with a faint blush on her cheeks. Praise Atoille, her eyes have already returned to their full color, a deep brown. She's dressed all in gold, a silken sleeveless dress, glittering with sparkling gold-tinted quartz. I can only imagine how it will shine in the light of the ballroom. There are gold quartz pieces in her hair. Jeru is thrilled about the length. Most of it is swept up into a twisting up-do, with strategic pieces left to curl around her shoulders. I've never seen her look so radiant.

I'm wearing a cobalt silk shirt and a gold sash with tinkling quartz pieces. I didn't pay much attention while Bernan was getting me dressed. I was too busy thinking about Norah.

"Are you ready?" I ask. "Are you going to be able to display the power Agriad expects?" I don't know what will happen if she can't, but I don't want to find out.

Norah gives me a brief nod. "I think so."

"What are you going to do differently?"

Norah opens her mouth, but Jeru cuts her off.

"They're ready for you," Jeru says.

I hold out my arm. "Shall we?"

Norah loops her arm through mine. We walk forward with bated breath.

"You're going to be perfect," I say.

"Our dance. We never practiced together," Norah says.

"Dance?" There will be dancing at the gala. Of course. "Don't worry." I grin. "I've got it."

She attempts to smile back. "Zadock." Norah pauses at the door. "Are you happy here?"

I stop and turn to look at her. "I'm—I'm happy to be with you."

What is she getting at? Worrying that I'm afraid Agriad doesn't want me around? "I wouldn't be anywhere else right now."

"I was thinking that…it's nice to be respected, for once."

I frown. "For once?"

"Never mind."

"Nors." I stop and take her by the shoulders, turn her to face me. "What do you mean?"

Norah meets my eyes. "Just that, for my whole life, I was different. I was an outcast. Here, I'm—not. I'm royalty. It's a nice change."

"Are you saying that you want to stay?"

Norah hesitates for too long.

"Nors, our people at home are starving. Shrey, your motah, *my* motah. Imwraeth, Lylahn. We can't forget that."

"I haven't forgotten," Norah snaps.

"Norah—"

Jeru opens the grand double doors to the ballroom, and we're flooded with light. "I present to you, Zadock Penvaren."

I let go of Norah and step through the double doors. Worry churns within me. What does Norah mean? She can't possibly want to stay.

Some in the crowd grow quiet and turn to stare, but most continue their conversations. They don't know who I am.

The ballroom looks even more impressive than the glimpses I've caught of it. It's enormous, with a high glass ceiling. Atoille is visible in an orange and purple evening sky, and soon, the stars will glitter up above. Tall quartz sculptures line the room, some abstract shards of quartz stacked into unique shapes, others flowing like water. In each corner of the room is a young potted tree, only a few black vines dangling from the branches.

I descend the grand staircase, praying to Atoille that I don't trip. I keep my chin up, and my head held high. The music hits me in full now, stringed instruments playing a lively tune interspersed with a quartz chime. Dancers fill the ballroom floor, twirling and spinning.

Groups of people gather and talk, and servants dressed in glittering livery wind their way through the groups, presenting trays of delicacies and sparkling wine.

It's glorious. Stunning. I've never seen anything like it.

Potah would've loved this. Or he would've been sick with envy. It's hard to say, but the thought makes me smile. It also makes me homesick.

I wonder how everyone's doing without Norah. *I've got to get her home. I've got to get her out of this, even if she doesn't want it.*

I finish my descent and wait at the bottom of the staircase.

The door opens again, and Jeru says in a loud voice, "I present to you Norah Saranyi, Great Sustainer, daughter of Agriad Zul."

The crowd quiets. All heads turn to stare at her.

This is the moment.

Norah stands at the top of the staircase. Her dress glitters in the light. I notice now that there are tiny bits of quartz somehow stuck to her bare shoulders so that even her skin seems to sparkle. Her eyes are lined with something dark, making them appear even larger than normal, and her lips have been painted red. These details I didn't notice before make my heart pound.

Atoille, I love this girl.

As she's been instructed, Norah begins her Sustaining display. The people need to know what she's capable of.

I hold my breath. She's told me how difficult Sustaining has been for her, how it's seemed even harder than it was on To'Rahn. Yet Agriad and the people are expecting a grand display, a display worthy of a great Sustainer. I don't know what Agriad will do if Norah can't pull it off, but I don't want to find out.

Norah lifts her arms, sand slipping through her fingers, and the trees in each corner of the room shoot up toward the ceiling. There's a cracking sound, and the pots they've been planted in burst. The crowd gasps. And still, the trees continue to grow, vines reaching from their branches. Roots dig into the ground, seeking earth, and the ballroom floor fractures. I wince. I assume that was part of Agriad's instructions. My mouth drops open when red fruit pops from the branches and grows to ripeness. The crowd gasps in delight and plucks the fruit from the trees, tasting and exclaiming over the sweetness. I applaud with the rest when she's done.

Norah smiles, a sheen of sweat on her forehead making her even more glorious, and she descends the stairs, maybe a tad too quickly, but I think Agriad will forgive her for that.

"You were magnificent," I tell her when she reaches me.

Norah grins. "I did it."

"What did you do differently?"

"Ambition," she says. "That was always the key, as Agriad kept trying to tell me." Her eyes slide to the side. "I just had to figure out what I wanted. Then it clicked."

I turn to follow her gaze. Raen Saranyi chats with a group of nobles.

I clear my throat. A tumble of emotions does flips in my stomach. "You have grown so much." The music swells around us, and people begin dancing and chatting again. Nobles head toward us to talk to Norah.

"I present to you Agriad Zul, the High Sustainer of To'Sharazad." Jeru's voice rings out over the crowd, and the people quiet.

"My daughter is a marvel, no?" Agriad stands at the top of the stairs, looking elegant in his finery. The people cheer. He descends, and I wonder how he can walk with the sheer weight of quartz jewelry around his neck and fixed to his sash. "Please, let us celebrate." He smiles. "Be seated for the feast in her honor."

The crowd cheers once more and turns to the long tables set up at the end of the room, places set with crystal plates and cutlery. The people take their seats, and Jeru leads us through the crowd to ours. I'm seated at the far end of the table, away from Norah, Elandor, and Agriad. I thought that might change tonight since he's going to announce that Norah and I are Anointed, but maybe Agriad is waiting.

Even more servants bring in trays of food, and I try to remember the etiquette that's been crammed into my brain. The servants are all Shakers, carrying in trays floating on sand, a feat of strength and balance, and another display of Agriad's power.

The now familiar crystal bowl of cooling green soup is placed at the top right of my place setting, but I don't touch it yet. A plate of roasted vegetables and meat is set in front of me. What did Kemelah call this?

Kemelah glances at me with a smile. Of course she's been seated near me. "You like the picuro?" She savors the bite. "Delicious."

"Is this what we—what you—?"

Kemelah nods and skewers another piece. "Try it."

I skewer a bite and put it in my mouth. It's meat, right? I chew and swallow. "It's good."

Kemelah smiles. "You're doing pretty well. For a lizard boy."

I turn back to her, my mouth full of food. I swallow self-consciously. "Lizard boy?"

Kemelah tosses her hair over her shoulder. "You lizard-dwelling To'Rahn have primitive ways. But I see that some lessons I've taught you have sunk in."

I swallow and lick the juices from my lips. I take a sip of sparkling wine. It's tingly on my tongue, and I have to remind myself to have just one glass. Course after course is brought, everything from exotic soups to rice dishes to more trays of meat whose origin I don't ask. When I take a final sip of the green soup, signaling that I'm ready for the next course, a servant brings a tray filled with tiny buttery pastries stuffed with a dark brown cream.

"What is this?" I ask.

Kemelah's eyes sparkle. "It's chocolate. Made from the cacao tree local to To'Sharazad."

"Chocolate?" I eye the dark stuff, but hey, we're here. Might as well get the full experience. I take a bite. Pastry flakes in my mouth, and sweet and bitter flood my tastebuds all at once.

I can't help it. I close my eyes and moan.

Kemelah laughs. "You like it?"

"I love it." I glance down the table, wondering if I can catch Norah's eye. She's got to try this.

Agriad and Raen engage in quiet conversation at the head of the table. It looks serious, and I wonder what they're talking about.

Norah is chatting with a plump woman seated across from her, but she's seen her potah, too, and she keeps stealing glances his way.

Some of the feasters have finished and are standing, making their way back to the dance floor, so I grab another pastry and stand. Kemelah winks at me as I walk away.

I make my way down the length of the table, weaving through Shaker servants bearing trays. I stop beside Norah and cut into the conversation with a clearing of my throat. "Might I borrow the Great Sustainer for a moment, grand lady?" I ask. "Your dress is lovely, by the way." Might as well put on the flattery so she's not offended. I ignore Elandor on purpose, and he busies himself with his food.

The plump woman smooths her purple skirt and laughs. "Oh, well, thank you. And of course. Enjoy." She lifts her glass of wine.

Agriad frowns, but Norah presses back her chair and stands. She turns, her eyes shining, and puts her hand in mine.

"Thank you," she breathes in my ear. "You saved me."

I pull her further away from Agriad's disapproving gaze and steal a moment of privacy in the shade of one of the great black trees.

"You have to taste this." I feed Norah a bite of chocolate pastry. Her lips graze my fingers.

Norah smiles and chews. She closes her eyes. "Holy Atoille above."

"Amazing, right?" I grin. "It's called chocolate."

"That's it. We're not going home." Norah laughs, but there's a bitter twinge at the end. "I'm joking, of course."

"I know." I do. I know that Norah would never abandon her people. I hold up the pastry and raise my eyebrows.

Norah grins and nods. I feed her another bite. I'm enjoying this way too much.

We finish the pastry together, and I extend my arm. "Now, about that dance? I'd like to get in at least one with you before the masses take their turn."

Norah frowns. "I think we're supposed to wait until Agriad announces us. Didn't Kemelah talk to you about that?"

"Um. I'm not sure. She didn't say—"

Agriad stands and claps his hands. A hush falls over the ballroom.

"Honored guests," Agriad says. "I am so pleased you can be here tonight to celebrate my daughter's return."

Cheers and smattered clapping rise through the crowd, and heads turn to smile at Norah. She smiles back, but she looks somewhat sick.

"I have a special announcement." Agriad's eyes glitter, their hollow, icy stare unnerving me. What does he have planned? "Norah and her Anointed will share their first dance together here tonight. Would you like to see that?"

The crowd cheers and claps.

Agriad spreads his arms wide. "I present to you Norah Saranyi, my daughter, and her Anointed, Elandor Thenahn."

34

NORAH

I freeze. My eyes go wide in horror, and I look to Zadock. His face is a sandstorm of shock, which quickly turns to rage.

Elandor stands and takes slow steps toward me. He reaches out his hand. I feel myself taking it without really deciding to. He leads me forward, and the dance floor clears around us. It's time for the dance. The dance I was supposed to share with Zadock.

Agriad has me under his thumb. I've done everything he's wanted, but this...this is too much.

Elandor bows, and I curtsy, going through the motions. Agriad is watching. His blank stare bores into me. The nobles around us are hushed, watching our every move. The music starts. Strings, flutes, and quartz chimes play long, measured notes.

When Elandor rises out of his bow, he mouths, "I didn't know."

Is he lying? It's convenient that he was the one who taught me this dance. But, of course, Agriad arranged that.

He takes one of my hands and places the other on my waist. I put a hand on his shoulder. We dance, following the music. I know the pattern by heart now because we've practiced it enough. I'm in shock, going through the motions.

When I can, I catch Zadock's eye. We'll sort this out. Somehow. And really, what does it matter what all these people, including Agriad, think? Zadock is my Anointed. One dance doesn't change that.

"I'm sorry, Norah," Elandor whispers. He dips me down low, and the audience claps in approval. This was supposed to be Zadock. I wanted to dance with Zadock.

I rise. "We are not Anointed."

Elandor's face falls. I've hurt him, but I don't care.

"I know."

We spin, and I feel almost faint. Heat presses in on my chest, and sweat drips down my back. I haven't had enough to eat. The few bites I was able to sneak in between conversations at the feast weren't enough, and the chocolate Zadock fed me feels like it was forever ago. "I'm sorry. I don't want to hurt you." I grit my teeth, fighting back dizziness. "And I know this isn't your fault. You didn't know this was coming."

Elandor nods once.

"You miss Cale. I know. I wish I could bring her back."

The dance ends, and people applaud. Couples around us begin to dance to the next tune. I breathe a sigh of relief. We made it through that. Now I just have to reassure Zadock that it wasn't real.

Elandor kisses my hand, and the nobles around us cheer. They want more, I know. I can see it in their eager faces. This is a society that hasn't ever had to dampen their love, and open expressions of affection are common. But I can't. Elandor looks into my eyes, and he doesn't see me. He sees Cale.

I take a step back. People are disappointed. Agriad is probably disappointed. Let him be.

My eyes search the crowd for Zadock, but I don't see him. The dancing and laughing around us continue. I feel another wave of dizziness. Where's Zadock?

I step through the crowd, grabbing a glass of water off a servant's tray and downing it. That helps a little. I push forward, but I can't make much progress. People stop me, calling out congratulations, wanting to touch and compliment my gown, fuss over my hair. It's stifling. I can't breathe.

I catch Agriad's eyes. He smiles and nods. Takes a sip of wine.

I glare back, furious. He has toyed with me enough. I'm done. Zadock and I are fighting back. We're going to take my potah even if we have to knock him unconscious and sail out of here.

And then it hits me. I stop right in the middle of the ballroom. Someone bumps into me and apologizes, but I barely notice.

Sailing. If I could take potah sailing, he would remember. He would remember me. Sailing with me was everything to him.

And then, there he is, my potah. My eyes fill with tears just seeing him. He stands before me in a dark green silk shirt. His wild dark curls have been combed and somewhat tamed. He notices the tears and walks forward with a frown. The crowd still feels too close around us, the room too hot.

"Are you all right, Norah?" Potah says.

"Yes. I'm fine. A little overwhelmed over the evening."

He gives me a kind smile. "I am, too, I have to confess." He grabs a glass of water from a passing servant and hands it to me, and I take a sip.

"Would you take me sailing?" I blurt.

Potah frowns. "Sailing?"

"Yes. On the ocean of sand," I say. "Please." I must look desperate, because his face softens.

"Norah, have you had enough to eat tonight?" He grabs an appetizer from another passing servant, some kind of rice ball on a stick. I take it, but I'm not hungry.

"Please. I want to learn to sail the ocean of sand." I lie. "It's an important part of military tactics, isn't it?"

"Well. You do make a good point. And I am pretty good at sailing." He winks.

I almost sigh in relief. He remembers that, at least.

"All right." He smiles. "With the High Sustainer's permission, we'll arrange a time for me to take you. I'm sure he wouldn't object to his daughter learning that skill."

My stomach clenches at his words, but I nod and try to smile. He agreed to go with me; that's what matters.

I finally see Zadock. I catch a glimpse of him behind Potah, talking with that white-haired girl who's been teaching him. She laughs at something he says, and something like jealousy squirms in my stomach.

"Excuse me." I curtsy to Potah, and he dips his head. "And thank you."

I take a bite of the rice ball on my way to Zadock, and it is delicious. I need to eat something. There's something sweet on the stick, too, a grilled yellow fruit. It's amazing.

I interrupt their conversation by clearing my throat. Kemelah looks at me. She's dressed in a pale blue gown. She inclines her head and gives the barest of curtsies. I return the nod but not the curtsy.

"Great Sustainer," Kemelah says. The words sound mocking in her mouth.

"Kemelah," I say.

She leaves without a word.

I turn to Zadock and open my mouth, but he turns away from me.

"Zadock."

He walks away.

For a moment, I can't breathe.

"Zadock, wait!" I push through the crowd of people, but they clamor to get to me. "Zadock!" I call over the crowd, but either he doesn't hear, or he chooses to ignore me.

My heart sinks right down to my toes.

"I'm just trying to keep you alive," I whisper. Zadock, my beloved, my Anointed...walked away from me.

Lady Robehla, with the owlish eyes, appears at my side in an instant. "Are you all right, Great Sustainer?"

A wave of dizziness comes over me. "I'm—I'm—"

And then I'm swept off my feet, lifted off the ground. I think for a moment that the dizziness has gotten the better of me, but then I realize that it's happening to everyone.

Screams sound through the crowd. My breath has been stolen from my chest. I'm floating out of control. Someone's foot smacks against my arm. And then we're thrown to the ground.

I hit the ballroom floor and choke out a gasp. Shattering glass sounds throughout the ballroom, and the terrified screaming around me doesn't stop.

What happened?

I look up through the glass ceiling. The stars are brilliant overhead, and Atoille shines in the sky.

When I scramble to my feet, Lady Robehla meets my eyes, terrified. "What was that?"

It happens again. I'm lifted off my feet into the air, kicking and flailing. Something is going terribly wrong. People around me scream and scramble over each other, clamoring to get out of the ballroom, to get anywhere. I hear Agriad's voice booming, trying to restore order, but I can't make out what he's saying over the screams.

"Norah!" I hear someone cry. "Norah!"

I land back on my hands and knees with a jolt and push myself to standing. "What is happening?"

I look up at the moon again and pause. Atoille seems closer. She is even bigger in the sky, the details of her craters clearer.

"No," I whisper. "No."

The ground begins to shake, and people stumble over each other. I scramble through the crowd, half falling, half floating, trying to get to Zadock, but I don't see him.

"Norah!"

I turn. "Zadock?"

Elandor grabs my arm and steadies me. "Look up."

I look up again at the moon. "Atoille," I gasp. "She's falling."

35

LYLAHN

We sail deeper into the white ocean of sand. The ocean of water is long gone. We don't know where we're going, and the crew is getting restless.

We made it across the ocean of water, but now what? Where are the people who took Norah and Zadock?

I sit in my tiny room, my knees pulled into my chest. The bed is narrow and hard, affixed to the floor and wall by a quartz rim. The privilege of being the Lady Lylahn is that the room is my own.

There's a pile of white sand on the floor. I take a handful and close my eyes, feeling the softness of it float through my fingers.

Absorb.

It used to be so easy. I was strong, a valued healer in To'Shahera.

Nothing.

It's gone.

I drop the sand with a shudder and pull my knees back into my chest. There's a soft knock at the door, and I take a deep breath. "Come in."

Imwraeth enters the room, an uncertain expression on his face. "The crew is all set," he says. "We're going to keep heading west, see what we can find." He hesitates. "We don't have much food left. We have maybe a week or so to explore, and then we'll be forced to turn around and go back." Imwraeth sits on the bed beside me and puts his head in his hands. "But we can't go back. We can't go back empty-handed."

I uncurl my legs and lay my head on his shoulder. I don't know what to say. He's right about everything.

We sit there like that for I don't know how long. I've never felt so useless in my life.

Finally, Imwraeth breathes, "Still no Absorbing?"

I shake my head. I don't trust my voice.

"Tell me again what happened?"

"When we were going through the ocean of water, it was like there was this green glow all around me." I choke. "I...I felt the urge to Absorb. I couldn't deny it. I Absorbed, and slowly, the green glow vanished."

Imwraeth wraps his arms around me and pulls me in close. He smells good, warm and just like him. I lean my head against his chest. "Oh, Lylahn."

There is a deep ache inside of me. A piece of me is missing. I swallow and brace myself for the lie. "I'll be all right."

He looks into my eyes.

I set my expression. Tell myself the lie until I believe it to be truth. He's got so much on his mind, so much to deal with. "It will be ok. If that's what got us here to rescue Norah, it will be worth it." I can't quite make myself believe that, but I try. For Imwraeth.

Imwraeth shakes his head. "I didn't see a green glow. I didn't feel any of that."

"I can't explain it."

"There's a lot about this that's hard to explain," he says. "Why is the sand white? Why do my navigators keep telling me that the stars are wrong for this time of year? Something's going on here. Something far beyond what we expected." Imwraeth trails off. "Maybe your sacrifice was what got us here, wherever we are."

I shut my eyes. Absorbing is a rare gift, and among all of us who came on this journey, only Danosrin and I are Absorbers. Now it's just him.

Suddenly, there's yelling up above. Imwraeth and I look at each other.

We rush out the door, me following after Imwraeth.

Sailors cry out in the desert wind, and warriors gather on deck. I turn to see what's going on.

My stomach drops.

A black ship. A black wooden ship with tan sails and strange markings carved into the side. Shakers on both sides attack, sand shooting between the ships. Warriors are shouting, and there's chaos on the deck.

A poison dart flies and strikes a man in the neck, and he goes down. My immediate reaction is to rush forward, to heal him, but a hand grabs my arm.

"Lylahn!" Imwraeth screams. "Get below deck!" He turns and joins the fray, shouting orders to his warriors.

"No, I—" I trail off. The chaos seems removed from me, my ears full of camehl wool. "I can help. I can help."

I wander on the deck, weaving between falling soldiers. I kneel beside one and grab a fistful of sand. I press the sand to his chest, where blood squirts between my fingers. Nothing. Nothing.

I scream in frustration.

Warriors cry out and rush up the stairs from below deck, more of To'Morat's finest joining the brawl, but I can already tell we're losing. These people, with their instant kill poison and their fine control of the sand, have the advantage.

Warriors fall around me, and I'm a liability on deck. I scramble between them. I have to get to Imwraeth. I have to make sure he's safe.

I see him ahead, reaching into his satchel of sand and Extracting, shouting orders that my numb ears don't process. Warriors fall around him.

"Imwraeth!" I try to push closer. Darts fly all around me, and warriors are yanked off their feet by sand and hurled into the ravenous waves.

"Imwraeth!" I press through the chaos.

He turns to look at me, stricken. "Lylahn, go below deck! Please!" He screams more orders. "The sand is different here!" I'm not sure if he's talking to me or the warriors fighting around him.

"Surrender!" I cry.

Imwraeth doesn't hear me, just keeps shouting.

I grab his shoulder, and he turns to me, eyes stricken. "We have to surrender." I look at him with wide eyes. "They'll take us to Norah."

"Or they'll execute us all."

"We're losing," I say. "We can't win."

Imwraeth swallows, but then he drops his spear. "We surrender!" He cries. "Warriors! Put down your weapons. Stop the fighting!"

It takes a moment for Imwraeth's voice to be heard over the chaos of battle and the rage of the desert wind.

The captain of the other ship steps to the edge, a woman with long blonde hair pulled back in a tail. Her black leather armor looks different than the others, with broad shoulder pads and decorations on her chest. She reaches out a hand. To my relief, the darts stop. The Shakers cease.

The woman smiles. Her eyes are cold and blank, calculating. "Do you surrender, Imwraeth Jeriyah of To'Morat?"

They know exactly who we are. I can only assume that they were waiting for us, that they knew we would try to follow.

"Yes," Imwraeth calls. His voice trembles. "We surrender."

Murmurs travel through the warriors on deck. The To'Morat surrender to no one.

Once again, Imwraeth followed my advice. I pray to Atoille that it doesn't lead us to ruin.

"You will follow us," the woman says, her voice tinged with an accent. She signals to her warriors, and long snakes of white sand stretch from their ship to ours, tying the two together. "We will take you to To'Sharazad for the High Sustainer to deal with. Any attempt at escape will be met with your immediate deaths."

"You have my word," Imwraeth says, though I can tell it gives him physical pain. "We will follow you."

The woman sneers like Imwraeth's word doesn't matter to her.

And then my feet are lifted off the deck. I scream and reach for Imwraeth. He grabs onto me. His feet, everyone's feet, are lifted into the air. The barge itself floats off the sand and then plummets back down.

"What's happening?" I cry.

We crash back onto the deck, and there's a spray of dust as the barge returns to the white sand. The captain of the other ship curses and shouts orders to her people.

Imwraeth looks at me. "What was that?" I can hardly hear him over the wind. The waves of sand crash and spray even higher than before, throwing sand onto the deck that Shakers work to shove back overboard.

And then we're flung into the air again, and I lose my footing, grabbing onto Imwraeth and tumbling to the deck with him. The barge tilts back and forth at a dangerous angle. My heart pounds. What is going on? The other ship seems to be faring no better than us, so I don't think it's something they're doing.

Then I look to the sky, and I see it.

"Atoille!" I point. Imwraeth and the warriors close by turn. "Atoille!" I scream again.

No. No no no. How could this be happening?

The moon is falling.

36

NORAH

I wrench my arm out of Elandor's grasp and rush over to Agriad. I scan the panicking crowd for Zadock, but I don't see him. That pricks my heart, but there's no time to think about it. Atoille is falling.

I see through the glass ceiling the huge white orb even closer in the sky. *Oh, Atoille. What is happening?*

I reach Agriad at the other side of the room. He's talking with my potah. "General Saranyi, gather my finest Sustainers and tell them to meet me on the east lawn."

Potah nods. "I will." He hurries away, shouting for Sustainers to follow him.

Agriad eyes me with a weighing glance. "Come with me."

I follow him through the ballroom, the crowd parting around us. I have to lift my skirts so I don't trip. My body feels lighter; my steps seem to bounce.

Everyone is wrenched off their feet again, and screams rip through my ears. We're floating for an instant, and then we slam back down. I hurry to my feet. I'm going to be bruised in a dozen places tomorrow, but that's the least of my worries. Sustainers join me in following Agriad through the hallways of the palace.

I catch glimpses of outside through windows that we pass. Atoille is closer. Closer.

My heart hammers in my throat. What will happen if the moon touches our world?

"Agriad!" I cry. It's hard to be heard over the screaming and the pattering of running feet. "Potah! What is happening?"

Agriad turns but doesn't slow his stride. "Trust me, Norah."

Sustainers join us in a crowd as we exit the palace and descend the steps. We turn right onto the east lawn. I assume the people following us are Sustainers, all dressed in their finery. I've been introduced to some of them, and they seem calmer than others who are fleeing the palace in terror.

We stop on the grass lawn and look up. Wind rages through the trees. Bits of quartz that were fixed to my dress and hair go flying. The cold hits my bare arms, and the hair of my arms and neck rises. I look up at the unobstructed moon.

Atoille is enormous, and a trail of white smoke cascades behind her. She's falling into our world.

"Agriad!" I scream. "What do we do?"

Sustainers around me murmur.

Agriad turns to us. "Everything in nature must be kept in balance. That is part of our job as Sustainers." He speaks with calm assurance. "That balance has been upset."

I swallow and lift my head. Maybe now he'll see that I *need* to get home.

"Heaven...and Hell." Agriad gestures to the space around him. "The white sand is Atoille's paradise, and the orange sand marks Atoille's Hell. I have made things right in the world, and still, the balance is upset." He glances at the moon.

My mouth drops open. "What?" My breathing speeds up. Where is Zadock? I need him.

Elandor appears beside me and puts a hand on my arm, even though he's a Forger, and there's nothing he can do here. "What is happening, Norah?"

I don't have the energy to shrug him off. I'm too terrified. "I don't know."

"We must restore balance to the way it was meant to be," Agriad says to the nodding crowd. "Our world is meant to be a paradise, so let us make it so." Agriad raises his hands, and the Sustainers around me join in, grabbing fistfuls of sand. I scoop up some sand and raise my hands. If I don't Sustain, Agriad will know because the glow of the sand will be missing.

The plants around us begin to grow at incredible speeds, and soon they're towering overhead and heavy with fruit.

"It's not enough!" Agriad shouts. "Keep going!"

I Sustain, but I try to direct it at the moon. *Atoille, what is happening? How can we stop this?* I think Agriad is making it worse.

This is so, so bad.

I try to Sustain the moon, not the plants around me.

C'mon. C'mon. I know this is wrong. Agriad talks about balance, and he's right. Our world is definitely not balanced. I grab more sand, drawing in more power.

Ambition. That is the key. Longing for the power to save those I love.

I'm going to fix it. I will fix it. Please, Atoille. Help me.

There's a jolt, and we fall backward to the ground. I land beside Elandor with a grunt, and I look up to the sky. It's hard to say, with Atoille being so enormous and so close, but I think she has stopped her progress through the sky. The trail of white ash and smoke behind her seems to be dissipating.

I let out a sigh of relief. I think the moon is stable for now.

Agriad stands and holds his arms wide, a smile on his face. "Well done, my friends. A crisis has been averted."

The group of Sustainers around me clamor to their feet and clap, grinning.

I stand, swallowing, and clap as well, but I don't share their joy. I get the sinking feeling that this isn't over; this was only the beginning.

I have to get out of here. I have to get home.

Potah strides across the lawn towards Agriad.

Tears fill my eyes, and I turn away from the celebration. I sit down on the grass and draw my knees into my chest, heedless of my gold gown getting stained. I'm shivering from the cold.

Elandor sits next to me. "Norah, are you all right? That was some Sustaining. It's probably taken a lot out of you."

It should be Zadock here, not you. The thought tears through my brain. "I'm just shaken."

Elandor slowly reaches out and puts an arm around me. He's warm, and I stop shivering. "Yeah," he says. "Me, too."

"Do you truly believe that where I'm from is supposed to be some kind of Atoille's Hell?"

"I don't know, Norah. Whatever Agriad did tonight worked, right?"

I grind my teeth in frustration. Nobles move around us, exiting the palace grounds and entering Extractor-powered carriages. "But why did Atoille start falling in the first place?" I shake my head. "He's wrong. This isn't how nature is supposed to be, and my people don't deserve this. They're good people. Bad people, too, just like here. And..." I trail off, my voice choking. "And they're starving because I'm gone. I need..."

I can't finish. I know what I need to do. The sacrifices I need to make.

I swallow and blink the tears out of my eyes. Elandor scoots closer and wraps both arms around me. Maybe some part of Cale is in me, like Agriad says, because I lay my head on his shoulder and let the tears fall.

A part of my mind is screaming right now, but I'm too exhausted to care.

"Maybe you're right," he says. "Maybe you're right."

I blink back the tears and sit up. Going back may not be enough.

If balance is what nature needs, then one Sustainer working to bring life to my home is not nearly enough. I need to bring back more

Sustainers. If I can convince some of them to go with me, that could change everything.

I glance up at the moon. What if this happens again, and I can't stop it?

I shift my gaze to the Sustainers celebrating and congratulating Agriad. I memorize their faces. These people. These are the ones I'll have to convince.

The balance of the world is broken. And I've got to fix it.

37

ZADOCK

Norah. I've got to find Norah.

I force my way through the walls of screaming people, trying to fight my way to her. I saw her leave with a group of Sustainers.

And she was...she was Anointed to someone else. Or at least, it was announced. And she came to me, probably to explain, and I just—

I growl in frustration, pushing past a screaming woman in an orange silk gown. My legs burn as I hurry up the ballroom staircase, crowded with terrified partygoers. This whole evening has been a disaster, and now the moon is falling. The moon is *falling*. Terror rises from the pit of my stomach.

"Zadock!"

I stop pressing forward. Was that Norah? Behind me? I turn around to look, and Kemelah waves. I scowl, but I stop.

Kemelah catches up to me. "Zadock, please. Help me calm these people down. The palace is chaos."

I turn away. "I know. And I have to get to Norah."

Kemelah grabs my arm. "Don't. Let the Sustainers do what they're supposed to do."

"And how are they going to fix this?" I gesture out the glass ceiling at the trail of ash following a falling moon. "Why is this happening?"

Kemelah shakes her head. "I don't know. But help me, please."

I yank my arm from her hand and run out the ballroom doors.

The corridors of the palace are even more crowded. Palace staff tear through the hallways. I hurry past them, trying to remember how to navigate the twisting hallways. Finally, I'm outside, and I see a crowd of Sustainers off to my right. I hurry toward them. My mouth falls open when I see the moon above. It's stopped its progress through the sky. Something must've worked.

I scan the crowd, looking for Norah. And then I see her.

She's sitting on the grass, looking overwhelmed and drained but utterly beautiful in that dazzling dress. She tells me that she feels awkward in it, but it looks like it was made for her, like she was meant to be a queen.

She's laying her head on Elandor's shoulder, and his arms are wrapped around her.

I stop. My stomach turns to ice.

I step forward but pause, unsure if should go on or if I should leave her alone.

Norah stands and makes her way through the crowd. She seems to be scanning the faces. She turns and jolts when she sees me. Norah runs up to me, and I catch her in my arms. She buries her face in my shoulder.

I feel better...a bit.

Elandor runs a hand through his perfect straight hair and looks away. Good.

I hold Norah tighter. "Nors, I'm so sorry. I'm sorry I walked away from you."

Norah's brown eyes meet mine. "You should've let me explain."

"I know." I sigh. We've got bigger problems. "What happened?"

"I don't know. Agriad said something about balance. The balance of the world is wrong. It's like what was happening to us with the famine, but a thousand times worse. Atoille...she's falling."

I take a deep breath. "Is she stable now?"

Norah swallows. "I think so. For now."

I grip her forearms tighter and lower my voice. "We've got to get you home. If the balance is what's wrong—"

Norah shakes her head furiously.

"We can't stay here—"

"It's not that," she says. "I'm not enough. I can't bring balance to the world alone."

My stomach sinks with her words. She's probably right, but what are we supposed to do about it? I glance around at the Sustainers, some heading for home, and some laughing on the lawn and downing more glasses of wine that have been passed out. "Are we supposed to convince these people to come back with us?"

Norah cringes. "Yes?"

I sigh. "It won't work. All it takes is one noble telling Agriad our plans, and we're through. I'll never get you out of here."

Norah's eyes flash. "I never said it was your job to get me out of here."

Her words slice through me like a knife.

"And what if I don't want to leave?" Her voice is barely a breath. A tear slides down Norah's cheek. "What if I can't do everything they need me to do?" She gestures in the direction of the ocean of sand. "What if I'm not the savior everyone thinks I am?"

I swallow down my anger and hurt. Pause for a few deep breaths. "I don't have the answers, Nors." I open my arms to her and breathe a sigh of relief when she moves forward into my embrace. I hold her tight. "I care about your happiness more than anything." I pause. "But we can't let everyone we love starve to death. We can't."

"I know."

For a long time, I just hold her.

"I can't do this, Zadock," she whispers. "I can't save everyone."

I bury my face in her hair and breathe her in. "We'll get some Sustainers to help you. You're right. You can't do it alone."

Norah tilts her head back to meet my eyes. "Thank you."

"Please. Will you be ready to leave if it gets too dangerous?"

Norah's eyes find her potah in the crowd. She turns back to me and takes a deep breath. Slowly, she nods. "All right. If it gets too dangerous, we'll leave." Her huge brown eyes lock onto mine. "Do you trust me to make that decision?"

I take a step back. Her words hit me like a fist of sand. "I—I—" I don't know what to say. "We'll—we'll decide together."

Norah frowns and opens her mouth.

"Norah!"

Agriad's voice. I whip my head to the side, and he's there, striding toward us. I frown, and my gut clenches. Norah steps in closer to me.

Agriad frowns when he sees that I'm holding her, but I don't let go.

Most of the Sustainers have already left, and Agriad waves away the ones that stick around. Some head to the palace, but most leave through the gates. I don't know where Elandor went, but I don't see him anymore. Soon, it's just us three on the deserted palace grounds. The night air is freezing, and I put one arm around Norah's shoulders, bringing her in close to me.

Agriad scowls. "Norah, I thought I made it clear tonight who your Anointed is."

Norah's eyes light up in a rage. "Zadock is my Anointed. I have never been Anointed to Elandor. Tonight was a lie."

I wince a bit at her bold words, but at the same time, I cheer.

Agriad takes a deep breath. "You do not remember being Anointed to Elandor, but it did happen. I will say it again. Norah, I thought I made it clear tonight who your Anointed is."

Norah's face pales. I tighten my grip on her.

Agriad glances from her to me, and his cruel eyes convey so much. Slowly, they bleed from white to black. "I'm sorry, my darling Cale. You leave me no choice."

Before I can blink, Agriad grips my shoulder. Sand glows in his hand. My right arm from the shoulder down goes completely numb. I gasp and try to wrench myself out of his grip, but I'm weak...so weak.

"Stop!" Norah screams. "Don't hurt him!" She steps away from me.

Agriad smiles and removes his hand.

I gasp for air and barely stay standing. I'm drained. Feeling inches back into my arm. What happened? What did Agriad do to me? Whatever it was, it seems to be fading, but *speck*.

"It has been a trying evening for us all, has it not?" Agriad says. "I believe you will be needing a new room, Zadock Penvaren."

It takes everything within me to swallow my retorts and nod. "I believe so." Prickles go up and down my arm, and I shake it out.

Norah cries silently beside me, tears falling down her cheeks.

38

LYLAHN

I sit at the edge of the barge, staring at the spray of the white sand, watching the black boat lead us to a plateau looming on the horizon, a plateau that could swallow To'Morat and To'Rahn together.

I'm falling apart. The vivid, bloody dreams are getting worse and worse.

At least the moon seems stable. Atoille fell through the sky, drifting even closer to our world, but then she stopped. I don't know what is going on, but this seems impossible.

From across the sands, the captain of the other ship looks back, as if she senses me watching, and smiles. I look away.

I've repeatedly given Imwraeth bad advice, and look where it's gotten us. I put my head in my hands.

Footsteps. On the deck. And then a hand on my shoulder. I jump and look up but relax when I see it's Imwraeth.

He smiles at me, though it's weak and strained. His red hair ruffles in the wind, and I want to reach up and touch it. I want to bury myself in him. I want all this to go away and for it to be just us in the world.

Imwraeth sits beside me with a sigh. "We still have a chance. We can still get Norah and Zadock and escape."

"How?"

Imwraeth meets my eyes. "I don't know."

Suddenly, I lean forward and press my lips to his. I don't know what's going to happen. I don't know what the future holds. I can't miss this opportunity.

"I love you," I whisper. I think I really mean it.

Imwraeth kisses me back, his hands coming to hold my neck. "I love you, Lylahn."

The sound of boots slamming on the ship makes me jump and break away from Imwraeth.

The captain has boarded our ship, and she surveys us with arms crossed and a smile. Imwraeth and I hurry to our feet. Warriors around us pause in what they're doing, scowling, going on alert.

The captain motions behind her, and other sailors from her ship sail over to ours on platforms of sand.

"Bind them," she orders.

The sailors move forward with ropes. Imwraeth's warriors don't know how to act. Some lift spears. Some prepare knives of sand.

Imwraeth stops them with an outstretched hand. "We must endure this."

The captain sneers.

The To'Morat quiet their protests, allowing their hands to be bound behind them with ropes. A sailor with pure white eyes comes for me, and I glance at Imwraeth. He nods, gives me a smile.

The sailor's rough hands take mine behind my back and tie them tight. Then he does the same to Imwraeth.

At a signal from the captain, our ship and theirs are lifted toward the top of the enormous plateau. I stay on my feet, swaying, feeling like the world is tumbling out from beneath me.

We don't have a plan. We have no idea what we're going to do or what they're going to do with us.

Yet, somehow, we have to get Norah and Zadock and escape this mess.

We reach the top of the plateau, and there are crews of boatmen and a fleet of ships tied in a boatyard. They bring in our barge and their ship to land on solid ground.

We're herded off the barge like camehls, poked and prodded by the butts of spears and loaded onto a flat platform made of the same black wood as the ship. Bodies are pressed around me, Imwraeth close by my side. Danosrin stands near the edge, looking out over the trees that grow so tightly together that their branches and vines intermingle.

Extractors with glowing sands move the platform forward, following a quartz path that cuts through dense forests of thick, black trees and curling vines. Guards stand at the edges of the platform, watching us.

An enormous city looms ahead, great quartz walls that have been Forged into swirling patterns. My mouth drops open.

Gates made of spires of quartz open, and we're allowed through. We travel through city streets at a rapid pace, passing camehls loaded with goods and quartz homes of all colors. People with bundles of food, spices, and goods to trade cry out their wares.

The city is definitely not hurting. They're not starving like we are. It's so unfair that it makes my gut curdle.

People stop what they're doing and point at us in our ragged brown clothes, white sand in our hair. I force my shoulders back to stand tall and proud. I blow the bangs out of my face.

Eventually, we reach a smaller set of walls, a large field of grounds and an enormous blue crystal palace beyond. We're ushered through the gates after the ship captain speaks with the guards, and then we come to a stop.

"Where are we?" Imwraeth speaks. "Where are you taking us?"

The captain turns back and smiles. "Welcome," she says, "to the palace of To'Sharazad. The High Sustainer will be pleased that you're here."

I exchange a look with Imwraeth.

"I wish to speak with Agriad Zul," Imwraeth says.

The captain grins. "Excellent."

We wait for a few moments more, the warriors around me getting antsy and shifting on their feet. Some flex their fingers like they long to hold a weapon or Shake the sand around them. The ropes are cutting into my wrists.

The palace doors open, and Agriad Zul descends the steps on a navy carpet. His image is seared into my mind from our first meeting. His long black hair is pulled back into a tail, and he wears a red silk shirt and a confident smile. A gaudy necklace is about his neck, three gems—orange, green, and purple—taking center stage.

Two guards flank either side of him. Norah and Zadock aren't anywhere to be seen.

Agriad Zul's cool white eyes take everything in. "Welcome, my friends. I'm so glad you've decided to join us." His voice comes out in a hiss, like a desert viper's. Chills go up and down my spine.

"Release us," Imwraeth says. "We are here to treat with you, and we do not deserve to be bound like prisoners."

Agriad shakes his head. "I wish I could do that. But unfortunately, I can't trust you."

"Where are Norah Saranyi and Zadock Penvaren?" Imwraeth asks. "What have you done with them?"

Agriad smiles again. "They are here, Imwraeth Jeriyah. They are safe."

I breathe out a sigh of relief.

"You must want your friends back," Agriad continues. "But Norah Saranyi cannot be allowed to leave."

Imwraeth doesn't say anything. Agriad, of course, knows why we're here. We have to look for an opening, figure out a plan.

Agriad shakes his head. "I cannot allow you to take her back with you. I'm afraid your journey has been a waste of time." Agriad's gaze shifts to me. He places one hand on the green stone about his neck. "What a shame that it cost so much."

My shoulders stiffen. Somehow, he knows.

My Absorbing. Could he know how I can get it back?

Agriad nods to the white-haired captain. "You have done well, Captain Shalen. You will be rewarded."

The woman preens under his praise.

Agriad turns to his guards. More have gathered on the palace steps behind him. "Show our guests to their rooms."

Guards in black leather step forward to escort us, and everything in me says to fight back. I try to still that response, to do what Imwraeth is doing and take this treatment with dignity, but it's so difficult.

One of the To'Morat warriors can't take it anymore. He cries out and Shakes, punching out at his captors with enormous fists of sand.

"Tahi, no!" Imwraeth shouts.

Agriad nods, and Tahi is rammed through the gut with a spear. He falls over to the green grass, bleeding and writhing.

I hear a scream, and then I realize it's me.

Heal him. Heal him. I have to—

"Cooperate!" Imwraeth cries. "We must cooperate with them."

Warriors stir and murmur, but then still.

"Very wise." Agriad Zul smiles.

39

NORAH

I'm sullen and quiet at breakfast the next day. First thing this morning, I checked Atoille, and she seemed stable in the sky. But I don't know how long that will last.

I sneak a glance at Zadock, down at the end of the banquet table. Guests from the gala the night before dot the dining hall, chatting in small groups, but Zadock sits alone.

Potah enters the room, his curly hair disheveled. He smiles when he sees me, and I smile back. My heart lifts just a little. He takes a seat next to Zadock, even though his rightful place is next to Agriad. I blink, surprised.

He's still my potah. He's still in there.

I turn to Agriad, feeling a little bolder. "Potah," I say. It's coming easier now. "I want to go sailing today. I want General Saranyi to take me."

Elandor glances at me.

Agriad takes a bite of yellow fruit, pineapple, I think it's called. "Why is this, daughter?"

I shrug, try to act nonchalant, even though my heart is

hammering in my ribs. "I think it would be a good skill for me to learn."

"It would be better for you to continue working on Sustaining." He pauses, chewing. "But you *have* improved. If you want to learn to sail, I will arrange for General Saranyi to take you. His skill is unparalleled."

I smile. I'm flooded with relief, but worry sits like bad lizard meat in my stomach. Does Agriad not see the connection in our names? Does he not know who my true potah is? And if he does, is he truly unworried that potah will remember me?

If that's the case, there must be a reason.

After breakfast, I stand, eager to make preparations to sail. Gerian, a middle-aged gentleman who walks with a cane, shakes hands with Agriad and leaves. I stride across the banquet hall, hurrying to catch up.

"Lord Gerian!" I say. He stops, and I lower my voice somewhat. "Might I speak with you a moment?" Atoille, what is this place doing to me? I don't even sound like myself anymore. My stomach is queasy with nerves. What I'm about to say could get me in serious trouble, but I don't have a choice.

Elandor, of course, is close behind me, following me around like a desert fox pup. I don't think he'd betray me to Agriad. I hope.

"Yes, Great Sustainer." Gerian nods.

"I was wondering..." Now I trail off, unsure how to proceed. I catch Zadock watching me from across the room. "Gerian, aren't you worried about what happened last night with the moon? I'm so concerned." I bite my lip, slipping into the role of the frightened little noble girl.

Elandor puts a hand on my elbow. I want to shake him off, with Zadock watching, but I focus on Gerian's response.

Gerian chuckles. "Oh, Norah. Don't worry about that. The moon is fine. What we did restored balance."

"But did it?" I dare to ask. "Did it really? Because I'm not sure that that's the case."

Elandor's hand on my elbow squeezes too tight, but I ignore him.

Gerian frowns. I press on before I can think better of it. I hear Agriad behind me, talking with my potah, so I'm reasonably safe. I think. "I'm from the other side of the ocean of sand, and there are no Sustainers there. I'm not sure you can call that balance."

Gerian's eyes widen. "The other side of the—Cale, really, what are you on about? This is preposterous." He looks at me kindly. "Get some rest, dear girl. You've been through a lot." He pats my hand once and then turns to leave. I start after him, but Elandor tightens his grip and stops me.

"Let it go," he whispers. "This is dangerous, Norah. What you're doing."

I turn to him, and our faces are way too close. "But I have to try. Something *is* wrong. Something is going wrong with nature again."

Elandor frowns. "Maybe."

Maybe. That's a start.

I watch Gerian go, twirling his cane without a care in the world.

A start, but not enough.

ZADOCK

I stare at Norah talking with the nobleman, Elandor gripping her elbow. She feels farther away than she ever has before, even when I was Anointed to someone else. She's so distant, trying to take on our problems on her own. She won't let me in. Won't let me help her.

"It's been a pleasure talking with you, Zadock," Raen Saranyi says. "But I'm afraid I must get on with my duties."

I nod, and he stands and crosses the room before he's stopped by Agriad.

"So, more lessons today?" Kemelah asks as she fills the seat that Raen Saranyi vacated. A servant brings her a breakfast plate, and she digs in.

"No more lessons," I say.

Kemelah eyes me. "Oh, grumpy today, are we?" She chews. "Look, Zadock. You'll get over her. Agriad wants her for someone else. And Agriad gets what Agriad wants."

"No," I say. "I won't get over her." Kemelah doesn't understand, so why bother explaining? Norah is the only one for me. That's always been the truth.

Kemelah shrugs and falls silent.

I try to eat, but my stomach protests.

What can I do to help Norah? I glance at her, still talking with that noble. She won't leave without her potah, and now she's talking about taking other Sustainers as well. How the speck are we going to do that? Sneaking just the two of us out is a problem enough.

Is there something I can do to help Raen Saranyi remember? Or something I can do to convince other Sustainers to return with us?

I turn to Kemelah to ask her about Sustainers, but a different question comes out. "Kemelah, why do your eyes look like that?"

She swallows and looks at me for a moment with those large, blank eyes. After a moment, she sighs. "I guess it can't hurt to tell you." She spears a piece of fruit with a skewer. "Agriad Sustains those that he calls to be his."

"What does that mean?"

Kemelah shrugs again, twirling the orange fruit. "His most dedicated warriors, those he favors the most, he Sustains. It changes our eyes." She laughs, strained. "At first, I was upset about it. I miss my eyes. They were green, very striking." She gives me a half smile, almost flirtatious, but then it disappears. "My parents begged Agriad to make me a soldier. They knew I had talent with sand Shaking, and they wanted the honors that come from having someone in your household close to the High Sustainer." Kemelah stares at her food. "They lived the high life of nobility because Agriad accepted. I went kicking and screaming."

My face falls. "Oh, Kemelah—"

She cuts me off with a shake of her head. "Don't pity me. Look, my eyes are different, but when Agriad Sustains me, I get a whole host of benefits. I'm physically stronger. I'm full of vitality and energy. Why do you think our warriors were able to overpower yours so easily?" She cocks one eyebrow.

"Umm. You had poisoned darts, and we didn't."

Kemelah laughs. "Good point. But also, we've been Sustained. We can take battle hits and heal from them faster, we can recover quicker, and our muscles are stronger." She shrugs. "It's worth it, in the end." She stirs her porridge. "There's another thing, Zadock. Something else you should know about being Sustained."

I lean forward. "Tell me. Please."

She looks me in the eyes with that creepy blank stare, her white hair falling around her face.

"Sustaining gives life, right?" she asks.

"Yeah."

"To plants around us. To the world. Sustaining is vital."

I nod. "Ok."

"Sustaining gives life," she repeats. She looks away like she can't bring herself to say the next part while looking at me. "And I've been alive for a very long time."

I blink. "Ok. Like, how long?"

Kemelah swallows. People around us are standing. Breakfast dishes are being cleared away. I glance to the side, and Norah's gone.

"How long, Kemelah?"

She looks at me again. "My parents are dead, Zadock. They've been dead for over a hundred years."

"Wait, what—"

"And I'm still here, still serving Agriad." Kemelah's blank eyes turn colder, darker. "My parents sold me for a life of luxury, and now their lives are over. And I'm still here. You'd think that eternal life would be a blessing." She whispers the last part almost to herself. "But it's not. I never age. I watch my friends and family grow old and die without me. And I will serve him for as long as he continues to Sustain me." Kemelah quiets. Startles and blinks. "Sorry, I—I shouldn't have—"

"No, no." I'm reeling. "Thank you for telling me. Kemelah, I'm sorry."

She looks away. "Don't. Don't."

"Why don't you leave him? Go somewhere else? Wouldn't the effects of his Sustaining wear off?"

She shakes her head. "It's been too long. I am bound to him."

"Kemelah." I pause. "How long has Agriad been alive? Can he Sustain himself?"

Kemelah stands. "We should go."

I hurry to my feet and put one hand on her arm. "Kemelah. Agriad Sustained Norah."

She freezes. "How many times?"

I pause. "Just once. I think. Her eyes are already back to normal."

Her voice is rigid like Forged quartz. "Be careful, Zadock."

(

I WANT TO TELL NORAH, but she's gone, and Kemelah drags me away for more lessons. What for, I don't know. We already had the gala. The moon is falling, for Atoille's sake, and somehow, Kemelah still feels the need to teach me which spoon is for soup and which is for dessert.

Instead of following her down the corridors, I take her hand and drag her to the front of the palace.

"Where are we going?" She yanks her hand out of mine with surprising strength. But maybe, then again, not so surprising.

"Let's ditch lessons," I say. "Just this once. Can you show me the city?" If I can get Kemelah to show me around, it will be a good opportunity to check out security around the boats. Maybe scout out a way to get Norah out of here when she's ready. Or even if she's not.

Kemelah rolls her eyes and crosses her arms. "Is etiquette not important to you?"

"Of course. But, just this once? Kemelah, please?" I give her my biggest smile.

Kemelah grins back. "Fine. But you owe me."

I follow her through the palace corridors and out the grand front doors. The guards see her and wave us through. She smiles as she descends the quartz steps.

"Should we walk? Or fly?" I ask.

Kemelah smiles. She goes to the right, to a small building made of black wood too ornate to be called a shed, but that's what it looks like. She grabs two of the gliders and hands one to me.

We soar toward the palace gates. Kemelah waves to the guards and gets us through. That is good to know. If I can get Kemelah more on my side, if I can drive the fissure between her and Agriad even deeper, maybe Kemelah will be willing to help us escape. It's a slim chance, but it's still a chance.

I notice that the guards usually trailing me are gone, leaving me in Kemelah's watch. Even better.

We glide through the city, and I feel the rush in my stomach and the thrill of the air blowing past my face. This is something we need to bring back to To'Rahn.

We soar over colorful quartz houses and people dressed in exotic colors, going about their day with chores or selling goods. It's a busy city, full of music and chatter. Even the day after the moon fell through the sky, people are going about their business like everything is normal. They trust their Sustainers to work it out.

Kemelah pulls to a halt in a busy market square, and I follow. "This way."

We hold the gliders and walk down the crowded street. Closer up, the people are even more interesting, the quartz stones making up the streets even more brilliant. Crystal fountains flow with water, and garden beds overflow from balconies. It's beautiful, and so, so different from the desert streets of To'Rahn.

This is what Sustaining can do.

Kemelah stops in front of a market stall. "You've got to try these," she says. "If you're going to experience To'Sharazad, this is the way to do it." Kemelah purchases two flatbread sandwich-looking things stuffed with browned vegetables.

She hands one to me and inhales before digging in. "Mmmm."

I take a sniff. "What is it?"

Kemelah grins. "Try it. You hardly ate anything at breakfast."

I take a bite. "Holy speck." Savory juices fill my mouth, and the bread is soft and almost sweet. "What is this amazingness?"

Kemelah laughs. "I knew you'd love it. They're mushrooms. Almost taste like meat, right?"

I nod around another bite.

We walk through the market as we eat, taking in more stalls. Jewelry, clothing, and spices I've never tasted. I wish I had some money so I could get something for Norah. I think back to her, centering myself on the true purpose of this visit.

"Can you show me outside the city walls?" I ask.

Kemelah glances at me through narrow eyes as if she's guessing my thoughts. "Maybe. But it's dangerous out there, Zadock."

"Then it's a good thing I have you with me, right?" I smile again, but I'm pretty sure I have mushroom in my teeth.

"Fine."

We hop back on the gliders and sail through the city once again. My stomach feels pleasantly full and more settled, and the practice with the gliders is doing me good.

After a long ride, we reach the outer city walls. They're enormous, and I find myself wondering how high a glider can fly. Kemelah gets us through the gates past the guards.

We're outside of the city. Kemelah watches me, probably wondering if I'll try to escape. She doesn't realize that I'd never leave Norah.

Still, I breathe a deep breath of fresh air. The quartz-paved path extends farther into the jungle, black trees and vines crowding it. Hoots and whistles from creatures I don't know sound in my ears.

I drift upward on the glider, experimenting, and after a while, it won't go any higher.

"Safety locks," Kemelah explains. "You can only go so high."

I nod, disappointed.

"Stay on the path," Kemelah says. "And watch out for frogs, snakes, or anything on the road."

I nod and follow her, zooming even faster now that we're out of the city. The gliders can work up some speed. I would be expending some serious energy to go this fast via sand platform.

We reach the boathouse at the edge of the plateau without incident. I look out over the ocean of white sand, and it's oddly comforting to see it again, to hear the swish of the sand against the plateau and watch the waves. It's choppier than normal, and I worry that Atoille's proximity is having a stronger effect. I'm worried about everything right now, and I feel so powerless.

"This what you wanted to see?" Kemelah asks.

"Well—"

"It's ok," Kemelah says. "I know you want to get her home."

I turn toward her. "You won't tell anyone?"

Kemelah laughs. "What's there to tell? It's not exactly a secret that you two don't want to be here."

I look away, uncomfortable. I still feel like Kemelah holds all the power here. I glance at the boathouse. A guard stands at each boat, and I see a group of three sailors signing a paper to get ready to take one out. Speck. It would be really tough to steal one.

Kemelah stands by me and notices where I'm watching. "Agriad doubled the guard as soon as you got here. He's not taking any chances."

I frown, feeling sick. "Kemelah, I—" I breathe out. "I have to get her home. My people are dying."

She looks at me again, compassion in her eyes. "You can't."

"Why?" My anger is getting the better of me. "You just said not to let Agriad Sustain her. Well, it's going to happen again, isn't it? That's what he's planning, right? So what am I supposed to do?"

She pulls back. "I—"

"Please." I step forward. "Help me."

Kemelah picks up her glider. "Look, Zadock. I want to. I like you. You're my...friend. You're my friend." She says it like it's a foreign word, and I can't help but feel sorry for her. "I want to help. Really. But there's nothing I can do."

I turn away angrily, and I feel her hand on my shoulder. A light touch, hesitant.

"Even if I helped you escape and somehow miraculously got you a boat, he would come for her. He would never leave her alone. He needs her."

I turn back around, and Kemelah's hand falls. "Why? Why, Kemelah? This is about more than just a father wanting his daughter back, isn't it?"

Her face falls, and she swallows. "Just...give this up, all right? You can't win."

41

NORAH

I breathe in the smell of the sand, and I'm home again.

I didn't realize how stifling the jungle and the palace had become until I was out here on a boat once more. I can almost pretend that I'm back home with Zadock, sailing the sands.

But I'm on an unfamiliar boat made of black wood. It's small, made for two people to crew. Zadock isn't with me. But my potah, he is here. He looks at me and smiles. He's steering the ship with his sand Shaking, just like he used to. My heart aches from watching him. Remembering all the times we did this when I was a child.

I have to look away.

The sand is white. Pure white, like starlight. It glitters in the light of the sun. And it stretches all around us, no other plateaus in sight besides To'Sharazad behind us.

We're moving forward with remarkable speed, and the wind is tangling my ridiculously long hair. I make my way to the rear of the boat so I can sit next to Potah. A group of sand moles pops out of the sand to my right, and I laugh with delight.

"Look how many there are!"

Potah smiles. "A whole pod."

I reach out to tap one on the shell, and it burrows back underneath the sands in a flash.

I study my potah's face. He's smiling but concentrating, moving the boat forward. I miss his eyes. They were warm and brown. His gaze, now white, makes my spine stiffen.

I can imagine Motah throwing her arms around him and weeping into his shoulder. I can imagine Shrey, showing him her cactus needles.

It's what I want more than anything in the world.

"General Saranyi." I hate those words in my mouth. "Thank you for taking me sailing today."

"My pleasure, Great Sustainer."

Ugh. "Please, call me Norah."

"Norah."

I lower my voice, afraid to let the next words out of my mouth free. "Do you not remember me?"

His arms move back and forth, directing the sand. "I wish I did."

"I'm your daughter." My voice falters, heavy with emotion.

He starts, and the boat dips at his loss of control, though he quickly regains it. "The Higher Sustainer has said—"

"He's wrong." I shake my head. "Your favorite food is Motah's bristlebrush stew. You like the way she spices it just right. You have another daughter, with curly hair like yours, but blonde. Her name is Shrey."

Shrey. I have to get home to her. I feel sick at how I've abandoned her for so long, left her to starve. Maybe Zadock is right. Maybe it's time to go.

Potah works the sand, staring straight ahead. His expression is thoughtful, his eyebrows furrowed.

I plow ahead, hoping beyond hope that he'll believe me. "Your favorite smell is the desert air after rain. Your favorite thing to do is sail the ocean of sand. With me." I choke on the words. "You taught me to navigate using the stars. We used to sit on the edge of the plateau, and you'd point out the constellations and tell me their stories. We—"

"Enough, Norah." His voice sounds pained. "I don't need to hear anymore."

I watch him in silence for several heartbeats.

"So, you don't really need me to teach you to sail?"

I bite my lower lip. "No." I stand and grab for the ropes, controlling the sails, expertly positioning them so that they catch the wind and give us a burst of speed. A small smile tugs at the corner of Potah's mouth.

My balance is wobbly after not being on a boat for so long, but my body is remembering the correct stance, the right ropes to grab and how hard to pull. "I don't know what Agriad has told you, but three years ago, you were sailing. With me." The pain of it hits me all over again.

Potah watches me, and he's listening.

"I had begged you to take me sailing. I loved it, even then. You said it wasn't a good idea, that Atoille was too high in the sky and the waves were too rocky, but I pleaded with you, and you gave in." Tears fill my eyes. "We sailed, and the sand was too rough. I stumbled, and I was about to fall overboard, but you grabbed me and hauled me to safety. The boat tipped at just the wrong moment, and your momentum took you over. The sand sucked you away instantly. I thought—I thought you were dead." *And it was my fault.* The small voice in my head is accusatory.

I close my eyes. I'm trembling. It never really leaves, this grief. I drifted in that boat for hours, at the mercy of the sands, praying to Atoille that it wouldn't tip before someone from To'Rahn noticed a lone boat and thought to check what was happening.

"I'm so sorry you went through that," Potah says.

I scan his face. He is contemplative, concerned.

He sighs, moving his arms to toss a splash of sand back overboard. "Agriad Zul has told me that I came through the sands, that I lost my memory because of it. Very few survive falling through the sands, and

I didn't come out unscathed." He hesitates. "Perhaps what you say is true. But..." He shakes his head. "The High Sustainer says that you are his daughter."

"I'm not." I shake my head vehemently. "I'm not." *I'm yours.* I want to say. *I'm yours. Remember.*

"I met Cale before she died. You look like her. How could that be possible if what Agriad is saying isn't true?"

I clench my fists in frustration.

Suddenly, the boat jerks upward, and we're floating. My stomach lurches, and I gasp. Only my tight grip on the ropes keeps me from going overboard. What—?

I look behind me, and I see Atoille. *Oh no.*

The boat drops to the sand, and we land in a puff. I scramble to the side of the boat and grab the railing. Potah furiously works his arms, trying to steady us.

The trail of ash and smoke streams behind Atoille again. She's falling, descending from the sky. She's so close to the sands it looks like she's about to touch.

"No!" I scream.

The boat lurches into the air again, and the waves are growing. Sand sloshes into the boat, and Potah uses one hand to Shake it away.

"Hold on!" he cries through gritted teeth.

I grip the sides of the boat. I watch Atoille, praying that she'll slow. Praying to the moon to stop her movement toward the planet.

I'm sure Agriad and his Sustainers are hurrying to "work" on the problem.

I stand, my legs shaking, but even though the boat is rocking, I feel steady. Potah screams for me to sit down, but I ignore him. I move to the center of the boat and raise my arms, a handful of sand in each one.

I Sustain.

The power of nature flows through me. I direct it at Atoille.

Ambition. I have it now in abundance. There are many things I want. And I yearn for the power to get them.

Sand glows in my palms with the brightness of the sun, a white-hot light. Waves of sand slosh around my feet. We may be sinking, but I'm focused. One with Atoille.

All my Sustaining, I direct at her.

I'm here.

I'm here.

STAY!

There's a jolt, and I fall, bumping the back of my head on one of the benches lining the boat.

"Norah!" Potah calls, but he can't run to my side because he's Shaking to steady the boat.

I look in the sky and breathe an enormous sigh of relief. Atoille appears steady, but she's even closer to our world than before. So close that any tiny pinch will make her touch down.

This is bad.

There's a weirdness in the way I move. Gravity has shifted.

I'm completely spent. The waves of sand are even higher, and Potah has to work twice as hard to keep sand out of the ship.

"We're going home," he says. "Agriad will know what to do."

Home.

Despair makes my vision go black.

42

LYLAHN

I wake in an unfamiliar bed. Lavish, even compared to the one I had in To'Morat. The blankets are downy, a shade of soft blue with gold accents. Sunlight streams through a clear glass window. There's a large round rug on the floor with gold tassels and a small crystal table and chairs off to the left.

Imwraeth rolls over on his side, and I jolt. I almost forgot that he slept next to me. These people put us in one room.

They captured us, and now they're treating us like royalty?

I roll over on the pillow to face Imwraeth. My heart flutters while I watch him breathe, in and out. His red hair is matted on one side, and his brows are furrowed in concern, even in sleep.

My home plateau of To'Shahera isn't as stiff and formal about the Anointings as To'Rahn is, and I don't know customs in To'Morat. But Imwraeth and I have been waiting for other reasons. It never seems like the time is right when your country is starving.

Imwraeth's eyelids flutter open. For a moment, he frowns, taking in the room sleepily. Then he turns to me.

I manage a weak smile just for him. Even though our situation is desperate, I always smile for him.

"Good morning," I say.

"Good morning. Did you sleep well?" He watches me with an expectant expression. So he knows about the nightmares.

"I did, actually." And it's true. No nightmares last night. For the first time in a long time. Which doesn't make any sense. Things are worse for us than they have ever been.

Imwraeth rolls back onto his back and stares at the ceiling. "What are we going to do, Lylahn?"

I put a hand on his arm. "Find Norah and Zadock. Get them out of here." I lower my voice. "Nothing has changed."

"You're right. You're right."

(

WE'RE FED A BOUNTIFUL BREAKFAST, and, even if the food is strange, it's a small wonder to have a full belly. Solemn-faced servants wait on us and dress us in fine clothes. I don't know what's going on, but the servants taking care of us are quiet and don't respond to questions.

We're hustled down endless corridors and hallways. I try to learn my surroundings, but after a few dozen turns, I'm lost. I scan the faces of everyone passing by, but no Norah and Zadock.

It's an effort to keep my shoulders straight, to walk tall with confidence. Where are we going? What is Agriad's game?

We're led to a sitting room, and the servants gesture for us to sit. They bow before exiting the room. Imwraeth and I take seats on a blue velvet couch. The room is spacious, with couches and chairs and potted plants on end tables of carved black wood.

And we wait.

Finally, the door is opened by a servant, and Agriad Zul strides into the room. My senses go on high alert.

"Agriad Zul, the High Sustainer of To'Sharazad," the servant announces. He turns to us. "The Lady Lylahn Velare of To'Morat and Imwraeth Jeriyah, the Favored One of To'Morat."

I swallow.

Agriad Zul takes a seat across from us, and the servant pours him a cup of something steaming. He takes a sip. The servant pours us drinks as well before leaving and closing the door behind him. Neither of us reach for our teacups, delicate things made of milky white crystal.

There doesn't appear to be any guards. Interesting. Agriad is very confident that we won't try to kill him.

Agriad Zul is as intimidating as I remember. More, even though he's at ease, reclined in his chair. We're seated close enough that I can see the tiny red veins going through the whites of his eyes. He studies us, unblinking, a small smile on his face. I want to take Imwraeth's hand, and I force my hands to clasp together in my lap.

Agriad takes a sip of his drink. "Ahhhh. Lylahn and Imwraeth. Welcome to To'Sharazad. I'm glad you're here."

My stomach turns.

"We are grateful for your hospitality." Imwraeth reaches for his teacup but doesn't drink. "You are most generous."

Ha. That's an understatement. We came to attack him and take back our people, and Agriad is treating us like royal guests.

Agriad's smile widens. "All of the hospitality my house can offer is yours. But first, we must discuss the small matter of why you're here." He lowers the cup to the table beside him. "You crossed the ocean of water. Came through the dunes of water. That is no easy feat. And the price," his eyes shift toward me, "the price was great."

I stiffen. Imwraeth glances toward me, worry in his eyes.

Agriad leans back in his chair. "No one can cross the ocean of water without hitting the dunes and paying the toll. It is a force of nature unto its own. Like the ocean of sand. Like Atoille herself."

"Is there any way..." I find myself saying, reaching for any sign of hope. "That I might get my Absorbing back?"

"I'm afraid not. I'm sorry for your loss."

Sorrow makes my shoulders slump. "Why did it take from *me*?"

The words come out small, a whimper. Imwraeth takes my hand, and I focus on the curl of his fingers going through mine.

Agriad lets out a breath. "Who can say? The ocean of water requires a steep price. Perhaps it sensed deep strength in you."

Does he mean the strength of my Absorbing? Surely there were others aboard who were stronger in their sand gifts. I straighten my posture and school my face to stillness. I tell myself the lie that I'm fine, I'm fine.

"Then how is it that *you* are able to travel across the ocean of water?" Imwraeth asks.

"I have other means." Agriad takes a sip from his cup.

"Where are we?" Imwraeth asks. "When we went through what you call dunes—"

"To'Sharazad is on the other side of the world." Agriad grins. "That is the inherent power within the dunes."

Imwraeth and I are silent, processing. Could that be right? When we entered the ocean of water, it was day, and when we reached the white sand, it was night. This is unbelievable.

"The moon is falling," I blurt out. I don't know where it comes from. Maybe some part within me is hoping to reason with him. "You must know something is deeply wrong. It's happened twice now." Twice, the moon has fallen closer to our world. I can only speculate as to why, but after seeing our desert nations fall into famine because nature was unbalanced, I think Norah is the key. "We need our Sustainer back." *I am bold. I am brave.* I use every ounce of skill I have to tell myself the lie until I almost believe it. Imwraeth gives me a small, reassuring smile that I see out of the corner of my eye.

Agriad frowns, a fake thing, overdramatic. "And here I thought you were coming to experience the wonders of To'Sharazad."

"Our people are starving without her," Imwraeth says. "Surely some sort of deal can be arranged. Let us continue our discussions from before."

"Discussions?" Agriad laughs. "There were no discussions. I have taken what is mine. This is how the world was meant to be." He gestures to the room around him. "Two halves of one world. The sand white, the sand orange. This is how nature was meant to operate."

Anger grows within me and replaces the fear. Does he truly believe that? "Then why is the moon falling? If nature has been corrected, then why is she still trying to right herself?"

Agriad scowls. "I wouldn't expect you to understand. There is more at stake here than you could possibly know." He takes another drink and his control returns. "I thank you for your visit to To'Sharazad. Unfortunately, I cannot let you or your people return home."

I freeze, shoulders tense.

"Where are our people?" Imwraeth asks, unruffled.

"Oh, they're being taken care of." Agriad nods. "Maybe not as well as you have been, but still. Don't worry about them."

"So we are to be prisoners here?" I burst out. "How long are you going to hold us?"

Agriad grins, and I wish I wouldn't have asked the question. "Oh. Not long, I think."

43

NORAH

I walk through the corridors. I need to find Potah.

I'm worried. I can feel something happening to me. Something is changing. He's always said I was so strong that I would likely have a Sustainer double, a partner, someone who looked exactly like me and was my foil, my counterpart. He says it's almost time for us to go find her, but I think it's past time.

Something is happening. I can feel it.

I move through crystalline blue hallways, brushing past tapestries of my ancestors hanging on the wall. Candlelight flickers. It's dawn, but I know Potah will be awake. He's always been an early riser.

I see him, finally, in his office, a grand room with a clear glass wall overlooking the palace gardens. He can watch Sustainers in training and make sure everything is growing the way he wants.

I am about to barge into the room when something makes me stop. The sound of Raen Saranyi's voice.

I don't like that man. The way he looks at me... It's strange. I wish Potah would get rid of him, send him back, or pit him against the bloodworm in Judgment, but Potah has instead made him his General.

I don't go into the room. Something makes me wait and watch.

"You don't have to do this," Raen is saying. He takes a seat in a chair in front of my Potah. I can barely see him through the open crack in the doorway. "I'm feeling much better."

Potah's voice. "Your ordeal through the sands was no trivial matter. And you still haven't gotten your memories back, have you?"

"Well, no. But shouldn't an Absorber take a look—?"

"Not for this kind of ailment. We'll keep trying."

My potah's hands go atop Raen's head. The glow of Sustaining slips through his fingers.

I'm confused. What is he trying to do? Sustaining can't bring back memories.

I jolt awake.

Elandor is next to me, sleeping, and the light of dawn creeps into the room. My heart is beating hard. I get out of bed and cross the room to the window. I can't sleep well next to Elandor anyway.

I stare out over the palace grounds, at the pink light of dawn grazing the trimmed grasses and flowers.

What I saw. That dream. It was one of Cale's memories. And she saw...she saw my potah, being Sustained by Agriad.

Sustaining can't bring back memories.

I throw on a robe and wrap it around my nightgown. The quartz floor is cold under my bare feet. I've got to find Zadock and talk this over with him.

I hurry through the hallways. I know where Zadock is sleeping now, in a tiny room by himself a few corridors from mine. Hopefully not for much longer. Especially if we have this piece of the puzzle.

I'm about to burst through the door, but I hesitate. The rift between Zadock and me is growing. Mostly because of Agriad, but a little bit because of me, too. It's enough that I knock on the door rather than burst in.

"Zadock?" I call. It's so early that most of the palace is dead asleep.

I'm about to knock again when the door creaks open. Zadock rubs bleary eyes. He's beautiful, and I want to throw my arms around him and kiss him, but something holds me back.

Zadock starts when he sees me. "Nors, hey. Come in." He holds the door wide, and I enter his room, not caring that Agriad would disapprove of me being here by myself in a thin robe. The room is tiny, with no windows. There's a narrow bed in the corner and a tall armoire in the other.

Zadock wraps his arms around me. "Hey."

I melt into him, feeling the comfort of his warmth, inhaling his smell. "Hey."

We stay like that for a moment, but then I can't wait any longer. I look up at his face. "I had another dream."

"A Cale dream?"

"Yes. And I saw something." Excitement rises within me. "I know why my potah can't remember. Agriad is Sustaining him and taking away his memories. He's probably still doing it. I saw it through Cale's eyes, heard her thoughts. She made it sound like an ongoing thing, something that needed to be done frequently." My mind whirs. "Maybe if we can somehow get Agriad to stop Sustaining my potah, he'll get his memories back!" Hope surges within my heart.

Zadock steps back with a sigh, releasing his arms from around me. "Are you sure? Are you sure that's what's going on? We don't know what Sustaining can do, but—"

"Exactly!" I say. "We don't know what Sustaining can do. Who's to say it can't take away someone's memories?"

Zadock frowns. "I just—I don't know, Nors. It seems like a stretch."

My heart drops. He doesn't believe me.

"I mean, what's more likely? That the trauma of traveling through an ocean of sand caused some irreversible damage to your potah's mind, or that Sustaining is messing with his head?" Zadock looks at me and shrugs.

I stare at him, hurt. "I know what I saw."

"Yeah." He rubs a hand over the back of his neck. "It's just…

Kemelah told me things that I haven't had a chance to tell you yet. She says that Sustaining can—can make someone stronger. Make them...immortal." Zadock sighs. "I don't understand it. But Kemelah says that that's what happened to her. Agriad Sustains her, keeps her alive and strengthens her, and that's why her eyes look like that. That's probably what's going on with your potah, too."

I take a step back. No. He's wrong. "You believe everything Kemelah tells you?" I grit my teeth in anger. "She's on his side, Zadock! Why would she tell you the truth?"

Out of the corner of my eye, I see satchels stacked within the cracked armoire door. I cross the room and open it. Supplies. Where there should be clothes, there are stacks of travel supplies. "You're preparing to leave."

"No one ever comes in here, so yeah. I am. Bernan stopped waiting on me, so I thought it'd be a good place to store what we need." He looks at me, excited. "I've been sneaking food from our meals and hiding it here. I found one of the kitchen's pantries, and I've been raiding it." He pauses. "Look, I think we should go now. We need to get out of here. We need to get you back home. And I just—I don't know what we're doing here anymore."

My mouth drops open. "We're convincing Sustainers to return with us. I'm not enough, Zadock. Don't you understand? That's what I've been trying to tell you! I can't do everything! And we're helping my potah remember." My eyes fill with stupid tears. "I can't go back without him. Not now...now that I know he's alive."

"I get that." Zadock doesn't move to comfort me. "I just don't know how we're going to get him to remember. You've tried everything. I think we should leave."

"No," I say. "Not yet." Why can't Zadock see? We're so close to discovering what's really going on.

Zadock looks at me with large blue eyes. "People are dying, Nors. We've almost been here the full moon cycle, do you realize that? That's how long Agriad said we had before the famine would start to get bad. Who is it going to affect? My family? Yours?" He pauses and scrubs a hand through his hair. "How long are we going to stay here? Please, give me a date."

I turn away. I'm trembling all over. Zadock puts a hand on my shoulder, but I shrug him off.

"I can't," I whisper. "I can't be the savior everyone needs me to be."

Zadock swallows. "Nors, you're all they have. These Sustainers here, they're not going to leave. Our people need *you*. There is more at stake here than the way you feel!"

The blow is physical. It hurts in my chest. I don't know how to respond.

"And what about this?" Zadock pulls a rose, an orange quartz rose, from his pocket. The flower Elandor Forged for me.

My hands go to my mouth. "Where did you get that?"

"I found it." Zadock turns the rose over and over in his hands. "When I was gathering my things out of our room. He gave it to you, didn't he?"

I nod.

"When were you planning on telling me?"

"It's only a—"

"Don't!" Zadock drops the quartz and runs his hands through his hair. I've never seen him like this. Anger rips through my gut. He's not even letting me explain.

"I've seen the way you look at him. What's going on?" Zadock turns back to me, sorrow heavy in his eyes. "Where's my Norah?"

I grit my teeth. "I'm right here. I didn't go anywhere. And I don't care about Elandor."

Zadock turns away. "Look, I'm tired. Maybe we can talk about this later."

"You don't trust me," I spit. "You don't trust me."

"Nors—"

I rush from the room.

44

ZADOCK

I stare at my plate at breakfast. Agriad decided that all the nobles would gather at a café this morning. We took several glider-carriages and paraded through the city, the Sustainers waving out the windows to people on the street. We stopped at a café—I had to ask Kemelah what that even was—and were shown to a beautifully furnished outdoor patio with tables and couches.

Cheerful fires blaze in stone pits in the center of each table, staving off the morning cold. The sun rises in a pink sky, and with yellow and orange flowers blooming all around a quartz fountain tinkling off to the side, it's paradise. It doesn't fit my sullen mood.

Speck, that fight Norah and I had early this morning was *awful*. She's so stubborn, so determined to rescue her potah. I have no idea what to do about it. Is there a way I can *make* Norah come home? I'd be saving her, but she wouldn't see it that way. She would hate me forever.

I'm seated at a table next to Kemelah, of course, and two other nobles who are familiar to me, but I can't recall their names.

The other two nobles, an older man and woman, quietly converse. Kemelah picks up a paper in front of her and scans it. She smiles when she notices me watching. "It's a menu. Choose what you want to eat from it."

"Oh." I glance over the paper, but most of the foods are unfamiliar to me. When someone comes and asks what we would like, I repeat whatever Kemelah says. I try to eat the food that's brought a short while later—fried plantains coated in cinnamon and coconut sugar, dates stuffed with some kind of nut butter, and a fruit salad with all colors of the rainbow, covered in lime and honey. I hardly even notice the tastes.

Agriad laughs and jokes with Raen and Norah at a table on the other side of the patio. Norah stares at her plate.

Kemelah notices my gaze. "You can't escape with her, Zadock." Her voice is low.

"I know." I'm getting Norah out of here, but Kemelah needs to think that I believe there's no chance of escape. "What am I supposed to do, Kemelah?" I turn toward her. She seems to be my only friend here. Besides Norah, of course. "You keep telling me, 'Don't let him Sustain her,' and 'He needs her for something bigger than this,' but I don't know what to do." I'm clenching my skewer in my hands, and I force myself to let it go. "Please," I lower my eyes to my plate, "tell me what to do."

Kemelah gives me a look of pity, her face softening. "Zadock, I—"

Raen Saranyi stands and pushes his chair back, excusing himself from the table. I stand as well, cutting Kemelah off. This is something I might be able to help with.

I follow Raen out of the maze of tables and chairs, past the sparkling fountain. Norah watches me. I try to smile.

Raen nods to the café owners and leaves through a wooden gate, heading toward a waiting carriage. I hurry to catch up.

"Raen! I mean, er—General Saranyi, wait!"

He pauses and turns. "Yes?"

"Do you...do you remember me?" I'm at a loss. Norah seems to have tried everything to get him to remember, but still. I have to try.

He looks me up and down. "No. I've seen you around the palace, but I'm sorry. I don't know who you are."

"We knew each other," I say. "Before you fell through the sand. I'm Zadock Penvaren, Norah's best friend."

He gives me a polite smile. "Nice to meet you again."

"You don't remember anything? Your wife or your daughters—"

"Zadock," Raen says. "Thank you for re-introducing yourself, but let me stop you there. I'm not going back across the ocean of water. Whatever my life was before now, it's over. This is what I remember." He gestures around him, to the people, the city. "I will not take Norah away from Agriad." He raises one eyebrow. "So please, don't ask. He will not take that lightly. It will be seen as a serious crime." Raen claps me on the shoulder as my face falls. "It's all right. Norah has a good life here. She's royalty. Can you say that about her life before?"

Raen enters the carriage, leaving me standing there as the glow underneath ignites, and the carriage takes off. I sigh.

Well, I tried. He's gone. His memories of his life before, vanished. But why? Why won't they come back?

Is there nothing Norah and I can do?

Other nobles are leaving the café patio now. They walk by me in their finery, chatting and laughing, splitting off to enter their carriages. What do the Sustainers do all day? Go about the city growing things?

If I can't convince Raen, maybe I can convince one of them.

"Excuse me, Lady," I say, not sure if I'm using the right words. A middle-aged woman in a deep navy gown twirls toward me. She looks me up and down, eyelashes fluttering. Gross.

I paste on my biggest smile. "Can I talk to you for a moment?" I watch out of the corner of my eye for Agriad or Norah, but I don't see either.

"About what?"

Here we go. "What's your name, Lady?"

"Lady Grasha, and you?"

"Zadock Penvaren." I smile. "May we talk in private?"

She winks at me. "Certainly."

I lead her on a walk down the city streets. People bustle by, carrying loads of goods. Now what?

"That stuff with the moon. So strange, right?" I try to give off a casual air.

Lady Grasha seems surprised. She eyes me sideways. "Yes. Very."

"And you are a Sustainer, right?"

"Yes, I am."

"Great Lady, the balance of the world is wrong." I don't know how else to say this. I stop in the road, letting the traffic flow around us. I'm no good at these sidestepping delicate politics. "Please, you must see that."

"Nothing that the High Sustainer can't fix." She glances behind her, seeming to realize that this is not what she thought. "Now, if you'll excuse—"

I put one hand on her arm to stop her. "Lady Grasha, would you come back to To'Rahn with me and Norah Saranyi, to help make things right? To fix the balance of the world, we need more Sustainers *there*. Please—"

Her eyes turn toward me slowly, widening in horror. "Do not speak of these things to me, boy. What you say is treason."

"Yes." The voice that speaks is familiar, and my heart sinks down into my shoes. "It is."

I peek around Lady Grasha and see Agriad striding down the street, a grin on his face. I swallow.

Oh no.

45

———

NORAH

Agriad returns to the café. I'm not sure where he went or why he hurried to excuse himself from the table, but now he's back. He insists that I come on a walk with him through the city. My skirt tangles with my feet, and my hair tumbles past my chest. I don't think I could ever get used to this.

We walk down the quartz-paved road, people bustling by, smiling and chatting, baskets of food carried on their hips. Children laugh and run in the streets. Gliders whiz by overhead.

Why can't To'Rahn be like this?

We keep walking, not saying much, just taking in the sights of the city. People cheer as Agriad walks by, and he smiles and waves back.

Agriad pauses by a fruit tree and takes a handful of sand from a pouch at his side. He's given me a similar pouch, and, at Agriad's nod, I join him in Sustaining the tree. It shoots toward the sky, faster than I've ever been able to get my Sustaining to work alone. Fruits sprout up, orange and round, and people scramble to pluck them from the branches, grinning.

Agriad beams back, and it's strange to see such an open, happy expression on his face.

"The people really love you," I say, quietly enough that I think he won't hear, but he turns to me with a smile.

"I take care of them." We keep walking, leaving the people to harvest the fruit. "I provide them the means to live the way we do in this thriving city. Along with all the other Sustainers, of course. I take care of my people because I care about them."

"Yes, I see that."

Agriad stops at a street food vendor and buys me a thin wrap. He hands it to me with a grin. "Your favorite."

I pause and swallow. He must've seen that I didn't eat much at breakfast. I take a bite. The wrap is soft, and the filling is bittersweet. Chocolate.

"Thank you," I say and take another bite. "Why are you doing this?" I can't help but ask as we continue our walk down the street.

"Do I have to have a reason to dote on my daughter?"

I keep eating the wrap—Atoille, it's so good—but the question remains on my mind.

Agriad pauses at another tree, one with bright yellow fruit this time, and Sustains with the same result. People crowd around this tree, but they also allow for the weak and small to go first, making sure that everyone gets taken care of.

"Potah, I—" I don't know how to ask what's on my mind.

Agriad turns to me.

"They love you. You are their savior," I say.

He pauses. "Yes, in a way."

I polish off the sweet wrap, and Agriad holds out a hand. Feeling like a child, I give him the paper wrapping. He puts it in a pocket.

"My people—I mean, the ones in To'Rahn, where I'm from—they didn't always love me."

Agriad stops. A jungle bird—black, with an orange and yellow beak—twitters overhead. "And now they need you."

"Yes." Atoille above, why am I having this conversation with Agriad, of all people? I should be talking my feelings over with Zadock. The fight we had this morning rips through my mind.

Agriad takes a long time to answer. So long that I wonder if he's going to answer at all. "Sit, daughter." Agriad gestures to a nearby quartz bench, and we sit. "You are angry at the way you were treated."

"Yes." It's true, I realize. A deep, burning resentment festers within me. "They treated me like an outcast my whole life. I was always looked down on, always pointed at and talked about. The only one who didn't have a sand gift. And then, as soon as I could Sustain and they *needed* me, it was different. I was revered. Loved." *And shipped around the desert to fix everyone's problems*, I don't add.

"That must've been hard for you to process," Agriad says. He seems willing to listen. Like a potah should. I have to blink back the furious tears that fill my eyes.

"It was. So hard. I don't know how to react. I feel—angry, like you said, at the way I was treated growing up. But now, they'll die without me. What am I supposed to do?" I turn to look at him. Study his face. The blue veins and pale skin, contrasting with the long dark hair, tied back in a tail now. He wears simple clothing of camehl cloth, and I wonder if when he goes out among the people, he tries to remind them that he is one of them.

It's a new perspective for me, seeing Agriad in this light.

"How can I be their savior?" I find myself asking.

"You don't have to be." Agriad reaches over and touches my hand. "You are here now, my daughter, where you belong. You can put the past behind you."

I bite back my sigh. I knew what he was going to say.

The unanswered question tumbles inside me as we stand and start our walk back toward the palace.

46

LYLAHN

All of Imwraeth's pleas to talk to the High Sustainer have been denied. We're not allowed to leave our room.

I stare out the window at the palace grounds, at the washed out moon on the distant horizon. She seems even lower, but it's hard to say if it's unnatural or part of her orbit.

Imwraeth paces the room behind me. Breakfast lies mostly untouched on the table beside him.

He stops and scrubs his hands through his hair. "Lylahn, I don't know what to do."

I stand and walk over to him. I take his hand in mine. I wish I could heal this. "We're doing the best we can."

He sighs and squeezes my hand. "I've made so many mistakes, so many wrong choices."

"What else could you have done?" I pause and realize I'm speaking to myself as well as him. "You did the best you could."

Imwraeth pulls me in close and holds me tight. "Thank you."

I take in this moment, the feel of him against me. I lay my head against his chest.

"I never thought that I would find someone like you, Lylahn," Imwraeth breathes. "You are everything to me."

The door opens, and we break apart. There are guards, four of them this time. At least the sight of their black fighting leathers doesn't make me react the same way To'Morat's red and black armor does. I wonder if I will ever have the chance to finish my quest, if my sisters' blood will ever be avenged.

"You will come with us," a tall guard in front says.

Imwraeth and I exchange glances. Are we going to get to talk to Agriad again?

"Lead the way," Imwraeth says.

We follow them down the corridors. Servants glance sideways at us, and nobles with curious expressions pause to watch us pass. We reach the great palace doors, and then we're outside, blinking in the blinding light.

The guard steps forward with quartz chains and motions for our hands.

I freeze, my spine stiffening. Imwraeth turns to the guard. "We will not be bound."

The guard doesn't move. "The High Sustainer has commanded that if you leave the palace grounds, you are to be tied."

Leave the palace grounds? I'm curious. And nervous. When Imwraeth extends his hands to be chained, I follow his lead. The slender chains are cold and heavy against my skin. The lock clicks shut, and the guard pockets the key. It feels final and unnerving.

"I must disarm you." The guard moves toward Imwraeth's shoulder to take his satchel of sand.

Imwraeth jerks back at the same time I cry out, reaching toward him with my chained hands. "I cannot be without a source of sand," Imwraeth says. "I have a weak heart and must Extract occasionally to steady it."

The guard hesitates. He withdraws his hand, and I breathe a sigh of relief. Tight-lipped, Imwraeth puts his chained hands into the satchel and Extracts.

The guard reaches for the curved quartz weapon at his side, but then he freezes, watching Imwraeth. "Keep your satchel. But at any sign of trouble, it's gone."

We're escorted to a carriage, a glider thing without wheels. The three guards take their places on the outside, holding onto rails, and the tall guard takes a seat opposite us.

He says nothing as the carriage moves forward at a rapid speed, flying through the palace gates and through the city. I stare at the people, the buildings, the sights. Nerves churn in my stomach. What is happening? Where are we going? I want to ask questions, but I doubt I'll get any answers.

Imwraeth is silent, staring forward.

The carriage slows. I glance over the side and see a crowd of people pushing to get into an enormous circular building.

"Where are we?" Imwraeth asks. "I am the Favored One of To'Morat, and I deserve—"

"The arena," the guard says. "You're at the arena."

Imwraeth and I exchange glances as the carriage inches forward.

People turn to watch us. I shrink closer to Imwraeth, trying to avoid the stares. Imwraeth reaches out, chains clattering, to put a reassuring hand on my knee. Finally, the carriage presses through the crowd.

We descend a guarded ramp and plunge into darkness. Sand glows in the guard's hand to light the way. An Extractor, then. We descend deeper into the tunnel, and then we halt.

"We're here," the guard grunts.

The guards on the outside of the carriage step down and open the doors for us. I stumble down the steps. My eyes adjust.

I gasp. Here are the To'Morat warriors who came with us. I want to rush forward and take their hands, reassure them that it will be all right, but I hold my ground. My own reaction surprises me. These are To'Morat warriors. Shouldn't I hate them?

They are trapped in a prison of quartz bars. I'm not sure where we are, except that we're underground. Torches line the walls. The warriors are silent and solemn, watching their leader. I see Danosrin in one of the cells to my left, and I almost cry out. He shakes his head.

I hear a whinny, and my heart leaps. At the end of the tunnel, I make out stables holding the retahn. Darkest Night fights against her stall, trying to get to me.

I long to help but don't know how. Imwraeth descends the steps beside me, and his breath catches.

"Will we be joining my people, then?" Imwraeth asks. "Tell Agriad Zul that I wish to continue negotiations with him. There must be some price he's willing to accept in exchange for Norah Saranayi and our safe return home."

The guard glances his way but says nothing.

My shoulders slump. Sweat makes my bangs stick to my forehead.

The tall guard gestures for us to follow him, so we walk on heavy feet down the tunnel past our friends. Imwraeth doles out reassuring words to his warriors, but I hold my tongue.

My heart sinks lower with every step.

The tunnel slopes slightly upward now, and we come to an enormous door. It's barred with quartz and locked. The head guard takes out a key and unlocks our shackles while the others keep spears pointed at our throats.

"Get your hands off me!"

I whip my head toward that voice. That voice!

Zadock Penvaren stumbles down the corridor, a guard wrangling him along. His wrists are also bound in chains. He freezes when he sees us.

"Zadock!" Imwraeth cries. He moves forward as if to throw his arms around him but then stops. "You're here! Where's Norah?"

Zadock takes in our faces with a look of joy and then anguish. "You crossed the ocean of water? How did—?"

The guard unlocks Zadock's chains. "Quiet," he says.

I'm about to open my mouth to protest, but then I hear another voice that sends chills up and down my spine.

"Ahhhh. My friends! Welcome." Agriad Zul strides down the corridor and comes to a stop in front of us.

Anger and loathing writhe within me. And beyond that, a deep, penetrating terror. We came all this way, faced so many obstacles, and it all led to nothing.

I don't know what's beyond that enormous door, but I have a feeling it's not going to be good.

"I apologize that I neglected you; I had something keeping me away," he says.

Imwraeth doesn't respond.

"Where's Norah?" Zadock says. "Is she all right?"

Agriad smiles. "She's fine."

"What's happening?" Imwraeth asks. "Our negotiations haven't reached a conclusion."

Agriad laughs, an echoing, grating sound. "Negotiations? What negotiations?" He laughs again, and Imwraeth stiffens next to me.

"It has been nice getting to know you, Imwraeth Jeriyah and Lylahn Velare of To'Morat." Agriad nods to Zadock. "And Zadock Penvaren, you as well. However, I'm afraid the time for socializing has ended." He shakes his head as if in deep sorrow. "Unfortunately, each of you has broken promises to me. Imwraeth and Lylahn, our deal was that I would leave To'Morat alone and Norah would be mine, yet here you are, coming after her. And Zadock. I've allowed you to stay here, treated you like royalty, and still, you spit upon me by trying to convince my own nobles to leave me." He tsks and shakes his head.

I see Zadock's face pale out of the corner of my eye.

Agriad smiles. "You've seen this once before, Zadock Penvaren. What happens to traitors."

Imwraeth reaches out to grab my hand, our chains clinking together. "Have mercy," he says. "Let Lylahn go. Let her stay with Norah and wait upon her. She had nothing to do with this; she is only here at my request."

Oh, Imwraeth. Agriad shakes his head. "Valiant effort, Imwraeth. But no, she will stay with you."

"I am the Favored One of my people," Imwraeth tries again. "If any harm comes to me or mine, there will be war."

"Oh." Agriad grins. "I'm counting on it."

"Don't do this," Zadock says. "Agriad—"

Agriad Zul turns to the guard. "Remove their chains. Then open the door."

47

ZADOCK

We stumble out into the glaring sunlight, my heart pounding. I know what's coming. And I have no idea how we're going to beat it.

I glance sideways at Lylahn and Imwraeth. What a shock it was to see them. How did they even cross the ocean of water? I wish I could ask. Imwraeth is whispering comforting things in Lylahn's ear. She's staring straight ahead, a blank expression on her face, a single tear making its way down her cheek.

Guards push us forward, farther into the arena. It's wide and dusty, covered in white sand. My eyes adjust to the light. Crowds of people boo and jeer at us. Agriad Zul strides past us to stand in the center of the arena.

The guards herd us forward like camehls until we stand behind him.

I scan the crowds, looking for Norah, and I see the special box where Agriad's cronies sit. She's there, sitting next to Elandor, of course. We lock eyes. Hers are filled with horror. She stands and reaches out to me, but Elandor pulls her down.

I'm in shock. I can't believe this is really happening. This is how I'm going to die. After everything Norah and I have been through, I'm going to be eaten by a giant worm.

I stand tall, trying to quell the pounding in my heart and the nausea rolling through me. I try to smile. I meet Norah's eyes again.

"I love you." I breathe the words, hoping she can read my lips.

Norah's far away, but I can make out her face and her lips as she repeats my words. That has to be enough.

"Welcome," Agriad Zul begins, "to the Judgment!" People in the crowd cheer. The sound is deafening.

"All three of these people have been found guilty. We shall let the bloodworm decide their fate."

A roar goes up in the crowd. I swallow. I don't know how we're going to make it out of this. We could run. I scan the arena for exits. There are only two. The one we came out of, and the giant one off to the right for the bloodworm. Two guards stand where we entered. No hope to make it past them.

We could try to climb through the arena stands, but even if we could somehow get over the high walls, the crowd would push us back in.

There's only one way out of this. I glance at Imwraeth and Lylahn, hoping they're ready for a fight.

Agriad's not done. He gestures off to the side, and the door we came through opens. A line of glowing Extractor platforms carrying cages full of people is paraded into the arena. Most of the cages are of quartz, but some are wooden bars; I assume that those are for the Forgers so they can't reverse Forge the bars into sand. Imwraeth and Lylahn gasp and cry out, and I am willing to bet that those prisoners are To'Morat warriors.

"We're raising the stakes." Agriad grins. "The lives of their crew members will also be decided by this match."

"Agriad, let us discuss this further—" Imwraeth begins.

Agriad rounds on him with a scowl. "No more discussions." He turns and strides from the arena. He passes the guards where we came through, and a few moments later, he takes a seat next to Norah.

I take a deep breath. In and out. Norah... I wish I would've known that this morning was my last with her. I would've kissed her and not let her out of my sight. Instead, we had that horrible fight. I swallow, ashamed and full of regret.

I do trust you! I want to scream.

"Zadock," Lylahn says, a frantic tone in her voice. "What's happening?"

I open my mouth, but a guard strides toward us. "Choose your weapons."

We follow the guard back toward a rack of quartz weapons, all varieties. The red and black armor of the To'Morat has been stacked off to the side, and it shines in the sunlight. "They are going to make us fight a giant worm thing." I wish I could be more specific. Imwraeth glances at me. Lylahn goes pale.

We are pushed forward toward the rack of weapons, and I choose a spear tipped with quartz. It's got a longer handle than I'm used to, but it's the closest thing to what I know. I doubt it's going to do me any good. I ignore the bulky armor. I've never fought wearing it before, and it would only slow me down.

Imwraeth and Lylahn glance over the weapons. "I've never used any of these," Lylahn says.

Imwraeth takes her hand and pulls her in for a kiss, and she melts into his arms before guards step forward to push them apart. Speck. I wish I could've done that.

The crowd jeers and shouts.

"Choose your weapons," the guard says again.

Imwraeth steps forward and takes an ax with a long handle and a pointed top. Lylahn copies me and grabs a spear. It's a good choice. The other weapons look too heavy for her. Lylahn pointedly looks away from the armor. Imwraeth sees her face, then ignores it as well.

The guards herd us back to the center of the arena. I grip the spear in sweating hands, sending all the prayers in my heart up to Atoille. Is there any way we can beat this thing?

Agriad's voice booms out over the arena. "Release the bloodworm!"

48

NORAH

No no no no no. This can't be happening.

I sit in the Sustainer's box next to Agriad and Elandor with a perfect view of the spectacle about to take place. The crowd's cries burn my ears, and my heart thunders in my chest. I grip the arms of my chair, watching Zadock, Imwraeth, and Lylahn stare at the enormous door on the other side of the arena.

Elandor puts a hand on top of mine, trying to be soothing, but I wrench my hand away from his.

"Potah, please!" I turn to Agriad. "Please, stop this."

Agriad turns to me with an understanding smile. The kind you give a child you have been indulging for far too long. "I'm afraid I can't do that, Norah."

Anger wars with the despair in my gut. "Please. You can. One word, and you can stop this."

Agriad gives a silent shake of his head. "Your friends have committed treason against me, and they must be tried for it. This is our way."

"But—" I swallow and lower my voice. "But you said...you said that if I did what you wanted, you wouldn't hurt him. You would keep him alive."

Why now, Agriad Zul? Why get rid of Zadock now?

Agriad turns to me, and his smile widens. "My poor, dear daughter. Did I say those words specifically?"

I scan my mind, racing through our conversations. I can't think. I can't remember. "Please." I try one more time. "Please, don't do this. I'll do anything."

Agriad's expression turns tender. The wide doors are being dragged open, and the crowd's cries elevate. "I'm sorry for your pain, but I have no choice."

Fury, white-hot. "I'll run. I'll leave. I will have no reason to stay here without him."

Elandor stiffens beside me.

Instead of a worried frown like I hoped I would see, Agriad smiles. "I'm sure you'll try."

I'm frustrated and fuming, but this is getting me nowhere. I turn back to the match.

The enormous doors are dragged open, and the bloodworm bursts into the arena. For such a bulky monster, it is fast. Its many clawed feet snake through the sand, and the central sucker whirs and clicks.

The crowd roars.

Zadock shifts into a fighting stance, his hands on the spear. Imwraeth pushes Lylahn behind him.

Oh, my friends. They came to rescue me, and now they're paying for it.

And Zadock. My precious Zadock.

This can't be happening. I can't lose him. My panic rises until I'm gasping for air.

Elandor puts a hand on top of mine. "Norah, deep breaths."

I try to slow my breathing, but it's not working. "I can't lose him, Elandor."

"Maybe they'll win..."

The bloodworm winds through the sand, heading straight for Zadock. He drops the spear and uses both hands to put up a wall of sand, redirecting the beast back the way it came. The sand wall is enormous, bigger than anything I've seen him create before.

The crowd jeers.

The bloodworm rears its head back and trumpets its anger. Lylahn screams.

"Is there any way to kill it?" I ask.

Zadock shoots knives of sand at the creature, but everywhere they hit, its skin glimmers and hardens, blocking the impact.

Imwraeth has a heart condition. He can't even run. *Lylahn can heal them,* I tell myself. So there's some hope.

But she's not a fighter. It's up to Zadock.

"Is there a way?" I ask again.

To my left, Agriad raises a fist and cheers with the rest of the crowd.

Elandor shakes his head. "I don't know. People have been fighting this thing as long as I've been alive. I've never even seen anyone injure it."

"So being accused of a crime is a death sentence here," I say bitterly. "There's no way to win." I stand. "I'm going down there. I'm going to help him." I move forward, but Elandor grabs my arm.

"No, Norah! No. There's nothing you can do." Elandor's eyes are pleading.

"Norah," Agriad cuts in. "You will stay here."

Elandor still grips my arm. "Please. You'll only die, too."

It would be better to die with him. I can't help the thought.

But I take my seat. I watch Zadock dodge out of the way of the body of the beast. And I pray to Atoille to help him figure out some way to defeat this monster.

49

LYLAHN

"Zadock!" I cry. "How do we defeat this?"

My mind is reeling. I can't believe this situation we've ended up in.

Zadock dodges venom that squirts from the mouth tube of the beast. It's focusing on him since he's the one doing the attacking.

Imwraeth reaches into his satchel. Sand glows between his fingers as he Extracts.

"I don't know!" Zadock cries. He throws a spear of sand at the thing, but it doesn't even try to evade. Where it hits, the skin turns shimmering metallic and then back to tan.

I clutch the quartz-tipped spear I chose, holding it forward, hands shaking. The boos and jeers of the crowd fill my ears. The creature makes a trumpeting noise. The sharp scent of iron fills my nose.

"Lylahn, I want you to stay back," Imwraeth says. "Get to the side of the arena. Will you do that for me?"

I turn to look at him. "I won't leave you."

"Lylahn—"

"I'm not letting you fight this thing alone, Imwraeth Jeriyah." My voice hardens in determination.

I dash toward the beast. It's enormous. Taller than the palace on To'Morat. Its skin looks sandpaper rough, and though it lacks eyes, it's covered in fine sensory hairs.

I hold up the spear, but I don't know how to use it. Fear rips through me. I don't think. I dash forward with my long spear, and I actually manage to jab the thing in the side while Zadock is distracting it, but the skin glimmers and becomes hard as quartz. The spear bounces off, and the creature doesn't even notice.

One of its six feet lurches forward, and I jump out of the way.

My heart pounds, and I take a few involuntary steps back. The claws at the end of its feet are wicked sharp. It turns toward me, sensing another threat, and the central tube of its mouth whirs and spins. Its claws click as it lunges forward.

I leap back, and I find myself lifted on a platform of sand. I cry out and fall on my rear, letting the sand support me. Zadock lifts me out of the way. I glance back behind at Imwraeth, who's frozen in horror.

"So if we beat this, we can go free?" I call to Zadock.

He raises himself up on a platform of sand next to me. "I think so."

The bloodworm turns its attention away from us, sensing weaker prey.

"Imwraeth!" I cry. "He's on the ground."

"I can't make more than two platforms!"

The bloodworm sprays a string of venom toward us. Zadock pushes our sand platforms apart.

"Get me down to him!" I scream. I plunge toward the ground, toward Imwraeth, a cry leaving my lips. Imwraeth jumps, dodging another string of venom, and he grabs onto me with both hands. Zadock lifts us and brings the two sand platforms closer together. He's using both hands, one to control each platform. There's not much else he can do while we're both flying like this. The beast trumpets, squirting poison. The crowd roars and boos.

"How do we beat this?" Imwraeth asks. He's still got both arms wrapped around me as if he can save me by holding tight enough.

"I don't know," Zadock says. We dodge out of the way again. "Don't get close to its mouth. It can drain all the blood out of you in an instant."

I gasp. Imwraeth's grip around me tightens. "We need a plan," he says.

"We can't hit it," Zadock says. "The skin gets hard instantly." He moves our sand platforms again, dodging the venom, staying out of reach of its enormous body and claws. The crowd is getting louder, calling for blood.

"What would happen if we left?" I ask. The arena is open. "What if we floated away on our sand platforms?"

Zadock hesitates. "I can't leave Norah."

He's right, I realize. If we left, we *might* be able to escape, but we could never come back here. If we were caught again, I doubt they'd give us the luxury of fighting a beast to declare our innocence. We'd be killed on sight. We'd be leaving Norah on her own, and we wouldn't get a second chance to rescue her. We could go back home and resign ourselves and our people to starving to death.

"And my warriors," Imwraeth says. "Their fates hang in the balance as well."

All those lives. I don't doubt that Agriad Zul would send them in to fight the creature after us.

"Your warriors," I say. "Is there a way to free them? Get them out of those cages so they can help?"

Zadock moves us around the arena, keeping one eye on the beast. It's still spewing venom. Doesn't it ever run out?

"It's a good idea, but those cages are locked," Imwraeth says. "And you can guess who's holding the key."

I glance toward the guards flanking Agriad Zul, sitting in his box, watching.

"We have to kill it," Zadock says, resigned. He glances toward the box, where we can barely see Norah watching us. "We don't have a choice."

"What if we try hitting it in tandem?" I say. "All of us at the same time?"

Zadock looks at me. "It's worth a shot. Maybe its skin can't harden in multiple places at once."

"Zadock, Lylahn lost her sand gift," Imwraeth cries out. "She can't heal."

It's a blow to my heart.

Zadock looks at me with wide eyes. "You can't heal?"

The bloodworm roars.

I shake my head. I have to blink tears out of my eyes.

Suddenly, the beast rears itself up, standing on its back feet. The bloodworm clicks its claws, hot saliva dripping from its mouth, its enormous head level with us.

50

ZADOCK

The beast lunges forward, and I blast our sand platforms apart. Fine sensory hairs brush my skin, and the heat of its body is searing.

Whew. That was close.

Lylahn can't heal. Speck. That's a letdown.

What happened?

I can't do much with both of us sailing around on sand platforms, so I lower Imwraeth and Lylahn to the ground. I stay in the air, hoping we can attack it from both directions.

The bloodworm turns to Lylahn and Imwraeth, who are racing away from it toward the arena's side.

"Hey, ugly!" I shout and move my sand platform in front of its face. "Come and get me." I spray sand right into the tube.

The bloodworm spits it back out, but I'm ready. I move up again, darting out of the way, and glance at Imwraeth and Lylahn. We need to time our attacks.

"You're just a big fat worm," I taunt. "I squish worms like you all the time." I doubt this thing can understand me, but it helps me feel a little bit better.

The crowd boos. I glance toward Norah's box. She's small and far away, but I can see her worried face.

Well, I've fought one giant beast for her once, why not again?

"Here we go," I mutter.

I throw spear after spear of sand, faster than I ever have before. My arms burn. I dart around the arena, keeping to the air. The bloodworm turns to look at me, spitting venom in an arc. I have to take care to stay away from the To'Morat in cages so they're not accidentally sprayed. My sand spears hit the bloodworm's skin, one after the other, but the skin glistens and hardens.

Speck. It's impossible to hurt this thing.

I'm breathing hard, sweating. Oh, Norah. I glance over to her one more time. Take in her beautiful face.

"Zadock!" Imwraeth shouts. "Together!"

The beast slides forward with impossible speed toward Imwraeth. He steps back, but he can't dodge fast enough. Lylahn darts forward to pull him back, but I sweep them both out of the way with a wave of sand. The bloodworm lands, and they're safe. They weren't crushed. That probably didn't feel great, but at least they're alive.

Speck. This is so bad.

I swirl sand in a raging storm around the bloodworm's head. It doesn't have eyes, but the majority of its sensory hair things seem to be located around that area. The beast whirls its head, and I smile. I hope I've made it so it can't "see" very well.

"NOW!" I scream.

Imwraeth stands and hurries forward. I curse under my breath. Running would be really useful right now.

Lylahn runs to the side to hit from another direction, clutching the spear in both hands.

I swirl the sand, trying to distract the beast so they can get close. The bloodworm rears its head, trying to escape the sand, but I move the dust cloud with it. I won't be able to keep this up for long. I'm going to need to drop the cloud to make an attack.

They're close. Just a moment more...

"NOW!" I cry. Imwraeth lifts his heavy ax and brings it down into the beast's side. Lylahn stabs forward with her spear, then jumps back to avoid a shredding claw.

I drop the dust cloud and throw a barrage of knives into its head.

I hold my breath and watch. Did that do it?

The sand knives hit just as Imwraeth's ax and Lylahn's spear do. The skin wavers, glimmering. But the shine isn't as bright. It flickers rather than giving off a steady glow. One of my sand knives cuts. Imwraeth's ax gets in a small wound before it bounces off. Lylahn manages a small gouge.

The beast lets out a guttural cry that mixes with the screams of the crowd.

We did it. We injured it. The bloodworm screams and rolls, legs flailing. I scoop up both Lylahn and Imwraeth in a swirl of sand. No time to make a platform. I hurl them backward to safety.

I land next to them.

"We hit it!" I say.

"Yes," Imwraeth says. "But the wounds are minor."

He has a point. The bloodworm writhes in the sand, angry, and its scarlet blood drips onto the dusty arena, but the cuts are relatively small.

It's going to take a lot more than that to kill it. Lylahn lets out a growl of frustration.

The bloodworm turns its head toward us. It stops writhing. It slithers forward through the sand, new purpose filling its movements. We've made it mad.

I'm breathing hard, panting. I don't know what else to do. I don't know how to kill this.

And I don't know how much longer I can keep this up.

51

NORAH

I sit on the edge of my seat, every part of my body bursting with adrenaline.

Zadock, my Zadock, is fighting for his life, and I sit here watching. Like it's a sport.

I can't take this much longer.

Elandor has one hand on my arm, and Agriad sits in his chair, watching with a quiet smile on his face. The nobles in the box around us mingle and chat, cheering occasionally, eating appetizers proffered by servants. It makes me sick.

"This is wrong, Elandor," I say. "This isn't how you judge someone."

Elandor shrugs. "It's the To'Sharazad way. It's how things have been done for generations."

"How old is this creature?"

"Oh, it wasn't always a bloodworm that criminals were pitted against," he says. "There have been other beasts that were brought out to fight. Whenever one is killed, a hunting party is sent to find a new one. It doesn't happen very often, though."

I can't take my eyes off Zadock. He's got his hands full, keeping himself and Imwraeth and Lylahn alive. There's not much any of them can do.

They split apart, each going for different sides of the beast.

The bloodworm whips toward Imwraeth and sprays a purple streak of venom. Imwraeth stumbles backward but can't get away fast enough. Zadock moves his arms and lifts Imwraeth back on a platform of sand, and the venom misses by inches. But Zadock doesn't have enough time to dodge out of the way of a flying claw, and it tears across his chest.

"NO!" I stand and scream. Elandor tries to pull me down, but I jerk my hand away. Agriad is frowning and saying something to me, but I don't hear. My ears are ringing. I only see Zadock.

Zadock.

He falls backward and lies in the sand. *No...* Please, Atoille, let him be ok.

Lylahn races across the sand to him. Zadock is no longer controlling the sand platform, and Imwraeth falls to the ground.

Lylahn kneels next to Zadock and does...nothing. There's no sand glow, no sign of Absorbing.

"Why isn't she healing him?" I cry.

Finally, Zadock gets to his feet. His shirt is ripped, and he's bleeding, but I think he's ok. Hopefully, it was a superficial gash, and not deep.

I sag to my chair in relief, letting Elandor pull me down.

Finally, what Agriad is saying registers. "Lylahn Velare has lost her sand gift."

What?

"She gave it up to cross the dunes of water."

My heart pounds in my ears. No. No no no no.

Lylahn can't heal.

Lylahn can't heal.

I grip the edge of my seat. Zadock and Lylahn split apart. Imwraeth is barely keeping the monster busy, poking and hacking at its legs with his axe. There's a glow of sand coming from his hands.

He's Extracting, and a lot. He must be using a massive amount of energy to keep his heartrate in check and to power his movements. When he swings the axe, it looks like he's using an inhuman amount of strength, disproportionate to the size of his muscles.

Lylahn and Zadock circle around the beast, trying to get closer. Blood drips down the front of Zadock's shirt.

I can't stop the fight. I've already tried.

Sustaining. Can Sustaining do anything here?

Agriad Sustained my hair. He's shown me that Sustaining can work on living things. I bring things to life.

But can it do the opposite?

Ambition. Ambition, Norah. Well, I want that power. I want that power more than I've ever wanted anything.

I grab a handful of sand from the pouch at my hip. I bury my fist in my dress so the glow won't be visible.

Sustaining comes easily now, in a burst of power and life energy.

I sense the bloodworm. Feel its life force. Zadock and Lylahn rush forward to attack it, but at the last minute, its blood sucker turns to Lylahn, and she can't get a hit. Zadock pushes her back with a wall of sand. Another claw flies out, but Zadock is able to throw up a wall to block just in time.

I try to force the life of the bloodworm down. Nothing. It trumpets its rage and squirms to find Zadock. It knows that he is the real threat. Imwraeth whacks it with his ax, but the bloodworm ignores him, the skin hardening and taking the hit.

I try pulling, pushing, poking at the force I feel, but nothing. It's not working.

My heart sinks, and I run out of sand. Sustaining shuts off.

I can do nothing.

5 2

———

LYLAHN

I'm gasping for air, sand coating my lungs. My movements aren't my own, powered by adrenaline and the deep animalistic part of my brain that wants to survive, *survive*.

I leap out of the way of a claw. Poor Zadock. The gash across his chest isn't deep, but it's long. He was lucky. A few inches deeper, and he would've been gone.

I have never felt so powerless. There is nothing I can do to take away his pain, nothing I can do to heal him. I tried.

Desperate, I race across the sand toward the cages holding the To'Morat warriors. Guards in black fighting leathers sit in the arena stands directly behind the cages. A few of them eye me as I get close.

All these warriors, right here. If only they could help.

The bars are quartz, locked tight with long chains. I run down the line of cells, coming to the cages made of wood for the Forgers. I rattle the bars, shaking them and crying out. Imwraeth's warriors watch me.

"We've already tried that, Lady Lylahn." Danosrin's voice. He makes his way to the front of the cage at my left.

He reaches his hand through the bars. I walk forward and grasp his hand. "We would help you if we could."

His kind expression, the hand squeezing mine, breaks something loose within me, and tears start to fall down my cheeks.

"You are strong, Lylahn," Danosrin whispers. "You are stronger than you think."

"Get back!" a guard yells. "Your friends cannot help you."

I let go of Danosrin's hand and step back.

The bloodworm trumpets, and I whip my head around. It dips its sucker down to Imwraeth.

"Imwraeth!" I scream and race forward. He stumbles backward, trying to dodge, but he can't go fast enough.

Zadock sweeps Imwraeth back with a wall of sand. The worm rushes forward, slithering across the sand, tube-like mouth poised to suck Imwraeth dry.

"ZADOCK!" I scream.

He lifts Imwraeth up in a tendril of sand, snatching him out of reach.

I gasp enormous breaths, still feeling like I can't get enough air.

Air. "Let Imwraeth attack from the air!" I shriek. Zadock glances toward me and nods.

"One," Zadock calls. "Two. THREE!"

He drops Imwraeth on top of the beast and shoots a volley of sand spears toward the creature with his other hand. I dodge through claws and feet, trying to get closer to the sand-papery skin. I stab forward with my spear, hoping that we can time our hits just right.

And then I scream.

There's a To'Morat warrior, blood dripping from his black and red armor, here in the arena. He's right in my path.

I turn and run, panicking, shaking. He's here.

I hear Zadock and Imwraeth shouting, but I can't make out what they're saying. I have to run; I have to get away.

"Lylahn!" Imwraeth cries as Zadock lowers him to the ground beside me. Zadock's shouting, sending spears of sand to distract the creature from us.

"Lylahn?" Imwraeth says. His face is covered in sand and grime, sweat dripping down his temples.

I bury my face in his chest and cry. "He's here. He's here."

Imwraeth strokes my hair, keeping one eye on the bloodworm. "Shhh. Shhh. It's all right. Who's here, Lylahn? Who did you see?"

I'm shaking, panicking, my whole being overwhelmed with fear. "The one who killed my sisters." I manage to gasp. "He's here."

Imwraeth stiffens, and his hold on me tightens. "Oh, Lylahn…"

"WATCH OUT!" Zadock screams.

The bloodworm rears its head above us. It's a blurred shape in the sky through my tears. And reality comes crashing back.

He's not here.

I stand. I grab Imwraeth and yank him out of the way as the bloodworm's enormous body comes crashing down.

5 3

ZADOCK

I throw up a wave of sand to redirect the bloodworm, and the beast misses them by inches. I look back at Lylahn, and she doesn't look good. Her face is pale, and she's shaking. Imwraeth pulls her back, away from the writhing bloodworm.

Every movement sends fire through my chest. Atoille, it *hurts*.

I'm tiring. I can feel it. My muscles are weakening; my Shaking is less finessed. It's only a matter of time before I can't Shake anymore, and then we're dead.

I swallow. The roar of the crowd and the trumpeting of the bloodworm rage in my ears. What are we going to do?

I soar over to Imwraeth and Lylahn on a platform of sand. "Lylahn, are you ok?"

She stands up straighter. "I'm fine."

The bloodworm shoots poison in our direction, and I put up a wall of sand to block. The sand in front of us turns dark, absorbing the poison.

"We've got to end this fast," I say. "I'm losing strength." I hate to admit that, but they have to know where we stand.

Imwraeth nods, red hair blowing in the wind.

"I have an idea," I say. "Can both of you get close enough to hit it?"

"We'll do our best." Imwraeth squeezes Lylahn's hand.

Lylahn and Imwraeth dash away, each going for opposite sides of the bloodworm. I'll distract it until they can get close.

This thing may have fought Shakers before. But none like me.

The bloodworm ignores Lylahn and Imwraeth. I stay on the ground before it. The bloodworm rears, the stench and heat of it overpowering. It blocks out the light above me, and terror grips my throat. The bloodworm lunges for me.

"NOW!" I scream. I muster all my strength. I give everything I have. I'm on the ground, without a sand platform to control, so I use both hands to sharpen the sand and send it in a sandstorm of knives at the bloodworm's head. I don't see if Lylahn and Imwraeth hit. I focus on the sand.

The mass of sand knives that pummels the bloodworm is staggering. It's more than anything I've ever done. The bloodworm's giant head is engulfed in stabbing daggers of sand.

The cloud of sand dissipates, and I fall to my knees, spent.

Blood drips from a dozen wounds on the bloodworm's head, making lines down its sandpaper skin, catching on the sensory hairs. It rears back, screaming in rage, droplets of blood flying. It roars, the sound tearing at my eardrums.

One clawed foot swipes out and strikes Imwraeth.

"Imwraeth!" I scream.

Lylahn is on the opposite side of the bloodworm, racing to get away from it, spear in hand. I hope she got in a hit. The bloodworm writhes on the ground.

I try to scoot Imwraeth back on a wave of sand, but I'm out of strength. I can do nothing. Lylahn dashes around the bloodworm, avoiding flying claws, and hurries to Imwraeth's side. When she sees him lying on the ground in a pool of blood, a strangled cry escapes from her throat. I step forward to help her drag him back.

Imwraeth lays on the sand, teeth gritted and eyes squeezed shut. Three deep gashes have torn through the muscles of both legs.

"I'm fine," he gasps. "I'm fine."

Lylahn's eyes fill with tears. "No, you're not." She shouts a cry of frustration. "I could heal this in moments." She grabs a handful of sand and throws it. "Why? Why?" Finally, she puts her head in her hands and sobs. Imwraeth places his hand on hers.

"I'm ok." He attempts to stand despite Lylahn's protests, but then falls back to the sand. His ripped pants are soaked with blood.

"Imwraeth, you are *not* ok." I glance behind me. The bloodworm is quieting.

Lylahn rips the shreds of Imwraeth's pants and ties them around his upper legs. "This will help stop the flow of blood until we can get you to an Absorber."

Imwraeth watches her work, face pale.

The bloodworm lifts its head. Blood drips from its wounds and lands on the sand with a hiss of steam. My heart plummets. It's not dead. After all that, it's not dead.

The bloodworm charges forward.

5 4

—————

NORAH

I grip the armrests of my seat, my hands white. My stomach is a churning mess of nerves. Imwraeth is out of the fight. Zadock will have to protect him because the bloodworm won't quit.

I hate this. I hate this so much. It's a miracle that they've lasted so long.

I turn to Agriad. "Please. They wounded it. Let that be enough."

Agriad turns to me, puts a hand on mine. "Norah, the judgment is out of my hands now. There's nothing I can do."

I tear my hand from his. No reason to go on with this charade. He's taken everything from me.

I scan the arena. Our box area is open, so sand and dust blows in, and the screams and cries of the bloodworm are clear.

Zadock lifts himself on a platform of sand to be level with the beast's tube. His arms are shaking, the sand platform wobbling beneath him. He's so weak. My heart sinks. He's using himself as a distraction, over and over. How long can this work?

The bloodworm darts forward. So fast. Zadock moves out of the way. Lylahn tries to hack at one of the feet, but it swipes its claws at her, and she manages to get back.

I stand. I step forward.

"Norah!" Elandor calls. "What are you doing?"

I look back at him. There's horror on his face. Agriad's expression is blank. His lips turn upward in what is the barest of smiles, but could I be imagining that?

I turn and run. I push past servants with trays of food and nobles with their sparkling gowns. My long hair flows behind me, and my dress gets in the way of my feet. I'll have to do something about that.

"Norah, no!" Elandor leaps from his chair.

I step up onto the quartz wall that separates our box from the arena.

And I jump.

55

ZADOCK

Lylahn cries out and points, and I turn around in time to see Norah. Norah, falling from the sky. Her skirt trails behind her, her long hair flying back.

What the speck?

The bloodworm trumpets and I spray sand in its direction, but I focus on Norah. She's falling and crying out my name. I form a platform of sand to catch her, and she jerks to a halt. I sigh in relief. I lower her to the ground and race over to her, hoping Lylahn can keep the bloodworm busy for a little while.

"Nors. What are you doing here?" I run to her and throw my arms around her, then bury my face in her neck. She smells so good, and I'm getting dirt and blood all over her.

She wraps her arms around me, taking care not to press against my chest. "I'm sorry, Zadock. About this morning. I'm so—"

I squeeze her tighter, ignoring the pain. "Me, too. I'm so sorry."

"Zadock. We're going to fight this thing together."

I pull back and keep one eye on the bloodworm. Lylahn is stabbing at the sucker with her spear, keeping it at bay. Barely.

"Zadock." Determination fills Norah's expression. "I can help you." She blinks moisture from her eyes. "I can't watch you fight this thing alone."

I can't lose her. I couldn't bear it. But I don't have much choice here. "What can Sustaining do?"

Norah smiles.

"ZADOCK!" Lylahn screams.

56

NORAH

The bloodworm storms past Lylahn and heads for Imwraeth. The smell of blood has driven it to a frenzy. He lies against the side of the arena, his face torn in pain. His legs don't look good. We have to end this. Now.

Zadock moves his arms, swirling sand to block the bloodworm, but the creature pushes through his meager efforts. Lylahn is struck by a claw. I cry out, but luckily, it seems to have only hit her upper arm. She stumbles backward, clutching the wound.

The bloodworm pushes on toward Imwraeth.

I take a deep breath and put my hands on the ground. I Sustain, and the sand glows. Power and light and life flood through me. I can feel a thousand possibilities at my fingertips. I choose one.

Out of the sand in front of Imwraeth shoots a wall of spiny cacti, the tall, tough kind with thick barbs. Shrey's favorite.

The bloodworm recoils back just before it hits the wall. I let out a breath of relief. I wasn't sure if its skin would be impervious to the spines.

Zadock turns to look back at me, his mouth open.

I smile. "Lylahn, give me your spear."

She hands it over, wide-eyed. I use it to cut the hem of my skirt off at the knee. This dress is going to be annoying to fight in, but I don't have a choice. I take another moment to cut the sleeves off at the shoulder, freeing my arms. Better. I blow hair out of my face in frustration and briefly consider using the spear to hack it off.

"Here." Lylahn pulls something from her pocket, a leather cord for tying back hair.

"Thank you." I set the spear aside and take the cord.

Out of the corner of my eye, I see the Sustainers' box. Agriad watches calmly. Elandor is in a frenzy, trying to get to me, but several guards are holding him back. Interesting. Agriad let me go, but he's ordered guards to restrain Elandor.

"Lylahn," Zadock gestures toward Imwraeth. "Take Imwraeth's ax. Guard him."

She nods, and Zadock lifts her over the wall of cacti and sets her down beside Imwraeth.

Zadock looks at me uncertainly. "What else can you make grow?"

The bloodworm turns around, giving up on the cacti. It faces us, and its sucker whirs.

"I'm not sure." The plants I've studied with Agriad flicker through my mind.

The bloodworm charges toward us across the sand.

I don't think. I put my hands on the ground and make a wall of black trees grow. They shoot up out of the ground, and I put all my strength, all my energy into making them grow faster, faster.

The bloodworm stops and moves to go around the trees.

"Norah!" Zadock calls. He lifts himself on a platform of sand. "Can you pen it in? Make it so it can't move?"

The bloodworm snakes its head around the trees. All that work and I barely managed to slow it down. Sweat pours down my temples, and I'm breathing hard.

I grit my teeth. "I can try."

I grab more sand and Sustain. I shoot up more black trees, trying to close the bloodworm in, but it's too fast. It's figured out what I'm doing and plows through the trees before they're fully grown. I'm not fast enough. *Atoille's ashes!*

The bloodworm writhes toward us in a fury. Pure terror grips me. Poison shoots from its mouth, and I leap to one side.

Zadock throws spears of sand at the creature, trying to distract it. The bloodworm turns to him.

I put my hands on the ground and Sustain. Agriad taught me about the medicinal plants of the jungle, but he taught me the poisonous ones as well.

I grow a swath of yellow oleander, the green vines and yellow flowers blooming in the bloodworm's path. The worm comes to a halt, but not before its skin comes into contact with the flowers and their nectar. Patches of skin glimmer and harden, but not enough. Where it's not able to defend, the skin reddens and blisters.

A thrill goes through me. Zadock looks at me in awe.

"Don't touch those flowers," I say.

"I wouldn't dream of it."

The bloodworm roars in pain. The poison won't be enough to kill it, but it's given us a moment to catch our breath. I reach out with Sustaining, feeling for the beast. I sense its lifeform.

I try to snuff it out, shove it down, but it doesn't seem to work. I don't even know if it's possible.

Zadock's arms shake as he works the sand. Imwraeth lies in a pool of his own blood, Lylahn standing above him and hefting the ax. This is not going well.

I grab more hot sand, draw upon more energy, making more trees grow in the creature's path, but I'm too slow.

Zadock looks at me and lowers his sand platform down. "What now?"

The bloodworm turns its attention to us, rearing up to its full height.

"I need to touch it," I say. "I think if I can touch it, I can bring it down."

57

ZADOCK

"Norah, no. It's too dangerous."

The bloodworm trumpets and plows through the sand toward us. We jump apart in opposite directions.

The bloodworm goes for her.

"NORAH!" I scream. I throw spears of sand, trying to distract it, but the worm doesn't even notice. I can't see Norah past its huge, ugly body. I can't see what's happening.

Vines grow and snap around the thing. They slow it down, but the worm pushes forward and breaks them off.

I Shake the sand under the beast's belly, trying to get in its way, slow it down. It works a little. The thing turns back to me. It lunges forward with its sucker with incredible speed.

I try to leap out of the way, and the bloodworm follows. The sucker is so close I can smell the iron emanating from it, feel the heat that resonates off the bloodworm's skin.

I spray sand into the sucker, but it doesn't care. It presses forward. It wants blood.

Suddenly, I see Norah. She's standing at the top of a growing tree. She's clutching the branches, sand glowing between her fingers. She stops Sustaining when she's level with the bloodworm.

"Nors, no!" I try to scream, but it comes out as a croak.

The bloodworm darts toward me, its bloodsucker poised.

Norah leaps from the tree onto its back.

58

NORAH

The bloodworm rears, and I scream. I cling to the fine hairs that cover its skin. Its hide is hot, and it reeks. I gag. But I manage to hang on.

I Sustain and send up cacti in a ring around Zadock. They grow, inching toward the sky. The bloodworm rears again, trying to throw me off, and I barely manage to hold on.

The worm crashes through the arena, bashing into trees, heedless of where it's going, just trying to get me off. I cling to it with a death grip. As long as I can keep it focused on me, my friends are safe.

I Sustain another handful of sand from my pouch. Heat and light course through my veins, and I direct the power at the bloodworm.

For a moment, it calms. I have time to take a breath, but I don't relax my grip. I project peace into the beast, swirling my energy into it. It goes quiet.

The crowd around me stills as well, holding their breath.

I feel the bloodworm's lifeforce. I'm connected with it in the most intimate way possible. I sense every particulate that sustains this creature's life, and, finally, something clicks.

Rather than direct energy into the creature, I funnel it away. The beast whimpers, a strangled screech. It attempts to toss me off, but its efforts are feeble. I hold on, and I don't quit Sustaining. The bloodworm slows.

Nausea makes my stomach churn. But I ignore it and keep pulling. I run out of sand, and I scramble for more, re-establishing the connection. I drag the life energy from this monster and throw it away.

The bloodworm quiets. It gives one last pitiful cry.

I feel it the moment it dies.

The body stills. The sensory hairs go stiff, and I use them as handholds to get down the thing. There's a numbness spreading through me, and when I look down at my hands, they're shaking.

I feel...wrong. What I have done is wrong.

Zadock squeezes through the cacti and runs toward me, but there's a whine in my ears, and I can't hear him. Dizziness makes my vision blurry.

Zadock grabs onto my arms and says something. I see his lips form my name, but I can't hear. And then his eyes drift upward, above my head. His mouth drops open.

I glance above me, and my heart drops.

Oh no.

Atoille is falling. I know, deep down, it's my fault.

59

LYLAHN

The moon is falling.

The spectators in the stand are screaming, running, tumbling over the arena benches.

When I glance behind me, I see Norah with her hands outstretched, the glow of Sustaining in her fingers. She's trying to fix the moon. I glance upward. It's falling, a trail of smoke and ash leaving a white path in the sky. It doesn't look like it's slowing down. If anything, it's speeding up.

Oh no.

I turn my attention back to Imwraeth and squeeze his hand. His face is pale, his skin cold like the desert night. His face is distorted in pain, and he lies in a pool of blood. He's lost so much of it.

"Please!" I turn and scream. "He needs an Absorber! Please, someone help!" Tears pour down my cheeks. I try in vain to Absorb the sand.

"Lylahn," Imwraeth says. I look at him. He's smiling. "I'm not going to die. I've lost a lot of blood, but I'll be ok."

"You say that because you're an Extractor," I say. "You feel better than you truly are. Danosrin. I have to get Danosrin."

Imwraeth meets my eyes and nods.

"I'll free our friends and bring him back to you." I kiss his fingertips.

Imwraeth cups his hand around my cheek. "I can keep Extracting. I'll stay alive."

"I'll be back soon."

I stand and squeeze through the cacti. Imwraeth can Extract energy and keep himself alive, but for how long?

ZADOCK

orah's arms are outstretched, trying with all her might to Sustain Atoille. But the moon still falls.

We're swept off our feet again by a wave of gravitational weirdness, and I wrap Norah in my arms, trying to save her from pain. We fall to the ground together. I grit my teeth against the fire across my chest.

"Zadock, it's not working," Norah cries. Her head is on my chest, her arms around my back. "Why isn't it working?"

I shake my head. "I don't know, Nors."

Her eyes are wild with fear, her face streaked with dirt. "What are we going to do?"

I help her to her feet. Everything feels specking strange. Like when Atoille is in our sky, and everything is lighter but multiplied by a hundred. I feel like if I don't hold on to Norah, she'll float away.

Norah glances toward the stands, where people are falling over each other to get away. Agriad has a group of Sustainers gathered around him. They raise their arms and Sustain.

"I have to get to him," Norah says.

"Nors, no." I turn to her. "We have to get out of here. We have to get you back home. Now's our chance to escape. Please." I hold her to me as the world tilts sideways. "Let's go home."

There's a long pause. Then Norah looks up at me. "No."

My heart falls. "Nors—"

"Zadock, I can't go. Getting me back home isn't going to stop this. It's not enough."

She glances toward Agriad, and then off to the side. At her potah.

I look back toward her, my heart racing. "Norah, we have to leave your potah. We have to *go*."

Norah meets my eyes with fire raging in them. "No, Zadock."

She turns and runs across the sand, across the tilting world, her feet flying out from under her.

Speck. I have no choice but to race after her.

NORAH

I clamber over the arena stands. Running feels strange. Atoille is still on fire behind me, tearing through the atmosphere. The stands have emptied, though I don't know where people have gone.

Zadock doesn't understand. We can't run from this.

When I glance behind, I see him tearing after me, but at least he's not Shaking sand to stop me. There's that.

I reach Agriad's box and scramble over the lip. My balance is off; the world is slanting sideways.

"Norah!" The guards release Elandor. He rushes to my side and helps me to my feet. "You—you killed the bloodworm." I brush him off and go straight to Agriad.

He's there, in the center of the box, at the head of a group of Sustainers. They close their eyes, raised hands Sustaining. Plants have sprung through the box from the ground beneath. Trees press through the wood, splitting and cracking it, and still they grow. Again, they're not Sustaining Atoille herself, not directly. Maybe they don't know how. Maybe they can't. But whatever I'm trying hasn't been working.

"Agriad!" I call. My heart leaps when I see my true potah off to the side. He's Shaking sand, trying to use it to steady the box to protect Agriad. He looks at me.

Agriad's eyes find me. I expect him to be angry, upset that I leapt into the arena and killed his precious bloodworm. But instead, he smiles. Agriad stops Sustaining and strides forward with a calm, purposeful walk.

"Norah!" He wraps his arms around me in an embrace, and I feel stifled, shocked. "Norah, my daughter, I'm so proud of you." He looks at me, and a chill goes through my spine. "You did it."

Zadock climbs over the top of the box and comes to stand beside me. Agriad glances at him with a frown. Elandor follows right behind Zadock.

"Atoille is falling," I say. "You're right, you're right about the balance of the world being wrong, and it's because there are too many Sustainers here! Please, you have to—"

Agriad cuts me off with a finger on my lips. "Shhh. Daughter, you're misguided, confused."

He goes on in a soothing voice. The rest of his Sustainers behind him continue to make plants grow, the sound of trees breaking the wood popping in my ears. The realization hits me like a slap across the face—I'm never going to convince him. Or them. It's all up to me.

I feel a dull ache settle over me, a despair sinking into my bones. What else can I do? What am I supposed to do?

"Norah." Agriad puts one finger under my chin and lifts my head. Zadock puts an arm around my shoulders, but I hardly feel it. Agriad's voice is quiet, his expression pained. "You never were going to become her, were you?" Agriad closes his eyes and takes a deep breath.

"I'm not her," I whisper.

Agriad opens his eyes. "I know. I know. I tried so hard... My darling Cale." His voice breaks, and I almost feel sorry for him.

He clears his throat, composing himself. Louder, Agriad says, "You're right. The balance of the world is wrong. I know you don't believe me, but I know how to fix this. It has to do with you." He smiles sadly. "And it has to do with me."

A chill goes over my body. What does he mean? What is he saying?

"And now," Agriad says. "You are ready."

LYLAHN

I rush to the side of the arena where the To'Morat are still trapped in cages. Some have tipped onto their sides from the shifting gravity, and our friends are crying out in the cramped space. The arena stands have emptied behind them; there are no guards in sight.

Through the bars, the warriors stretch out their fingers.

"Save us, Favored Lady!" one of them cries.

I'm not—I'm not the Favored Lady.

"How can I get you out of here?" I ask, glancing around for a key or any way to open the cages.

Gravity shudders, and my feet fly out from under me.

When I look up, I see legs and black fighting leathers. One of Agriad's guards.

He frowns down at me. "What are you doing here?"

I hurry to stand and brush off my ragged clothes. "W-we won. We beat the creature. And now the moon is falling!" I add, just in case he hasn't noticed. "Free my friends." I stand tall, willing my voice not to quake.

The guard holds up the pointed tip of a spear. "I've been told to guard these prisoners at all costs until they are released by Agriad Zul, the High Sustainer himself."

My heart sinks. "But we won."

I don't know what to do. Imwraeth needs me. He needs an Absorber. He's lying on the sand, bleeding.

Red flashes before my eyes. No. I shove the panic back.

You are stronger than you think.

What can I do here? What can I do?

"I'm going to ask one more time," I say.

I am calm. I am supposed to be here. I am in charge.

Lies.

I hold out my hand. "Give me the keys."

NORAH

"Come with me." Agriad pushes through the group of Sustainers, still with glowing sand cupped in their palms, sweat dripping down their faces. One glance behind me tells me the moon is impossibly close and getting closer.

It's going to hit the planet.

Not seeing many options, I hurry after Agriad. Zadock follows close behind. When I glance back, I see Elandor watching us go. His face is stricken, pained. But I think it's finally hit him that I've made my choice. Because he doesn't follow.

We push past Sustainers and leave the arena, heading back down the quartz road for the palace close by. The tattered shreds of my dress swish around my knees.

"Where are we going?" I plead. "How is this going to help?"

Agriad turns around. His expression is somber. Gravity jolts, and we're thrown to our knees, but Agriad stays standing. Only he seems unaffected, utterly calm. "Trust me. I know how to fix this."

I don't know what else to do, so I scramble to my feet and follow Agriad. People scream and run through the streets. It's chaos. Atoille is enormous in the sky, the deep gouges of her craters getting closer and closer. She blots out the sun, and a dark pallor falls over everything. My heart leaps into my throat.

We run across the palace grounds. Zadock breathes hard beside me.

"Norah, what are we doing?" he asks.

Agriad strides ahead of us up the palace steps.

"I don't know. I'm hoping that Agriad knows something that can stop this."

We follow Agriad through the palace and up flights of stairs, higher and higher. I'm breathing hard from the exertion, my muscles on fire.

At last, we pass through the small library that leads to the astronomy tower. We clamber up the stairs and enter the room, the highest part of Agriad's palace. Zadock glances around at the telescopes, but I continue to follow Agriad across the floor and to another door. We ascend one last short flight of stairs, and Agriad pushes aside a panel in the ceiling that allows us to go up above, on top of the tower. Zadock hurries to join me.

My stomach lurches when I realize how high we are. The people dash through the streets of the city far below us like tiny ants. I can see out past the dark jungle and to the white ocean of sand beyond. The waves are bigger than I've ever seen them, and I hope no one is out sailing in this. They'd be capsized immediately.

We are almost high enough to touch Atoille, it seems. The wind howls in rage, and I worry I'm going to be flung off the tower. It's only about a dozen paces across. A narrow, waist-high railing of quartz is all that separates us from falling off the edge.

Is this what Agriad had in mind? Getting closer?

Sand is scattered across the floor, and I gather a few handfuls into my pouch before the wind can take it away. Zadock stands close by, glancing around us in awe.

Atoille! I scream in my mind. *I'm here.* I Sustain, like I did on the ship, trying to hold the moon in place. I feel...nothing. The connection I had earlier is gone.

The moon continues to fall. Smoke and ash billow in the sky.

I put a hand over my mouth, the dread and fear overwhelming. Something I've done has caused this separation from Atoille. The connection has snapped.

Life was never meant to be Sustained away.

"What are we doing here?" I shout to be heard above the wind.

Agriad turns his attention to me. I'm shocked when I see that his eyes are full of tears.

"Norah." He tucks a strand of loose hair behind my ears. I meet his eyes, keeping my gaze hard and cold.

"How do we fix this?" I ask.

"I must ask you something," Agriad says.

Zadock puts a hand on my arm.

"What would you give to make this right?" Agriad says. "Would you give your life?"

I step back, conscious of the tower's edge behind me. "I—I don't —" I've had to contemplate this decision before, on a different edge.

The white intensity of Agriad's stare bores into me. Zadock's hand grips my upper arm.

I swallow. "I said yes to that question once before." *And where did it get me?* I wonder. I would've sacrificed my life for the people of my plateau, the same people who scorned me for being different. I would've done it because it was the right thing to do.

And now they expect everything from me.

A single tear slides down Agriad's cheek. "I accept that you are not Cale."

My mouth drops open. I stagger backward, jolted by the moon's changing gravity. Zadock steadies me.

"I tried to make you her." Agriad is oddly solid on the tower. The necklace of moonstones glints about his neck, even in the fading light. "I tried so very hard. Because Cale was my daughter. My beloved—" He chokes. "And you are not her. It seems that the balance nature has struck by creating doubles does not extend as far as I thought."

Thunder booms in my ears, and I glance to the side, wondering if

Atoille has hit, but not yet. She's falling, streaming through the planet's atmosphere.

"Agriad," I shout over the wind. No point in calling him potah anymore. "What can we do about the moon?"

Agriad stares at me for too long. "You say that you would give your life to save your people." He pauses. "Would you give your life to me?"

I take another step back. "What—?"

"Never!" Zadock cries.

"Let me explain something to you, Norah," Agriad says. He walks, circling around us on the tower. The world tilts, and we're floating off our feet. I scream. Zadock's hand is yanked out of mine, and gravity throws him across the tower to slam into the railing.

This is not a good place to be.

I collide into Agriad. "What are we doing here?" I scream.

Agriad wraps his arms around me, a furious embrace. "I love you, my darling Cale." He pushes me away from him and meets my eyes.

I hate this man. I hate him so much.

"I need to Sustain your life."

I jerk back. "What?" I breathe, my words carried away on the wind. "How is Sustaining me going to help?"

Agriad stands, towering above me. His black hair whips back and forth. "You misunderstand."

Zadock cries out, trying to fight his way across the tower floor.

"I must Sustain your life into *mine*," Agriad says. "Only then will I become powerful enough to correct the world."

"What?" I gasp. Terror squeezes my heart with a quartz fist.

Agriad doesn't have an answer. He doesn't know how to solve this.

I furiously push myself out of his arms and stumble backward.

Agriad reaches out a hand. "Come, Norah."

ZADOCK

No. No no no no no. Did he say what I think he said?

My eyes widen in horror. Agriad steps forward, and Norah stumbles back, but there's nowhere to go. He puts a hand on her shoulder, and she screams.

I lunge forward. My only thought is to get to her.

Agriad doesn't even look up from Norah. His hand jabs my arm, the glow of Sustaining emitting from the sand. Where he touches me, my arm goes weak, limp.

"What just happened?" I can't move my arm. I can wiggle my fingers, but the rest feels numb.

Norah's face is torn in pain. She's still screaming, her eyes closed.

"I Sustained away your life, Zadock," Agriad says. "But I don't have to. I cannot take your life force within me, only hers. She is a powerful Sustainer, tied to the balance of the world. It's Norah's life that I need. You must see that this needs to be done. Be reasonable."

I plant my feet. Sand swirls to my fingertips. I hardly feel the sting across my chest or the blood dripping down my stomach. "I've never been reasonable. Not when it comes to her."

I charge forward.

LYLAHN

Fear pulses through my veins.

I stand up straighter, forcing my shoulders back. Lies. My whole life has been rife with them. And once they saved my life. Maybe they can again.

Sisters. Thank you.

I become a new person. I am confident, haughty. The guard holds up his spear, but his expression wavers.

I am a great lady. "Agriad Zul will be very displeased to hear if anything happens to me."

The guard frowns. "But—you were just, you were—"

I give a tittering laugh. I nearly place a hand on the guard's shoulder, but I pull back as if he's beneath me. "Oh, that? That was my and Agriad's secret." I lean forward, hooking my finger to get the guard to come closer. He leans in. "Agriad Zul and I are working together, and you'd better not get in my way." The last comes out in a growl. "You do not know the things that will happen to you."

The guard hesitates, just for a heartbeat. A heartbeat that lasts for eternity. Then he straightens. "How can I help you, my lady?"

I smile. I am calm. Confident. "Agriad Zul will hear of your dutiful service. Now, unlock these prisoners."

☾

THE WARRIORS BURST from the cell doors, rubbing their unbound wrists. Danosrin runs to me, his hair disheveled. He glances behind me to the enormous body of the bloodworm, to the guard standing at attention off to the side. "I cannot believe that just happened."

"Neither can I." I give a hiccupping laugh. The world wobbles, and I'm reminded that our problems are not over. "Hurry, everyone!" I call. "Grab weapons, get ready. We're getting Norah, and we're getting out of here."

The warriors cheer and hurry to the side of the arena, where the weapons and armor available to fight the bloodworm are still stacked.

The guard's mouth falls open. "What? That can't be—"

"And someone watch him," I say. A To'Morat warrior puts a spear to his neck. The guard drops his weapon and glares murder at me, but I only smile.

"Get the retahn!" someone screams.

"Hurry, Danosrin," I urge. "Imwraeth needs you."

To'Morat warriors are all around me, putting on their armor. My heart pounds harder. I swallow the lump of fear in my throat. I turn to get away, but everywhere, there's red and black. Blood and smoke.

I shut my eyes and grit my teeth to hold in the scream.

"Lylahn," Danosrin's voice. "Are you all right?"

"I'm fine. Get to—" I open my eyes. I freeze.

There he is.

Danosrin has put on armor, something I've never seen him wear before. The crimson and ebony panels shine in the sunlight. Recognition slams into my brain like a spike of Forged quartz.

It's him.

It was *him*.

I fall to my knees, trembling all over. No. It can't be. This person who I worked with, counseled with, sat at meals with. Who has shown me kindness.

He was the one who killed my sisters.

Hatred courses through me. I'm shaking with it. I look up at Danosrin and meet his gray eyes.

NORAH

Pain lances through my shoulder where Agriad grips me. The sand in his hands emits the glow of Sustaining. My arm is a mass of excruciating pain, and I can't move it. What is happening?

Zadock collides with Agriad and knocks him to the ground, and I gasp in relief. The pain vanishes, but I still can't feel my arm, just a lingering numbness.

Agriad turns his efforts on Zadock with a crazed grin like this is what he's wanted to do all along. He puts both hands, glowing from Sustaining, onto Zadock's shoulders. Zadock collapses, folds in on himself like a rag doll.

"STOP!" I scream. "What are you doing?"

"What must be done. For the good of all."

I have nothing. No weapons. Only sand.

I charge forward with a scream and shove Agriad with all my might. He's more solid than I thought, but he releases Zadock. Zadock staggers back with a gasp. His face is pale.

"Zadock..." I reach out to him.

I glance down and notice that black tree branches have climbed up the tower and around Agriad's feet, rooting him in place. That's why I couldn't push him over.

I step back, and the tree branches snake backward. Agriad has reverse-Sustained them.

I take a handful of sand from my pouch. "I'm done, Agriad."

His eyes alight with anger. The white bleeds to black.

"I'm not giving you my life." I Sustain, and light fills my body. I bring up sharp cacti to get in his way, growing them out of the wood of the tower, growing them through sheer will. There's no earth here, nothing to work with, so the plants fight me, but I grit my teeth and draw more life energy. I *will* push Agriad back.

Killing him is the only option. I can't run. If it's my life he needs, he will always come for me. I have to end this.

Atoille is still hurtling toward the planet.

Agriad touches the cacti. They shrink back down into the ground in mere moments. I gasp. "That won't work, Norah," he growls, any semblance of the loving potah gone.

Zadock moans behind me and gets to his feet. His face is pale but determined. "We can fight him, Nors. We got this."

Agriad steps closer to me, his expression twisting into a snarl. "I wanted you to be Cale!" he shrieks. "I wanted to bring balance to the world together! You are leaving me no choice here."

"Zadock!" I cry. The world tilts. There's a ringing in my ears, a change in pressure. I feel as if one step could take me off the tower and make me fly into the sky. "Get out of here!"

He looks at me, his face hurt.

"We're leaving!" I say. *And we're taking my potah, too.* "I need you to get a boat. Get everything ready—"

Agriad leaps forward, and his hands squeeze my throat. They are icy cold. I feel it, the slow drain. The weakening of my limbs. The pain, radiating through my body.

"Yes," he whispers. "Yes."

Zadock screams and moves his arms, trying to Shake, but there's not enough sand. A few flurries blow through his fingertips, but the rest has been swept off the tower. "Norah, NO!"

Agriad releases one hand from around my neck and reaches toward Zadock.

I Sustain, and a sharp tree branch juts into Agriad's stomach. He cries out and loosens his hold. I gasp in relief. I'm weak all over. This isn't working. I can't win like this. I can't protect Zadock and me.

I scuttle across the tower top like a desert lizard, trying to get away. I am so drained. My sand and strength are both nearly gone.

"We'll run," I shout. "We'll run together."

A hand clamps down on my leg, and I scream. Agriad has me. I feel weaker...weaker.

Then, a thunderous sound. A boom tearing through my ears. I glance to the side. A firestorm of sand erupts on the horizon.

Atoille taps down onto our world.

ZADOCK

"**N**ORAH!" I scream.

Agriad has her. I want to Shake, because that's what comes naturally, but there's no sand. I stumble across the tower, trying to get to her, but then I'm falling, falling, and the tower ground comes up to meet me.

"Norah!"

Norah jerks her leg away from Agriad and turns around and punches him in the face with a *wham!* He's so shocked that he's still for a moment. *That's my girl.*

I lunge toward her, but I slip on the tilting world and stumble down. The pressure in my ears is unbelievable, the sandstorm in the sky spectacular. Agriad yanks my hair. And there it is again, the suffocating weakness taking over my body, my life force being drained away. I scream, but I can't move—I can't—

Sand is flying through the air now, and the desert is rippling. The tremors will hit the plateau soon. I try to stretch out my arm to Shake the sand, but it slips away. I'm weak, too weak.

I feel the icy drain of my life going into Agriad. No. Not into him. The energy shimmers around him like it did around Norah when she killed the bloodworm. He can't take my life force within him. Only hers.

"ZADOCK!" Norah screams. She barrels into Agriad, and he releases me. I fall to my knees, gasping. But it's what Agriad wanted. He catches her, grasps her skin, and she falls against him, weak.

"No!" I try to get to my feet, but the world is tilting, and I am so drained. "Norah—"

I don't see what happens, but somehow, she gets away from him.

Norah turns to me. "Zadock, you have to trust me. I need you to go."

I look up at her, dazed. "What?"

"Go! Get a boat!" Norah turns her fiery gaze on Agriad. Sand glows in her palms. Around her shoots up growth and life, a wall of thick black trees. "Trust me!"

"I..."

Agriad grins and walks toward me. He will use me against her, I know. But I can't make myself leave.

Norah looks up at me. "Go." Her eyes soften. Fill with tears. "I love you. Trust me."

Trust me.

Can I leave her alone with this monster, knowing that it might be the last time I see her?

The wall of trees behind Norah is shrinking, Agriad tearing it down bit by bit. He'll have her soon. I know. I clench my fists and scream.

"I love you, Norah."

With a cry, I turn and run.

LYLAHN

R age.

Rage blinds me.

Rage powers me.

Danosrin's the one who killed them. He's been right in front of me all along.

I grip the handle of a spear fallen in the sand.

"Lylahn?" Danosrin frowns.

I could ram the spear into his gut, slip between the cracks in his armor before he knew what was happening. I could kill him right now.

My sisters. Their faces flit before my eyes.

Their screams. Fire and blood.

I step toward Danosrin. The world is gone. It's just me and him in this white space, this blank area in time, where everything is frozen. Just me and my choice.

"Lylahn?" Danosrin whispers.

"It was you," I say. "You killed them."

"Killed who?" He frowns, confused. The warriors around us

climb onto retahn. They're ready to ride, ready to charge and push for freedom, but they wait. They look to me.

"My sisters," I gasp. "On To'Shahera. You don't even remember?"

Comprehension dawns on Danosrin's face. "Yes. I did. I killed many on To'Shahera."

His admission should make me more furious, but instead, I feel a cold numbness settling in. Acceptance of what I have to do. My vision is tinted red.

"It was you." I grip the spear. One forward lunge, one quick movement, and he'd be dead.

Suddenly, a different kind of flashback strikes my mind. Bellah, holding me and reading me stories after our parents died of the plague. I was filled with hatred then, too. A hatred that had no aim, nowhere to go. It filled me until it boiled over.

Bellah saw the deep pain within me.

"Lylahn," she would whisper. "Lylahn. Remember that they loved you. Only remember that they loved you. Do not let the hate poison your heart. Remember the love."

I fall to my knees. Tears pour down my cheeks, and sobs wrack my body. Kaera tried to tell me on the plateau, but I chose not to listen. Bellah's last words to me were this—remember my love.

I'd forgotten.

For an eternity, I kneel there, letting the pain course through my body. Trembling and crying. Letting the memories, the good ones, flood my mind. My parents had loved me. They didn't care if their sand gifts were weakened. And my sisters...they had loved me, too.

They wouldn't have wanted this.

I stand and brush the tears from my face. Danosrin watches me, but I can't look at him. A warrior brings Darkest Night forward, and I put my foot in the stirrup and mount her, my back straight and tall. I remember what Sharise said, although it feels like ages ago. *The retahn can sense who has true courage.*

"The Favored One needs an Absorber," I say.

"I will go to him," Danosrin says.
"Hurry."

NORAH

Zadock yanks open the floor panel and dashes down the steps, and my heart goes with him. I don't know if I can survive this, but at least he will be safe.

Agriad doesn't move to stop him. "So touching."

"I love him," I say. "Something you could never understand."

Agriad's face contorts in anger. The shockwave from Atoille smashes into the plateau, and I stumble to the ground. The jungle surrounding the city is roiling. I hope Zadock can find a boat that will sail.

"You were supposed to be her!" Agriad's hand shoots up, and jungle trees with vines reach out to entrap me. I cry out and leap out of the way.

The rough bark of a tree presses up behind me. I try to step forward, but then branches lock around my hands and wrists, holding me in place. I scream. I can't move.

Agriad steps forward. He takes a deep, steadying breath and wipes the moisture from his cheeks. His palm covers my forehead, fingers gripping tight. "This is what you were made for, Norah. I see that now. This is your purpose."

Needles, stabbing into my skin, all over. I struggle and writhe, but the life seeps out of me. My muscles slacken, and I stop fighting against the branches holding me. At least Zadock is safe. At least he can get out of here.

He'll hate me. I told him to trust me, and he did. He did.

"The doubles that Atoille creates, this is the reason." Agriad's black stare holds mine. "I've always been able to find them. I've been to your world before, you know."

I stop moving, trying to conserve energy. I strain, reaching into my pouch for more sand, and my fingers scrape the bottom. It's gone. Hope drains from me with my life.

"I'm old, Norah." Agriad glances to the side. The shockwave is rumbling closer. "Old enough that I thought it might be time to die. I was ready to pass on the mantle to you, my beautiful Cale." He takes a deep, shuddering sigh. "But in the past, when I felt my body weakening, I would go to your world. There used to be so many Sustainers there, oh, generations and generations ago. Many strong ones who had doubles in our world. I always knew that I could take life from them."

I glance up at him, my eyes wide, not believing what I'm hearing. "What...?"

"Oh, yes." He laughs. "You thought that the Sustainers on your world died out on their own? That was a rumor planted by me."

I'm weak, so very weak. It's almost over, I think. I can feel my body fighting him even as it gives up its reserves. I struggle. I want to get back to Zadock, my love, my family.

"They...sacrificed...themselves." Each word is a delirious battle.

"Some." Agriad nods. He's glowing, I realize. A vibrant light is seeping into his skin. My life. My light.

"Some gave themselves up to try to save your world. They would die, bringing forth life for decades. But in the end, it always served my purpose."

Hatred writhes within me.

"Oh, Norah." Agriad seems younger, his skin youthful and shining, his features softer. "Now, thanks to you, I will live. My life will continue, and, with my power and yours, I will make the world right. Your world will die, as it should." He smiles. "Balance."

ZADOCK

I fly through the city on a glider with all the supplies I can carry. I know it won't be enough, but I'm hoping that if I can find a boat, I can scavenge supplies from the city and load it up. Have it all ready to go. For Norah.

Norah...

My heart is shredded. It cost me everything to leave her there.

Trust me, she said. *Trust.*

I break free of the city walls. I can see across the black forest of trees to the white ocean of sand. The shockwave from the moon tapping down is roiling closer. The glider jolts, rocketing into the sky. My stomach drops in fear. What is going to happen when that blast hits the plateau?

I approach the boatyard. The place looks deserted, and there are several of the pointed black ships that the To'Sharazad use, along with one fat ship made of brown wood that seems out of place. I head for the nearest one.

Kemelah steps out from behind a ship. "Zadock." She doesn't look surprised to see me, only disappointed. "You're here."

I stop moving forward and swallow.

Kemelah takes in my glider, my bundles of supplies. "You're leaving." Again, no surprise. She crosses her arms and shakes her head. "I told you, Zadock. That won't work."

"Kemelah, please." The slash across my chest burns like it's on fire. "I have to get a boat ready for Norah. I have to get her back home. Look at what's happening." I gesture behind her to the shockwave rumbling closer. "This is because of Agriad, because of the things he's done. I need to get Norah back." I've never been eloquent or good with words, and I'm desperate right now. Desperate to make her see.

Kemelah looks...sad for a moment. Behind her, from the boatyard, walks out a group of a dozen warriors. Their eyes are blank and white.

A dozen warriors. Against me, exhausted and wounded.

"Come with us," I plead. "Leave Agriad. He's forced you to serve him for this long? So end it! Come with us."

She shakes her head. "I can't."

"Yes, you can! Leave—"

"I physically cannot leave To'Sharazad or get farther from Agriad than I am now," Kemelah snaps. "Because he's Sustained me—us—" She gestures to the warriors around her. "—for so long, we are tied to him. I can't go."

My heart sinks. "Then please, let me go."

"I can't. I'm sorry. He will hurt me." Kemelah sucks in a sharp breath. "You don't know what kind of torture a Sustainer is capable of."

I climb off the glider and set down my packs. Sand swirls through my fingertips.

"I will get that boat, Kemelah," I say with a fierceness and intensity I didn't know I had.

Her white eyes turn steely hard. "Zadock, don't make me do this. I don't want to hurt you."

I bring sand up, forming a dozen knives. The warriors prepare sand. Some bring blowguns to their lips.

The shockwave hits.

The boat house explodes. The plateau growls and breaks, and the ground beneath my feet is torn in upheaval.

I scream.

71

LYLAHN

We tear through the city, flying on our retahn. I scanned the arena and the stadium for Norah and Zadock but didn't see them anywhere. We just have to hope that they make it to the ship.

I have never urged Darkest Night to go so fast. I push her harder, one hand on her neck, whispering in her ear.

It's exhilarating.

Despite everything, I feel free. I'm soaring down the quartz road, the wind blowing my hair wild behind me, Imwraeth at my side, and a host of To'Morat warriors in full armor behind me.

I don't fear them.

Danosrin is there, at my left, eyes focused on the road ahead. My heart squeezes when I see him, but there are no visions. No flashbacks. My sisters would've wanted me to live in love.

I glance to the side at Imwraeth. I love him, and it's enough.

I let my need for revenge die. I let it die with a scream into the wind.

The people of To'Sharazad cry out and run every which way, pointing at the shockwave up ahead. The moon has touched the desert.

The shockwave hits the plateau, and sand and rock explode into a cloud of debris. It rolls over the black forest, tearing apart trees like they're twigs. It hits the city wall, and the magnificent quartz barrier cracks and breaks, falling in huge chunks onto the city it once protected. I hear the screams even from here.

I slow the retahn and signal for the others to do the same. Imwraeth reaches into the satchel at his side, sand glowing in his fist.

The shockwave slams into us.

It rolls through the retahn and overturns their feet. I fall from Darkest Night, and I'm pulled into the sand and rubble. I scream, inhaling a lungful of sand.

Fear makes me hyperventilate, clawing through darkness and grit.

Then, a hand grasps mine, and I come up for air. "Imwraeth!" I cry.

But when I open my eyes, gasping, it's Danosrin who grips my hand. I look at his face. Pause. "Thank you."

He nods, solemn.

Imwraeth surfaces next to me, debris sliding off his clothes. Most retahn, thankfully, scramble to their feet, but some stay down with broken legs or other wounds. Danosrin moves among them, grabbing sand and Absorbing. I turn away.

"Lylahn!" Imwraeth scrambles to my side. I watch the city behind us, the destruction rolling through it, bringing down homes and streets. It hits the palace, and the walls crumble.

"Go!" I cry.

We can't ride the retahn over rubble, so we do our best to lead them on.

I pray to Atoille that there's an undamaged ship we can use to get home.

72

ZADOCK

A dart whistles through the air, dangerously close to my ear, but I manage to duck. Kemelah swirls her hands, Shaking sand. She's strong. I know this from all our practice sessions.

This is not going to be an easy fight.

I shoot sand knives into the dozen warriors emerging from the boats. They drop and cry out, and one hits its mark.

I'm already breathing hard, already exhausted from my fight with the bloodworm and my ride through the city.

I stand on shaking legs, sand swirling around me in a storm.

This is for Norah. I can do anything for Norah.

"Kemelah, let me go."

She scowls. "You know I can't. Don't make me do this."

She Shakes the sand beneath my feet. I feel it shift and move out from under me. Darts whistle through the air, and it will only take one hit to bring me down. I bring up a wall of sand for cover with one hand and steady the sand underneath me with the other.

A male warrior leaps out of the wreckage and strikes at me. I take a whip of sand and wrap it around his neck, yanking him backward. He screams.

More darts sail through the air, so I lift myself up on a platform of sand to get above them. I am the strongest Shaker on all of To'Rahn.

Time to show them what I can do.

I sail through the air, moving through darts and spears of sand. A few warriors are Extracting, I can tell from the glow, to make them stronger.

Kemelah's eyes are on fire as she raises herself up to my level.

"All right," she says. "We're doing this."

Kemelah throws a dagger of sand in my direction, and mid-flight, it glints steely hard, becoming quartz. One of the warriors below me is a Forger.

I can't control this knife, can't direct it away, so I sail to the left. My heart thunders in my chest, my muscles are tense and taut, my whole body burning with adrenaline. There's no room for fear.

A dart whistles up behind me, and I duck. I don't know how long I can keep this up.

For Norah.

Kemelah brings herself closer and assaults me with a wall of sand. I fling up my hands and direct it back toward her, and she hurls it to the side.

Flying on the sand feels strange. Gravity is definitely off. My movements take me higher than I'm used to, and the platform is hard to control.

Kemelah launches spear after spear of sand up toward me, each becoming quartz, and I maneuver out of the way.

But then, behind me, something strikes.

I cry out and tumble from the sky, losing control of my sand platform. Something sharp is lodged in my shoulder blade. Blinding pain and panic strike me.

Another warrior lowers himself on a platform of sand. He came up behind me.

I fall to the ground, and Kemelah lands beside me. She shakes her head. "You shouldn't have chosen to fight, Zadock."

With a cry, I jerk the quartz knife out of my shoulder. I try to push myself to my feet, one hand on the wound, but Kemelah shoves me down with a blow of sand.

"I didn't want to have to do this." Kemelah nods to a warrior, who puts a blow gun to his lips.

I try to Shake the sand off me, but I'm so weak. I can't lift it. I'm trapped.

"Kemelah, listen—"

She nods. "But at least the poison will be quick and painless."

The warrior inhales.

"Don't do this," I plead, struggling beneath the sand she's holding in place to keep me down. The warriors gather around her in a circle, watching.

I try in vain to Shake, but my strength is spent. "I'm—"

From out of the wreckage, the warriors of To'Morat ride their beautiful retahn, armor sparkling in the sunlight, spears held aloft. With a cry, they charge toward the To'Sharazad.

Lylahn grins at me from their head.

Relief floods through me. "I'm not alone."

73

NORAH

Agriad reaches out to take the last dregs of my life. I'm still trapped by the trees he's made grow, the rough branches tight around my ankles and wrists. I can't fight him, and I'm so weak. Energy slips from me.

No. No no no no.

Out of the corner of my eye, through the pain and terror, I register that the rumbling shockwave from Atoille is getting ever closer, closer. It hits the wall around the palace and cracks it into pieces. The grounds roll and break.

It slams into the palace.

Agriad cries out and lets go, giving me blessed relief. He screams and slides across the tower. The palace foundations shiver and fracture. The tower tilts. I cry out, but the branches trapping me hold fast. The wind shrieks, and with it, white dust. Dust from the ocean of sand.

I open my fist and let it coat my trembling hands. I Sustain. Pure power flows into me, and I Sustain the life out of the trees that are holding me. They shrink down until I'm free. Agriad gets to his feet, leans against the tower railing for support. The tower is at an angle, but it seems to have stopped tilting for now.

"You are done, Agriad." I stand tall and straight. "Your time is over." My limbs feel weak, completely drained, but I take shuffling steps forward, my hands alight with sand. "You will never hurt anyone again."

I put my hands on Agriad and Sustain. My own energy flows back into me with a jolt.

Agriad growls. He grabs onto me, and sand glows between his fingers. "No!" There's a war between us that lasts for eternity. He fights to take back his power, but I pull and pull. He's fighting to keep himself alive while I'm fighting for so much more. Zadock. Potah, Motah, Shrey, all the people I love.

Sand on the wind covers my arms, and I use that, taking it within me. I feel it when the balance shifts between us, and I have more of the power. Agriad's face twists in horror, and he screams. "Norah! Please..." He fights to get away, but I grip his arms with a newfound strength.

Just like I did with the bloodworm, I tap into Agriad's life energy. It's even easier, maybe because he's like me.

Agriad goes limp, weak. "My daughter...my darling..."

It hurts. It hurts my heart to hear those words, to imagine them coming from not him, but my true potah, who's been here all along.

Agriad's eyes meet mine as he falls to his knees. He's aging, skin growing wrinkled and spotted. Rage distorts his expression, and he surges forward, fighting back.

I take more sand within me, using every particle on my face and exposed shins, and shove him down. Agriad sinks to his knees.

What I'm doing feels wrong. Life is not supposed to be Sustained away. I know that. I hope Atoille will forgive me for this. I'm trying to do what's right. I'm trying to make the balance of nature *right*.

The glow of Sustaining fills me, and I *pull*.

Agriad's eyes go enormous, and he falls to the tower floor. He writhes, his body wrinkling and drying like lizard meat left too long in the sun. He seems to rot in three heartbeats, becoming a dried husk. My stomach turns over, and I collapse to the ground. My mind is weary despite the life energy coursing through me.

It's over. He's gone.

I feel his power. It's there before me, nebulous. The power of hundreds of Sustainers, harvested over centuries.

I could take it.

But there's a wrongness, a darkness swirling about the power. Agriad is the reason everything is out of balance. His choice to Sustain his own life by taking from others has caused this.

The wind rages around me, louder, faster. Atoille is still colliding with the planet. Off to the side, I see her, booming into the desert, jets of sand and dust flying. Our world is being torn to shreds.

I touch Agriad's power. The pure power of Sustaining.

It burns and it freezes. It fills me with life at the same time it sucks me dry. I gasp. It's mine. To do with what I wish. A heady giddiness fills me. I can do anything. I am the most powerful person in the world.

I feel...everyone. Zadock. He's down by the boats, fighting a group of To'Sharazan warriors. Imwraeth and Lylahn battle alongside him. Every pinprick of life, I feel it.

Potah.

I find him, and I feel him. His mind is there, a comfort and a familiarity. He's—

"Norah."

I gasp and turn.

He's here.

Potah glances at the husk of Agriad and then at me. His eyes go wide in surprise.

He kneels. "High Sustainer."

My eyes fill with tears, my heart dark with sorrow. "Potah."

I could heal him.

I can feel the darkness in his mind, the darkness put there by Agriad. I could take it away easily.

But somehow, I know. I can't have both. I can heal my potah or I can heal the world.

He looks up at me. "Norah. What can I do to help you?"

My name in his mouth is too painful. I reach out. All I have to do is touch him. That's it. And the blackness Agriad put into his mind would be gone.

I could do this one thing for myself. I could have him back.

I once chose to give up my life for my people, and all it got me was their expectations.

It was a hollow, lonely feeling.

I didn't want to be revered. I didn't want to be their savior, when before I had been nothing. *Nothing.*

With all the power of the world, I see Zadock. He's fighting to get us a ship. I connect with his mind for the briefest instant.

You're not nothing, Norah. You were never nothing.

I reach even farther, across a white ocean of sand and an ocean of water, to the orange desert that I know so well. I find Motah's mind and Shrey's easily, feel their love in an instant, even if they don't know what's happening.

You're not nothing, Norah. You were never nothing.

With a scream, I turn toward the moon.

Atoille. Take it.

I give it up. All the power in the universe. I give it up.

There's a flash of brilliant light, and gravity shifts. I can't see. I can't feel. The power zaps from my body, draining me in a single breath. I collapse to the tower and fall across the floor, barely holding onto consciousness. The world is spinning out of control.

I feel myself slide through the tower railing and fall over the side, open air below me. I scream.

A hand reaches out and grabs mine.

74

ZADOCK

The To'Morat are ferocious.

They charge forward, teeth bared, spears aloft and sand ready. I shoot sand at Kemelah while she's stunned and push her backward.

The To'Morat clash with the To'Sharazad, a flurry of battle cries and screams.

Lylahn is at the head, wielding a spear. Her form is not great, but she's on a retahn, and that gives her some advantage. And she's fierce and fearless.

I smile.

"We cannot let them take a ship!" Kemelah cries. The warriors of To'Sharazad who are left rally around her.

The fight rages on. Strength renewed, I aim spears of sand at two warriors converging on me, and then I sail above the battle to get closer to Kemelah. Lylahn and Imwraeth fight beneath me. I see her directing warriors to attack.

"Kemelah, stop this!" I lower my sand platform. "We don't want to fight you. Just let us go."

Kemelah looks up at me. She opens her mouth.

Suddenly, the To'Sharazan warriors stop. All of them. They look at each other with horrified expressions. Gasps sound through the crowd. Lylahn gestures for the To'Morat to hold.

The To'Sharazan warriors are crumbling away to dust. Their skin flakes off in bits of ash, like flakes from a burned log of wood. Like sand blowing in the wind.

I cry out and take a step back. "Kemelah. What's happening?"

Kemelah looks up at me, horror in her blank eyes, but then they soften with understanding. She gives me one tiny smile. "He's gone," she whispers. "I'm free." Her skin splits and rips like paper.

"Kemelah!" I cry.

"Goodbye, Zadock." She sighs, her form shifting into fluttering particles. To'Morat warriors around me murmur and step back.

The pieces of Kemelah blow away in the wind.

The To'Morat cheer, and Lylahn and Imwraeth scrabble down from their retahn to embrace. I breathe out a heavy sigh. It's over.

Suddenly, a blinding light fills the sky.

I shut my eyes against the brightness. There's ringing and popping in my ears. The world shifts and tilts, and warriors cry out. I stumble and try to open my eyes to see what's happening, but it's just *so bright.*

Finally, the redness over my eyelids fades, and I blink my eyes open. Warriors around me open their eyes in a daze, stumbling over wreckage. Imwraeth still holds Lylahn in his arms.

The moon is in the sky again.

Norah did it. I gasp and grin. Somehow, she did it. The To'Morat around me cheer.

I glance back up the jungle path. The tower of the palace is visible in the distance, tilted at an angle.

"C'mon, Nors. C'mon."

I decide to scrounge for the lost supplies, sifting through rubble to see what I can find. Imwraeth turns to his warriors and organizes a scavenging effort to gather from the city. One of the To'Morat, a tall man with a long face, checks over everyone and Absorbs away their injuries. He puts his hands on me, and the tear across my chest reseals, the throbbing pain in my shoulder blade vanishes.

I let out a sigh of relief and hold out my hand. "I'm Zadock."

"I know." He smiles and shakes my hand. "Danosrin." He moves on to continue healing.

Lylahn pats her retahn before it's led away. "Where's Norah?"

"She's coming." I keep my gaze on the path. "She's coming."

We wait. Many ships were damaged in the collision, but a few are still sailable. Everyone's loaded onto the fat ship that I assume was To'Morat made, and we wait. Lylahn, Imwraeth, and I stay on the path and stare. To'Sharazad seems quiet after what happened. The wall is rubble, the city destroyed.

A figure emerges from the dust.

"Norah!" I cry and run forward. *It's her! She's alive!* Her face is pale, and she's shaking.

"Zadock!" She runs toward me and falls into my arms, sobbing. I stroke her hair and hold her tight. Relief floods my body. "Shhh," I say. "It's over. It's over. You did it."

"He won't come with me," she whispers. "He won't come with me."

I rest my head on top of hers. "I know."

"I took this from Agriad." She holds up her hand, green light shining through her fingers.

The moonstone.

I catch my breath. "Well, that will be handy on the journey home." I pause. "What about orange and purple?"

Norah sighs. "I can't leave the people here with nothing. They need something to power their sand gifts and to rebuild. I left the orange and purple moonstones with—" She chokes. "With potah."

I hold her tight in my arms.

Norah looks up, beautiful, eyes full of tears. Her face takes on a grim determination. "Let's go."

She takes my hand and walks onto the ship.

75

LYLAHN

After days of travel, the ocean of water swells and crashes before us, making our barge seem insignificant and small.

My whole body stiffens at seeing it again, but Norah has assured me that now that she has taken the green moonstone from Agriad, traveling through the water will be much easier. I'm still spending the trip strapped in below deck.

I start down the steps, but I feel a hand on my shoulder. I turn.

Norah gives me a tiny, sad smile. "I hear...that you don't have a sand gift."

The pain twists within me. Sometimes, it still strikes me out of nowhere. It's gone. My Absorbing is gone forever.

"If anyone understands," I find myself saying. "It's you."

Norah's hand on my shoulder squeezes. "It's hard. So, so hard. And I'm so sorry, Lylahn. You sacrificed so much to rescue me."

I want to say that it was worth it to save her, to save both our peoples, but the words get stuck in my throat.

"Nothing makes that kind of pain better," Norah says, removing her hand.

I can only nod.

"I'm grateful to you for everything." Behind Norah, the crew scrambles about, taking down the sails and readying the ship to cross the ocean of water. The roar of the spray grows louder. "You have so much to give, Lylahn. You are not your sand gift. And you are not defined by the loss of it."

Tears fill my eyes. "Thank you, Norah."

She turns to help the crew prepare the barge, and I finish making my way down the stairs.

Imwraeth is waiting for me, already sitting down, the straps of his chair loose around him. The glow of Extracted sand lights up his face. He pats the seat next to him, and I take it.

"I'm surprised you're here," I say, snapping my buckles together. "I thought you'd be up top helping everyone get ready."

"Some things are more important than that," he says, looking at me.

My heart flutters.

"Lylahn...are you all right?"

I reach out and take his hand. I'm not going to hide the hurt. Not anymore. Imwraeth needs to know. Everything. "It was Danosrin," I say. "It was... I can't..."

Imwraeth scoots closer and wraps his arms around me. I bury my face in his chest. "Shhhh."

Finally, I let it all go.

I cry for my sisters. I cry for my friends and neighbors who were slaughtered. I cry for my simple life on To'Shahera, reading books and caring for camehls. I cry for my utter helplessness, for the feeling that it should've been me. I should've been the one to die.

I don't hold back. I sob. Imwraeth holds me tight.

"I've been getting flashbacks," I say. "Every time I see black and red armor, I'm thrown back to when they were killed."

Imwraeth's arms tighten around me.

It is so hard knowing that I'm burdening him, but this load can't be lifted by only me. Not anymore. "I was planning to find the warrior who murdered my family and kill him." The words strangle my throat, and I take a moment to breathe. "I kept a knife under my pillow. Danosrin woke me one morning, and I—I stabbed him."

Imwraeth jolts with surprise, but he says nothing.

"I healed him right away, of course, and I begged him not to tell you." Another tear falls down my cheek. "I didn't want to burden you. You were already going through so much."

Imwraeth tilts my chin up to look at him. It's hard to meet his eyes. "Lylahn." He pauses for a moment. "You are more important to me than anything. Don't you know that?"

"I know," I say. "I know, Imwraeth."

Imwraeth nods for me to continue, and I tuck my head into his chest. "I should've told you all of this sooner. I shouldn't have tried to bear it alone."

Imwraeth kisses the top of my head. "I'm glad you're telling me now."

"I don't—" I swallow. "I don't know how to forgive him."

Imwraeth cups my face in his hands. His thumbs wipe away my tears. "It's going to take time to heal, but I'm right here with you."

When I let out a breath, some of the hurt ebbs away. I look into Imwraeth's perfect, dark eyes. "I know."

He leans down for one soft kiss.

NORAH

At long last, To'Morat is in sight.

Atoille is a washed-out orb fading into the blue sky, just rising on the eastern horizon. But she's there. The moon is stable.

We traveled during the day as well as the night for the last stretch of the trip. Everyone is eager to be home, anxious to see how our families are faring.

The plateau on the horizon gets closer and closer. I stand near the edge of the barge, watching, comforted by the familiar orange sand.

Zadock comes to stand by my side. "We're almost there."

"Almost there," I repeat.

It feels like a bitter homecoming. I don't know how I will face Motah. How I will tell her that Potah is alive, he's alive...

I look down, the hurt cutting my heart all over again. Zadock puts an arm around me. "I'm here with you, Nors."

I lean into him.

"Nors..." Zadock begins. "Your dad's eyes—they were blank, like Agriad's. Like Kemelah's. Did he—?"

Zadock told me what happened in the shipyard at To'Sharazad.

What happened to Kemelah and Agriad's warriors when I took his life force.

"He's all right." I shake my head. "He wasn't affected."

The barge rocks gently beneath us.

"I'm so relieved," Zadock breathes. "Why do you think that was?"

I shrug. "I don't know. Maybe he hadn't been Sustained as long as the rest of them. Maybe it's because he was touching me, and my Sustaining protected him. I—I fell, Zadock. I slipped off the edge of the tower."

Zadock's grip tightens around me, and I hear his sharp intake of breath.

My eyes fill with tears. "And Potah was there to catch me."

Zadock swallows. "I'm glad you're all right. I'm glad we're going home."

"Me, too." We still failed in so many ways. I am still only me, the lone Sustainer on this side of the world working to make things right.

I find that the thought doesn't fill me with knots of worry like it used to. I will do my best to help my people, and that is enough. It's who I am.

And now, without Agriad harvesting and hoarding centuries of Sustainers' power, maybe things will be easier. Bringing balance to the world might not be out of reach.

I look into Zadock's eyes. "Zadock, I'm—I'm so sorry. For the things I said. For all of it. I put you through so much, I—"

"Nors." Zadock turns to me and takes both of my hands in his. "I'm sorry, too," he says. "I should've trusted you all along."

The sand waves are a calming swish against the side of the ship. "Are we ok?"

Zadock smiles. "Of course we are, my wild girl."

☾

WHEN THE BARGE docks on the lip of the plateau, Shrey and Motah are waiting, watching the ship come in. They're here, in To'Morat!

Right away, I notice the expanse on the edge of the plateau is covered in dead, brittle plants.

Shrey bounds across the sand, breaking through shriveled stems, her blonde curls flying behind her. I descend the ramp, and she throws her arms around me.

"Norah!" she shrieks with delight. "You're home!"

Shrey feels wafer-thin, like she could float away in the desert breeze. I feel sick thinking of what everyone went through while we were away.

Motah's cheeks are hollow, and her eyes are bloodshot, but she stands tall, and there's a smile on her face.

"Motah." I throw my arms around her. She holds me tight.

When I look up, tears are pouring down her cheeks. "Norah. I was so worried. We didn't know where you were or if you were coming back—"

"I'm here, Motah," I say. "We made it. I'll tell you everything."

Behind me, Imwraeth directs his warriors to start unloading. I see out of the corner of my eye the people of To'Morat emerging from homes and cheering at the sight of our return.

I have a lot of work ahead of me. Even though we fixed the world, it's still just me, the lone Sustainer trying to keep everyone alive.

But.

Something *has* changed.

I entrusted Zadock with holding the green moonstone once we got through the dunes of water. He's keeping it in a pouch at his side until we can council together with the leaders of both To'Morat and To'Rahn and decide what to do with it.

I don't need it anymore.

I bend to grab two handfuls of sand, looking around at the charcoal husks of plants littering the plateau's edge. People stream from the city, exclaiming and pointing at me. Others go to help unload supplies and retahn down the ramp of the barge, grateful that their warriors have come home safely.

I Sustain the sand.

Love. I'm full of it, to bursting.

Gasps sound around me. The withered plants go from brittle and black to firm and green, blooming in full health. Red, spiny bristlebrush fruit pop into existence at my right. Yellow bushels of plantains spring from the ground at my left.

Date palms shoot upward, their spiny branches heavy with brown, squishy fruit. Shakers raise themselves up on platforms of sand to gather it, laughing and tossing sweet dates to waiting people below. The entire expanse of the plateau becomes something that would rival To'Sharazad's deepest jungles, every inch of space crowded with plant life. I direct it all, smiling.

Sustaining feels right again. If anything, I'm even more powerful than I was on To'Sharazad.

People weep with joy and walk among the plants, gathering and eating straight off the bushes. Zadock looks up from helping to pick plantains to give me an enormous grin.

I am only one person. But I will do what I can, and that is enough.

When the sand I've gathered dissipates, Sustained away, I take a break and turn to my motah. Her eyes are shining, and the pride on her face sends a surge of joy through my heart. Shrey looks up at me with a grin, red berry juice staining her teeth.

I step forward and take Motah's hands into my own. Sorrow closes in on the brief happiness I felt.

"Motah." I look into her dark brown eyes. "There's something I have to tell you."

77

———

ZADOCK

Two moon cycles later

I sit at my workbench, tinkering with some shards of quartz. Motah added this bench to my bedroom once I was received into the guild of engineers, and I love it, even though I haven't had much time to use it lately. I'm trying to build something new, but it's not coming together like I want. My brain seems backed up. Filled with thoughts of Norah.

For a week, we stayed on To'Morat, helping rebuild and restock, and then we made the three-day journey to To'Rahn. Norah is Sustaining like never before, trying to fix everything, save everyone. We've rotated through all the desert nations, bringing life and food to them all. But it's never enough. Norah can only do so much.

I pound with my hammer over and over. Nothing's working.

I throw it down in frustration. Norah's been so distant, so distracted, so...sad. I just don't know how to help her.

I cross the room and lie back on my bed. I stare at the quartz ceiling.

Atoille's back in place and solid, no more gravitational weirdness.

And with Norah back, food is growing once more. Both our families made it through. I should be happy.

There's a soft knock at the door.

I sit up. "Motah?"

The door creaks open, and there she is.

Norah.

She's back to her plain brown V-neck shirt, laced up at the front. She's wearing brown pants and sandals, her usual clothes. No more dresses flowing about her feet, no more fancy hair and quartz jewelry. Her hair is back to its normal length, just touching her shoulders.

She's the most beautiful thing I've ever seen.

"Norah." Her name is soft in my mouth.

She smiles, a shy, quiet smile. "May I come in?"

I scoot over and make room for her to sit. She enters the room fully, and she's holding—

"I brought you a gift," Norah says.

I grin. "You brought back a glider? How?"

Norah crosses the room, a new elegance in her walk, and sets the glider on my desk, where she knows I'll want to examine it later. Figure out how it works. Then she sits next to me.

"I grabbed one as we were loading up the ship with supplies to leave To'Sharazad," Norah says. "Shrey wanted to try it out for a little while, which is why I didn't give it to you right away." She smiles. "If anyone can figure out how to recreate these, it's you."

I beam. "Thank you." I take her hands in mine and run my thumbs over her fingers.

"We're both different, aren't we?" she asks after a moment. "After what we've been through."

I put my arm around her shoulders and hold her close. "Yes," I say. "But I don't think that's a bad thing. Our experiences shape us. Make us who we are."

Norah breathes in and out. "Who am I, Zadock? Who am I without him?" A single tear drips down her cheek.

My heart hurts so much for her. I lift my thumb and wipe the tear away. It was so painful for Norah to tell her motah about everything that had happened and what she chose. Her motah just held her. Said she did everything right, everything right.

But something's different in Norah's motah as well. She goes to the plateau every night and stares out over the horizon. Just stands there for hours, watching the sand.

"You're my Norah." I don't know what else to say. "Like you always were." I lift her chin. "We have the future together, and that's what matters."

She smiles, and my heart lifts. "I love you, Zadock Penvaren."

"I love you, Norah Saranyi. I want to marry you." My breath catches. "Soon."

Norah's smile widens. A faint blush creeps into her cheeks. "Soon," she repeats. "We never got to have that dance." Norah bites her lower lip and watches me.

I smile and stand, then help her to her feet. "My lady."

She grins and places my other hand around her waist, then puts her hand on my shoulder. There's no music, but we move around the room to an imagined rhythm. I'm clumsy. I haven't practiced this as she has. But the feel of her waist in my hand, and her eyes staring into mine... It's everything.

I squeeze her hand, heat igniting within me at that simple touch. Then I dip her, as I watched Elandor do. Norah gasps and laughs out loud. I grin, happiness jolting through me at her genuine laugh. I haven't heard it for a while.

I lift her back up, clumsily, and Norah laughs again. I pull her in close, and we sway. Norah rests her head on my chest. I close my eyes, savoring the feel of her.

Norah pauses and looks up at me. Her dark brown eyes soften. She wraps both of her arms around my neck and buries her face in my chest. I hold her tight to me like I can push back the world, the pain, if I just hold her tight enough.

"I miss him," Norah says softly.

"I know," I whisper back.

She pulls away to meet my eyes. "But I'm going to be ok."

I press my forehead to hers and breathe in her smell. I bend my head toward her, and our lips touch with soft, sweet kisses. Then faster, more urgent, hungry for each other. I tangle my fingers in her hair, and her arms wrap around my back. A husky moan escapes my lips.

I can't get enough of her. I will never get enough of her.

LYLAHN

I sit up in bed and stretch, yawning. The morning sun is streaming through the curtained window. No nightmares.

I smile. I'm home.

Danosrin avoided me as best as he could on the trip back to To'Morat, and I was all right with that. I am not ready to see him. I don't know if the hurt will ever go away, but its edges have softened.

I look to my left. Kaera is sleeping, her long brown hair splayed over the pillow. I smooth back the loose strands. She's been sleeping with me since we got home, and I don't mind one bit.

There's a soft knock at the door.

"Come in," I say.

"Lady Lylahn?" Amantha pokes her head in the room. "Are you awake?"

My smile widens. "I could hardly sleep in on a day like today."

She grins back.

I climb out of bed and down the ample breakfast that Amantha has brought for me, but I don't taste the food. Kaera wakes up sometime partway through and joins me at the table with a sleepy smile.

When we've finished eating, Amantha dresses me in a scarlet gown, traditional to To'Morat. The waist folds with ruching in a way that's flattering to my curvy figure, and the skirt swirls and shifts like a desert storm.

"I love it," I breathe.

She goes to work on my unruly curls. "It's stunning on you, Lady Lylahn."

"You look beautiful, Lahnnie," Kaera says, tracing her hands over the smooth fabric. Amantha will dress Kaera after she finishes with me.

Today is a big day, and we both have to look our best.

Amantha does my hair in a way that emphasizes the curls. She pulls half of it up into a twirling bun and pins it with sparkling quartz. She lines my eyes with black and touches up my cheeks. When she's done, I gasp. I look stunning, fierce.

Like I belong here.

"You're ready, Lady Lylahn," Amantha says.

"Favored Lady." I smile. "It's Favored Lady."

☾

Dust billows around the folds of my skirt at the edge of the plateau. The enormous quartz pillar of To'Morat looms overhead. Imwraeth's name was Forged into it after the battle of To'Rahn, and I scan the names until I find his. My heart swells.

I look out over the ocean of sand, take in the rise and fall of the waves. It's beautiful, wild and free, but I will be glad if I never have to travel it again.

An enormous crowd is gathered. Nearly the whole of To'Morat has come to witness this moment. They shuffle through the sand, talking. Kaera stands off to the side, a huge smile on her face.

I'm waiting, breathless.

Sharise, newly appointed retahn master, stands next to Kaera.

Sharise grins when we meet eyes. She's nervous about the job, says she doesn't know enough yet, but we'll learn. Together.

Because I'm going to be her new assistant.

I don't know how much spare time I'll have as Favored Lady, but I've promised Sharise that working with her to train new retahn will be a priority. Imwraeth has sanctioned it. In fact, Imwraeth was the one who suggested it.

The crowd hushes and parts, and through them strides Imwraeth Jeriyah, the Favored One of To'Morat.

I beam.

He looks incredible. He's wearing the red formal robes of the Favored One, and he stands tall and confident. His face is tender when he takes me in, and his dark eyes shine.

"Lylahn," he breathes.

I nearly melt.

Imwraeth steps forward until he's standing opposite me. "You look absolutely beautiful."

Warmth creeps onto my cheeks. "Thank you."

The religious leader of To'Morat steps forward, wearing white robes with gray marks meant to represent Atoille. She's carrying a quartz pitcher of water.

"I am Ki'Rhen Dorahna, and I will perform your Anointing today," she says.

The Anointing Ceremony of To'Morat is similar to To'Shahera's, yet different. Some words are said that I barely register because I can't stop grinning, and a laugh keeps threatening to escape my lips. I don't think I've ever been this happy.

Imwraeth grins right back, squeezing both of my hands in his.

The Ki'Rhen leader holds aloft the pitcher. "With this water, you are Anointed." She turns to Imwraeth. "Imwraeth Jeriyah, Favored One of To'Morat, do you accept this Anointing?"

Imwraeth's eyes never leave mine. "Yes."

Three drops of water are poured on his hands.

Ki'Rhen Dorahn turns to me. "And Lylahn Velare, do you accept this Anointing?"

Imwraeth catches his breath.

"Yes." Tears fill my eyes, so I can hardly see Imwraeth's smile, the water being poured.

"You are Anointed," she says. "To rule over To'Morat together."

The crowd cheers. Imwraeth holds up my hand.

Tears of joy fall down my face. I glance to Imwraeth, my heart full of love. I lean forward for one perfect kiss.

And then I look out over the cheering crowd.

My people.

NORAH

I go to the edge of the plateau every night. With Motah, I stare out over the ocean of sand, watching, waiting.

I don't know for what.

Motah puts one arm around my shoulders. She's got a blanket wrapped around her, and she opens it to let me into the warmth.

We stand, silent and staring.

"You and Zadock seem happy together," Motah says at last.

I smile up at her. "We are."

"I'm happy for you. He's a wonderful man."

"He is."

We stand there until the moon brightens and the stars blink overhead.

"We better go back," Motah says. "Shrey will be wondering where we are."

I turn to go, but then I see it.

A ship.

"Motah." I point.

Motah glances behind her, and her eyes widen. She freezes. We stay that way, watching the ship draw closer and closer.

It's narrow, pointed. And made of black wood.

Could it be—?

The ship rises and docks at the edge of the plateau. My heart thunders in my chest. That wood is definitely from To'Sharazad, but who is it? And what are their intentions?

Motah wraps her arm around me again. The guard towers at the edge of To'Rahn light up, and I hear shouts from within.

Figures appear at the railing of the ship, but it's too dark to make out who they are. A ramp is extended from the boat, and down walks—

"Elandor!" I cry.

Disappointment and joy are at war within my heart, but I run forward to meet him. "It's all right!" I call to the warriors gathering. "He's a friend."

Elandor smiles and throws his arms around me. Just a brief hug, and then he steps back.

"Norah!" He grins. "I'm so happy to see you."

"And I, you."

The three tears of his tattoo crinkle when he smiles.

I gesture behind me. "Let me introduce you to my motah, Katiyah Saranyi."

Motah steps forward, looking regal and proud, even with an old blanket wrapped around her. "Elandor. It's a pleasure to meet you."

I keep my eye on the other visitors descending the barge while we chat.

My mouth drops open. "You brought—the nobility."

Sustainers. Elandor brought Sustainers.

Elandor grins. "Yes. I managed to convince some of them to come live here to help you, at least for a while." He shrugs. "It's a big world. We've all got to help take care of it, right?"

I grin and throw my arms around him again. "Thank you! Thank you, thank you!" I step back. "How did you even get here? I took the green—"

Elandor lifts a chain around his neck, and I see orange glinting in the moonlight. "I'll have to take this back eventually. The trip was a little rougher without the green moonstone—it's the one that's most connected with the dunes—but the orange still got the job done."

I smile. I still can't believe it.

The nobles glance around with distasteful expressions, dusting off their fine clothes. I see many faces I recognize. I glance through the crowd. "Did my—did Raen Saranyi come?"

People are gathering behind us now, To'Rahn citizens coming to see what's happening. I see my friend Saeri and wave. She grins and walks over to join us.

Elandor shakes his head. "No. I'm sorry, Norah."

My heart sinks, but I try to focus on the joy of this moment. I try to smile. "Thank you, Elandor. Thank you."

Motah steps forward. Her voice carries through the crowd. "Honored guests, please, come with me. My name is Katiyah Saranyi, and I am part of the council that governs the village of To'Rahn. We will find you places to stay."

The nobles go, grumbling, following after Motah.

Saeri steps closer tentatively, and I grab her arm and pull her over to me. "Elandor, let me introduce you to my friend. This is Saeri."

Saeri and Elandor lock eyes. She smiles shyly. Saeri extends her hand, and their fingers interlock.

"Hi." She clears her throat. Their hands are still intertwined, and she seems to realize this with a start, jerking back and removing her hand.

"Hello." Elandor smiles.

Even though there is still pain in my heart, even though it may never be healed, I grin. The joy of this moment is real.

8 0

NORAH

I look up from within the grow wall at the sun high above. Lady Grasha works in the dirt beside me. The nobles were surprised and disappointed to realize that they are not royal here. And yet, they stayed. Some returned almost immediately to take the orange moonstone back, but they said they would stop at other plateaus on the way and see what they could do to help. It's unreal—this relief.

I have help Sustaining my home. It's more than I could have hoped for.

Lady Grasha looks very different with her plain clothes and dirt smudged on her cheeks. "It's so beastly hot," she mutters, grabbing a handful of sand and Sustaining. "And why is there so much dirt?"

I shake my head. She complains about it, but she does the work. It's enough.

The grow wall is thriving, the drip system bringing the plants plenty of water. I reach out, touch a plant, and Sustain it with more growth. It blooms before my eyes.

I climb the ladder out of the grow wall, and I'm surrounded by plants. Fruits, berries, bristlebrushes, they're everywhere. People walk among the plants, harvesting and smiling, and it lifts my heart. Life is good.

"Norah!" Zadock runs down the sandy path, grinning. He catches me in his arms and lifts me up, twirling me around his head. My heart races.

"Zadock!" I laugh and throw my arms around him, kissing his neck.

We're already planning our wedding. Neither of us can wait. I only wish Potah could see it.

"Norah." Zadock puts me down, breathless. "Someone's out there on the sands, traveling by sand platform."

My senses go on high alert, but I don't want to get my hopes up. I nod. Hand in hand, we run to the edge of the plateau.

I look out over the orange ocean of sand, the waves peaking and crashing, and I'm taken back to the many times I've been sailing on that ocean. Everything it's given me—the thrills, the joys, the adventures.

A tiny figure flies by sand platform, steadily getting closer to To'Rahn.

I clasp Zadock's hand. We watch and wait as whoever it is gets closer and closer. I catch a glimpse of purple shining in the light.

"Is that—?" I breathe. I don't finish what I'm thinking. I've been disappointed day after day, night after night. I can't let my hopes rise.

But I swear I see the purple moonstone, glinting around the neck of whoever is flying closer. I recall my potah telling me that Agriad's purple moonstone is what let him safely travel through the sands. My heart rises to my throat. Could it be?

"What will happen to To'Sharazad without a moonstone?" Zadock asks. "Because that looks like—"

I shake my head. "It can't be good. But there's already a party heading back to bring them the orange. Hopefully, they won't be without one for long." Because, despite it all, I want To'Sharazad to heal and thrive again.

Zadock readies sand, swirling it through his fingers as the figure gets closer. "It could be a threat."

And then I see him. I see my potah.

Tears spring up in my eyes, and I wave. I can't hold back a cry. Is it true? Is it really—?

He lifts his arm and waves back.

"Zadock, it's—"

Zadock drops the sand and wraps his arms around me. Then he whoops for joy.

"It's him."

When I wrote Oceans of Sand, I had no idea it was going to be a duology. I was thrilled with the direction Norah's story took. She and Zadock could love, her relationship with Motah was fixed, and all was ending happily ever after.

But. Some questions kept nagging at me. What else is out there? What's across the ocean of water, and how would people travel it, if they could?

Oceans of Sand was still a few months out from publication when I was in Florida with my family on vacation. The beaches were this gorgeous pure white sand. I was like, "Wow, this sand is awesome! I wonder what Norah would've thought about it."

On that vacation I woke up in the middle of the night with this KILLER idea that would not let me go. What if this evil guy showed up holding a body that looked just like Norah? Who is he? Who is the body? All these possibilities spiraled from there.

So I added in that lovely cliffhanger into Oceans of Sand that kept so many of you up at night (sorry about that!) and got to work on this sequel, Dunes of Water.

Norah's story is done for now, but head to jessicaflory.com to get a free book! You can also sign up for my free newsletter and get giveaways, sneak peeks, and behind-the-scenes.

Also, would you take a second and leave reviews for Oceans of Sand and Dunes of Water? Reviews really do so much to help me out, and they put a huge smile on my face! It doesn't have to be long or eloquent. A simple, "I loved this book!" is fantastic.

I am so immensely grateful to you for reading, sharing, reviewing, and enjoying my work. It means the absolute world to me.

ACKNOWLEDGMENTS

Wow. What a journey it's been, putting this book out into the world! Thank you, you wonderful soul, for reading.

Thank you to my incredible husband, Devin, who supported me through writing a second book and got me through all the highs and lows—the moments when I didn't know if I could do it, to the moments when I signed the contract or typed "the end" and we went out to celebrate. (Also, thanks for freaking out with me and doing a happy dance in the kitchen when Oceans of Sand won an award! Eeeek!) Thank you for all the dishes, child-watching, and mountains of laundry you have done so this book could come to life. You are wonderful, my darling Devin. I don't know what I'd do without you. All the best Zadock moments are inspired by you.

Thank you to my editor, the magnificent Lindsay Flanagan. (She is an author, too! You should check out her book!) As always, you caught the vision of this book and magnified it. When I turned in that first draft, I felt like something was missing, especially with Norah's character arc. You picked up right on it and your suggestions were invaluable! Thank you for being an amazing person to work with. (And just an amazing person overall.)

HUGE thanks and lots of credit goes to my incredible writing group, the Hot Mess Writers Group. Jordan Wright, Valerie Doll, Patrice Hale, Tracy Daley, Heidi Rogers, Tamara Bailey, and David Munk, you guys are the absolute best writing group in the world. Period. Heidi, credit for the title goes straight to you! I adore you all. Thanks for taking my ideas from good to great.

Thank you thank you thank you to the team at Immortal Works, including Holli Anderson and Jason King. What a wonderful experience it's been working with you all!

Lenore Stutznegger, the covers you created for Oceans of Sand and Dunes of Water are absolutely gorgeous. Thank you so much for your hard work and incredible art.

Special thanks to Penny Flory, Jessica Henrie, Carissa Quinn, and McKenna Hooker for their horse training expertise. I felt so much more confident with those scenes thanks to you amazing ladies!

I cannot thank enough the wonderful readers, reviewers, and amazing people who have read my work and cheered me on over social media.

In particular, I must thank Madelyn, the Squeaky Clean Reader. You were one of the first people who read my book (who didn't know me personally) that reached out over social media and gushed over how much you loved it. You have no idea what a wonderful confidence boost you gave me!

I must also thank Rachel of the Instagram account, Closed Door Romance, for reading, reviewing, and celebrating my books over social media. Also for answering my bajillion questions about how to grow on Instagram. (Seriously. I started out asking, "What's a reel and why are people changing their voices?")

To my amazing friends and family who help launch my books, thank you so much! Your enthusiasm just puts me over-the-moon, and your early reviews and thoughts are invaluable.

Mom and Dad, thank you so much for everything you've done and continue to do for me, but especially for supporting me in my dreams and believing that I can accomplish anything. I'm so, soooo lucky to have you as parents! (And the kids don't even know how lucky they are to have you as grandparents!)

To my wonderful siblings, thank you for your support and your love. Jenny, thanks for all the times you've made me laugh until I cry, staying up way too late so that Dad came down and yelled at us, hugs when I was crying, and generally being my best friend. Nate, thanks for being an awesome dude. And for reading all the way until the acknowledgements even though you didn't want to. Danny, you're looking cut, bro! And thanks for the workouts, protein shake recipes, and being a fantastic uncle to my kiddos.

Last, to my sweethearts, Sam, Grant, Owen, and Gwen, what would I be without you? I adore you, little stinkers. Thanks for being patient every morning while I get my writing done. Sammy, that moment when I came around the corner and found you reading my book made my heart soar. Grantie, you asking Daddy to read you Oceans of Sand did wonders for my confidence. Owie, your reaction when we first opened my author copies of Oceans of Sand was priceless and so, so sweet. Gwen, your snuggles and kisses are the best part of every day. Thank you all for your support and excitement as I do this whole author thing. I love you kiddos with all my heart.

ABOUT THE AUTHOR

Jessica Flory has a bachelor's degree in Molecular Biology from BYU, Provo, and she uses that science background to dream up cool settings and magic systems. Jessica has been a proud member of the Hot Mess Writers Critique Group since 2013.

Jessica is a mom of three crazy boys and one girl, a fitness instructor, and an avid baker. When she's not writing, she can be found chasing her kids, making a mess in the kitchen, or reading with her husband. Connect with her at jessicaflory.com.

This has been an
Immortal Production